The Living List

Tamia Blaine

THREE BEES
PUBLISHING

Three Bees Publishing

For Uncle Colin

I hope that the clouds are fluffy and the pints are cold.

You deserve nothing less.

Love always Xx

Coming Soon

Chapter One

Elsie

Elsie Bellamy leaned back in the chair and stared vacantly at the poster on the wall behind the doctor's head. Outside the consultation room, the general hubbub of daily hospital life continued with people chatting as they walked past, the low hum of trolleys being pushed, and the soles of shoes squeaking on the sheet vinyl floor. Cars whizzed along the busy road outside and seeped in through the open window, carrying blasts of cool air mingled with exhaust fumes. Elsie would never have paid attention to such inconsequential things before today. They were just the insignificant noises of an ever-moving world that had no bearing in her life, but now, with her senses in complete turmoil, the confusion that her brain was attempting to process had brought them to the forefront.

'Elsie. Do you understand what I've just said to you?' The doctor asked as he leaned slightly towards her across the desk.

Did she understand? Of course she understood. She wasn't stupid. Elsie had heard every word that Doctor Stanford had said, but at that current moment in time, they were just a jumbled mess inside her skull: Returned. Metastatic. Several affected organs. Terminal.

She felt a gentle squeeze on her hand and turned to look at the nurse beside her. Her name, according to the name badge, was Marion. Marion was a plump middle-aged woman, but the dark circles that sat beneath her eyes and the deep frown lines and crow's feet indented into her skin made her appear older, but, Elsie reasoned, that was what working long hours for the NHS did to a person. Despite attending the hospital over several years, Elsie had never met Marion before today. Maybe she was new on the ward? Still, Elsie was grateful Marion had sat with her as Doctor Stanford had delivered his body blow, even if it was only to squeeze her hand.

Elsie's eyes drifted back to the doctor, who was watching her carefully. She sat upright in the chair. 'Yes. I understand, Doctor. But...are you sure?'

The doctor gave a solemn nod. 'Yes. I'm sure.'

'Not the diagnosis,' blustered Elsie. 'Just the part about there being nothing that can be done. Surely, there's something? You see it on the news all the time about new cancer treatments being discovered. I'm sure I read somewhere about a person's stem cells being used to attack cancer cells. I can't remember the exact details, but it said it had a high success rate.'

She was babbling. She always babbled when she was nervous.

He gave a sorry sigh, but there was a tinge of frustration hidden beneath the surface. Undoubtedly, the good doctor had to deal with this line of questioning constantly.

'I'm sorry, but that's not an option for you, not for your type of cancer. The scans show multiple tumours in several of your organs. Even if it were widely available on the NHS, stem cell therapy has certain limitations that would eliminate you from being a suitable candidate.

Marion squeezed her hand again, and this time, Elsie squeezed it back. Suitable candidate? It was offensively formal, given what she'd just been told. She could feel the tears burning behind her eyes, and she quickly blinked them away.

'How long?' she asked him.

Doctor Stanford's gaze dropped to his hands, and Elsie held her breath. Finally, after what seemed like hours, he looked back up at her.

'In my experience, I'd anticipate a life expectancy of nine to twelve months. I'm so very sorry, Elsie.'

She slouched back down in the chair as her muscles crumbled under the weight of news. Nine to twelve months. How quickly would that go by? How many times had Elsie drunkenly seen in a new year in an overcrowded club, only to blink and find herself doing another midnight countdown in another overcrowded club the following year? Life had a way of flowing from one month to another without her even noticing the change in the seasons. Nine to twelve months was nothing. What could she achieve in such a limited time? The silence in the consulting room seemed to highlight the heavy atmosphere, and an intense pressure pushed down on her shoulders, enveloping her body. She could feel the heaviness constricting her chest as her ribcage pushed against this invisible force. Her breathing became shallower until her breath emitted from her mouth in short, sharp bursts. The tears that had threatened to come earlier now fell freely from her eyes and trickled down her cheeks.

'This can't be right,' she said. 'That's not enough time. There must be something. Anything! I can't die yet. I'm not ready.'

The doctor's professional composure finally broke, and his brows crumpled together. She wondered how often he'd sat in this room to deliver a death sentence to patients. Would there be others today who would be told the same? Would they walk out of this room as she would, feeling like her whole world, her dreams and goals, had been stolen away from her? Elsie knew as well as the next person that death was always going to come knocking at some point for her; it was the inevitability of humanity and the only certainty that every person could expect from life. How ironic it was that the one certainty in life was actually death. But it shouldn't be yet. It shouldn't be at thirty-four years of age. It should be when she was older — an aching, arthritic old woman dithering around in a nursing home. It should be when Elsie had accomplished absolutely everything she'd wanted to do in her life. It should be when she'd visited every country on her wish list and taken a smiling selfie next to some national monument or other. Or when she'd sampled every possible cuisine. Drank every different type of tequila. Blew half of her life savings at the roulette table. It should be then that she left this world.

'We could look at treatment to prolong the time you have left,' said the doctor, 'but this would only give you a few extra months. Ultimately, it's entirely up to you on how you wish to proceed.'

He continued to talk, and Elsie stared back, nodding occasionally when she thought she ought to, but his words muffled in her ears. She doubted that she'd remember much of what he said by the time she had got home.

Less than twenty minutes later, she was standing outside the entrance to the hospital with a series of leaflets clutched in her hand that Marion had given to her. She opened her bag and pushed them deep inside. It was strange how the mere thought of looking at the pamphlets made her diagnosis more real and more final than the doctor's words themselves. Perhaps she'd be brave enough to read them later, she thought. Perhaps.

She unlocked her phone and ordered an Uber, and looked across the road. An old lady was waiting at the bus stop. Elsie guessed the woman to be well into her seventies. She was holding onto the handle of a rather florescent shopping trolley in her right hand whilst using the other to shield her mouth as she coughed up what sounded like the contents of her lungs. The hacking noise drifted across the road to Elsie's ears and no sooner had the woman vigorously cleared her throat than she delved her hand in her pocket, retrieved a pack of cigarettes, and proceeded to light one. This was what was wrong with the world, thought Elsie, what was wrong with life in general, as she watched with disdain as the pensioner puffed away. Elsie worked out at the gym six times a week, only drank alcohol socially, and had never even held a cigarette in her life. And yet, somehow, her body had still failed her. She was being denied the fundamental right to live whilst the old woman in the bus stop, overweight and with a chest full of toxins and smoke, had managed to survive some thirty-plus more years than her. Life was unbelievably cruel.

The Uber pulled up at the kerbside, breaking Elsie's thoughts, and she climbed inside.

'Elsie?' asked the driver, to which Elsie nodded her head.

'St Paul's Square, please,' she said on autopilot, even though Elsie knew full well that he would already have this information on the little screen attached to his dashboard. She leaned back in the seat, closed her eyes and sighed heavily.

'One of those days, eh?' said the driver.

Elsie's eyes pinged open, and she saw the driver peering at her in the rear view mirror. *Well, yes, actually. I've just been told I'm dying, and I'll be lucky to see the year out. You know—one of those days. What about you? Having a good day?* But seeing that Elsie had no intention of offloading onto this stranger, she feigned a smile instead.

'Yes. You could say that,' she replied.

She unlocked her phone and aimlessly clicked on app after app in an attempt to look busy and keep the chattiness between them to a minimum. She opened Facebook and quickly closed it again after seeing a holiday post from Jenny, who worked in the bistro below her apartment. Jenny, who described herself as all 'tits, teeth and tan', was currently sunning herself in the Maldives with her equally gorgeous boyfriend. They were stood together, her boyfriend's arms wrapped around Jenny's tiny waist, with the backdrop of the clearest and bluest sea possible. The photo was the epitome of blissful happiness, and it tore straight through Elsie's soul.

Instead, she opened her sudoku app and stared hopelessly at the screen, willing her brain to engage as it always had done so easily before today. Numbers whirred through Elsie's mind, but they refused to find their rightful place on the grid. She kept the app open and continued to stare vacantly, her brain now drifting to thoughts of what her ending might look like. What it might feel like. Would it hurt? Would anyone be there with her when she went? Would she die warm in her own bed at home or in a hospice? Did you have to request a hospice, or did the nurses organise that? Would Marion be there if she was admitted into the hospital again? Elsie hoped so. Marion had a smile as warm as her hands had felt that morning. She needed a friendly face looking down on her when her chest rose and fell for the last time.

The traffic, as always in Birmingham city centre, was heaving. It trailed along slowly towards traffic lights, which only seemed to turn green long enough for a few cars to pass each time. Elsie's eyes went to the car in the next lane, where a woman sang along to whatever was pumping out of her stereo. She watched the woman's hands tapping rhythmically against the steering wheel of her shiny new Range Rover and felt a ball of bitterness twist inside her stomach. Why had *she* been afforded the luxury of life? What made *her* so special? Finally, the lights changed, and the singing woman and her super-clean car sped off before the ominous red light forced them to stop again.

The taxi driver took a left turn, leading them through the side streets of the city until they finally reached St. Paul's Square.

'Anywhere in particular?' asked the driver.

'No. Here's fine,' said Elsie.

She needed to get out of the car. She couldn't breathe. She needed to gulp down the fresh air.

'Thanks,' she said breathlessly before pushing the door wide open.

She almost fell out of the car in her bid to escape. Her breathing was so fast now that her head was starting to spin. It was just a short walk to her apartment door on the other side of the square, and she hurried across the green in the square's centre to reach her home before she passed out. As she neared, she saw Julian, the owner of the bistro, spot her scurrying across the road. He smiled, raising a hand in greeting. Elsie flicked up her own hand to return the gesture but continued towards the front door. She didn't want to speak to him. She couldn't. A heat suddenly cascaded down from her head and into her body. She fumbled for her key and slid it into the lock, pushing the door open forcefully, slamming it into the wall behind. Once safely inside, she closed the door and felt her legs buckle as the blackness came.

Chapter Two

Elsie

Elsie was lying in a clammy heap on the floor by the front door. The cold tiles brought a welcome chill to her skin as her breathing finally began to normalise. Was that what it felt like to die? she wondered. Would she feel that same sense of hopelessness as she struggled to breathe, or in the end, would her body just shut down and force her dead?

Elsie sat up against the wall and looked down at the contents of her handbag, which had spilt out when she'd collapsed. There, as though taunting her, were the leaflets that Nurse Marion had pushed into her hand at the hospital. Where was the humanity in a leaflet? It was so disgustingly impersonal—death leaflets—a handout for the walking dead. Elsie grabbed them off the floor and tore them.

'Fuck you!' she screamed at the top of her lungs. 'Fuck you. Fuck you. Fuck you!'

She ripped them into confetti and let them flutter to the ground. Only then did the tears come, and Elsie sobbed. She cried until her throat hurt, guttural and raw. It was the sound of a wounded animal who'd lost all hope. It was the sound of the condemned waiting to be taken to the noose. It was the sound of a woman who'd been cheated out of life.

***

She had no idea just how long she'd sat in the hallway, but the light coming through the frosted window above the door had darkened. The stairs were right there, but they felt too much of an effort to climb. Her bones felt heavier than when she'd woken that morning. She knew she couldn't stay sitting on the floor for much longer; pins and needles were stabbing at her skin, and she roughly rubbed her limbs to wake them up before she stood. The scattered remains of the leaflets could stay there until the morning, thought Elsie as she slowly made her way up the stairs. She couldn't look at them any longer.

Opening the door to her apartment, she was greeted with the sweet smell of jasmine and pomegranate from the wax melt strategically placed on the side table by the door. She surveyed her pristine home. Everything in it was expensive. Everything had been bought more for a visual impact rather than a functional one. It was the type of home that made everyone who walked inside go 'wow', and that was just how Elsie liked it. The plush white rugs and sofa and stark white walls may have been impractical, but they made every piece of colourful artwork she'd purchased pop against its backdrop; Elsie wouldn't even sit on the sofa to drink or eat for fear of spillage and instead opted for the hard plastic (but equally pricey) dining chairs instead. There wasn't a single piece of clutter to be found. Everything, in Elsie's opinion, had its place, and if she couldn't find a place, then it was unceremoniously dumped straight into the nearest bin. The work surfaces of the kitchen housed the essential kettle and toaster. The coffee table had a lone peace lily in its centre. Even her wardrobe had been organised with only that season's latest fashion, which would then be promptly removed and taken to her local charity shop the moment one season bled into another.

The few people who knew Elsie would call her wasteful. Others assumed she had OCD. But Elsie knew exactly what fuelled her living choices; it was to prove to her mother that she was nothing like her. It was to prove that despite the shitty life she'd bestowed upon her only child, despite all of the disadvantages, she, Elsie, had made it through to the other side and had not only achieved but had excelled. Her mother. The junkie. The one whose love of heroin had been stronger than love for her daughter. The one who systematically sold off any possession of remote value to fuel her destructive habit. The one whose actions saw her daughter removed by social services while she lay comatose in hospital after overdosing for the third time. The one who hadn't even attempted to see Elsie when she'd been discharged. The one who eventually died with a needle sticking out of her scrawny arm on a filthy sofa in her flat. Elsie couldn't even bring herself to say her name.

She went to the fridge, took out a bottle of wine, and poured herself a large glass. The first gulp burnt itself down her sore throat, and Elsie savoured it. She felt it trickle all the way down into her empty stomach, which grumbled its thanks to her. Going to the sofa with her glass in hand, she glanced down at the pristine material.

'Fuck it. Live a little, Elsie Bellamy,' she said with a quick shrug of shoulders before dropping herself heavily onto its plumped-up cushions. She scoffed at her choice of words and took another swig from her glass. How stupid all of her life decisions seemed now.

She supposed she should call somebody to let them know what had happened at the hospital, but when she looked at her phone, there were no missed calls. No text messages. No WhatsApp messages. Why would there be? She'd only told one person what was happening, and he didn't even have a phone. Who didn't have a phone in this day and age? Jack may have been old, but Elsie had seen plenty of pensioners on the streets with a mobile phone pressed against their ear. She'd once offered to take out a contract for him, but he'd just smiled softly at the suggestion.

'Why would I need a phone?' he told her.

'To keep in touch,' replied Elsie.

'With who?'

Elsie paused. Who indeed? She may have sat for hours with this man, but he'd given her little to no information about his life. Their conversations had never strayed far from current affairs, the latest MP scandal, or celebrity gossip. They were inane conversations where there were no expectations from either of them. Elsie had never asked him about his personal life, and in return, Jack had never queried hers. There was something profoundly comforting in knowing that somebody wanted to spend time with you, just because you were you; not for what you had, or what sort of life you led, or what somebody might be able to get out of you. It was just the two of them sitting on a park bench and talking nonsense while they threw chunks of bread at the greedy pigeons. It gave Elsie a sense of calm that she'd never experienced before. Jack was worldly and wise, almost philosophical. Was that just because he was old? Elsie didn't know. And it was something that she'd never know.

Not now.

Chapter Three

Elsie

The following morning brought a hazy mist, which hung low in the air. It was decidedly cooler than it had been recently, following an unexpected October heatwave that had seen a flurry of people rush to the nearest coastline in a bid to savour one last week of sunshine before the winter months set in. Elsie loved winter. She loved the dark mornings looking out from her living room window and seeing the blare of car headlights as the city began to wake. She loved the cold days, bundled up in a chunky coat with a scarf wrapped to protect her from the biting wind. She loved the short days and the nights that drew in ridiculously early at four o'clock in the afternoon. And she loved the days when she peeled off her coat, drenched with the rain from a heavy downpour and heated a bowl of tomato soup to warm herself again.

That morning, she'd managed to eat a piece of heavily buttered toast despite having no appetite whatsoever. Her stomach hadn't seen food at all yesterday, just an entire bottle of wine that had left Elsie a little woolly-headed when she'd woken. She pulled on her Ugg boots, slid on her coat and headed out the door. It was just under an hour's walk to Cannon Hill Park from Elsie's home, and one which she did every day, seven days a week, ever since she'd found herself with an abundance of time after selling her digital marketing company after being diagnosed with cancer the first time. It was where she'd first met Jack and struck up their unlikely friendship. He'd been sitting on a bench under a tree, sheltering in the shade from the intense August sun. The park, unsurprisingly, was busy with visitors as families and tourists walked around the grounds or whizzed by on the land train. In the distance, the sound of a brass band drifted across the green from the bandstand. Despite the hectic surroundings, Jack sat alone, watching the families and groups of friends have fun all around him. Was it pity that made Elsie go over to him? Possibly. Maybe it was the feeling of being two loners together that drew her to sit next to him. She ambled over and mused about how to start the conversation. Elsie was adept when talking about work: targets, clients, and profit were the only languages she truly felt at ease with. But when it came to small talk, she quickly realised she was clueless. There was an art to chatting. You had to be utterly unguarded for it to flow naturally, and that was one thing that Elsie could simply not do.

'Lovely day, isn't it?' said Jack as if sensing her discomfort.

'It is,' replied Elsie.

She closed her mouth and frantically wracked her brain for something to say. Something interesting and witty, but the harder she thought, the more difficult it became.

'Of course,' continued Jack. 'I still come here every day regardless of the weather. It's such a tranquil space, considering it's just off a main road.'

'Every day? Like seven days a week every day?' she asked.

'Yes. It really clears the chest, all of this fresh air.'

I doubt it'll clear my chest, thought Elsie sarcastically, thinking of the cancer that was currently cultivating inside her.

'Yes, it's good for the body and good for the soul sitting here,' he continued.

Elsie looked over at the old man. Did he really come here to clear the body and soul? Or was it a case of accosting anybody who'd listen to ease his loneliness? Did he live alone? she wondered. She took in his crumpled black t-shirt, khaki shorts, which had a slight tear in the pocket, and an aged pair of extremely worn sandals and stripey socks and guessed that, yes, he must definitely live alone. No self-respecting partner would allow somebody to leave the house in that state.

'I'm Jacob, by the way,' he said, leaning towards Elsie and offering his hand. 'But I prefer to be called Jack.'

'Nice to meet you, Jack,' said Elsie, shaking his hand. 'I'm Elsie.'

'I thought you looked like an Elsie.'

She raised a quizzical eyebrow. 'Really? Nobody in the history of my life has ever said that I look like an Elsie.'

'It's one of my many superpowers,' replied Jack. 'And it was quite a popular choice of name when I was younger.'

'Well, any decent parent steers clear of calling their children archaic names. It makes them ripe for bullying, believe me. My name is like a hundred years old or something. No offence.'

Jack smiled. 'No offence that you don't believe I have superpowers or no offence that you think I'm a hundred years old?'

'Both,' said Elsie.

'I once knew a girl who was called Philomena. Now that's cruel,' continued Jack.

'Cruel?' said Elsie. 'I'd say that's a hanging offence.'

They both chuckled. Perhaps there was something in this small talk malarky? It felt good talking to Jack. Elsie watched a young mother chase her toddler daughter around a picnic blanket on the grass. The little girl squealed with delight as the woman caught up with her, scooped her up in her arms, and planted a big kiss on her little chubby cheeks. Elsie wondered what it must feel like to want to have children. She'd decided many years ago that there was no way she would ever bring a child into this world; the years of children's homes in the nineties had instilled that into her.

As she watched the mother and child together in the sunshine, she suddenly realised just how lonely she was. Elsie had no children, no husband or even boyfriend, waiting for her to get home. In reality, she didn't even have any real friends. Just work colleagues and general acquaintances with whom she'd never made any real effort. She'd spent her life keeping everyone at arm's length, too scared to open up and let anybody in. And where did that leave her now? Now that she needed support and somebody by her side. Who did she have to confide in? Maybe she wasn't that different to poor Jack, who spent his days sitting on his own on a park bench.

'I have cancer,' she blurted out before she could stop herself.

How did that feel? To unburden herself on this man who was probably only being polite in talking to her in the first place. Did he really want to hear this? Elsie couldn't bring herself to look at his reaction. She didn't want to see the pity in his eyes. The last thing she wanted was *pity*.

'How long?' asked Jack.

Elsie turned to face him. He hadn't even turned in his seat.

'How long have I had it?' she asked, confused.

'No. How long have you got left to live?'

'Oh. Well...I don't know. It's not terminal. At least, I don't think it is – stage three. I was diagnosed a couple of weeks ago.'

'Then stop feeling sorry for yourself,' said Jack nonchalantly. 'You've still got everything to live for.'

Elsie was taken aback and, for a brief moment, dumbstruck. 'I didn't think I was feeling sorry for myself,' she said, finding her voice again.

Jack shifted in his seat and looked her in the eyes. 'No? It sounded like it to me. You tell a complete stranger you've got cancer and with an air of such finality, too. You didn't say, *'I've got cancer, and I'm going to beat it,'* just, *'I've got cancer,'* like it's already beaten *you.'*

'I didn't say it'd beaten me,' Elsie snapped back. 'Just that I had it.'

Jack turned away from her again. 'Good,' he said. 'Glad we've got that cleared up. Now, tell me what your treatment plan is.'

Well, Elsie said she didn't want pity, and in that moment, and for the first time in her life, Elsie realised that she had just made her first proper friend. He was just what she needed.

She went on to meet up with Jack as much as she could. There had been times when she'd been too tired following chemo to make the journey. Or there had been periods where she'd been travelling, ticking off the destinations on her extensive bucket list: Every country she'd wanted to visit had been visited, every city break suitably broken, and every crazy-arsed experience day experienced. But outside of those times, she met Jack at the park, where they sat for a few hours talking about everything and nothing. Jack was like the father, the brother, the uncle, and the best friend that Elsie had never had, all rolled into one.

How would that morning's conversation go, she wondered. As she walked, Elsie glanced at the clock on her phone. It was just coming up to 9 a.m., which meant that Jack wouldn't be there for another hour, but that didn't matter. Elsie would wait. She'd needed to get out of her apartment. She'd had a restless sleep where the duvet had felt heavy on her body, and no matter which way she turned, her mind had refused to switch off as it replayed, over and over, the conversation with Doctor Stanford the previous morning. She'd turned on the television for distraction, but still, Doctor Stanford's voice sounded inside her ears, as clear as if he was standing right next to her. Exhaustion had finally taken over in the early morning hours, and Elsie had fallen to sleep for what felt like no more than an hour or so until her eyes pinged open again. Her head felt heavy and her eyes sore, and there was still a rawness in her throat from screaming and crying. The atmosphere in her apartment was thick with negativity and tiredness, and all Elsie wanted to do was escape.

She rounded the corner and entered the park, passing through the open gates. A groundskeeper smiled at her as she passed, and Elsie lowered her eyes to the ground. She didn't want him to say anything to her. She didn't want to hear a cheery 'good morning' when, in truth, that morning was anything but good. It was the start of her horrific new reality and one which she had no hope of escaping. As Elsie headed towards her and Jack's bench, she stopped dead in her tracks. Jack was already there, waiting. He was bundled up in a thick woollen coat, the collar of which turned up to protect his neck from the gentle but cold breeze that was flowing in the air that day. He was looking out towards the grass as he always did during their meet-ups, and as Elsie approached, he didn't even look up.

'Morning,' he said as she passed and sat beside him.

'You're early,' she replied.

'Likewise.'

They sat in silence. Elsie could feel a fresh wave of tears burning in the corner of her eyes, threatening to fall at any second. When she thought they were about to come, she felt Jack shuffling along the bench closer to her.

'How long?' asked Jack.

She let out a slow exhale. It was the same question that he'd asked her when they'd first met almost three years previously.

'Nine to twelve months. And this time, it *is* final. It's beaten me.'

***

They'd been sat on the bench in the park for just over two hours, and no more than a few words had been exchanged between them. Jack seemed to have lost his ability to make quick-witted responses, and Elsie was grateful for it. It was neither the time nor the place for them.

When she'd first told Jack her devastating news, he'd silently reached out and placed his hand on her shoulder. It wasn't quite a hug; they weren't the hugging kind. Finally, after what felt like an age but was probably no more than a few minutes, Jack spoke.

'Do you want to talk about it?' he asked her.

Elsie shook her head. No. It was the last thing she wanted. What could be said? There was no sugar-coating her situation. There was no hope of a miraculous recovery. The doctor wasn't wrong. All that was left for Elsie to do was purely logistical now. She had to think about the practicalities of dying. She'd have to find a solicitor and and have a will drawn up first of all, but who would she leave her possessions to? There was only Jack, and during their friendship, the man hadn't ever accepted a single thing from her. It didn't matter whether it was a bar of chocolate or an offer of a mobile phone. It was always a firm but appreciative no from him. Maybe she should leave her estate to a charity? That's what people did. But which one? Or did it even matter for that fact? One charity was the same as any other. Perhaps she should sell everything in preparation and find a fancy nursing home? She owned her apartment, and the apartment above her, and the shop premises below. Of course, Julian in the Bistro might not be happy, but then again, he might buy it himself. That's it – she'd give him first refusal. The apartment above her she'd listed on Air B&B, so there were no long-term tenancy issues there. She'd just have to delist it from the website. All three properties were mortgage-free, owing to the fact that she'd cleared them with the money she'd made from the sale of her business. So, that would leave her with a nice, tidy sum to find an exclusive nursing home.

'What are you thinking about?' asked Jack.

'I was thinking about practical stuff. You know – end of life and all that.'

'So, you're thinking end game now?'

'What else is there to think about?' said Elsie. 'I've only got a year left, give or take a few months.'

'Exactly. So, why are you thinking end game when you still have a year left...give or take a few months.'

Was he shitting her? What else was she supposed to think about?

'Jack,' she said, sighing deeply. 'I don't think this is the time for one of your epiphanic speeches. Do you?'

'On the contrary. I think that this is the perfect time. Now's the time to start thinking of the present – the here and the now. Now's the time you really get to live.'

Elsie abruptly stood to her feet. She didn't need to hear this; She didn't *want* to hear it.

'Jack. Don't! Just...don't. Okay? Do you know how absurd you sound? Have you listened to yourself? What in the world has possessed you to think that I want to hear any of that bullshit right now? As if I'm going to let an old man who does nothing but sit on this fucking bench all day, every day, tell me that it's time I started to live my life. What life? Didn't you hear? I don't have one anymore. Do you know what? Save it! Save for the next person who sits next to you.'

She pushed her clenched fists deep inside her coat pockets, turned, and stomped angrily away from him.

'I'll be here waiting when you're ready to live, Elsie,' he shouted after her.

'Fuck you, Jack. Fuck you,' she shouted back without turning.

***

Elsie had been sitting in the corner booth of the bistro since it opened. She'd seen the lunchtime rush come and go and endured the boringness of the post-lunchtime lull as staff prepared for that evening's covers. She'd also managed to see off an entire bottle of wine, which had worked its alcoholic magic straight to her head. A sharp pain tore through her stomach, a not-so-kindly reminder that it probably needed feeding, and she caught the attention of one of the waitresses, Ellen, to come over to her table.

'Could I order some food, please,' said Elsie. 'And another bottle of this.' Her fingernail tapped the side of the empty wine bottle, almost toppling it over.

Ellen reached out and steadied the bottle. 'It's a little early to take dinner orders,' she replied. 'Chef won't accept them before five o'clock.'

'Even for me?' slurred Elsie. 'I practically live here.'

This wasn't true. At best, she went to the bistro twice a week, but they generally didn't see her from one week to the other, apart from when she was walking towards her apartment door.

'It's okay, Ellen. You can take this order,' said Julian, appearing behind the waitress.

She nodded at him and somewhat reluctantly pulled out a notepad from her back pocket. 'What'll it be?'

'The grilled chicken, please. And could I have a side order of onion rings with that?' said Elsie.

'We don't do onion rings here,' replied Ellen.

'Even for me?' Elsie repeated, to very much her own amusement. She laughed but stopped when she noted that neither Julian nor his rather non-plussed waitress were laughing with her. 'God! It was just a joke. Fine. I'll have a side order of potato skins instead.'

'We don't do pota...' started Ellen but was quickly hushed by Julian.

'Potato skins. No problem. We can do that for you,' Julian told Elsie, and he flicked his head, motioning for Ellen to leave, which she duly did.

He sat down at the table and picked up the empty wine bottle. 'Good choice,' he said to her before setting it back down.

'Are you sure you want that second bottle, though? It's a strong vintage.'

'The stronger the bottle...no wait..., the stronger the better,' said Elsie. She laughed again despite Julian, once again, not laughing with her.

He leaned in towards her. 'Are you okay, Elsie? You seem out of sorts.'

'Do your customers need to be not okay to come here? Can't it be that they're perfectly fine but just want to get pissed on cheap but very strong wine?' she said.

'That's not cheap wine. It's fifty quid a bottle,' he said flatly.

'Oh well,' said Elsie, throwing her arms up. 'Can't take it with you.'

A smirk ghosted Julian's lips, but his forehead was crinkled with concern. 'You sure you're alright?'

Elsie leaned back in the booth and blew her cheeks out with her breath. 'Well. Yes and no. Or rather, no and yes,' she said. 'No, I'm not alright, but yes, I am out of sorts.'

'Do you wanna talk about it?' he asked.

Elsie looked at him. He was a delicious specimen of a man. He was in his fifties, a little older than she would normally go for, but he had bright blue eyes and a mop of dark hair that was slightly greying at the sides. He looked refined. That's what they called men when they aged, wasn't it? He was also gay and married to a man called Richard, which Elsie only discovered last year when she'd tried to drunkenly kiss him when they'd had one too many drinks for his birthday.

'Not really,' replied Elsie. ' I just want to drink, eat my potato skins and go home to bed.'

'Then I'll leave you to it,' said Julian, rising to his feet. 'But if you get a chance, maybe we can meet up sometime later in the week? I need to talk to you about something.'

'No problem,' said Elsie, 'We'll sort something out.'

Julian nodded and walked across the dining room and into the back office, leaving Elsie wondering where the hell Ellen had gotten to with her bottle of wine.

Less than an hour later, she stumbled out of the bistro and into the early evening darkness. It had rained while she'd been inside, and the pavements glistened under the streetlights as the smell of damp grass drifted over from the centre of the square. As she rooted inside her pockets for her keys, she heard a voice behind her.

'Excuse me. Do you have any spare change?'

Elsie turned and spied the shabbily dressed man with disdain. He had long matted hair, dark with dirt, and an overgrown beard and tatty clothes, which appeared to be far too large for his thin frame.

'Sorry. I spent it all in there on expensive wine and chicken,' she replied without a hint of sarcasm.

The man smiled. 'Lucky for some,' he said, to which Elsie immediately felt a flush of anger rising up her chest.

'Don't you dare do that?' she slurred at him, pointing an unsteady finger at his face.

'Do what?' he asked, genuinely perplexed.

'Money-shame me.'

'Money-shame you? What the fuck are you on about?' said the man.

'Yes. Making me feel bad about spending fifty quid on a bottle of wine,' said Elsie, stumbling.

'You spent fifty quid on a bottle of wine?'

'No! I spent a hundred pounds on *two* bottles of wine, I'll have you know.'

The man laughed and held his palms up in defence. 'Hey. If you want to waste your money on wine that you're going to piss out eventually, then be my guest.'

Elsie's fingers wrapped around her front door key in her pocket, and she pulled it out, holding it aloft as though she'd just pulled Excalibur from the stone. But as she pulled out the keys, it sent a flurry of coins flying through the air, which clinked as they hit the wet pavement.

'There. You can have that,' she said to the man, and she turned and headed towards her front door.

'Keep your money,' the man said flatly. 'Put it towards your next bottle of wine.'

'Get a job,' Elsie shouted at him without turning.

'Get a life,' he retorted.

She laughed sardonically. 'Wouldn't that be nice!' she said. 'If you can tell me where I can buy a new one, I'll gladly sacrifice my wine for it.'

She turned the key in the door, and the lock clunked open. She stepped inside, and as she turned to close the door, she saw the man shaking his head at her with disgust.

Chapter Four

Mack

It was just after 2:30 a.m., and with the last of the stragglers leaving the club on the square and most likely stumbling their way to the nearest takeaway, Mack decided to call it a night. He sat and counted the money people had given him; it was mainly coins, but one kind, but highly intoxicated, man had given him a ten-pound note. In total, he'd collected almost twenty pounds. It was enough to buy food for the next three days, five if he was especially frugal.

Thankfully, that evening hadn't bought its usual tirade of abuse he experienced most weekends. Apart from that one woman, of course. Generally, it was men who took offence to Mack's existence – not because they didn't like him, they didn't even know him, but it was more to do with the fact that they considered him an easy target. The homeless were not only seen as a scourge on humanity but inhuman altogether. Up until his homelessness, Mack had never been involved in a fight in his life, but in the six years he'd lived on the streets, he had gotten into more scrapes than he could remember. He was pretty sure that most of the bones in his body had broken at one point or another, and all of the attacks had been inflicted upon him by 'normal' people: Well-dressed, well-spoken, from normal homes, in normal streets, and who led normal lives. And it was these well-dressed, well-spoken, normal people who, at the end of what Mack assumed to be a good night, had decided that it was perfectly acceptable to beat the shit out of another person for no other reason than the fact that he wasn't well-dressed, well-spoken, or normal – not by their standards at any rate. Mack wasn't considered to be one of them where society was concerned. Of course, not everybody was like that towards him. There were plenty of people with good intentions and charitable hearts who'd pop a few coins in his cup at the end of the night and others who would buy him a meal deal from the little supermarket for his lunch. Alcohol was always the catalyst for the abuse that Mack received, which made it all the more riskier to stand outside a club on a Friday and Saturday night. Unfortunately, it was a risk that he had to take.

Mack plodded through the soft rain toward the high-rise car park. A lot of homeless people felt safer sleeping there where it was less exposed than being huddled up somewhere in a shop doorway, and although it was open to the elements to some degree, the structures did provide some protection against the sometimes cruel and harsh British weather. The roads were quieter now than in the daytime, but the heart of the city continued to beat until around six in the morning, and so there were still plenty of clubgoers entering and leaving clubs with late-night licenses, and where taxis queued in an orderly fashion at the sides of the roads at the designated taxi ranks.

As he continued the short journey, his mind again drifted back to the woman on the square. She had clearly been drunk when she'd left the bistro, but it still irked Mack at how spiteful she'd been. He didn't usually get abuse from women, and it bothered Mack at how she'd expertly flipped the situation to make him the aggressor. What had she said he'd done? That was it; money-shamed her. Despite his situation, Mack had never felt envious of anybody else's life. He was well aware that he was the creator of his own situation, something that he could now see and accept now that he was clean. He doubted that woman could be shamed into anything if he was being honest.

Was she always so rude to people? Or had it just been the booze pumping through her veins that had caused her to mouth off at him that night, he wondered. How would she feel in the cold light of day when she woke later that morning? Would she even remember it? Even if she did, Mack doubted she'd care. Wariness meant survival when you lived on the streets. It allowed you to make a character judgement in seconds; unblinking eyes, hard stares and even a slight twitch at the side of a mouth, if noticed, could potentially save you from being hurt. That woman, in her expensive coat, walking into her expensive home in one of the last Georgian squares in Birmingham, clearly had a high opinion of herself and a lowly one of others. Good luck to her, he thought to himself, and to the poor bugger who ended up stuck in a relationship with her. She must be a complete nightmare to live with.

Mack entered the lower entrance of the five-story brick car park. It stank of piss, and even Mack had to shield his nose from the stale stench as he trudged up the concrete staircase to the fourth floor. When he reached the brushed steel sign of level four, covered with numerous graffiti tags, he pushed open the door and walked over to the large bundle on a cardboard base, flanked by several carrier bags. Mack gave it a gentle nudge with his foot.

'Hi, honey. I'm home,' he said.

The cover of the sleeping bag was pushed back, and a dirty face squinted back at him. 'What time is it?' said the man, his voice croaky from sleep.

'Just coming up to three. Go back to sleep, Sid. I'll keep watching for a bit.'

But Sid was already pushing himself up out of the bag. 'No. No,' he said. 'My turn. Get some rest, lad. You've been standing in the rain for hours.'

Mack knew better than to argue with Sid, so he unfurled his sleeping bag and slid his body inside. 'Cheers, buddy. Wake me up when the traffic starts to get busy outside.'

Sid patted the outside of Mack's sleeping bag. 'Will do. Get yer head down.'

Mack had grown accustomed to surviving on a few hours of sleep in the same way he'd also gotten used to sleeping in shifts with Sid. He lived in a permanent state of exhaustion, surviving on a few hours of sleep each night, but those few hours were deep and restful, knowing that Sid was keeping a watchful eye over him. He thought of that woman again. She was probably out for the count in her king-size bed with Egyptian cotton sheets in her big posh apartment. Now that, thought Mack with a smile, was what you called money-shaming. Within minutes, the familiar echoes of life around him muffled into silence as he finally allowed sleep to come and transport him through dreams to a place where he was back, living his old life.

***

'Remind me. Why are we going again?' Sid asked Mack as they made their way across the pedestrian crossing.

Mack had woken that morning to the roar of a diesel engine as it had made its way up to the top floor. He had slept well and much later than usual if the morning rush hour had started. It was unlike him. Mack always liked to be up and out of the way to avoid the contemptuous looks shot in his direction through the glass of the car windows. But that morning, his first thought hadn't been to rush off and hide away. It had been fixed again on that woman from the previous night. Not in a weird, stalkerish way. She wasn't his type at all; far too hoity-toity for his liking and much too young for him at that. No. It was something different. Inquisitiveness perhaps? No, that wasn't it either. Maybe he just wanted to see if she was different without a belly full of booze. Maybe she was a nicer person without it? Whatever it was, there was some inner sense forcing him to see her again.

'I told you,' he replied to Sid. 'We're going to St. Paul's.'

'Don't tell me. We're off to see a man about a dog?' said Sid.

'No. To see a woman about an apology,' replied Mack.

'Her to you? Or you to her?'

'A little bit of both...but mainly her,' said Mack.

They continued to walk, and a Ferrari pulled up at a set of red lights.

'Gorgeous car,' said Sid, eyeing up the red paintwork.

At that moment, the passenger window of the Ferrari slid down, and a suit-clad man leaned over and shouted. 'If you got a job, maybe you could afford one of these too.'

Prick, thought Mack rolling his eyes.

'We could have at least stopped and picked up some breakfast first. I'm starving,' complained Sid as the Ferrari sped away.

'They'll be somewhere to eat up there,' said Mack.

Sid scoffed. 'We're not eating up there with those prices. We've only got that twenty quid from last night.'

'Oh. Stop whining, Sid. I'll get some more money tonight.'

When they'd reached the square, they made their way over to the church and sat down on the bench, and Mack looked over towards the bistro and, in particular, the woman's front door.

'You're getting me worried,' said Sid as he tightened his coat over his chest. 'You're behaving a little odd.'

'I'm not stalking her,' he said, smiling. 'I just need to see her again.'

'Why? Trust me. She doesn't give a shit about you.'

'It's more like I *need* to see her. And don't ask me why. I don't know why. I just know that I have to.'

A large van pulled up outside the bistro and began to unload a delivery of fresh vegetables. A man from inside the bistro came outside and nodded at the driver, pointing to inside the building.

'Wait there,' instructed Mack. He hurried across the green and to the bistro. 'Alright, mate,' he said to the man as he approached.

The man's bright blue eyes looked him up and down. 'Alright,' he replied cautiously. 'Listen. We're not even open yet, but if you come back later, I can ask the chef if there's any food we don't need. You know, the stuff we have to chuck out.'

Mack shook his head. 'No. It's nothing like that,' he said. 'I was just wondering if you could tell me something about a woman who was in here last night.'

The delivery driver handed the man a clipboard. 'There were lots of women in here last night,' he replied. He took the clipboard, signed his name and handed it back to the driver without looking at Mack once.

'Yeah. But you might know this one. She lives just here,' replied Mack pointing at the freshly painted black door next to the entrance to the restaurant.

The man paused and narrowed his eyes. 'What do you want with her?'

'Nothing. I just, err...' said Mack, stammering under the man's suspicious glare. 'There was a little bit of a misunderstanding last night. I just wanted to clear things up with her.'

'Well. I'll let her know when I see her.' He turned to head back inside the bistro.

'Hey. Wait,' Mack called out. 'Do you know her name?'

'Yes,' he replied bluntly.

'Can you tell me what it is then?'

The man turned and walked back towards Mack. 'No, of course I can't. Listen, we don't need people like you pestering residents. So just go, please.'

Mack shook his head slowly. 'You know, that's exactly what you said to me last time.'

The man tilted his head as if trying to place him. 'Last time? I don't think we've ever...'

'Yeah. I came to see if you had any work available in the kitchens, and that's what you told me. Cheers, mate.' said Mack.

The man shrugged his shoulders. 'Listen. No offence, but I get excellent and highly qualified chefs contact me all the time about working here.'

'Who said I wasn't excellent and highly qualified? You didn't even let me past the door.'

'Apologies. I didn't realise they were handing out Michelin stars at the soup kitchens,' said the man with a sarcastic grin, before turning and walking back inside.

'They don't. But they do in London, which is where I trained. And under Michelin-starred chefs you could only dream of meeting,' Mack shouted back a fraction too late as the door slowly closed.

Mack went back over to Sid, who was still sitting on the bench beaming, seemingly having enjoyed the show. He sat down next to him with a heavy, dejected sigh.

'Making friends again?' said Sid.

'You know me. I must have one of those faces. Come on,' he tapped him on the knee. 'Let's go and get some breakfast. I've got a feeling that it's too early for Sleeping Beauty to be up and about anyway.'

Chapter Five

Elsie

E lsie's mobile phone rang out and echoed around the bedroom. She rolled over in bed from her foetal position and groaned as she reached for the phone on the bedside cabinet. Opening one eye, she saw the hospital's number on the screen and, with the click of a button, muted the ringing and turned back on her side. She didn't want to speak to any doctors. There wasn't any point. She'd already made up her mind that she wasn't going ahead with any further treatment. She couldn't face her hair falling out again or the pain and burning sensation that coursed through her body after each round of chemo. Alcohol would be a no-no as well if she decided to go ahead with chemotherapy. Good God, if she was going to die, she at least wanted to be able to enjoy the time she had left. If she wasn't going to be cured, then Elsie didn't want to know.

She rechecked her phone and looked at the time. It was almost eleven o'clock, too late to meet Jack. Not that she had any intention of going anyway. He'd infuriated her with his shabby attempt to put a positive spin on things yesterday. What was there to be positive about? It was absurd and pretty bloody selfish of him if she was being honest. What she needed yesterday was for Jack to tell her that he was sorry that this was happening to her. That he was going to be there for her. That he'd be by her side until the very end. Instead, he'd shuffled a whole two inches closer to her, rested a hand on her shoulder and told her to start living.

She hoped that he was feeling guilty. She hoped he was sitting on that bench and frantically thinking of ways to make things up to her. It'd do him good to be sat there alone – it'd give him a taste of what it would be like next year when she was gone. She didn't need people like Jack in her life. She didn't need anyone.

Elsie slowly sat up in bed and clutched her head. God, it hurt so bad. Why did she have to go for that second bottle? Julian should have told her no and sent her on her way. Any other self-respecting landlord would have. She'd have a word with him about that later. He'd mentioned something about needing to talk to her anyway; she could kill two birds with one stone.

She peeled back the duvet and kicked her legs out of the bed. She was just about to stand when the image of the man outside the bistro dropped into her head, and she slowly lowered herself back down. What had happened exactly? She didn't remember leaving the bistro, but snippets of an altercation were beginning to materialise in her mind. Had she thrown money at him at one point? The image of the man became clearer, and she remembered how he was dressed and the overgrown hair and beard. Oh god! He was homeless. And she'd thrown her pennies at him! What sort of monster was she becoming? No, thought Elsie. It couldn't have been her fault. He must have said something to antagonise her. She'd never do something like that. Thankfully, she doubted she'd ever see him again, but she made a mental note never to order a second bottle of wine again.

***

Elsie had always believed that to cure a hangover, you needed something stodgy in the stomach – preferably greasy. After showering and dressing, she'd gone to her fridge and pulled out an open packet of bacon. Checking the date stamp on the front of the packet, she frowned, seeing that it was three days past its used-by date. But she pulled back the plastic cover and gave the contents a cursory sniff. It didn't smell like it had gone off, but it was pork, so you never could tell. She tossed the packet back in the fridge, closed the door, and then immediately opened it again and took it back out.

'Fuck it,' she said, retrieving a frying pan from one of the kitchen cupboards. What was the worst that could happen? She was dying anyway.

Elsie fried the bacon just the way she liked it, to the point of cremation, and threw a few chopped mushrooms into the pan just before it was finished. She turned off the hob and then placed the bacon and mushrooms onto two almost stale pieces of buttered bread and went and sat on the sofa. She hungrily bit into it, taking a large bite. Mushroom juice spurted out of the side and landed all over the sofa's fabric. She watched the greasy liquid slowly soak into the cushion, making no attempt to clean it up and then turned her attention back to the sandwich. With her other free hand, she plucked her phone from the pocket of her jeans, unlocked it and Googled local nursing homes. Her screen filled with home after home in the search results, and Elsie sighed. She clicked on the first result in the list and pulled a face at the image on the website's homepage where a group of pensioners stood smiling in a garden. All around them were badly photoshopped flowers and plants in full bloom. The whole thing screamed amateur, and immediately, Elsie was put off; if they skimped on the quality of the website, then what did that say about the business? And if that wasn't enough to send her screaming in the opposite direction, then the reviews certainly did the trick.

I caught a member of staff stealing my mother's jewellery,' said one.

'My father was left in soiled clothes for over four hours,' said another.

She wrinkled up her nose, went back to the original search results, and clicked the next one on the list, but a quick location check showed that it was plonked straight in the middle of one of the most notoriously dangerous estates in the city where the crime rate soared off the scale, gang warfare was rife, and muggings commonplace. Definitely not somewhere she intended to visit, let alone see out the rest of her days.

She aimlessly scrolled one after the other, and just when she was about to give up all hope, her eyes settled on a tiny picture of a large white Victorian house. It had probably started life as a gentlemen's residence, assumed Elsie, ostentatiously grandiose and close enough for any self-respecting, middle-class banker to quickly get to the city centre. It was located only a few miles away in Moseley, and the generous garden was beautifully landscaped into different sections: There was a Chinese-themed ornamental garden, an English cottage garden complete with wildflower beds, and a more modern area with an immaculately manicured lawn and a large metal pergola. In the centre of the garden, there was an imposing water feature, and Elsie closed her eyes, imagining the soft trickle of water splashing back down into the base. The downstairs of the property appeared to be entirely communal, with a living room, an ornate library, and a sensory room, with the kitchen and the staff room set at the back of the property. The upper floors housed large bedrooms for up to eight residents, with the remaining three bedrooms allocated to staff. The whole house was tastefully decorated in muted colours, soft and subtle and even though they were just a group of photographs flickering on a screen, Elsie felt a calmness inside her just looking at them.

She clicked on the 'About Us' section of the website, and a photograph of a middle-aged woman appeared. She had short, silvery hair cut into a fashionable style, and she flashed a broad, genuine smile.

Meet Ingrid

Ingrid Smythe-Owen, is the founder and owner of The Orchids Care Home. She purchased the property seven years ago, in 2016, after her husband passed away from Motor Neurone Disease. Following her husband's diagnosis, Ingrid struggled to find a small nursing home which could not only provide the care that her husband required but one which also felt like a home-from-home for residents during their final years. Ingrid dedicated her time to finding the ideal location, providing the high-quality care that residents require but without the look and feel of a generic and large traditional nursing home. The home can cater to up to eight residents at any one time, and whilst only three staff members remain on-site overnight, there are several additional staff members during the day, ensuring that no resident is left wanting at any time. Activities and entertainment are organised frequently for residents, along with regular outings for those who are able to attend. The Orchids has since received three major care awards and several commendations from local charities and hospices, sealing its reputation for undisputed excellence.

Elsie saved the care home's number in her phone and closed the page. It seemed promising and just what she was looking for, but the sceptic in her didn't quite believe that The Orchids could be that perfect. Perhaps she'd order an Uber and drive there to check out the area and see for herself. But that was something for another day. Not today. She wasn't ready.

Right now, she needed to get out of the apartment. Usually, she would have thrown on her trainers and made her way to the park to see Jack, regardless of whether she was late. He had this uncanny way of just being there. But that was another thing that she wasn't prepared to do that day.

Perhaps she'd go down and see Julian instead to see what he wanted to talk to her about. She went over to the window and peered outside to see Julian's silver BMW parked outside of the designated parking bay with a bright yellow parking ticket stuck to the front window. She grabbed her house keys and made her way downstairs. As she opened the door, she let out a scream. Julian was standing on the other side, his hand in the knocking position.

'Christ! You scared me to death,' She winced at her own choice of words.

'Good timing,' said Julian. 'I was hoping to catch a quick five minutes with you.'

'And I you,' said Elsie. 'Shall we?' she added, gesturing for them to go to the bistro.

Julian shook his head. 'I'd prefer to talk away from there if that's okay. I don't want people overhearing.'

Elsie shrugged and ushered him inside. When they were in her living room, he flopped heavily on the sofa and then leaned forward and sunk his head in his hands.

'It's all gone to shit,' he said.

His voice wobbled, and Elsie didn't know whether she should go over and console him but decided against it. Apart from the drunken kiss incident, which still made her cheeks flush red at the thought, they'd never really bonded.

'What's wrong?' she asked, praying that Julian wasn't having a domestic with his husband. She hated stuff like that.

'I'm going to have to close the bistro,' he said, his head still in his hands. 'Covid hit us so hard, and we only just managed to cling on to it. But now there's this cost of living crisis, and people just aren't spending their money as they used to. Bookings are down, and for the past few months, we haven't turned a profit at all. I'm putting every spare penny into the place, and Richard is moaning that our savings are dwindling to nothing. He's transferred them now to another account, so I can't access them at all. Honestly, Elsie. It's devastating. Everything I've worked for just gone.'

'I'll make us some coffee,' said Elsie purely because she didn't know what else to say. She could offer to help in some way, she supposed. After all, there wasn't a mortgage on the property, so she could technically forgive some rent payments, but would that really help in the long run? At some point, she was going to die, and the property would be sold, and who knew what the new owner would want to do with it. Even if she did offer to forgo the rent, it wouldn't solve the dwindling customer numbers, and it would only be a matter of time before Julian was admitting defeat again, but this time with a much larger debt and, no doubt, a great deal more stress.

'You're a businesswoman,' said Julian from the sofa. 'You know how stressful it can be.'

'Humm,' said Elsie, not wanting to agree with him.

In truth, Elsie had found the whole process of running a business easy. She'd set up as a one-man band from the bedroom of the crappy flat that the Housing Department offered her after she left the care system. Her overheads had been minimal, and the layout to start had been nothing more than a cheap laptop and the monthly cost for the internet connection. She'd spent hours pouring over YouTube channels: How to start a business. Digital Marketing 101. Digital Marketing – Your first client. Basic Booking Keeping. How to submit tax returns.

Elsie had time on her hands and a desire to be rich that was so strong that she didn't care that she spent all day alone in the flat. She didn't see a living soul from one day to the next, but that was a sacrifice she was prepared to make as she grew her little business, carrying out all of the daily duties on her own.

With time, her newfound knowledge increased her confidence and with confidence came new clients. Soon, her little business had grown to a point where she could afford to rent a small office above a shop on the outskirts of the city and employ somebody to help with admin. Within two years, she had a bigger office and seven employees, until eventually, she became one of the most prominent digital marketing agencies in the UK.

The kettle clicked off, and Elsie poured the steaming water into the cafetière and inhaled the bitterness of the coffee beans.

'What are you going to do?' she asked, joining Julian on the sofa.

'I'm going to have to close. I can probably trade for the next couple of months, but then that's it,' he threw his arms up in the air. 'Last orders at the bar.'

Elsie kept quiet as she did the mental maths in her head. Two months before Julian stopped trading and probably another two months to close everything down and empty the building. She didn't know how ill she'd be at that point, but either way, it wasn't worth her advertising for a new tenant; they'd probably only get a six-month tenancy at best.

'Do you know when it feels like life is against you?' said Julian.

More than you know, thought Elsie.

'Of course, you don't know,' added Julian. 'Look at this place. Look at everything you've got. You've no idea.'

Rage filled her body. How fucking dare he. He was losing his business. She was losing her life! As her blood coursed through her veins, she took a deep breath to calm herself. She was being unfair, and she knew it. He didn't know what was happening with her, and actually, she didn't want him to know either. They'd never had more than a landlord/tenant relationship, and she wasn't about to unburden herself on him. He could close down but start again somewhere else. Julian had the rest of his life to start again. Elsie, on the other hand, was out of options, choices and time. Her doomsday clock was ticking perilously close to midnight, and when the big hand finally aligned, it was game over for her.

'Here. Have this,' said Elsie as she held a cup of coffee for him. 'I've put three sugars in for you.'

Julian removed his head from his hands and took the cup from her. 'I don't take sugar, but thanks,' he said. He sipped and wrinkled his nose as the sweet liquid hit his taste buds. 'I'm sorry to land this on you, but I won't be able to see out the term of the lease.'

There were eight months left to run, but Elsie shook her head. 'Don't worry about it. There are worst things that could happen in life, you know.'

Julian let out a derisory laugh. 'Is there? I'd like to know what could be worse than being an utter failure at life.'

Elsie bit her lip. *Yeah, but at least you still have one*, she thought silently as she drank her coffee.

Chapter Six

Ingrid

Ingrid plumped up the cushions on the sofa and straightened the magazines into a fan shape on the coffee table. She went over to the window and opened it to let in some fresh air, and as she looked through the glass, she spotted a woman lurking outside by the front gate. She tilted her head and watched as the woman started to walk up the path before changing her mind and returning to the pavement outside the gate. Ingrid took a step back and peeked out from behind the curtains.

'Who are you spying on?' said Amanda as she entered the living room carrying a vase of fresh white lilies.

'Shush. I'm not spying. Just watching,' said Ingrid in a whisper.

Amanda set the vase down on the table and walked over to Ingrid. 'I don't know why you're whispering. She's hardly likely to hear you from over there.'

Amanda stood in the centre of the window, and Ingrid gently pulled her to the side. 'Don't stand there. She'll see you.'

'So what?' said Amanda.

'Take a look at her,' she replied. 'The poor love is scared stiff.'

Amanda pulled back the curtains and stared at the woman, and Ingrid tutted and whipped the curtain back out of her hand.

'Do you want me to go out and see what she wants?' said Amanda, but Ingrid shook her head.

'God, no. I'll go. You'll scare her to death.'

Amanda blew a kiss at Ingrid. 'You love me really.'

'For my sins,' she said, smiling. 'Now bugger off. Haven't you got something useful to do?'

Ingrid walked out of the room and into the hallway.

'You don't pay me enough to be useful,' she heard Amanda shout after her. Ingrid chuckled, shook her head and headed out of the front door.

The clicking of her heels announcing her arrival caused the woman to turn around, but upon seeing Ingrid, she lowered her head, turned and began to hurry away from the house. Ingrid rushed after her.

'Wait,' she shouted out to the stranger. 'Is there anything I can do to help?'

The woman stopped walking. 'I doubt it,' she replied.

'How do you know if you haven't asked?' replied Ingrid as she took a tentative step towards her.

'Nobody can help me.'

'I suppose,' said Ingrid, 'that entirely depends on what help you need.'

The woman's shoulders shook gently, and before she could reach her, she let out a piercing cry. It was filled with a heart-wrenching sadness that Ingrid recognised only too well. It was the same cry of pain she'd made when the doctors told her husband was going to die. It was the pain of being told no hope was left for you. The woman's legs buckled and gave way, but before she hit the pavement, Ingrid rushed forward to steady her.

'I've got you, my love. I've got you.'

***

The woman sobbed uncontrollably for almost half an hour. So far, all Ingrid had managed to ascertain was that her name was Elsie, and she didn't want to talk about anything. Amanda had immediately sprung into nurse mode when she'd heard the wails coming from outside and rushed to help Ingrid bring the woman into the house. The sobbing eventually subsided and was replaced by a series of snorts and sharp intakes of breath as the woman's lungs attempted to calm themselves.

Amanda walked into the living room with two glasses of whiskey, and she set them down on the table in front of Ingrid and Elsie. Ingrid gave her a grateful smile, and Amanda winked back at her before silently exiting the room.

Elsie wiped her puffy eyes with the back of her hand, reached for the glass and took a large gulp of the amber liquid.

'Are you here to look at the home for yourself or somebody close to you?' she asked in her third attempt to get Elsie to talk.

Elsie took another drink from the glass, emptying it, and set it back down on the table. 'It's a beautiful place,' she replied, avoiding the question. 'It's nice that it matches what I saw on the website. You've got amazing reviews as well.'

'We like to think that we've got something special here that people are looking for,' said Ingrid, not wanting to push Elsie. It was clear that this young woman's barriers were firmly up. She'd have to be patient and tread carefully if she wanted to get her to open up.

'Would you like me to show you around?' offered Ingrid. 'You'll see that the rest of the home is just as we described, and you might want to...'

'Do you do palliative care?' interrupted Elsie.

'We do,' confirmed Ingrid. 'We offer both long-term and short-term care. However, it does depend on what kind of palliative care you require. If it's a complex illness, we have to make sure that we have the appropriate staff and equipment.'

'Cancer,' said Elsie.

'May I ask where in the body?'

'Pretty much everywhere, according to the doctors at the hospital.'

'And the prognosis?'

'Nine to twelve months,' said Elsie.

Such formality wasn't Ingrid's usual style when talking about end-of-life care, but it clearly was Elsie's, and if it helped her feel comfortable enough to talk, then Ingrid would carry on.

'And when would you be looking at moving in?' It was a strategic question on Ingrid's part, and it appeared to pay off.

'I want to settle my estate first. You know, sell property, get rid of possessions and all that, so it wouldn't be imminently. But I am happy to pay for the room from now to secure it.'

So the room was for her. How utterly heartbreaking. Elsie looked as though she were in her thirties. It was no age. At least when Phillip had passed away, he'd lived an almost full life. It had hurt Ingrid. Of course it had. When he'd first received the diagnosis, she'd been completely broken, but she did take some comfort in the fact that they had lived a life of almost forty years together. They'd travelled all over the world; experienced everything together. No doubt, Elsie had lived too, she supposed, to some degree. She was obviously a woman of means if she could afford to pay for a room that she didn't need to use, and Ingrid guessed that she'd probably travelled at some point in her life. But did that constitute a full life? It wasn't even close to it.

'That won't be necessary, Elsie. You probably won't even need to think about moving for a good six months, but I'll block the room out for five months' time to make sure that it's free for when you need it. You'll start to be charged from when you choose to move in. But wouldn't you prefer to be at home when the time comes? I only mention it because it's something that I hear a lot of people say. They prefer to,' she stopped herself from saying 'pass away', 'go surrounded by their friends and family.'

'That won't be applicable to me.' Elsie said, quickly standing to her feet. 'Thank you for your time,' she said, offering her hand to Ingrid.

She shook it and resisted the urge to pull her into a hug.

'You're more welcome. I usually take contact details so that I can check in with my clients prior to them moving in. Don't worry, I shan't bombard you; just send the odd message from time to time.'

Elsie nodded and reached into her handbag, pulling out one of her old business cards. She handed it to Ingrid, and her mouth opened as if she were about to say something, but she quickly closed it again and headed out of the living room and towards the front door.

Ingrid followed behind her. 'It was nice to meet you, Elsie. I'll be in touch soon.'

Elsie turned and gave Ingrid a courteous half-smile but said nothing as she made her way down the path and out of the front gate, disappearing from view behind the hedges that lined the bottom of the garden.

Ingrid went back inside.

'She's one tough cookie,' said Amanda, emerging from the staff room.

Ingrid thumbed the edge of the business card. 'I think she's had to be. It sounds like there are no friends or family to support her. But she's obviously struggling with being that person now. I doubt she even knows who she is anymore.'

Amanda draped her arm over her shoulder. 'Well, if that's the case, then I'm glad she came here and found you.'

Ingrid reached up and squeezed her friend's hand. 'Me too,' she said. 'Me too.'

Chapter Seven

Jack

It had been three weeks since Jack had last seen Elsie. He'd returned to the park every day since their fall-out and waited, and every day had brought a fresh wave of disappointment when she hadn't shown.

Jack had expected her reaction. You didn't spend three years with someone and not pick up on their traits and personality. Sometimes, he even felt that he knew Elsie better than she did. She came across as hard-faced, unfeeling, and heartless. When in truth, Elsie was nothing more than the product of a broken society and a broken system. She'd learned from a very young age that emotions served no purpose. Her mother hadn't cared whether Elsie's stomach was swollen through starvation; she hadn't given a damn about the cries of pain from her child when her appendix was dangerously close to bursting. When Social Services finally became involved and removed Elsie from her mother's care after yet another drug overdose, the woman did no more than leave the hospital and head straight for her dealer for another fix. Jack curled back his lips at the thought of the woman. He believed in the power of redemption. He believed that everybody deserved a second chance and that everybody was entitled to an opportunity to change themselves for the better. But some people didn't want to change, and Elsie's mother was one of them. The beauty of life just passed her by, and all because she sought solace at the end of a needle.

Was it any wonder that Elsie's walls had been built high, brick by brick, until nobody could climb over them any more? It was a technique that Jack had seen time and time again. Elsie was protecting herself from more hurt and pain; she didn't want to get close to anybody for fear of them letting her down, but she was missing out on some of the most incredible connections a human can have because of it.

Building up Elsie's trust had been a slow process, but as the weeks and months passed, she'd slowly lowered her walls, and Jack felt confident enough to talk so candidly to her. He knew her cancer was back before she did, in the same way that he knew that this time the diagnosis would be terminal: He'd watched her wince as she sat down on the park bench or complain of chest pain and headache far too often.

He had hoped that his nonchalant personality and erudite discussions over the years had been something that Elsie had grown to expect. She seemed to like him that way. But he'd misjudged her feelings altogether that day. He had known that she'd react to what he said. He even knew that she would walk away from him, but as her initial shock and anger subsided, he'd expected her to be intrigued enough by what he said to come back.

Three weeks!

Secretly, Jack worried that if he left Elsie alone for too long, he'd lose his opportunity to help her altogether. Maybe he should go to her apartment and sit outside on the bench by the church? But he quickly changed his mind. Elsie needed to come to him. He couldn't force her, not even subtly. This was her chance to change, and it was a decision that she needed to make without being prompted. No. He'd wait for her. She'd come. He knew in his soul that she would.

Chapter Eight

Elsie

It had been five weeks since she'd last seen Jack. Five weeks since she'd last heard his voice telling her about some latest conspiracy theory or offering up one of his pearls of wisdom. And five weeks was too long, considering that Elsie didn't have much time left to play with. She missed him in ways she never thought possible. It was as if *he'd* died, and without him in her life, Elsie was slowly falling apart, figuratively and literally. Her body was being defeated cell by cell, and each new day brought an unexpected pain in a new area. The pain she could live with – or die with, to be factually correct. It was the influx of feelings that Elsie's fragile brain couldn't process. They were becoming overwhelming to the point of embarrassment. She'd even cried at the end of *Toy Story 3,* a film that she would never normally watch, but she'd spent twenty minutes aimlessly flicking through channels looking for a distraction from the gritty crime documentaries or reality TV programmes she usually opted for. She didn't want to watch real people in real-life scenarios. A children's film seemed like a sensible idea, but as she watched the little toys grab each other's hands in the incinerator as they accepted their fate, a fresh wave of tears burned at her eyes. She angrily wiped them away and threw the remote control at the TV. The screen smashed with a sickening series of cracks and promptly turned green. Elsie let out a shout of annoyance even though it had been her own fault, and then she cried again as she decided whether or not it was worth her investing in a new television.

This crying business was exhausting and had only recently started to become a significant issue for her since her unexpected outburst in front of Ingrid. She had gone to see the care home a few weeks ago with the sole intention of confirming whether the pictures she'd seen on the website were accurate. Elsie hadn't wanted to go inside, see the rooms or speak to Ingrid. That would have been a step too far, an admission that she needed help when, only a few weeks previously, that sort of pre-planning was the furthest thing from her mind. It had been Ingrid's fault for coming outside and accosting her when all Elsie wanted was to hide behind the privet and check that the paint wasn't peeling from the front door and windows or that there wasn't a collection of bins spilling rubbish all over the front garden. If Elsie had been left alone to carry out her investigations in private she doubted that she'd been in this position now. But no, Ingrid had hurried down the garden path towards Elsie with her flowery skirt billowing in the wind.

What made it worse was that Elsie had spotted Ingrid peeping from the window in the front room. She'd seen the nurse, Amanda, join her who was more brazen, standing in the window and staring directly at Elsie. She should have left immediately at that point, but like an utter idiot, she'd stayed and retreated behind the bushes. She hadn't heard the front door opening. It was only when she heard the footsteps tip-tapping their way towards her and getting closer and closer that she knew she'd messed up. Had Ingrid's manner been a little more brusque. Had her opening question been anything other than *'Can I help you?'*, she knew that she wouldn't have reacted the way that she had. She wondered whether Ingrid's line of questioning had been deliberately leading. She'd probably done it before with other people. Whether it had been deliberate or not, the result was Elsie turning into the type of hysterical woman that she despised. She saw it as a weakness, the kind that other people, ordinary people, suffered from. Not her, though. She wasn't like ordinary people. She'd spent her life bottling up her emotions, hiding them away along with her heart, and believed that she could do exactly the same with her diagnosis, but there was only so much you could fit inside a bottle before it overflowed, she guessed.

The kindness and sympathy she'd received from Ingrid after her breakdown had left Elsie ashamed and embarrassed. She didn't doubt for one second that Ingrid's intentions were genuine, but Elsie felt as though she'd been exposed to her bones, and Ingrid could see her raw shame in all of its glory. She'd beat a hasty retreat that day and spent the rest of the afternoon huddled up inside her duvet, hiding from the world.

Now, she was a bubbling wreck of a woman who'd lost her ability to compartmentalise her feelings. Every emotion, thought and feeling was etched on her skin's surface for all to see. She'd even got teary when the old lady at the newsagents told her that she had beautiful eyes, 'they're as blue as the Caribbean sea,' she'd said to Elsie, 'so full of life.' Before Elsie could burst into tears in front of her, she threw a ten-pound note across the counter and hurried out of the shop. She'd sobbed the entire way back to her apartment. She'd only gone in there for a copy of Vogue and a Mars Bar.

Elsie didn't know what mood would greet her when she woke in the mornings anymore. She was so up and down; crying one moment, laughing the next, or organising her funeral with impartiality at other times. It was too much for her, and the more unpredictable and unstable she felt, the less she went outside. She ordered greasy takeaways, watched shit daytime television programmes and ignored all phone calls.

Julian had stopped by on several occasions, flicking the letterbox an annoying number of times to get her attention. Each time he left, he walked out into the road and looked up at her windows, and each time, Elsie had ducked below the window sill to hide from him.

You're rubbish. I saw you trying to dip out of sight. He'd texted her once.

Elsie rolled her eyes. 'Fuck,' she muttered under her breath.

Apologies. I'm not feeling great at the moment. I don't want to see anybody. She wrote back, pleased with her explanation, as it wasn't technically an untruth.

So you're not avoiding me because I'm letting you down? Julian replied.

What? Why did he have to make everything about him?

Not at all. You have to do what you have to do. Put yourself first, be happy, and don't apologise for it.

He sent her a smiley emoji with a thumbs up, and she closed her phone again. It rang as she set it down, causing her to jump, and The Orchids flashed up on her screen. Ingrid was certainly persistent; she'd give her that. It was the fifth phone call Elsie had received from her, and it would also be the fifth one she'd sent to voicemail, although she always listened to the voicemails afterwards.

Ingrid's voice was actually quite soothing, and Elsie would always text a polite response, but she didn't want to give her carte blanche to become her unofficial counsellor. Anyway, there was no point in getting close to Ingrid now. In a few months' time, Elsie would be gone, and the expensive room that

Elsie had paid for would have a new tenant quicker than the sheets could be changed.

What she needed right now was Jack. She needed to speak to him. He was the only person in her life that she'd ever trusted and the only man she was likely to ever trust. Maybe she should have given him the opportunity to explain? He shouldn't have said something like that at that time though. Jack should have kept it to himself until she was ready to hear shit like that. And if she was never ready, he should have kept it to himself permanently. She glanced at the wall clock above her now broken television. It was coming up to 9 a.m. If she bypassed her shower, threw on some clothes and hurried, she should make it to the park for just after ten.

***

Elsie entered the park with a heavy sense of trepidation weighing down her stomach. She couldn't believe that she was so nervous about what Jack's reaction might be when he saw her. He didn't seem the type to hold a grudge or reprimand her publicly, but she had shouted 'fuck you' to him several times, and for that he was owed an apology in the least. She hoped that he'd accept it. She also hoped that he apologised to her too. Did she deserve an apology? Was poor timing a reason to apologise to a person?

Yes. She decided. It absolutely was, and if it wasn't, then perhaps being an insensitive arsehole was.

As Elsie debated with herself on the just causes of an apology, she turned the corner at precisely the wrong moment and was smacked head-on by a low-flying ball. It was one of those soft ones, the kind that bounced with an echoey boing when it hit the floor, but it still smarted as it ricocheted off her nose. Impressively, it flew straight into the hands of a little boy who clearly hadn't been expecting the bounce-back. He smiled a wide grin back at Elsie, minus two front teeth, and then rushed off again in the direction of the green. The feral little shit hadn't even said sorry, Elsie thought to herself. He was the next generation of little fuckers growing into bigger fuckers who thought the world needed to bend to accommodate their whims, beliefs and generally ridiculous ideologies. At least there were some benefits in dying soon.

She thundered past the said problem child as he rejoined who Elsie assumed to be his family. There was one woman, presumably his mother, and four children, whose ages ranged from about two years old right up to the ball-throwing hooligan at about eight years old. The woman looked fraught and downright exhausted as she attempted to placate all four children at the same time. The littlest one, a boy harnessed inside its pushchair, was screaming at the top of his lungs and pointing to a teddy on the grass. Two girls, aged around six, and who looked to be twins judging by their matching outfits, were practising some kind of dance routine which they'd probably seen on the internet as the twerks they were, well, twerking, seemed completely inappropriate given their age. And then there was the eldest boy, the asbo-waiting-to-happen dickhead. No further words were needed about him.

Elsie thanked god that she'd never had children. What a world they would have been born into. She stole a quick glance at the mother; the dark circles stained her under-eyes and told Elsie all she needed to know. Better get used to looking like that, thought Elsie. You can kiss goodbye to life for the next eighteen years at least. But at least she'd have a life. Would Elsie swap with the woman? If there was some magical way that she could switch places with the habitually tired, panda-eyed woman with four children, would she do it? No, Elsie quickly decided. I'd rather be dead, and she chuckled to herself which both worried and surprised her at the same time.

Her smile quickly faded when she looked ahead to her and Jack's bench and found it empty. Elsie looked at the time on her phone. It was 10.20 and Jack should have been there by now. Panic filled her chest. What if he was ill? What if he was lying in bed at home in utter agony and unable to get help? The bloody man didn't have a mobile, so how would he call anyone? What if it was worse than that? What if Jack had fallen down the stairs and was lying cold and dead at the bottom of the stairs? Did Jack even have stairs or did he live in a flat or a bungalow? She had absolutely no idea, and Elsie cursed herself for not having asked him before. And then another possibility came forward, one that was worse than Jack being ill or dead in Elsie's mind. What if Jack simply didn't want to see Elsie again? What if she'd pissed him off to the point of him not wanting to return to be verbally abused by her? What if Jack had moved onto another park, to another bench and with another Elsie? Perhaps he was sitting there right now, chatting and laughing with them as if she had never existed.

Elsie's breath refused to calm. If only she'd taken the time to ask Jack more about himself. How could anyone possibly know somebody for three years and not know where they lived? It was a disgrace and Elsie was ashamed of herself on so many levels. Please, God. Let him be okay. Let him not be ill or dead. Let him come back here, she said silently to herself with her eyes closed.

She heard footsteps on the path, and she opened her eyes with the insane expectation that God had answered her prayer with the instant manifestation of Jack. Unsurprisingly, it wasn't Jack, and although Elsie was disappointed at this, she was more annoyed when she saw it was the tired-looking woman with too many children heading her way with the youngest child who, although was still being restrained in the pushchair, was much happier as he gripped onto the teddy he'd earlier screamed to take possession of.

'Do you mind if...?' asked the woman, pointing to the bench.

Elsie shook her head, but she knew full well that her face was saying anything but yes.

'Help yourself,' she replied, secretly hoping the woman took the hint and wheeled the brat and herself to another bench.

But the woman smiled. 'Thank you,' she said and sat down.

Elsie could hear the tinge of an accent but couldn't place it. They remained there in extremely awkward silence; the woman staring out at her brood and Elsie doing the same because there was nothing else to look at in front of her. Then she looked at her feet because it just felt weird looking at someone else's children playing when you had no children of your own playing near them. The two girls did a synchronised cartwheel as part of their dance routine. The boy threw the ball at the right moment, hitting one of the girl's feet and sending it flying through the air. They all found this deeply hilarious and fell to the ground laughing hysterically. It was a little over the top, in Elsie's opinion but she felt the stare of the woman next to her and turned her head to find her looking at her. Elsie faked a laugh and smile.

'That was a good one,' Elsie said, feeling obliged to say something now that she'd gone to the effort of acknowledging her.

The woman responded with a half-hearted smile. 'Can I tell you something?' she said to Elsie.

Elsie nodded. 'Of course you can.'

The woman leaned forward, cupped her hands over the toddler's ears and whispered.

'I can't stand the little bastards.'

Chapter Nine

Agata

G od, that had felt good. Apart from her family back in Poland, Agata had never told anyone about the King's children. They were a complete nightmare and utter brats, thanks to Mummy and Daddy King, who seemed to think that the sun shined out of their privately educated arses. The only one who was an exception to the rule was little Arthur, but he was already showing signs of liberal parenting affecting his personality. When Agata used to tell Arthur no, he would jut out his bottom lip and sulk for a few minutes until Agata distracted him with a silly voice or a piece of fruit. Now, though, no was a defunct word and meant nothing as Mr and Mrs King failed to reprimand his toddler tantrums and had banned Agata from doing the same.

It had been the same process with the other children, who had been beautiful little souls as babies. Agata first became the King's Au Pair following the birth of their eldest, George. He had been the most lovely little baby Agata had ever seen, with the rosiest cheeks and the cutest of button noses. He was the picture postcard of babies, the kind that always stopped passers-by in their tracks to look and coo over in the pram.

Little George had turned into a demon child after three years of indulgence and poor discipline routines. He'd kicked, bitten and spat at Agata. He'd laugh at her attempts to tell him off, refuse to do as he was told, and basically did whatever he wanted inside and outside the house. His parents laughed off his behaviour, telling everybody who would listen that George was 'special'. They'd meant this in an entirely serious way and deluded themselves into thinking that George was destined to become the next child genius: He behaved in the way that he did because his brain was far too superior for the likes of mere mortals who frankly couldn't compete with him intellectually. Agata knew differently. She once caught George eating rabbit poo in the garden a couple of years ago because he thought they were raisins. It was a simple mistake for any six-year-old, but it was a definite confirmation that he wasn't the next Stephen Hawking in the making. She doubted that the late, great Mr Hawking had ever eaten rabbit shit.

The twins, Isabella and Penelope, were the same as George, albeit a little less wild than him. But they still refused to listen to a word that Agata said, ran rings around their parents and pretty much did whatever they wanted to, whenever they wanted to.

To put it bluntly, this job was the pits and not at all what she intended to do when she'd first arrived in England over nine years ago. She was a qualified accountant back in Poland and had built herself quite a successful career freelancing for various businesses. But the lure of the opportunity to earn over four times her monthly wage in one month had proven too great for Agata to resist, and she had secured accommodation, packed her suitcase and waved goodbye to her family without so much as a backward glance.

Her rude awakening came the moment the plane door opened, and she was greeted with cutting rain hitting the side of her face. Outside departures, she hailed one of the waiting taxis and baulked at the cost of her ride as she watched the meter steadily rise with each passing mile. Her accommodation, which looked stunning on the website, had proven to be a major disappointment and was nothing more than the front room of a standard semi-detached house. Every available space had been turned into a bedroom, leaving only one small and severely mouldy bathroom and a kitchen so dirty that Agata refused to cook in it. There were eight occupants in that tiny house, and it wasn't until she opened the door one morning to several housing officers and the police that she discovered it had been let illegally. All eight tenants were swiftly removed from the property and left to seek an alternative accommodation on their own, or face living on the streets.

But the worst was still to come. Agata had mistakenly believed that her pigeon English would be enough to secure herself a job with any accounting firm she chose, but with each rejection letter she received, and with each failed interview, she quickly realised that she needed to rethink her options and quickly. Her money was dwindling at an exponential rate, and if she didn't find a job soon, then she'd be back in Poland before the end of the following month, much to the delight of her family, who had been less than happy at Agata leaving in the first place.

Her poor English skills left Agata with few employment options; cleaning, fruit picking, and warehouse jobs were in abundance for migrants, but they also paid poorly, and she calculated that she would have to work at least forty additional hours overtime each month if she wanted to meet the monthly rent on her new, and much improved, flat. No. What Agata needed was a job which offered accommodation as well. That way, at least, she wouldn't have to work every hour she could just to survive. So, when she saw the advertisement for a live-in nanny pinned to the notice board in the local Polish centre, she tore it off the corkboard before anybody else could see it and rushed outside to call the number, arranging an interview for the following morning.

She had woken early the following day, ironed her black trousers and white shirt to precision, and washed her hair until it squeaked when she drained the excess water from her locks with her hands. She'd arrived at the imposing house ten minutes early and was shown in by a woman called Maria, who she later found out was the maid. Agata waited nervously on a chair in the hallway and counted the black and white tiles on the floor to keep herself calm and when the door to the front living room, or drawing room as Mrs King corrected her not long after she first started working there, was finally opened she was greeted by a towering but painfully thin man, who introduced himself as Esra King.

'If you'd like to follow me, Miss Rutkowski,' he'd said, leading Agata into a beautifully decorated and immaculate room.

The ceilings were so high that Agata suddenly felt claustrophobic at the thought of her little flat. A sparkling chandelier glistened above her, and there were plush leather sofas that looked like they'd never been sat on. The fireplace was black, with little black and white tiles flanking either side and the fire that crackled cast a comfortable warmth that Agata was grateful for. A low-backed, leather chair had been placed opposite two ornately carved ones, and Mr King indicated for Agata to sit down. Opposite was an exquisitely dressed woman whose hair had been fashioned into an impossibly tight chignon and who, despite clearly wearing heavy makeup, had mastered the art of making it look natural.

'So, Miss,' Mrs King consulted her notepad, 'Rutkowski. Do you have any experience working with children?'

Agata had expected this question. The truthful answer was no. She'd never worked with children in her life, but her elder sister did have two children, so she felt that it wouldn't be a total lie to say yes.

'I have indeed, Mrs King,' replied Agata, hoping that she had pronounced all of her words correctly.

'And for how long?' continued Mrs King.

'For four years,' said Agata. It was the age of her eldest niece – again, not a complete lie.

'And did you enjoy your work? Were you involved in any disputes?' continued Mrs King.

Agata opened her mouth to answer, but Mr King's mobile shrilled, and he looked apologetically at his wife.

'It's the hospital. I have to take this,' he told her before rushing out of the room.

'My husband is a surgeon at City Hospital,' said Mrs King. 'He's on call. So, you were saying, Miss Rutkowski?'

'Yes, I enjoyed my work tremendous. And no. There were no disputes,' said Agata.

'Tremendously,' corrected Mrs King. 'We'd have to work on your English if you were lucky enough to get the job. Children's brains can be little sponges when they're young, and I wouldn't want my son to pick up any bad habits as far as the English language is concerned. He would, after all, be in your company for much of the day.'

Agata felt her cheeks flush, and she hoped her neck hadn't gone blotchy as it often did when she was nervous or embarrassed.

'Mrs King,' she said confidently. 'If I am lucky enough to get the position, I promise I will study English all the time until I speak perfect.'

Mrs King raised a perfectly-plucked but doubtful eyebrow. 'Perfectly,' she corrected again, scribbling something in her notepad. Agata gulped loudly.

'Of course, we're advertising for a live-in nanny. You'd work six days a week, with Sunday being your scheduled day off to do whatever it is you choose to do. We wouldn't tolerate any guests in the house at any time. If you wish to meet with friends or family, this must be done outside our house. Your hours would be from six o'clock in the morning until seven in the evening, and if my son wakes during the night, you'll be expected to tend to him. There will be no alcohol consumption at all whilst you're in our employ, and it goes without saying that absolutely no drugs unless you have a medicated condition. Do you?'

Agata shook her head.

'Good,' continued Mrs King. 'You'll be entitled to two weeks paid holiday per year to be taken separately and to do with as you please, with a further two weeks holiday with us, which you'll be expected to attend and care for little George. Do you have any questions at all?'

Indeed, Agata did. The most obvious question of all being how much was she going to be paid. But Mrs King projected an air of superiority that made Agata uncomfortable even to ask, and she thought that it might have been a ploy by the woman to check and see if the lure of money was more important than the job itself. Would it go against Agata if she did ask? Agata decided it was best not to risk it.

'No. No questions. It all seems quite acceptable,' replied Agata.

Mrs King seemed happy with her response, and she grinned smugly. 'Wonderful. Well, I shall be in touch,' she held out a limp hand, and Agata wasn't sure whether she should kiss it, shake it or curtsey. She opted for the shake.

The phone call to say that she got the job came a few days later, and Agata had been thrilled. She'd packed up her minimal belongings, returned the keys to her landlord, and headed to the King residence with a renewed sense of hope inside. All she needed to do was use this opportunity to brush up her English, and the second she had, she would start to apply for jobs at accountancy firms.

When she arrived at the King's home, Agata was ushered upstairs by Maria and shown to her room. It was painted stark white and had minimal furniture, with only a bed, bedside cabinet, wardrobe, dressing table and mirror inside. There were no pictures on the walls, and the whole room appeared to be an afterthought, contrasting heavily with the expensive furnishings in the rest of the house, but it was clean, comfortable, and warm.

Her first month as a nanny passed unremarkably. George, thankfully, slept through the night and napped for much of the day. He only grumbled when tired or hungry, and Agata thought herself lucky for landing such a cushy job. Her first payslip, however, had proved more of a shock than a disappointment when she discovered that she had only been paid £980 for the month.

'Excuse me, Mrs King. But is this correct?' she asked after finally plucking up the courage.

Mrs King shot a contemptuous glare at Agata. 'Of course it's correct,' she spat back. 'You can't expect high wages with your level of experience and your shocking English skills.'

Agata wanted to shout at the woman and rip that ridiculous chignon straight off her scalp. She didn't need English skills to realise that the Kings were exploiting her. They spent more money on eating out almost every night than they did for Agata to care for their son full-time. Agata had had enough. She was tired, bored and lonely. By the time she finished work in the evening, there was nowhere for her to go, and her only day off coincided with the Polish Centre being closed. She saw nobody outside of the house.

As Agata slowly walked back up the stairs to run George's bath that evening, she vowed that first thing on Monday morning, she'd call around some accountancy firms and see if there was any work available. She'd have a free run of the house with Mr King being at work and Mrs King at her yoga class.

But every enquiry had resulted in disappointment, and disappointment quickly turned to despair as Agata realised that, as it stood, no business wanted her the way that she was. She was stuck, albeit temporarily, but stuck nonetheless. Within two years of her starting, Mrs King went on to give birth to Isabella and Penelope, and four years after that, little Arthur had arrived. Although Agata was now expected to care for four children, each new addition hadn't resulted in an increase in wages, and all these years on, she still only received the measly £980 per month wage she'd started on. Quite frankly, the Kings were taking the piss out of her; they knew it, and Agata knew it. She had spent years perfecting her English, but Agata soon faced a new problem. According to the businesses she was applying to, she'd been out of the accounting loop for far too long and now suddenly lacked experience. She couldn't believe it. She'd inadvertently shot herself in the foot.

She had grown to hate living and working in that house. She despised Mr and Mrs King, whose penchant for popping out children was conditional on someone else looking after them. They were completely unaffected by their children, and the only time they showed a smidgeon of interest was when it was one of the children's birthdays or on Christmas morning. Agata's life was one of banal housewifery, and she hated it. It wasn't that she was averse to motherhood, but if she were going to spend her days raising children, she'd prefer it if they were actually hers and not the by-product of two entitled cretins who didn't even know, or care, what their children got up to.

Agata had been craving somebody to talk to for years. Somebody on the outside who could tell her she wasn't going crazy but trying to make a new friend when she had four rude and annoying children in tow made it difficult. She'd seen that woman several times in the park. She had wanted to go up and speak to her before, but every time one of the children had run off in the opposite direction or was screaming because one of the others had done something to them, or they were just generally being little shits and complaining that they wanted to go home.

Thankfully, the woman was there almost as much as Agata, but even when the ideal opportunity had arisen to speak to her, which it had on several occasions, Agata had stopped herself from going over. She seemed a little weird – unhinged even, at times. It wasn't that long ago that she'd watched her scream 'fuck you' at the top of her lungs before storming out of the park. But oddly, she admired the woman for being able to do something like that. How Agata would love to scream that in Mrs King's face! It was probably for that reason alone that Agata had been determined to speak to the woman the next time she saw her in the park. She needed somebody as vocally free as her in her life. It might be liberating. But after that incident, the woman went on the missing list, and Agata panicked that she might have missed her chance.

But then, one day, she was just there. Sitting in the same spot, on the same bench she'd been at so many times before. The children were playing nicely together, mercifully, and she seized the opportunity to go over before they started to shout and scream or before Agata lost her nerve completely.

'Do you mind if...?' she'd asked.

The woman shook her head and smiled politely, but Agata could see the annoyance behind her eyes. It was hardly surprising. She'd seen how George had launched the ball in the poor woman's face, but Agata thought it best not to bring that up.

'Thank you,' said Agata, and she'd sat down, thinking of what she could say next.

It was a little uncomfortable at first, but then the children started laughing at something that George had done, and Agata turned to watch the woman's reaction. The woman then turned, and when she saw Agata staring at her, she laughed and smiled, but it was clearly strained. God! Agata was making herself look a complete fool.

'That was a good one,' said the woman, and all Agata could do was smile back because she couldn't care less what the children were doing. She needed to say something, and it had to count. She's already made herself look like a complete moron already.

'Can I tell you something?' she said to the woman.

'Of course you can,' the woman replied.

Agata leaned forward and cupped her hands over Arthur's ears. 'I can't stand the little bastards,' she whispered.

The woman stared back at her wide-eyed, and Agata thought for a second that she was about to whip out her phone and call Social Services on her, but after a few seconds, the woman's eyes crinkled at the sides, and she chuckled. The chuckle turned into a laugh, and the laugh grew louder and louder. The woman threw back her head and laughed until tears ran down her face. Agata relaxed and laughed with her, relieved that she hadn't misjudged her. Finally, after two or three minutes, the laughing subsided, and the woman wiped away the tears on her cheeks.

'God. I needed that,' she said. She leaned over towards Agata and held out her hand. 'I'm Elsie.'

'Agata,' she replied, shaking Elsie's hand.

'I take it that they're not yours then?' asked Elsie.

Agata shook her head. 'If they were my children, they wouldn't behave like that. I wouldn't allow it.'

'So whose children are they then?' asked Elsie.

Agata told Elsie everything—the whole story of the last eight years. With every sentence, she felt relief washing through her veins. She was finally able to cleanse herself, and after fifteen minutes of ranting, she let out a deep exhale.

'Wow!' said Elsie. 'I didn't realise that people still exploited foreign workers. And I thought I had it tough.'

Agata cast a look of concern. 'Why? What's going on with you?'

But Elsie waved her hand and looked away. 'Nothing that can't wait until another day.'

The alarm on Agata's phone blared, and she tutted and turned it off.

'I'm sorry. I have to go. The children have their piano lesson in an hour. I have to get them home. Mrs King says they shouldn't be rushed. She says they won't be able to concentrate properly.'

Elsie nodded and smiled. 'Mrs King sounds like a right royal...' she looked at Arthur, who was happily sucking the foot of his toy, and then mouthed the word, 'bitch,' at the end.

Agata smiled.

'Yes. A total bitch,' she replied, without bothering to censor herself.

Chapter Ten

Elsie

I t had been almost two months now since Elsie had last seen Jack. Each morning, she'd left her apartment and trudged her way to the park with a semblance of hope inside her that Jack might actually be waiting for her when she got there. But each day she arrived, her heart sank at the sight of the empty bench. It wasn't just disappointment that she felt; the guilt swelled inside her, and the anger that she'd had initially directed at him now sat firmly in her lap and refused to budge. She shouldn't have spoken to him like that. He was only trying to help her in his own unique, if not unconventional, way.

Elsie needed to see him again. She needed to apologise. She needed him back. Her life, or what was left of it, was ever creeping towards oblivion. She was tired all the time, and Elsie wasn't sure if it was the cancer or the rollercoaster of emotions that she went through every day taking its toll on her body. She woke most mornings now with aches in her bones and joints and sometimes migraines that were so intense that she wanted to tear the hair out of her head. She was running out of time.

Where the bloody hell was he? She never imagined that he was the type of person to hold a grudge, especially given her situation. He'd always seemed so considerate. But then again, maybe he didn't want to be at the end of a dying woman's beating stick? Perhaps he'd lived through something similar with somebody else? Somebody he was once close to. Had he lost somebody to cancer before? It could just be something he didn't want to live through again. Jack never spoke about his personal life, and at one point, Elsie assumed that he was secretly gay. Not that that mattered in today's world, but Jack would have lived through a time where you were criminalised, imprisoned and sometimes castrated simply for being who you were; He might have gotten used to just not talking about it.

Elsie tutted as she took another Louis Vuitton handbag out of her wardrobe. She wiped the dust away from the handles and shook her head. This one still had the price tag attached. What a wasteful bitch she was spending thousands on a bag that she hadn't even used, and it wasn't the only one. She'd pulled out so many brand-new designer clothes that had never been on her back that, eventually, she was ashamed of it all. Clearing out her wardrobe had certainly been an eye-opener. She dropped the handbag into a cardboard box destined for the local charity shop; at least some good would come out of it.

She'd been sorting through her things for the past few weeks. It kept her mind off everything, and Elsie was surprised at how much lighter she felt inside the more empty her cupboards and drawers became. There was something soothing about it all that she couldn't quite put her finger on. For years, Elsie had spent her time hiding behind her work, away from people and relationships, and compensated her loneliness with expensive treats. Her mental walls were built with handbags and shoeboxes, papered over with the photographs of her standing in front of a landmark somewhere in the world and the menus of Michelin-star restaurants. Her life was nothing but *things*. Things which could be sold. Or given away. Or thrown away. In the end, with her *things* all gone, all Elsie would be left with would be her memories until she closed her eyes for that last time, and even they would disappear into the ether.

People, not things, were important. Jack had said that to her once during a conversation about something that Elsie couldn't even remember now. People are the ones that live on in other people, he'd told her, and at the time, Elsie hadn't paid it much thought, but now, with all things considered, she could finally relate to what Jack meant.

Who was going to remember her when she was gone? Aside from Jack, there was only Agata. It was a relatively new friendship if you could call the odd text, and a couple of meet-ups in the park friendship, but that suited Elsie. After all, what would be the point in it being anything more when she had so little time left? She hadn't even told Agata she was ill. It seemed unfair to burden her with that knowledge when Agata herself had so much going on in her own life. No. It was better this way. One day, soon, Agata's messages would go unanswered, and their meetings would abruptly stop. Agata would assume that Elsie had gotten bored and moved on. She'd probably be a little upset but not as distraught as watching Elsie get sicker and sicker until she eventually died. She was doing Agata a favour by not telling her. She was too nice to put her through that kind of trauma. Elsie was surprised at just how much she liked having Agata around. Maybe her illness was mellowing her? Agata had this remarkable ability to make scathing and cutting remarks sound so nonchalant, and coupled with her Polish accent, it always made Elsie smile.

But keeping Agata at arm's length meant that Elsie had nobody to talk to. She was dealing with it all on her own, from her illness to doctors and hospital appointments to clearing out her home and speaking to funeral directors. In some ways, she was grateful for the normality of it all because at least it gave her something to do, but she needed that outlet of talking candidly to somebody about it all. It was the pressure valve that needed to be released, and without that, Elsie frequently found herself exploding, or crumbling, depending on what mood she had woken up in that day, over the slightest thing. She hadn't realised just how much Jack helped her through her first cancer diagnosis. He had sat and listened and talked and then listened some more. It didn't matter what Elsie had spoken about. Jack had sat on the bench, his eyes fixed on the grass and trees ahead, and he'd listened to whatever it was she had wanted to speak about that day, and only when she'd finished and fell silent did he speak. Elsie hadn't realised just how lucky she was to have him back then. It was only now that she was going through it all again that his presence made complete sense to her. If only she could see him again and tell him how sorry she was. Elsie had never believed in God, not even now, but if he did exist, her only prayer would be to see Jack again.

***

Nine weeks and three days, and there he was, sitting on the bench with his legs crossed and arms folded across his chest. The wind was particularly cutting that morning, with icy blasts chilling the skin, and Jack had his nose buried deep inside his scarf, which he'd wrapped several times around his neck like a brace.

Elsie had stopped walking into the park with expectations. It made it easier to deal with when she found he wasn't there, so when she looked further along the path that morning and saw him sitting there, her heartbeat picked up pace.

'Thank you,' she whispered to the grey sky above her, not that she gave any credence to the silent prayer she'd sent out a week or so before, but she still felt the need to say it.

As she walked closer to him, thoughts of what she would say evaporated like steam out of her head. When she was almost at the bench, Jack turned his head and smiled, and he stood to greet her with his arms outstretched. Elsie fell into them, and he wrapped them tightly across her back. She sucked in the smell of him and felt the first flood of tears in her eyes. She nuzzled her head into his shoulder and allowed a small sob to escape her mouth, only for it to be muffled by Jack's coat. Instantly, Elsie felt safe again. Jack was here, and he was hugging her and the world, for the briefest of seconds, felt right again. He broke away from the hug and looked into her eyes.

'I'm glad you came back,' she said to him, wiping her tears with a gloved hand.

'I never went away,' he replied.

He slid to her side, and together, they walked to the bench where Jack eased Elsie down as though she was incapable of doing it herself. Maybe she wasn't?

'I'm so sorry,' she blurted out between sniffles.

'You have nothing to apologise for. I should have thought more about your feelings. It wasn't the right time to speak like that to you,' he replied.

'Still. I shouldn't have told you to fuck off.'

'You didn't. What you actually said was, "Fuck you, Jack. Fuck you."'

They both laughed.

'Well. I apologise for that then,' said Elsie.

He batted it away with his hand. 'I've been told worse. Occupational hazard.'

As ambiguous as his comment was, it was the first time that Jack had ever hinted at having an occupation, and part of Elsie wanted to probe him further, but she stopped herself. Not now. Maybe another time.

'Why did you stay away for so long? I thought you weren't coming back,' she asked him instead.

Jack sighed. 'I realised that you needed time. Time to process what was going on. Time to accept it. Until then, having me around would have delayed that. With me gone, you had the chance to question everything.'

'I thought you'd had enough of me.'

He let out a soft chuckle. 'You think you can get rid of me that easily?' He reached his hand over to hers. 'I will always be here for you. Always.'

Elsie shuffled closer to him and rested her head on his shoulder. Considering she'd always pushed people away, she liked the feeling of being so close to him. He was more than a friend. Jack was like having a father of her very own to confide in and to support her. It was all the things that she'd missed out on growing up, and now, she finally understood what all the hype was about. Jack had been right. His absence had made everything so much clearer to Elsie. She felt his arm move across her back and his hand rest on her shoulder, and she closed her eyes, savouring the feeling of being somebody's something. They sat there in silence, listening to the wind rustling through leaves on the trees and the sounds of the cars speeding along the busy road in the distance. If Elsie was to die right then and there, she would die happy. She sucked in a lungful of cold air, the coldness in her warm chest was somehow comforting. Then she closed her eyes and smiled.

***

'I'm ready,' said Elsie.

She had no idea just how long they'd been sitting there, staring off into the distance and not saying a single thing. It felt like minutes, but Elsie suspected it was probably much longer. She thought she might have even fallen asleep at one point when she'd suddenly jolted and found a small trail of spittle trickling down the side of her mouth. She hoped that she hadn't snored. There was nothing more humiliating than public snoring.

'Ready for what?' asked Jack.

'To live. You told me you'd be here for me when I was ready to live. What did you mean by that?'

Jack was still embracing her. 'It's about making the most of the time you have left. It's about really living.'

'I am making the most of the time I have left. I've almost sorted everything out. I'm just working through the final details with the solicitor so the estate can be settled when I go.'

'Elsie. That's not living. That's admin.'

She smiled. 'Yes. But unfortunately, it still has to be done. I don't want things left all topsy-turvy. Otherwise, everything I own will eventually end up going to the state. I'd rather give it all away to donkey sanctuaries.'

'Yes. I can just see those donkeys hobbling around in your Louboutin shoes.'

Elsie gave him a playful nudge in his side. 'The money, I mean. Smartarse.' She pulled away and looked up at him. 'I didn't have you down for a fashion connoisseur. How on earth do you know about Louboutin?'

He shot her a wry smile. 'I know more than you give me credit for, Missy.'

Elsie smiled and settled back down into his shoulder.

'What I mean when I say start living is to do just that. Live. Spend every second of every day doing something you wouldn't normally do,' continued Jack. 'Make every experience matter. Make it count.'

Elsie wrinkled up her nose. 'I did the whole bucket list thing after I was told I had cancer the first time. I pretty much ticked off everything, although I drew the line at wing walking. I can't see why anybody would want to do that.'

She felt the gentle shake of Jack's head, and he broke away from the hug. 'No. No. No. People always look at bucket lists in the wrong way.'

'And what way's that?'

'A bucket list is for the living. It's personal to them and them alone. It's a series of day trips and experiences they feel they need to do before they die, to say that they lived this extraordinary life.'

Elsie furrowed her brows. 'Your point being?'

'Those experiences die with the person. What impact does that have on the people around them? The people who are left after that person's gone? Most people start a bucket list when they've still got their whole lives ahead of them. Even they'll forget parts of it eventually. Like I said, a bucket list is for the living. A *living* list, however, that's for the dying.'

Elsie turned towards Jack. His green eyes shone through the morning's misty haze. 'I don't understand what you're saying,' she told him. 'They're both the same thing.'

'A living list is about doing things for other people in a way that changes *their* lives, not yours.' Jack's hands moved wildly in the air as he spoke. 'A living list is about creating a legacy that lives on through other people so that, ultimately, you're never forgotten. It's selfless. And thoughtful. And the most beautiful thing that you can do for another person.'

'So I give strangers my money? Is that what you're saying?' Elsie didn't see how it was any different to leaving her estate to an animal charity. Either way, she was just an anonymous donor.

'No. Not strangers. It's...' He stopped as his eyes settled on an ageing Labrador that was idling its way towards them. The owner followed closely behind, immersed in his mobile phone. The dog sniffed at Elsie's shoes, and she leant forward to stroke it. It titled its head, and Elsie stroked behind its ear, much to the dog's delight.

'Come on, Oscar,' the owner said when he finally looked up from his screen. 'Leave the nice woman to enjoy her morning. Sorry,' he said, looking at Elsie. 'He'll have you doing that all day if you let him.'

Elsie gave Oscar a final ruffle of his fur. 'No problem. He seems lovely.'

The owner gave a polite smile and carried on walking. The dog, seeing his master stride on without him, followed slowly behind.

'Sorry,' said Elsie, looking at Jack. 'What were you saying?'

'Just start thinking about ways that you can use your money to help people. Think big! Don't just be a faceless deposit in a charity's bank account.' Jack adjusted his scarf to bring it closer to his chin and stood. 'Listen. Take some time and think about what I've said.'

What he'd said? What had he said? Elsie had no idea. 'Wait,' she shouted after him as he walked away. 'I don't understand.'

'You will. I'll see you tomorrow. Same time? We'll talk more then.'

She slouched back on the bench and shook her head. Honestly, that man made her feel like she was trying to have a conversation with an enigma machine at times.

Chapter Eleven

Mack

'Wait. There she is!' Mack said urgently.

He nudged Sid, causing his head to jolt away from his hand, which had been propped on the arm of the bench in the square.

'Fucking hell,' said Sid. 'Be careful, will you.'

'Look. Over there,' continued Mack, ignoring his friend.

He pointed across the square, and Sid followed the line of his finger. His eyes settled on the woman strolling on the pavement on the other side. She was wrapped up warmly in a longline puffer coat, ideal given the day's weather, and she walked straight into the bistro.

Mack tutted. 'I thought she'd be going home.'

Despite his repeated return to the square, he hadn't seen her since that fateful night when she'd been so rude to him.

'Well. Go on then,' said Sid. 'Get it over with so we can get out of here. It's bloody freezing.'

Mack went to stand and then lowered himself back down again. 'Nah. Give it a few minutes for her to settle. I don't want to bombard her in there.'

'Good grief, man!' exclaimed Sid. 'What on earth is wrong with you? Get in there, say your piece and let's get the hell out of here.' He looked up at the darkening sky. 'It's going to piss down by the look of it.'

But Mack shook his head. 'No. Not yet. Just give it a few more minutes.'

Sid shook his head in dismay and propped his head back on his hand. He sighed loudly. 'Fine. Whatever you say, Romeo.'

Mack scoffed. 'No. It's not like that. I need to talk to her, that's all.'

'If you say so.'

Mack ignored Sid. There was no point in trying to explain to him. It wasn't that Mack was attracted to her, not that she wasn't attractive, but deep inside, Mack just felt a pull towards her. Ever since their altercation, there had been something inside him guiding him back to the square. He couldn't explain it. He'd counted how many times he'd been back. Fifteen! Fifteen times in the hope that he'd see her again. See her to do what exactly? He wasn't sure. Talk? Argue? Who knew? He'd knocked on her door on quite a few of those occasions, but each time, the door went unanswered, even when he'd been sure that somebody was home.

He was hoping that by the end of the day, he'd be able to resolve whatever it was that lured him here and put it to bed once and for all.

Sid was snoring softly again, and Mack marvelled at his ability to fall asleep in any position, in any weather and at any time of the day. But, he surmised, Sid had had plenty of time to master this feat. It wasn't fair to keep dragging him along, either. Sid's hip had been playing up again, and he couldn't walk as far as Mack. Hopefully, Mack could finally move on and carry on with his life as he had done before he'd set eyes on that woman, if you could call what he had a life, at any rate.

Chapter Twelve

Elsie

'A bucket list is for the living, and a living list is for the dying,' Elsie whispered as she slowly followed the rim of her wine glass with her finger.

'I'm sorry?'

Elsie's eyes darted upwards to see one of the restaurant's waitresses staring curiously back at her.

'No. Nothing,' she said, flustered. 'I was just talking to myself.'

The waitress shrugged. 'No problem. I just came over to see if you wanted another?' she pointed at Elsie's almost empty wine glass.

Elsie nodded. 'Yes, please.'

The waitress tottered away, and Elsie sank back into the softness of the cushions in the booth. She looked around at the restaurant and sighed. Despite Julian not notifying his customers that he would soon be closing for good, there were signs all around that closure was imminent. The normal menus had been removed and replaced with a shorter and more succinct menu hastily printed out on low-grade A4 paper. The special's board had been erased and now sat stark and empty against the brick wall. And a lot of the bottles of hard liquor behind the bar were empty and unreplaced.

Julian had kept her informed of his progress, and thankfully, he'd stopped breaking down and crying in front of her about it. He seemed to have accepted the Bistro's fate, and although he wasn't happy, he and Richard had booked a three-month world cruise pretty much the second the doors closed on the business. The first thought that had leapt into Elsie's head when Julian had excitedly presented her with the travel brochure was just how much something like that had cost them. Maybe she shouldn't have been so forgiving with the rent? Business may have been bad for them, but they clearly had a tidy sum tucked away somewhere to be able to afford something like that. Elsie quickly gave herself a proverbial shake. It wasn't her place to question their finances; she wasn't their bookkeeper. For all she knew, they might have taken out a finance agreement to pay for the cruise. And why should she care anyway? A few months' leeway on the rent would hardly make a massive difference to her. It would be a shame to see the bistro close, but looking around the place now, it was practically empty, with only a few other customers enjoying a late but somewhat limited lunch.

The restaurant business was a difficult industry at the best of times, but with the pandemic and now a cost of living crisis eating up almost all of people's spare cash, only the strongest or more unique eateries seemed to survive.

The waitress returned with a new glass of white wine, and Elsie nodded her thanks. She should have just bought the bottle. She knew that even after this drink, she would have another. Already, the bubbles were making her feel light-headed, but Elsie didn't care. She wanted to mull over what Jack had said about this whole living list business, and being drunk might help her make more sense of it all.

Jack had told her to give it to people she knew, but seeing as Elsie only knew him and, more recently, Agata, it would hardly take too much effort to organise that. More importantly, Jack had never struck as the type of person who would accept something so extravagant, so that would mean leaving a huge windfall all to little Agata. Christ! Elsie could just imagine her face. Although she reasoned it would be nice to give her an opportunity to escape that wretched family.

Elsie smiled as she imagined what Agata would say to the King family when she realised she wasn't trapped into working for them any longer. Her smile broke into a little laugh as her mind played out a fictitious scene of Agata telling the Kings precisely what she thought of them.

'I'm glad to have caught you in a better mood,' she heard a voice say, breaking Elsie away from her daydream.

She looked up and saw two men staring back at her. They were scruffy and dirty and wearing layers of tatty clothes and, with their messy, overgrown hair and beards, quite clearly, homeless. One man was older than the other, rubbing his hands together and blowing onto them to warm them up. The other was much younger, but his straggly hair and dirt-engrained skin aged him an extra ten years. As Elsie looked at him, she felt a flicker of recognition, and she narrowed her eyes.

'You don't remember me, do you?' he said, still smiling. 'I'm not surprised. You were pretty tanked when we met the first time.'

Suddenly, the waitress hurried back over to the table. 'I'm so sorry, but you can't be in here,' she told the men.

The older one cast a dramatic glance around the desolate restaurant. 'Why? It's not like you'll struggle to find us a table.'

The waitress flushed red. 'I'm sorry, but we don't allow...' she hesitated.

'Hobos?' said the older man. 'Tramps? Vagrants? What word are you looking for, Sweetheart? Don't worry, we've heard them all before – and worse.'

'Erm. I wouldn't have used any of those words,' the young girl replied, her face now a fetching shade of crimson. 'It's just that unless you're buying something, you can't stay.'

'I think we both know that your prices are a little bit out of our range,' said the old man, tapping the other man on his arm. 'Come on. Let's get out of here.'

Then it hit Elsie. She snapped her fingers together and pointed at the man. 'You're the guy from outside here a couple of months ago.'

His eyes opened wide with genuine surprise that she'd remembered him.

'That's right. You threw money at me,' he replied.

'No. I pulled my front door key out of my pocket, and the change fell out,' she corrected him. 'I wouldn't be that horrible to somebody.'

'But you did tell me to get a job.'

Elsie opened her mouth to respond but thought better of it and closed it again. 'You've got me there. I'm sorry. That was completely out of order.'

The older man's eyes sprang open, and he looked over at his friend, who was standing mutely beside him. 'Well, say something then,' he prompted. 'You look deranged.'

The man ran his fingers through his hair, stepped forward and offered out his hand to Elsie. 'I'm Mack. And this is Sid.'

Elsie, in response, stood and noted that both his hair and hand were filthy, but she shook it anyway. 'Elsie. I truly am sorry for treating you that way. Please,' she indicated at the spare seats, 'join me. It's on me.'

Sid, it seemed, didn't need asking twice and quickly took a seat opposite Elsie.

'You don't have to...' said Mack but was halted by Elsie.

'Yes. I do. Please.' She gestured to the seat opposite, and this time, Mack nodded his head and sat down. 'Order anything you want.'

Sid picked up the flimsy piece of paper and frowned. 'Not what I expected from an establishment such as this,' he said, and Elsie smiled. 'I'll have the gastro burger, whatever that is, with the triple-cooked fries.'

The waitress looked behind her at the chef, who was peering out from behind the pass.

'Is there a problem?' asked Elsie. 'You said they weren't allowed to stay unless they were buying. Well, they are, so what's the hold-up?'

The chef shrugged and motioned for the waitress to take the order. She turned back to face the table and whipped out her notepad. 'Would you like anything to drink with that?' she asked.

'A pint of...,' Sid began to say.

'Unfortunately, the lager and bitter are both off at the moment,' interjected the waitress, 'but we do have quite a nice selection of craft ciders still available.'

Sid shook his head. 'I was going to say a pint of water if you'd have let me finish.'

She flushed a shocking shade of red once more and coughed away her embarrassment. 'And you, Sir?' she asked Mack.

His eyes scanned the menu quickly. 'I'll have the same as Sid,' he said. 'But not the water. I wouldn't mind sampling one of your craft ciders if that's ok?'

The waitress jotted down his order and then looked at Elsie, who gave a quick wave of her hand. 'Nothing for me thanks. I'm sticking to a liquid lunch today.'

Sid tutted his disapproval. 'You shouldn't, you know. Drinking on an empty stomach is lethal. You'll feel like dying in the morning.'

'Trust me,' replied Elsie. 'I feel like that most mornings lately.'

***

As it turned out, Mack and Sid were quite the double act, and Elsie hadn't laughed so much in a long time. Yes, there was an element of drunkenness at play, but apart from that, it was clear that the bond between the two men was a strong one, and the way they bounced off each other was fun to witness.

Sid, as Elsie discovered, was a former army veteran with thirty years of service tucked under his military belt. He'd served during The Troubles in Northern Ireland and The Falklands, among other less dangerous and aggressive postings. He did a tour of Iraq during the early stages of the war before retiring in 2004. There were no addictions to speak of, according to him at least. He didn't drink and had never tried drugs of any sort, but he admitted to struggling to adjust to civilian life in a world that he didn't recognise any longer before suffering a complete mental breakdown.

'I left to protect them,' he'd told Elsie when referring to his wife and son. 'For years, I'd been the one to provide for them. I was supposed to be the one who looked after them, and then all of a sudden, I was this gibbering mess who couldn't even take care of myself. It wasn't fair on them. It wasn't right. I had to leave.'

Elsie could see the sadness behind his eyes, and part of her wanted to probe Sid further and find out more, but before his eyes could glaze further, he changed the subject, and Elsie knew that it was a conversation that he no longer wanted to continue.

'Enough about me. Ask him about his life,' said Sid, jabbing a thumb over in Mack's direction. 'It's much more interesting than mine.'

Mack rolled his eyes as he supped on his third pint of cider. 'It really isn't that interesting,' he told Elsie as he placed his glass back on the table.

'Can I be the judge of that?' she said.

Mack sighed. 'Fine. What would you like to know?'

'Everything,' said Elsie. 'How did you end up on the streets?'

He folded his arms across his chest. 'In a nutshell. I came from a very happy home: Mum, Dad and a brother. My Mum's a Brummie born and bred, but Dad is from Scotland, hence my rather Gaelic name of Mackenzie. I excelled at school despite the ridiculous name, went onto catering college, which again I excelled at...'

'Swot,' interrupted Sid.

'And then I found myself in London, working at a two Michelin-starred restaurant. I spent eight years working myself up from the bottom right up to sous chef. And things were going great, and I mean just fucking great. I had this amazing life. Don't get me wrong, it was exhausting, but I loved every second of it. And then I got cocky, and that's when I fucked everything up.' Mack paused and drummed his fingers on the table. 'Sorry. I can't. I don't want to talk about it. Anyway, let's not bring the mood down with my ramblings.'

Elsie was intrigued, but she, more than anybody, knew how difficult it was to talk to people about personal matters, and she'd be damned if she was going to be the one to force it out of him.

'Cool,' she said. 'Let's leave it there. And you're right – let's not ruin the afternoon.'

Five hours later and they were still sitting in the bistro drinking. Admittedly, Sid was only drinking pints of water, but Elsie and Mack had sunk about six drinks each, and her bar tab was steadily increasing. Elsie was enjoying the fuzzy effects the wine was having on her body. Everything felt so beautifully numb.

'So,' said Sid, taking another sip of tepid tap water from his pint glass. 'What about you? What's your story?'

'My story?' said Elsie. 'I don't have one.'

Sid shook his head. 'I don't believe that for a second. Everyone has a story. Granted, it might not be as outrageous as ours, but it's a story nonetheless.'

Elsie took a deep breath, followed by a large gulp of wine. There was no way in the world she was going to divulge everything that was happening to her at the moment, but Sid seemed like the type of man who wouldn't let something drop, so she gave them the censored version of her life. She missed out the part about her junkie mother and growing up in care and the bit about having terminal cancer and the fact that they would probably outlive her. Instead, she gave them the fluffier, nicer life story, where Elsie was a driven young woman who'd built a successful business, which she then went on to sell and who now spent her time doing whatever the hell she wanted, whenever the hell she wanted to do it. When she'd finished, she sat back.

'You're right,' she told them, 'not nearly as interesting as your lives.'

Sid stared at Elsie, and for a second, it felt as though he was gazing straight into her soul. She could tell that he knew that she was holding back, but like Elsie with Mack, he didn't push her for details. Instead, he clapped his hands together, making Elsie jump.

'Right,' he said, sliding the menu towards him. 'I don't want to take the piss, but all of this chatting has got me hungry again. Would it be rude to...' he pointed down at the paper.

Elsie shook her head and smiled. 'No. Help yourself. I should probably eat something as well before I get too drunk.'

'I think that ship has already well and truly sailed, love,' replied Sid.

Chapter Thirteen

Mack

Well, that night had taken an unexpected turn. They'd finally left the bistro just before eleven in the evening and stumbled to Elsie's front door, or at least he and Elsie had stumbled their way.

Elsie had slid her key into the lock, turned it, and walked inside, and Mack was on the cusp of thanking her for generosity when Elsie suddenly asked them if they wanted a bed for the night. He should have come straight out with it and said no. She was clearly heavily intoxicated and, like all people who have too much alcohol flowing through their bloodstream, wasn't making a sensible decision. No doubt she'd regret it first thing in the morning when she realised the gravity of just what she'd done. But the lure of sleeping in a proper bed for the night with soft sheets draped over his skin and a squashy pillow beneath his head was just too much for Mack to refuse. It was also something that Sid didn't want to miss out on either, as before Mack could respond, Sid had already gratefully accepted the offer and was practically barging his way through Elsie's front door.

'Don't mind if I do,' said Sid as he followed an unsteady Elsie up the stairs to the apartment.

Mack rolled his eyes and followed them inside, closing and bolting the door behind him.

Elsie had given them a not-so-in-depth tour of her apartment when they were finally inside.

'Living room,' she slurred. 'Kitchen. Bedrooms and the bathroom are through there,' she pointed into a dark corridor. 'You'll have to share. And on that note, gentlemen, I bid you goodnight.' She bowed as she said it and lost her footing, and Mack rushed forward to catch her. 'Very good of you,' she said and then proceeded to disappear into the blackness, bouncing off either side of the corridor before going into a room at the far end.

Sid laughed. 'She's going to have one monster of a headache in the morning. She should have eaten more than that little salad.'

Mack walked over to the open-plan kitchen and searched the cupboards until he found the glasses. 'You ate enough for all of us. Did you see how much the tab came to?' he said as he filled the glass with tap water. 'We shouldn't have agreed to stay, though. We should have just made sure she was home safely and then made our way back to...'

'Back to where?' interrupted Sid. 'The car park? I'm sorry, you may be a young 'un, but I'm a pensioner now. If somebody offers to put me up for the night, then there's no way I'll be turning that down.' He looked around the apartment. 'It's a bit sparse in here, don't you think?'

Mack glanced around the apartment and shrugged his shoulders. 'Maybe she prefers the minimalist look?'

'There's minimalist, and then there's looking like you've been burgled. Oh well, so long as there's a bed.'

He walked into the corridor, turning on the light as he went. As they moved further along, they pushed open the doors. There was a small but almost empty cupboard on the left; opposite, there was another door, which, when they opened it, found that it was the spare bedroom. The room Elsie disappeared inside at the bottom end of the corridor was obviously her bedroom, which, by process of elimination, meant that the last remaining door was to the bathroom. The men walked into the spare bedroom, and Mack eased off the large rucksack from his shoulders and let it drop on the floor. He stood with his hands on his hips and spied the double bed.

'I'll take the left side. No spooning!' Sid said to Mack.

Mack chuckled. 'You always have to spoil things. I'll go and wash.'

He headed out of the room and towards the bathroom. The door to Elsie's bedroom had been left open, and he took a cursory glance inside. Elsie was splayed out, fully clothed on the bed, snoring softly. He smiled and gently pulled the door closed.

The bathroom was huge. Stark-white brick tiles in the shower cubicle clashed against the dark blue of the painted walls but in an artsy way. There were expensive bottles of shampoo and conditioner and something in another handpump bottle which had the colour of mushroom soup but was most likely an overpriced body wash. He went over to a large free-standing cupboard and found a number of fluffy white towels. Surely, Elsie wouldn't mind if he took a quick shower? She'd probably prefer if he did if he were sleeping on her sheets. He'd be quick, and in Elsie's comatose state, it was unlikely she'd hear him.

Mack undressed, his dirty clothes dropped to the floor with a disconcerting thud, and he reached inside the shower cubicle and turned the handle. Powerful jets of water pumped out of the shower head, and when he saw the steam filling the cubicle and seeping into the rest of the bathroom, he stepped inside.

Showering had to be one of the most underrated experiences a person could have: that and a decent pillow. All of the silly things Mack had taken for granted during the years were now such a luxury that he realised just how lucky he'd been. He let the hot water run all over his hair and down his body, and after a few seconds, he looked down and grimaced at the trail of filthy water going down the drain. Just how grubby had he been? He pumped a generous blob of body wash into his hands, held it under his nose, and sniffed. Coconuts! It smelled delicious. He used it to wash his hair and body, opting to steer clear of Elsie's shampoo; some girls could be funny about that sort of thing. When he washed all of the suds away, he stood still, letting the heat from the water permeate his skin and warm his bones, and after a few minutes, he turned off the shower and stepped out of the cubicle to dry himself.

He frowned at the heap of dirty clothes on the floor. It felt wrong putting them next to his clean skin, but the only other option would be to sleep naked and had Sid not been sharing the bed with him, he most likely would have, but the thought of sleeping in his birthday suit next to an old man would have given Mack nightmares for years to come. He compromised by putting his boxer shorts back on and scooped up the offending clothes from the floor.

When he returned to the bedroom, he found Sid cocooned in the duvet and fast asleep in bed. Poor Sid. He was getting too old for this game. He smiled at his friend, and then his eyes drifted down to the bottom of the bed, where he saw another heap of clothes. Sid must have had the same idea as him. Would Elsie think he was a cheeky bastard if he popped them in the washing machine and put them on a quick wash? It'd be nice to leave the apartment tomorrow one hundred percent clean. Mack was prepared to take that risk. He walked over to Sid's clothes and went to pick them up but recoiled in horror when he saw a pair of rather old and holey Y-fronts.

'For fuck's sake,' said Mack as he used the other clothes to pick them up. Mack wasn't sure what he was most repulsed by: the fact that he had to touch a crusty old pair of underwear or the fact that it meant that Sid was lying naked in bed.

Chapter Fourteen

Elsie

What the actual fuck! Elsie's initial thoughts when she had first woken up still wearing yesterday's clothes were of the fun she'd had with Mack and Sid in the bistro. She felt the first thump of pain resounding in her head and groaned. Then her memory banks finally caught up with the rest of her body, and she sat up in bed with a start. Mack and Sid! She'd let them stay last night! What kind of imbecile was she? She, a grown ass, and what Elsie always considered herself to be, mildly intelligent woman, had let two homeless men stay in her apartment last night. Not the apartment above hers, which she rented out on Air B&B, but her very own safe space. Anything could have happened.

She jumped off the bed and winced as her head pounded. Elsie ignored it and tiptoed to her bedroom door. She could hear the radio playing quietly in the kitchen. As softly as she could, she edged along the corridor and glanced inside the empty spare bedroom. The bed had been stripped, and the duvet and pillows folded and neatly placed on the bed; nothing seemed to be out of place. Okay. So far, so good. She continued noiselessly towards the kitchen and living room and slowly poked her head inside.

Mack stood bare-chested at the hob, his hips moving in rhythm to the music on the radio. Elsie looked around the room. Nothing seemed to be out of place or, more importantly, missing. The fact that there wasn't much left in either of the rooms made it even easier to spot if something had been taken. However, Mack's hair appeared to have changed colour overnight, and the dark brown it had been when Elsie had first met him was now a lighter, more mousy brown: He'd clearly helped himself to a shower. The cheeky fucker! He better not have used her shampoo! She'd have to check the state of the bathroom. Men weren't renowned for their cleanliness, and considering the state Mack and Sid had been in yesterday, images of her white tiles splattered with dirt marks made her want to gag. God! They would have sat on her toilet seat!

As Elsie made a mental list of cleaning products she would buy the minute Mack and Sid left, Mack suddenly turned around and jumped when he saw her standing there.

'Christ! You made me jump.' His shoulders relaxed, and then he smiled making Elsie immediately think of her toothbrush. 'I hope I wasn't making too much noise. I tried to be as quiet as I could.'

'No. No. It's fine. You didn't wake me,' Elsie said, trying to act as normally as possible. 'Did you sleep okay?'

Why the fuck had she asked him that? Mack was used to sleeping on concrete, for goodness' sake.

'Like a baby,' Mack smiled again. 'Listen. It was a pretty heavy night last night, and we all know that in the cold light of day, you probably regret asking Sid and me to stay.' Elsie opened her mouth to protest politely, but Mack held up his hand to stop her. 'But we won't outstay our welcome. We'll soon be on our way. I wanted to cook you something to say thank you, but unfortunately, you don't seem to have much in your fridge and cupboards, so the best I can offer you is a mushroom and cheese omelette, I'm afraid.'

'You didn't have to,' said Elsie, pleased that she wouldn't have to be the one to mention them leaving. 'But it's very kind of you.'

'Sit down,' said Mack, pointing to the dining table. 'I'll bring it over.'

Elsie found it odd taking instructions from somebody in her own home, but she did it regardless. The dining table had been laid out with cutlery, a placemat, and a pint of water, complete with an Alka-Seltzer fizzling away inside. She smiled and felt her heart soften – just a little. Mack came over and laid a plate down in front of her with a flourish.

'Et voila,' he said. His eyes sparkled with delight as he did so, and then Elsie remembered him talking about being a chef last night. The passion was still there.

The last thing that Elsie wanted to do at that precise moment was eat, but she didn't want to hurt Mack's feelings. She picked up her fork, cut away a section of omelette, and popped it into her mouth.

'Umm,' she said as she chewed. But her reaction was a genuine one. It was the most delicious omelette she'd ever had. 'How did you make it taste this good?' she asked him.

Mack beamed. 'Seriously? You're not just saying that to be kind?'

Elsie cut off another piece and nodded. 'I mean it. It tastes amazing. I can't believe you made this in my kitchen.'

'Great! I'm glad you like it,' Mack said. He turned and headed back to the kitchen and started to wash the pan. 'It's all about seasoning when it comes to an omelette. I added a pinch of parmesan and a flutter of paprika to give it a little extra punch.'

Elsie demolished the omelette in minutes. When she'd finished, Mack came over to the table, took her empty plate and then proceeded to take it to the sink and wash it.

'You don't have to do that,' she told him.

'It's not a problem. Please. It's my way of saying thank you,' he replied.

Elsie leaned back in the chair and rubbed her stomach. 'You know, I can see that you must have been a good chef,' she told him. 'Why did you stop?'

This was Elsie's not-so-subtle way of reigniting the conversation from last night. She just hoped that he didn't take offence.

'Thank you. I was...I still am, I suppose. But years ago, I had this unstoppable belief that I was the best, and I took it too far. I decided I could set up my own restaurant, and so that's just what I did.'

'There's nothing wrong with self-belief. That's what determines a person's success.'

'Or their weaknesses,' replied Mack. He was staring absentmindedly out the window, still washing the plate in small circular motions. 'I may have been a great chef, but I was a shit business owner. I didn't have a clue about the day-to-day running of a business. There's more to a restaurant than just cooking and pumping out good food. There's marketing, staffing, stock control, ordering, and that annoying thing of making sure all the bills are paid. I just wasn't prepared or experienced in that sort of thing, and then suddenly, I found out just how important that stuff was. I missed a few bills and tried to catch up by not paying other stuff. Then, when some staff left, I wasn't on the ball with replacing them quickly enough. I messed up with the stock, ordering too much – not ordering enough. And then, all of a sudden, my little place started to get negative reviews. Customers waited too long for their food. Or there wasn't enough of a selection because so much had been taken off the menu when stock didn't come in on time. It was a shit show. All my fault.'

'So, you lost the business in the end, I presume?' said Elsie.

Mack placed the plate in the draining rack and nodded. 'Yep. I was in debt up to my eyeballs. I lost my business, my home, and eventually my girlfriend. I was under constant stress, and it affected me so badly that she didn't recognise me in the end. I was a completely different man from the one she'd met.'

'That must have been tough.'

'It was the worst period in my life. People think that it's easy to close a business, and in some respects, it is, from a legal point of view. But the stigma of failing crippled me. I couldn't move past that. I'd never failed at anything in my life, and then all of a sudden, I felt like I'd plummeted to rock bottom, and I was scrabbling around in the dirt, trying to get myself up again. It was suffocating. And so,' he paused, and Elsie could tell he was deciding whether or not he should continue. 'And so, I found something to help ease everything I felt. To take all of that hurt and embarrassment away.'

Her heart thumped in her chest. 'What was that?' she asked, even though she knew what was coming.

'Heroin. Just one puff, I told myself. Just something to take the edge of it all. But of course, it's never just one puff when it comes to that stuff.'

Elsie did know. She knew only too well. She thought of her mother and her addiction, and suddenly, it was like she couldn't breathe. Mack glanced over at her.

'I don't want you to worry,' he said, seeing her discomfort. 'I got clean. I haven't touched the stuff in years. But unfortunately, the damage was already done.'

Elsie's chest rose and fell in quick succession, and she was aware that she was panting. She'd been transported back to when she was a child and back to all of those terrifying days when she was left alone in the flat while her mum went off to score. The times when she'd been left to fend for herself and eat scraps of food that she'd found in the bin because there wasn't anything in the cupboards. Or the strange men that came into their flat at all hours of the day and night.

'You said you lost your girlfriend, but what about your family? Did they support you?' she asked.

Mack's jaw tightened. 'They tried to at first. Mum and Dad paid for rehab more times than I can count. My brother, Marcus, watched me like a hawk. And off I'd go into a clinic and come out a few months later miraculously reformed, but it wasn't long before I was stealing money off them all and scoring again. It was a vicious cycle that went around and around and around, and in the end, I think they just couldn't cope anymore. My dad had a massive heart attack, and Mum blamed me for causing it. Marcus was just tired of it all. He was younger than me and had his own life to live. He didn't need his big brother dragging him down.'

'Did they disown you?' asked Elsie.

'No,' said Mack, shaking his head. 'I disowned them.'

Elsie's brows crumpled with confusion. 'I don't understand.'

'It was just after my dad's heart attack. They'd paid for another round of rehab, and there was this beautiful moment of transition that I'd noticed before when you've gone through the pain, and the cramps, and the sickness of withdrawing. It's like your brain suddenly starts to clear. Like, you see things so clearly it's as though you can touch your ideas and thoughts. And I thought to myself that as long as I was around my family, I would always do this to them. I was always going to let them down and hurt them. I would always be a disappointment or the stress in their lives. When I was discharged, I decided that I wouldn't go back home to them. I didn't want them living on a knife's edge while I was under their roof, so I decided that I wouldn't go back until I was clean and stayed clean. Until I was absolutely certain that I would never let them down again.'

'That must have been difficult for you,' said Elsie.

Mack leaned against the kitchen counter and folded his arms across his chest. 'It was heartbreaking,' he said flatly. 'But sometimes, when you know that your presence brings pain to somebody you love, then the best and kindest thing you can do for them is let them go.'

Elsie had never thought about it like that. Was that what her mother had done for her? Did she know that she was causing so much damage to her child that she thought abandoning her was her chance to save her? Was that her motherly instinct kicking in and putting Elsie first?

'What did they say when you told them that you weren't going back home?'

Mack pushed himself away from the countertop and busied himself, wiping them down, even though it was obvious that they were perfectly clean. 'They didn't say anything. I didn't tell them. I just never went back.'

Elsie's eyes widened. 'Do they know where you are now? Do they know that you're clean?'

Mack cleared his throat. 'No. I couldn't face them again after such a long time. I'd let them down – badly. I thought it best to leave them be and let my parents enjoy their retirement years. And I definitely don't want them to ever know that I've been living on the streets. My dad's heart would probably explode.' He gave a hollow smile. 'Anyway. Moving on.'

There it was again. Mack had closed off, but Elsie could hardly blame him. He'd given so much, considering they hardly knew each other. He'd been brave to share that, braver than she had ever been, and what he'd said about his reasons for not contacting his family had shaken Elsie's beliefs to their core.

'No. Of course,' she flustered. 'I have to get ready anyway. I'm supposed to be meeting my friend soon.' She stood and went to walk out of the room but stopped and turned back to him. 'Listen. Don't leave just yet. At least not until I get back.'

Mack nodded. 'If that's what you want, I certainly won't say no.'

Elsie smiled at him and headed to the bathroom. She needed to shower away last night and start the day afresh. Mack had given her a new perspective on her childhood, and inside, she'd felt a shift. She didn't know what she'd shifted from or what she'd shifted to but there was just something inside that made her feel differently. Maybe Jack could help her understand it all. She pushed open the bathroom door and was hit by a blast of steam. Elsie screamed as she saw Sid in all of his glory stepping out of a very full and very bubbly bath. He quickly cupped his manhood with his hands.

'Bloody hell. You could have at least knocked,' he told her.

Chapter Fifteen

Ingrid

Ingrid walked into the living room to find Amanda looking out the window.

'Is that all you do,' she said jokingly, causing Amanda to jump.

'Tsk. You love doing that to me,' she admonished. 'I'm looking at what's going on out there.'

She pointed out of the window, and Ingrid joined her to see. Outside, a man was erecting a for sale sign in the front garden of the neighbouring property.

'You always said you'd love to expand,' said Amanda.

Ingrid pulled out her phone and Googled the website of the estate agent. She tutted.

'It's doesn't look like it's been listed yet,' she said with a frown. 'Perhaps it'll be on there tomorrow.'

'Give them a call,' instructed Amanda, 'It'll be at a knockdown price. Look at it. It's a right dump and needs a tonne of money spending on it.'

Ingrid knew this only too well. The front and back gardens were an utter mess, with overgrown hedges and trees, and the grass was peppered with bald patches and weeds. She'd never stepped foot inside, but the original wooden window frames were rotten and falling apart, and the single pane glass they held was either cracked or smashed completely and covered with small squares of cardboard. The property was owned by an old lady who had bought it over sixty years previously when house prices were as low as the cost of a designer coat in today's world. Over the years, her large brood of a family had left, and her husband passed away, leaving her all alone. She had refused to move on several occasions, much to the frustration of her children, who were all too keen to see the back of their former family home that was slowly going to rack and ruin. Inevitably, the woman grew too old to keep on top of the upkeep such a large and old property required, and it slowly fell into its current dilapidated state. Ingrid remembered the day the woman left. None of her six children bothered to attend as paramedics wheeled her out through the front door, flanked on either side by social workers and police. She looked so withered and small under the blanket, and she covered her head with her hand and sobbed as they pushed her down the path, straight into the back of a waiting ambulance and away from the only life that she'd ever known. If the house was up for sale now, it meant that either the family needed the money to fund her care costs, or she'd died, and her children now wanted their share of the money.

Ingrid pushed the phone back into her pocket. 'It'll keep,' she said. 'But I doubt that we'll be able to afford it anyway. We could cover the mortgage, but the money it needs to renovate the place would be astronomical.'

'It's nice to have a dream, though,' said Amanda. She checked the nurse's watch pinned to her uniform and tutted. 'I'd better get on with my rounds.'

She gave Ingrid a supportive tap on the shoulder and headed out of the room. Ingrid stepped closer to the window and sighed. Yes. It was always nice to have a dream. Her mind drifted back to her former neighbour and her grotesque family. How awful was it to have such a large family and for none of them to care enough to be there when it mattered? Ingrid had never been blessed with children – her body rejected all four of her pregnancies. She'd been examined repeatedly by numerous doctors, and none of them could find the cause, and as much as Ingrid would have loved to have been a mother, there were only so many miscarriages that she could endure. In the end, her husband gently suggested that they stop trying after seeing the pain it was causing his wife. They'd had a good life together, and every day, Ingrid counted the blessings she *did* have in life:

the laughter, the pure love they had for each other, their friends and family.

She was one of the lucky ones. Not like Elsie Bellamy. Ingrid hadn't been able to get that poor woman off her mind. She'd called her several times since they first met, but all had gone unanswered. However, she did text her to let Ingrid know that she was okay. Granted, she'd completed and returned all of the forms that Ingrid had posted to her. Elsie had even included a cheque which covered six months of basic care at the home, which Ingrid had chosen not to bank. It seemed too uncouth to cash the cheque of a dying woman who hadn't even moved in yet, and judging from what Elsie had written down on her forms, she was a woman who deserved to know what it was like to experience some form of human kindness. She'd written a big N/A on the form in the section for the next of kin details. Maybe it was the thought that Elsie would have no loved ones beside her at the end when she passed away that made Ingrid feel the way she did about her. She could just about believe that there might not be any family; perhaps Elsie was an only child to only child parents? It was easy to see how quickly a bloodline could die out, but for Elsie not to have any friends? That just seemed unbelievable.

Would it be too much if she went and checked on her? No. That was a terrible idea and something that she had never done before. But the more Ingrid thought about it, the more she couldn't let the idea go. What if something had happened to her? What if she was lying on the floor in her home, having had some terrible accident, and there was no one around to notice her missing? Well, she had put N/A in the next of kin section. It wasn't too much of a stretch to imagine that it was possible. That's it. I'm going, Ingrid decided, and if Elsie had a problem with that, then she would cross that bridge when she came to it.

She went into the staff room, retrieved her coat from the hook, and headed towards the front door just as Amanda was coming back down the stairs.

'Where are you going?' she asked Ingrid. 'I thought you were going to help me with Mrs Foster's catheter?'

'Sorry,' she called back. 'Something's come up. I'll be back in time for the doctor's visit this afternoon.'

***

Ingrid hadn't visited the city centre for years. In many respects, it was similar to what she remembered all those years ago when she and Phillip used to come for a night out with their friends. Ingrid smiled as she remembered those days with fondness. It was the age of the baby boomers, whose carefree outlook on life was nothing like those of their parents, who had struggled through the rationing, bombing and death of the Second World

War. She recognised a lot of the old buildings but built among them were newer ones with shiny glass facades and some with white rendering with strips of bright colours running across the front. Ingrid wrinkled her nose. She was all for modernisation, but they looked monstrous in her opinion.

She pulled up in the square and thanked the parking gods for the spare space that had just become available. She quickly reversed into the spot and went to get a parking ticket, popping it back in the window of the car before heading to Elsie's door. She rang the bell and stepped back – she hoped that she hadn't overstepped the mark with this.

'I'll answer it how I bloody like,' she heard a man's voice shout from behind the door.

Was this Elsie's problem? A domineering father? Or was it a controlling boyfriend?

The door opened and Ingrid's eyes opened wide with surprise at the sight of a bare-chested old man whose lower half of his body had been covered with a white fluffy towel.

'Yeah?' he said, looking at Ingrid. 'Can I help?'

This couldn't be Elsie's father. It just couldn't be. His hair and beard were long and straggly and even though he'd only spoken a few words, they were at odds with those spoken by the woman that Ingrid had met.

'Um. I've come to see Elsie. May I come inside?' she asked.

'She's not in,' he replied bluntly.

But Ingrid didn't believe him. 'May I come inside?' she sternly repeated.

The man shrugged and turned and started to walk back up the stairs. 'This way.'

Ingrid followed him inside and cautiously went up the stairs behind him. She kept her eyes set firmly on her feet as she ascended, fearful that his towel might drop. The last thing she wanted to see was the wrinkled arse of an old man. He led her into an open-plan kitchen and living room area, where Ingrid was greeted by the sight of yet another semi-naked man.

'Oh,' he said upon seeing her. 'I'm sorry. We've just had a bath. Not together though,' he added hastily when he saw the rise of Ingrid's eyebrow.

Like the man who had answered the door to her, this man, although younger, was equally unkempt. Just what was going on here?

'Is Elsie in?' said Ingrid, feeling like a stuck record. 'I'd like to talk to her.'

The younger man shook his head. 'No. She's meeting a friend this morning. She said she'd be back just after lunchtime. You're welcome to wait if you'd like?'

Ingrid had no intentions of sitting and waiting in the company of two men in bath towels, and she shook her head.

'No. It's okay. I'll pop in another day. If you could tell her that I called around, I'd be grateful.'

'Of course,' nodded the man. 'Who shall I say called?'

'Ingrid.'

The older man, who was now sprawled over the sofa, piped up. 'Ingrid. That's such a lovely name.'

'Thank you,' she said with a smile. Maybe he wasn't too bad after all.

'I had a dog called Ingrid. It got hit by a lorry and died,' he said.

Ingrid's smile faded and she turned and walked out of the apartment without bothering to say goodbye.

Chapter Sixteen

Elsie

'Have you given what I said yesterday much thought?' asked Jack.

Elsie pulled back her lips into a grimace.

'Some thought. Yes.'

'How much exactly?' probed Jack.

'Okay. Not very much, if I'm being truthful. It's just that I bumped into somebody yesterday, and we had a little too much to drink. You know what it's like. Before you know it...'

'You got drunk,' finished Jack.

It was yet another cold day, and Elsie thought she might suggest meeting inside the comfort of a coffee shop going forward. Her bones seemed to ache all the time lately. Jack pulled up the zip on his coat and shivered, and she wondered how he coped with freezing temperatures when she struggled so much. She glanced at him; his eyes fixed ahead on nothing in particular and Elsie worried that she might have upset him by not taking what he'd told her with serious consideration. A chainsaw was revved into action by the tree surgeons working on a low-hanging broken branch on the other side of the park, breaking Jack's concentration.

'Who was it that you bumped into?' he asked her.

'Yesterday? Oh. It's a long story,' replied Elsie. She didn't want to tell him about her being so drunk that she allowed two homeless men to sleep in her home. She doubted he'd be happy about it, and she wasn't in the mood for a lecture.

Jack opened his hands, his palms facing upwards. 'We've got the time.'

Fuck it, she thought to herself. If Jack wanted to know, then so be it. Above the racket of the chainsaw, Elsie told him everything. From her and Mack's first meeting to the appalling way that she'd spoken to him, right through to inviting them to join her for lunch, getting drunk and eventually asking them both to stop overnight in her apartment. She missed out the incident in the bathroom that morning. Jack might have taken offence to her obvious revulsion at Sid's old man nakedness. When she'd finished, she sat back and closed her eyes, bracing herself for his reaction, but hearing none, she opened them again and looked over. He was smiling at her.

'What are you smiling about?' she asked him.

'I think that you took in what I said yesterday more than you realise,' he said.

'In what way?' she asked with a tilt of her head.

'You did something that you wouldn't normally do,' he said with genuine happiness. 'You let two strangers, who most people would cross the street to ignore, into your space. You talked to them. Made them feel normal.'

'Got drunk with them,' added Elsie.

'That too,' agreed Jack. 'But you laughed with them. You listened to them. You treated them in the way that every person deserves to be treated. Can you imagine just how much that meant to them?'

Elsie pouted. She hadn't thought of it like that. She thought back to her conversation with Mack that morning; the evening before, he'd been reluctant to share anything in the bistro, but after a good night's sleep in a bed, a full stomach and a shower, he'd told her everything. In the space of twelve hours, she'd made Mack feel comfortable enough to trust telling her his story.

'How did it make you feel?' asked Jack.

How *did it* make her feel? Elsie wasn't sure exactly. Kind? Considerate? If she felt anything, those feelings were weak and paled into insignificance to what her actions had made her *think*. Mack's comments about letting people go for the sake of the other person had cast all of those long-held perceptions of her mother into a whole new light. She'd always held onto the belief that her mother had been a selfish bitch who had wanted drugs more than her daughter. When, potentially, it might have been something completely different. Maybe, just maybe, her mother hadn't chosen drugs over Elsie; maybe she'd actually chosen Elsie's safety over a substance that she was struggling to quit.

'I suppose it made me feel philanthropic,' said Elsie, not wanting to tell Jack of the confusion in her mind surrounding her mother.

'Philanthropy is more of a concept than a feeling,' he replied. 'But I'll let you off. You're on the right track. Keep thinking about what you can do for other people, and you can't go wrong.'

Jack adjusted his coat, and Elsie could tell that he was preparing to leave. She didn't want him to go just yet. The emotional cogs in her brain had rusted to a halt years ago, but now it felt as though the red rust was flaking away, and they were slowly turning again. She just couldn't make sense of anything.

'What's the point?' she asked. 'I'm nice to other people and make them feel better, and then what? I bag a place in heaven because of it? Is that what this is all about?'

Jack stooped to tie his shoelace. 'Elsie, Sweetheart. You've always had a place up there,' he thumbed the sky above. 'It's about going up there more enlightened than you were when you were alive. It's about feeling lighter in your heart and soul and being truly at peace with yourself when you do, well, pop off.'

Elsie smiled at Jack's choice of words. 'How eloquent.'

He gave her a wave of his hand. 'Until tomorrow.'

He turned and started to walk along the path, and Elsie watched his long strides, the slight limp in his left leg that Jack had told her was from a riding accident years before. She would miss that man so much when she was gone. She'd never really given the whole heaven and hell debate much thought until recently – for obvious reasons. But she did hope that there was a heaven and that Jack was right about her place already being secured there. But what she wished for more than anything was that if there was a heaven, and she did float up there or whatever the hell happened when somebody died, it wouldn't be too much longer before Jack was with her again. Wow! Has she just secretly wished Jack dead? What a selfish cow.

She checked the time and her phone. She should go home; she'd been out for over three hours, and there was still the journey home. She hoped that Mack and Sid hadn't claimed squatters' rights in the short time she'd been gone. Elsie smiled, knowing that they weren't the type of people who would do something like that. How did she know that exactly? She had no idea. Just something deep in the pit of her heart that made her know without question that the two men wouldn't do anything to her, or anybody else for that matter. So what should she do with them now? The logical answer would be to go home with two Subway sandwiches, hand them over and tell them how wonderful it had been, but off they went now. Back to the car park they go. The moral answer, however, wasn't as simple. Let them stay for another night or two, perhaps giving Elsie time to find Mack and Sid a hostel to stay in. There you go, Jack – another thing that she wouldn't normally do. This whole living list thing was easy.

Elsie pushed herself up off the bench and started her long walk home. As she looked ahead, she could see Jack further down the path. He was looking over at the tree surgeons as he walked, who were now in the process of sawing the large branch into smaller sections and loading them onto the back of an open-top van. Heading straight for Jack was a jogger who, despite the fact his head was up, was heading straight for her friend. Elsie cried out, but at the last second, Jack veered to the left, allowing the jogger to continue on his merry way without skipping a step. The man hadn't even apologised to Jack for nearly crashing into him, and as he jogged closer towards Elsie, she mulled over the idea of sticking out her foot to trip him over but decided against it. She was pretty sure that wouldn't be allowed according to the rules of Jack's living list, but she did glower at the man as he ambled past. He gave her a confused look and adjusted his jog to give Elsie a wider berth. She turned on the spot as he went past, satisfied that he'd registered her displeasure, and as she did so, Elsie found herself staring at Agata standing behind her.

'Oh! Hi,' she said. 'I wouldn't have expected to see you here at this time. I thought you said that you took Arthur to toddler group in the mornings.'

Upon hearing his name, Arthur looked up at Elsie and brandished a salivary smile and in return she gave the little boy a quick wave of her hand.

'Not today. The centre is closed,' replied Agata. 'There is problem with heating.'

She was looking oddly at Elsie, and Elsie instinctively wiped at her nose, hoping that she didn't have anything hanging out if it.

'Are you okay?' asked Agata.

'Never better,' she lied. 'Why?'

'You seemed quite angry just then. With that running man.'

Elsie laughed. 'What, him? No. I was just teaching him a lesson. He nearly jogged straight into my friend just now. He didn't even acknowledge him, let alone apologise.'

Agata nodded but appeared unconvinced. 'Okay. As long as you feeling alright.'

Had Agata heard any of the conversation between her and Jack? She was acting downright bizarrely. Maybe it was a Polish thing?

'Nope. All good. Anyway, I was thinking about messaging you. Are you up for a night out somewhere? It doesn't have to be anything too messy, just somewhere local for a meal and a couple of drinks.'

In truth, Elsie hadn't thought about it at all. She was just keen for Agata to stop looking at her in that way, scrutinising her for God knows what reason. That was the thing about keeping secrets, she supposed. You lived on knife's edge waiting for it to be exposed by some eagle-eyed friend or by a simple slip of the tongue. But Agata beamed at the suggestion. Elsie's plan had worked.

'That would be amazing. Yes, I love that,' she replied.

'Great. Maybe this Saturday evening then. You have Sundays off, so at least you won't have to get up early the next day.'

Agata nodded enthusiastically. 'Yes. Perfect.'

'Cool. I have to get back home but message me later and we'll organise where to go. See you.'

Agata rushed forward and planted a kiss on Elsie's cheek, taking her by surprise. Displays of affection just weren't in her repertoire, let alone public ones. She gave an awkward smile in response.

'Right. Bye then,' said Elsie.

'Bye bye,' said Agata. She knelt down besides the pushchair. 'Say bye bye to Elsie,' she said to Arthur.

The boy looked up at Elsie. His face crumpled and he burst into tears, kicking his feet and screaming wildly. Elsie gave Agata an apologetic shrug, turned, and walked away. Good grief. How did Agata put up with that sort of nonsense? No wonder the poor woman was so excited at the thought of a night out away from that house.

***

She walked back into her apartment to find Mack and Sid playing a game of Scrabble at the dining table. Elsie had come across it in the back of the sideboard and had promptly placed it into one of the cardboard boxes which was destined for the charity shop.

'There you are. Gunnu. Now how many points is that worth?' said Sid.

'Gunnu? There's no such word,' replied Mack.

'What are you on about? We use it all the time.'

Mack shook his head and reached for the dictionary that he must have found on Elsie's bookshelf. They certainly have been making themselves at home, she thought to herself.

'No. Just as I thought. Gunnu is not a word,' said Mack, his finger scanning down the page.

Sid reached over and whipped the book from under Mack's nose. 'What are you on about? It has to be in there.'

Elsie gave a little cough, and the men jumped in their seats.

'I think Sid is referring to Birmingham slang: Gunnu instead of going to,' she said as she walked over to the kitchen worksurface and set down the carrier bags in her hands.

Sid pointed over at Elsie and gave a vigorous nod of the head. 'See. I told you.' He folded his arms over his chest and leaned triumphantly back in the chair.

'I'm sorry, but Mack's correct. It's not allowed,' said Elsie.

Sid huffed and tossed his little notepad across the table. 'Bloody stupid game.'

Elsie laughed. 'Sorry. But that's the rules.'

'He's just a sore loser. Pay no attention to him,' said Mack. 'Did you have a nice time with your friend?'

'Yes. It was nice, thanks,' she replied. 'Listen.' Elsie pushed the carrier bags across the countertop. 'I hope that you won't be offended, but I've bought you both some bits and pieces. Nothing fancy. Just some new clothes: underwear and socks and that sort of thing. And some deodorant and body wash.'

Sid and Mack looked back at her silently, making Elsie suddenly wish she'd checked with them first. 'And, again, please don't be annoyed with me,' she added, not wanting the silence to linger. 'I booked you both in for a haircut and shave at the barbers around the corner.' She looked over at them and held her breath.

'That's really kind of you,' said Mack. 'Thank you. You didn't have to do that for us.'

He was genuinely touched, and Sid got up from his chair and went over to Elsie. She hoped that he wasn't going to kiss her like Agata had earlier. She couldn't cope with two lots of affection in one day. Thankfully, Sid didn't. He slid one of the carrier bags towards him and peered inside. He said nothing as he analysed the contents, but Elsie caught sight of a watery glaze in his eyes, and she felt an unfamiliar pang inside as those emotional cogs jolted once again.

'If you'd like,' she continued as she attempted to push whatever she was feeling to one side. 'I thought you could stop for a few more days. Just while I try and find you somewhere safer to stay.'

Mack blinked back at her. She wished that he'd say something, but instead, he looked back down at the Scrabble board and nodded his head numbly.

'Thank you,' said Sid. He smiled, and Elsie was surprised at just how straight and white his teeth were. 'That is quite possibly the nicest birthday present I've had in a long time.'

Chapter Seventeen

Agata

A gata hadn't had an evening out since she'd started this stupid job. It had completely caught her off guard when Elsie had initially suggested it, and she'd thought she might have blown it when she'd kissed her on the cheek to thank her because Elsie had looked absolutely mortified. They hadn't known each other that long after all, and Elsie didn't strike her as somebody who was easy to get to know.

Each time Agata had any contact with her, whether it was in person or over the phone, she just couldn't shake the feeling that Elsie was the type who preferred to keep people away. This surprised Agata as whenever she'd seen Elsie at the park, she appeared to be so desperately lonely and craving attention. Look at what had happened that morning with the jogger. Agata had thought Elsie was going to punch him at one point. She had stared so coldly at him, and even the jogger must have thought she was a little odd, judging by the way that he'd swerved to avoid her. But Elsie's behaviour was forgiven and forgotten as far as Agata was concerned. Maybe Agata could be the calming effect on Elsie's life that the woman so clearly craved.

This Saturday! Gosh, she needed this night out so badly. It would be nice to have adult company and not just be lying on the bed waiting for a child crying in their bedroom to ring out and disturb her. It didn't give her much time to prepare. When she first got home, she'd settled Arthur into his afternoon nap and hurried to her bedroom to rummage through the contents of her wardrobe, even though she knew exactly what she would find draped over the hangers, which was nothing, to be precise. Over the years, Agata had accepted that her current role didn't require her to have an array of fancy, fashionable clothes, and her wardrobe consisted of several pairs of blue jeans, black leggings and oversized chunky knit jumpers. She'd have to go shopping. There was no way that she could venture out of the door without something nice to wear. Thank goodness that Arthur's play centre was closed. She could catch the bus into the town centre tomorrow with him and trawl the shops for something to wear. Mrs King would never know; she'd just assume that Agata had taken Arthur out for a walk.

The mere fact that she had to think in that way irked Agata. All of the sneaking around made her feel as though she was in an abusive relationship, and in many respects, she supposed that she was. Agata had to ask permission to do anything. She was expected to look after four children and was only allowed to clock off when they went to bed. The zero tolerance rule on alcohol and drugs was, of course, something she agreed with; she was caring for children after all, but the fact that she wasn't allowed to come home if she'd been drinking, even if it was on her night off, was unreasonable. If the Kings wanted a nun to care for their children, they should have hired one. Agata had every intention of making the most of her night out with Elsie, including consuming copious amounts of cocktails, or cheap vodka, or whatever the hell she could get her hands on.

She heard the front door open and close, and she started. She hadn't been expecting anybody to be home so early. Mr King was giving a lecture at a hospital in Bristol and wouldn't be home for two days, and Mrs King had told Agata that morning that she was out with friends all day. Agata left her bedroom and leaned over the bannister to peer down the stairs. She could hear the click of her employer's heels on the tiled floor and hushed talking between her and another person. Curious, Agata leaned further over the bannister, straining to hear, but suddenly jumped back when Mrs King came into view at the foot of the stairs.

'Oh darling,' she heard her coo. 'You're such a worry wort. I've told you. There's nobody here but you and I. I sent the maid to run some errands, and that fuck-wit won't be back until later this afternoon with Arthur.'

Agata felt her blood pump with anger, and she wondered whether she could spit on Mrs King from her position at the top of the stairs. But her anger quickly seeped away at the sight of the mighty and self-righteous Arabella King, who was at that moment in a passionate kiss with a man who was most definitely not Mr King. He was tall and stocky, with biceps visibly bulging through the arms of his tailored suit jacket. He had Mrs King pressed against the wall, and she was running her hands through his thick dark hair as he slipped his hand under her short skirt and snaked it further up between her legs. Mrs King let out a loud groan, and Agata froze. Should she really be watching this? She felt like a pervert, dirty like Peeping Tom spying through windows and keyholes.

Mrs King tilted her head upwards as she let out another groan of pleasure. She looked up to the ceiling with a pleasurable grin filling her face until her eyes moved across to the top of the landing, where she saw Agata staring back down at her. She let out a huge scream, pushed the man away from her, and hastily straightened her skirt back down.

'What the hell are you doing here? You're supposed to be out with Arthur!' she screamed up the stairs.

Agata's legs wobbled. Inside she was crippled with fear, certain that she was about to lose her job. But then a sudden thought hit her. If Mrs King sacked her, then she would have to explain to her husband exactly why. No doubt Arabella would lie, but she ran the risk of Agata retaliating and telling Mr King precisely what his wife was getting up to when he was away from home. Agata stood firm. Unwittingly, Mrs King had just granted Agata the perfect excuse to really take advantage of the situation. She straightened her back, steadied her legs and made her way down the stairs in slow and deliberate steps.

'I think I should go,' said the man, tucking his shirt back into place.

'Yes. I think you should,' said Agata in the most confident tone she could muster.

The man was a beat away from practically running out of the front door, which he didn't even bother to close behind him. With her head held high in the air, Agata strode straight past Mrs King and watched the dust spin off the mysterious man's Porsche wheels. She closed the door, locked it and then slowly turned back to Mrs King.

'Now. Listen to me,' she said to Agata, jabbing a pointed nail close to her face. 'What you think you saw...'

Agata held her hand just inches from her employer's face to quieten her. 'I know exactly what I saw,' she replied sternly. 'And so will your husband.' She let the last sentence linger for a few seconds. 'Unless...'

'Unless what?' asked Arabella.

'I think that things need to change around here,' Agata said bluntly. 'I think this...arrangement,' she sucked her teeth as though the word was distasteful, 'not suit me anymore.'

Arabella King, usually so quick with her responses and scathing comments, was unsurprisingly silent.

'To start,' continued Agata. 'I would like more money for the work I do. So, let's say triple what you give me each month. And then,' she held up her hand again to Arabella, whose mouth dropped open to talk. 'Then, I want more time off starting,' Agata consulted her wristwatch, 'right now. I go to shopping...*without* Arthur. And Saturday, I go out with my friend.'

'So, this is who you really are? A common blackmailer? Just wait until my husband hears about this,' shrieked Arabella.

'Just wait until your husband hears about man who come to his house and seduce his wife while he is away,' retorted Agata.

Arabella King folded her arms over her chest defiantly. 'He'll never believe you,' she said smugly.

'Maybe not,' said Agata. 'But maybe he might. Do you want to find out? And I memorised the registration of your *friend's* car so maybe your husband can find out his details. It's your choice.'

Agata's heart was beating wildly. She held her breath, watching Arabella closely. This might possibly be the greatest moment in her life. For once, she was empowered and in control, and she relished it. Arabella was glaring at her, her eyes flitting from one side of her face to the other as the realisation that she'd been outfoxed by the lowly hired help finally sank in.

'I'll get you back for this,' she spat at Agata. 'Just you wait.'

Agata smiled. 'No. You won't. And you want to know why?' She leaned in closer and whispered in Arabella's ear. 'Because this fuck-wit is cleverer than you think.'

Chapter Eighteen

Mack

Mack let out a deep sigh as the piping hot towel was wrapped around his face. He and Sid had walked into the stylish barbers with a sense of trepidation, feeling outlandishly out of place. Even when Mack had had a home and a job, he'd only ever gone to his local barber, a real spit and sawdust sort of place with tatty furniture and décor straight from the eighties.

Into Eden, as it was called, despite the fact that it bore no resemblance to the blessed garden, was the epitome of modern male grooming. White-washed bare brick walls set the backdrop for the trails of open black piping that lined the walls, even though Mack was pretty sure that they were for aesthetic purposes only and weren't actually plumbed into anything. The far wall held a series of open shelves on which sat expensive-looking black bottles of hair and body products. It was the type of place that men in suits walked into after they'd finished work. Even the air smelled expensive, with wafts of sandalwood floating in the ether.

When the little bell above the door first tinkled at their arrival, it was as though the whole of the barbers stopped and stared. The barbers working on clients glanced a curious side-eye before returning their focus to the men on the chairs in front of them. There were two vacant barber chairs at the end of the row, which could only be for them, and Mack felt the urge to immediately announce that they'd been booked in before anybody had the chance to ask them to leave.

A man suddenly appeared from a back room holding a cup of steaming coffee in his hand. His eyes lit up at the sight of Mack and Sid, and he placed down his cup and clapped his hands together with glee.

'Ah. Mack and Sid, I assume. Miss Bellamy told me that we'd have fun with you two,' he said, walking over to them. 'I love a good transformation cut. Such fun! And it does wonders for our Instagram.'

Mack's muscles relaxed, and he smiled back at the man. 'Mack,' he said, reaching out his hand. 'And this is obviously Sid,' he added, thumbing over to his friend.

'Daniel,' he replied, cupping Mack's hand with his. 'Come. Come. Mack, you're with me, and Sid, you're with Adam over there.'

Adam gave a friendly wave, and Sid grunted in response. 'Oh dear,' said Daniel, frowning. 'Maybe when we cut all of this fluff away, we might find a smile somewhere underneath. Come now. Let's take you over to Adam so that he can work his magic on you.'

He stepped behind Sid and gently pushed him by the shoulders towards an enthusiastic Adam. Sid turned his head back to Mack, his eyes pleading for help, but Mack simply smiled and gave a quick wave. Sid's lips curled back with derision.

'You're dead to me,' he said.

Daniel had asked Mack to keep his eyes closed while he worked on him. Mack was only too happy to oblige. He was completely relaxed after having his hair washed; the young girl had even gently massaged his scalp, using her fingers to press down on pressure points. He closed his eyes and listened to the scissors clip, enjoying the soft tugging on his hair as Daniel expertly cut away over three years of growth.

He had no idea how long he'd been sitting in the chair; all concept of time disappeared the moment he heard the buzz of hair clippers. God knows how Sid was faring, but the fact that he hadn't spoken a word was a promising sign that he hadn't tried to drown Adam in the funny-shaped sink.

'Now,' said Daniel, breaking Mack's reverie. 'To beard or not to beard? That is the question.'

At that moment in time, Mack couldn't give a shit about facial hair. 'You decide. My face is in your hands. Literally.'

Daniel giggled with dizzy excitement. 'So be it,' he said.

He snipped away at the coarse hair, cutting close to the skin, and applied foam to the lower half of Mack's face. 'Keep perfectly still,' he instructed Mack. 'We don't want any Sweeny Todd incidents.'

Mack felt the gentle scrape of the cutthroat razor gliding over his cheeks and skin. Not to beard it is then, he thought to himself. He'd forgotten what he looked like without facial hair. The only part that brought tears to Mack's eyes was when Daniel had unceremoniously shoved two large wax-covered cotton buds into each nostril. He waited a few minutes before telling Mack to brace himself and tugged them out again. Christ, that was a kind of pain that he'd never experienced before and he secretly wished Adam well if he was going to try that on Sid.

But now, with all of the washing, and clipping, and snipping, and scrapping at an end, Mack's body relaxed under the heat of the towel, which was partially smothering him. He thought of Elsie's kindness. She didn't have to do this for them. It must have cost her a small fortune. Mack thought of ways he could say thank you. This was definitely more than an omelette's worth.

Daniel removed the towel and proceeded to rub all manner of lotions into Mack's scalp and face. 'Just a few quick piccies for the socials,' he said, as the sound of a phone camera clicked all around him. 'And there. All done. You can open your eyes now.'

Mack's eyes fluttered open, and he stared at the man facing him in the mirror. It was a face that he both knew but didn't at the same time. In the space of a few years, deep age lines had formed in his cheeks and around his mouth. And yet, in a bizarre way, with his hair cut and beard gone, he somehow looked younger. He ran his hand through his hair, loving the feeling of the short cut in between his fingers.

'Wow! I mean, just...wow!' he said. 'I look – I look...'

'Amazing,' said Daniel. He clapped his hands again. 'Wait until you see Sid.' He turned the chair so that Mack was facing his friend just as Adam removed the towel from his face.

Sid sat up, and Mack gasped. For as long as he'd known Sid, he had always had long, bedraggled salt and pepper hair and an overgrown beard which touched the top of his chest. In short, Sid, to him, had always looked like the poor man's version of Santa Claus. But now! Now, it was like meeting Sid for the first time. The man Mack knew had been replaced with a younger version. The neat crew cut had de-aged him by around fifteen years, and although he still had a beard, it was now cut short and tidy against the skin.

Sid's green eyes stared back at himself in the mirror. He was silent as he rubbed at his chin with his hands, and Mack couldn't tell if Sid was happy with the reveal or not. It was usually a bad sign if Sid went quiet and he waited for a retort, a grunt or a sharp comment.

'Well? What do you think?' asked Adam as he nervously nibbled the end of his finger.

Sid's eyes twinkled, and a grin spread over his face.

'I'm a handsome fucker, aren't I? he said, admiring his reflection in the mirror.

***

Sid stopped to look at himself every chance he got, pausing to look in shop windows as they made the short walk back to St Pauls Square.

'Will you stop it,' said Mack as he caught him staring, yet again, at himself in the mirror of a van window parked on the side of the road.

'Sorry. I can't help it,' said Sid, ruffling his hair for the umpteenth time. 'It doesn't feel like it's me. It's like I'm a new man.'

Mack didn't reply as he knew precisely what Sid meant. His old t-shirt and cargo trousers, which were torn at the knee, were at odds with the sudden newness he felt inside. It was as though his body no longer matched his clothes. It was almost as if he'd been reborn as a different person. No. Not a different person.

It had turned him *back* into the person he once was. The same person that Mack had pushed away under the haze of heroin and the person he'd been struggling to find again ever since the opiate fog had lifted from his life.

Two old ladies who were deep in conversation walked in the opposite direction towards them, and Sid slid over to give them more space on the pavement.

'Ladies,' he said, with a slight bow at the waist.

The women looked at Sid, who cheekily winked back at them. They giggled at each other.

'Why, thank you, kind Sir,' said one, her cheeks reddening.

When they were a safe distance away, Sid turned to Mack.

'Still got it,' he said, smiling.

'Bloody hell, mate. They were too old even for you!' replied Mack.

'You cheeky bugger. I was quite a catch back in my day, believe it or not.'

Mack could quite easily believe it as it happened. Well, at least now he could now that the years of the streets had been cut away from Sid's face.

They turned the corner and walked towards Elsie's apartment, passing the bistro and the man who owned it, who was busy watering the two large potted bay trees on either side of the doors. He glanced up at them as they neared.

'Gents,' he said with a polite nod. But as his eyes drifted from their faces and down to their clothes, his face crumpled with confusion.

'Good day to you, Sir,' replied Sid, doffing an imaginary hat.

Mack chuckled to himself and rang the bell to Elsie's apartment, feeling the burn of the man's eyes on his back, and he wondered whether or not he realised that they were the same men whom he'd been so judgemental to before.

Mack heard the patter of footsteps coming down the stairs and the clunk of the locks being drawn back. The door opened, and the split second it had taken Elsie to recognise them made Mack smile again. He was enjoying himself.

'Oh my word!' said Elsie. 'You two look fabulous. I never thought it would be such a dramatic change.'

'Neither did we,' said Sid. He turned on the spot, holding out his arms. 'Seriously? Do you like it?'

Mack couldn't get to grips with the change in Sid's personality. It was as though all of his anger and bravado had disappeared, swept away, and dropped into the bin with the rest of his unwanted hair.

'Honestly. I love it,' replied Elsie. She stepped to one side. 'Now get in quickly before my neighbours start to question why I've got two dapper gentlemen loitering on my doorstep. I'll get myself a reputation if I'm not careful.'

Sid went inside and followed Elsie up the stairs.

'Too late for that, it seems,' said Mack, closing the front door as the man from the bistro stood with his hands planted firmly on his hips as he stared back at him.

Chapter Nineteen

Elsie

E lsie slipped herself into a body-hugging black dress and smoothed it over her hips. She pinched the skin between her fingertips, feeling the jutting of hip bones and pulled a face. She'd lost more weight in the last few weeks than she'd expected, despite the fact that she still tried to eat three meals a day, but admittedly, it was getting more and more difficult now that her appetite had practically disappeared.

Beneath her expertly applied make-up, she looked incredibly gaunt, and her skin was tinged with a faint yellowish tint. Soon, she wouldn't be able to hide the fact that she was ill, and it wouldn't be long before people started to ask questions. Jack, of course, knew everything, but Agata, Sid and Mack had no idea, and she intended to keep it that way for as long as possible. She needed to cling to the last few scraps of normality before the cancer tore her life away from her forever.

She took one last look in the mirror and flicked her hair onto her shoulders with her hand. Not bad for a dying woman, she thought to herself. She slid her feet into her black patent high heels and entered the living room. Mack was cutting vegetables on the chopping board, prepping for the ratatouille he was making for himself and Sid later that evening. Sid was sat on the sofa, one leg crossed over the other, nose deep in her copy of *Oliver Twist.*

Elsie had called a few local hostels over the last couple of days, each promising to put Sid and Mack's name down on their waiting lists and call her back when something became available, but as yet, she'd heard nothing. It was still early days in reality, and she was only too aware of the current housing crisis that appeared to be gripping the country. As it stood, she was surprisingly okay with having them stay with her. Neither had caused any issues nor given her any reason to be concerned. In actual fact, they were both quite boring, enjoying the quiet and peace, either reading or listening to the radio. Mack had made himself the unofficial chef of the household, which suited Elsie as cooking was most definitely not her forte. He seemed at home in the kitchen, and each day, he would politely suggest a meal he could cook for them, handily leaving the ingredients list on the side for Elsie to find. He'd never once asked Elsie directly for the money to buy them himself, and she wondered whether that was because he was embarrassed that he didn't have any money of his own or because he was worried that Elsie might think he'd spend it on drugs instead. All Sid did with his time was read and bathe, sometimes doing both simultaneously. She was enjoying them living there with her. It eased the loneliness that ebbed away in the day and gave her something else to occupy her mind that wasn't to do with her illness. Elsie knew that it couldn't continue, though. At some point, it would have to end, and selfishly, she hoped it would be sooner rather than later. With any luck, one of the hostels would call any day now and offer them both a room. At least there'd be support workers there to help them apply for welfare benefits and find a more permanent home. Elsie had her own life to organise, or to be more precise, her own death to organise. The for sale board had finally gone up outside the bistro, and her own apartment and the one above had been listed on the same estate agent's website, but she'd asked the agent to delay those boards going up until after Mack and Sid had left. It would only lead to uncomfortable questions otherwise.

'You look great,' said Mack, giving Elsie a quick look of approval. 'Where are you off to?'

'A cocktail bar on Temple Row,' she replied. 'The one where the drinks come out looking like they've just ladled them straight out of a witches cauldron with the amount of dry ice they use.'

Mack smiled and continued to chop courgettes at lightning speed. 'Well, fingers crossed that they taste nice,' said Mack.

The doorbell shrilled, and Sid rose from his chair. 'I'll get it,' he declared, walking out of the living room. Elsie and Mack exchanged a surprised glance.

Sid had changed beyond recognition to the man she had first met. Gone was the bitter and ragged-looking man from that first day in the bistro, replaced with a calm and surprisingly helpful one whose quick-witted responses never failed to make Elsie laugh. She was amazed at the power of a good haircut! He returned moments later with a glamourous Agata tailing behind.

'Hi,' Agata said to Elsie before turning her gaze to Mack. 'Hello. Nice to meet you. I'm Agata. Elsie's friend.'

Friend. Elsie caught the smile before it materialised on her face. It was strange how nice it made her feel. Mack stopped his sustained attack on the vegetables and placed down the knife.

'Hi,' he replied. 'I'm Mack.'

Mack stared at Agata for a fraction too long for Elsie not to notice; Sid too, for that matter, as he gave a polite, but not indiscreet, cough.

'And this is Sid. Who...of course, you've already met just now, downstairs at the door,' fumbled Mack.

Oh dear. Elsie most certainly had not been expecting this. Agata smiled bashfully and tucked one of her freshly curled locks behind her ear.

'Pleased to meet you, Mack,' she said, still smiling but too shy to look Mack directly in the eye.

Enough of this nonsense. This was the last thing that Elsie needed.

'Right,' she said briskly. 'Time to go.'

Before she had time to flutter her eyelashes again at Mack, she took Agata by the hand and led her straight back out of the door and into the cool air of early evening.

***

'And then I turn to her, and I say,' said Agata. 'Because this fuck-wit is cleverer than you think.'

Elsie's mouth dropped open, and Agata threw back her head and laughed.

'You,' said Elsie, shouting above the thud of the music 'are a total queen!'

She held up her hand, and Agata high-fived her. Elsie had never high-fived anyone in her life, which showed when their hands failed to connect fully, but that could also be put down to the fact that they were on their sixth over-priced cocktail.

Agata had just regaled Elsie with juicy details of the virtuous Mrs King, and Elsie was astounded. The whole scenario was unbelievable, but Elsie was so proud of Agata for standing up for herself.

'You do realise that you've got her eating out of your hand now,' she said, chinking her glass with Agata's. 'You can get away with anything you want.'

Agata sipped at the luminous green liquid in her glass and gave a quick shrug. 'All I want is to be treated fairly. That's all. Then nobody can say that I take advantage.'

Some people might have said that Agata was wasting an opportunity. Still, Elsie found it heart-warming to know that Agata wasn't the type of person to manipulate a situation, even if it was deserved. In another lifetime, she and Agata could have been the best of friends.

Within the hour, they were dancing away on the tiny dance floor with men whose names they didn't know. Agata had bagged herself a tall, Mediterranean-looking man with light green eyes and Elsie, a fair-haired, thin man who spoke with an Irish accent.

Fast forward one hour later, and Agata was holding Elsie's hair out of the way as she hunched over the toilet in the ladies, throwing up the brightly coloured contents of her stomach. The remainder of the evening blurred like screenshots, little snippets of one event flicking to the next: Elsie remembered being hoisted up by a burly doorman and escorted out of the club. The next, she was in the taxi, resting her head on Agata's shoulder. Then, all of a sudden, Mack was helping her up the stairs and into her apartment.

'She drink too much' she heard Agata say to Mack.

'It's not the first time,' replied Mack. 'She always seems to drink a lot.'

'Whaatt do yooouuu know,' slurred Elsie.

The next time she opened her eyes, Elsie was lying in bed. She was still wearing her dress, but she felt the soft tug of her shoes being removed, and she lifted her head to see Agata.

'I'm so sorry,' said Elsie.

Agata covered Elsie with the duvet. 'Shush now,' she said. 'No need to be sorry. You're sad about something, I see it. Just sleep now.'

Agata lay on the bed next to her and started to stroke Elsie's forehead. She felt her eyelids close and the room span as she lay there motionless, her muscles paralysed by alcohol.

'Thank you,' she managed to murmur, but if Agata replied, Elsie didn't hear it as she drifted into sleep.

Elsie was running. Fear ripped through her body as she pushed away the branches that blocked her way. A low growling rumbled behind her like thunder, and she turned to stare into the darkness, which was spreading like a low-hanging fog. It crept forward, enveloping the landscape, sucking in the trees and pulling the grass beneath her feet towards it. It was like she was on a treadmill, running as fast as her legs would move as the green of the grass was pulled away and replaced with a monotonic grey. She could see a light in the distance. A brilliant white orb that was as small as a firefly. She reached out her hand even though she knew that she was too far away to reach it. It pulsed like a heartbeat, calling her to come closer, and Elsie felt her own heartbeat thumping in sync with its rhythm. It felt like home. It felt like it was somewhere she belonged, somewhere she needed to be to feel safe. The abyss behind her was swallowing the land, gaining pace, and she felt a tug on her clothes as it seized her body. She felt her weight shift as she was lifted inches from the ground. Unable to get traction, Elsie felt the panic rise as she was dragged away from the comfort of the orb and into the pitch of chasm of the monster that stalked her. Colour faded from her eyes, the glow of the orb becoming smaller and smaller until finally she blinked again, and it was gone, and Elsie was alone in a gulf of black terror.

She woke up with a start. A film of sweat coated every inch of her skin, and her dress felt clammy and damp against her body. She pushed the heavy duvet away from her and lay on the bed spread-eagled, trying to calm her pounding heart. She turned to the side and saw a pint of water placed on her bedside cabinet. She grabbed it and gulped it down greedily. Unsurprisingly, her head hurt and her stomach and throat were raw from the previous night's retching and vomiting. She thought back to the things that she could remember, which didn't account for much. Everything that had happened after eleven o'clock was a bit of a blur. She remembered Mack helping her up the stairs and into bed and Agata taking off her shoes and covering her with the duvet. They were talking about her. What was it they'd said? Elsie narrowed her brows as she willed herself to remember, but all of the cocktails she'd drunk the night before had wiped her memory. She retrieved her clutch bag from the floor and pulled out her mobile phone to check the time, but it was dead. Seeing as the light was breaking through the curtains, she knew that it wasn't too early.

She felt the swell in her bladder, and she staggered her way to the bathroom. When she finished, her initial intention was to head straight back to her room and flop onto her bed for the rest of the day, but the din of hushed voices in the living room made her stop in her tracks. She could hear the low dulcet tones of Mack and Sid quietly chatting, but then she heard a woman's voice, and Elsie strained her ears. Maybe it was Agata? She'd probably stayed last night to make sure that Elsie was okay. She should go and say thank you, really; she had, after all, completely ruined the end of the evening.

Elsie shuffled along the corridor, her legs refusing to work properly, and she pushed open the door. They were all sat around the dining table with large mugs of tea in front of them. Mack, Sid, Agata.

And Ingrid.

Elsie's breath caught in her throat.

Chapter Twenty

Ingrid

Ingrid didn't know what had made her come that morning. It was a Sunday, for goodness' sake, and for most people, it was a day of rest, but somewhere in her head, it made sense as it was more likely that Elsie would be at home.

When a petite blonde woman opened the door, Ingrid had been surprised yet again. For somebody who claimed to have nobody, there sure were a lot of people who had access to Elsie's home. Ingrid asked to speak to Elsie, and the woman told her in an accent that Ingrid couldn't quite place, that Elsie was in bed sleeping.

Ingrid consulted her watch. It was almost 11 a.m.

'Could I please come and wait then,' she told the woman. 'I'd really like to check that she's alright.'

The woman seemed taken aback. 'Of course, she alright. She just drank too much. That's all.'

Far from it for Ingrid to judge anyone, and maybe it was Elsie's choice to get paralytic drunk, but she believed that if this woman *was* her friend, then she could jolly well find a better way to support Elsie during the last few months of her life.

'Do you think that she should be drinking in her condition?' she spat back at the woman.

Her hand went to her chest. 'Her condition? You mean Elsie is pregnant? Oh my god! Why she not say anything to me?'

'Huh?' replied Ingrid, scrunching her face. 'No. Elsie's not pregnant, she's...'

Ingrid stopped herself from finishing. She was about to break a confidentiality agreement between herself and a client, something that she'd never done before. Over the years, she had been privy to people's innermost personal secrets, usually divulged in the final moments before their deaths. It was their final opportunity to unburden themselves in a world where people no longer sought solace and absolution from religion. Ingrid had been told all kinds of revelations in those quiet moments as she sat holding the hands of some of her residents; most of them weren't too shocking, relatively tame really. Apart from the spinster, Ms Newhaven, who'd told her that she'd run over and killed a small child when she was drunk-driving back in the seventies. And the frail Mr Hatton, who told Ingrid that he shot dead Nazis indiscriminately even after they'd surrendered at the end of World War Two.

It wasn't her place to let Elsie's friends know what was going on, and at the same time, Ingrid knew that she wouldn't be able to turn around and go home without doing just that. For some unknown reason, Elsie Bellamy plagued her thoughts from the moment she woke until she went to bed at night.

The woman was still looking at Ingrid expectantly, waiting for an explanation.

Ingrid took a deep breath.

'Elsie has terminal cancer.'

The woman grabbed Ingrid by the coat and pulled her inside, pushing her up the stairs and through the front door of the flat, where two men stared back at her with surprise.

'Hello again, Ingrid,' said the older man, and it took her brain a few seconds to register that this was the same man who had compared her to a dog the other week.

'Tell them what you just told me,' instructed the woman. But before Ingrid had the chance, she blurted, 'She said that Elsie is dying.'

The two men exchanged bewildered looks.

'What?' said the younger man.

'She has cancer,' continued the woman, who then burst into tears.

The young man went over and embraced the woman, pulling her into his chest.

'I'm sorry,' said Ingrid, even though she wasn't sorry at all. These people cared for Elsie. She could see that now. They deserved to know just what was happening to her.

'I think you need to tell us everything,' said the older man.

Ingrid looked into his eyes, which seemed kinder, softer, than before. He pulled out a chair at the dining table for her to sit down, and as she lowered herself, he pushed the chair back underneath her legs.

'Start from the beginning,' he said softly.

Ingrid nodded, took a deep breath and started talking.

Elsie's expression when she walked into the living room was a mix of fear and downright anger. Ingrid could hardly blame her, and she was sure she would have acted exactly the same had she been in Elsie's position.

'You had no fucking right! How dare you?' screamed Elsie at the top of her lungs. 'I could sue you for this. You signed a contract with me.'

Ingrid said nothing. She felt terrible for breaking Elsie's trust; of course she did, but she knew there was nothing that she could say at that precise moment that would calm Elsie. She needed this. She needed to let out all of her anger, sadness, and pain, and if Ingrid was in the firing line, then so be it. She didn't have a defence anyway. Elsie was one hundred percent right to say all of those things. Ingrid didn't have the right to tell anybody about her illness, and yes, Elsie could technically sue her for breach of contract. Still, she doubted very much that anything would come of that due to the unfortunate limited time that Elsie had left.

'You should have said something,' said the woman who Ingrid now knew was called Agata. Her eyes were swollen and red from crying.

Elsie scoffed. 'And what would you have done? What could any of you,' she pointed to Mack and Sid, 'do to help me?'

'We could have supported you. We could have...' Mack's voice trailed off.

'Exactly!' spat Elsie. 'Nothing. There's absolutely nothing that you could have done or said that would have made a difference. Do you know what? Why the fuck am I explaining myself to you anyway? I hardly know you. Any of you! I owe you nothing.' Elsie turned to leave the room, but she spun back around quickly. 'Why am I leaving? This is my fucking home. You go—all of you. Go on. Fuck off!'

'Elsie, please. Just sit down for a minute. Let's talk about this,' said Mack.

'What's the matter? Worried about losing your cushy set-up?' she replied.

'Now, that's not fair,' said Sid. 'You asked us to stay, not the other way around.'

'And now I'm asking you to leave. And you can go too,' she said to Agata. 'I only started being nice to you because I felt sorry for you.'

The words hit Agata like a slap in the face. 'You don't mean that,' she replied as her eyes filled with a fresh wave of tears.

'Don't I? Don't presume to know me. How can any of you sit there, at my table, drinking tea from my cups, and presume that you know anything about me at all.' Elsie stomped over to the table and pulled the cups away from them, sending tea splashing all over the table. 'And you,' she said to Ingrid. 'You're a disgrace to your profession. Suffice it to say, I won't be using your services any longer. Now get out of my home, all of you, before I call the police.'

Ingrid nodded, picked up her handbag, and rose from the chair. 'I'm not sorry for what I did,' she said, looking Elsie square in the eye. 'And I'll keep the room available for you. You're angry right now, and I completely understand why, but tomorrow or the next day, you might feel differently. Don't push people away who are here to help you, Elsie. It'll be the mistake of your life.'

Elsie shrugged. 'Well, it's lucky that I don't have much of a life left then, isn't it? Now get out.'

Ingrid pushed back her chair and stood. 'If you change your mind, you know where to find me. Don't feel that you're alone in all of this.' She gave a solemn nod to Agata, Mack and Sid and left.

Once she was outside, a swell of tears filled her eyes and flowed down her cheeks. It wasn't the fact that she'd deliberately betrayed Elsie that upset her, nor was it Elsie's anger towards her. It was the sad realisation that Elsie probably felt more alone than she'd ever done before. Her only wish was that as the trauma subsided, Elsie would realise that Ingrid was only trying to help her. Hopefully, she'd reach out to her again.

Hopefully.

Ingrid would be there in a heartbeat.

Chapter Twenty-One

Mack

After Ingrid's departure, Elsie marched into the spare bedroom and returned to the living room with arms filled with his and Sid's meagre belongings. She dropped them in a big bundle on the sofa and went over to the kitchen cupboard, retrieving a roll of black bin bags. She threw the roll at Mack, and he caught it in his hand.

'Pack your stuff and get out,' she shouted at him.

'Elsie,' Agata said tentatively. 'You're not thinking clearly.'

'Oh. I'm seeing things crystal clear, thank you. And you can piss off, too, by the way.'

'Elsie. Just listen...' started Mack, but he was cut off by Sid, who placed a hand on his shoulder.

'I think we should leave,' he said, taking the roll of bin bags from Mack's hand.

He tore one off and filled it with their clothes. When he'd finished, Sid silently went over to the small cupboard in the corridor and took out their backpacks and coats. 'Come on. Let's go.'

Mack slipped his arms into his coat and draped his backpack over one shoulder. 'Come on, Agata,' he said, taking her gently by the arm.

Mack didn't want to go. He wanted to stay and let Elsie scream and shout at them until her throat hurt, and only then, when she was utterly exhausted, would he rush over to her, take her in his arms, and hold her tightly to him. He may not have known Elsie for very long, but from their first meeting, he'd known deep down inside that there was something seriously wrong with her. He'd spent years hiding his own internal pain from everybody around him, and as a result, he'd sunk into a sea of despair where, no matter how hard he kicked, he couldn't find his way to the surface again. The thought of another person feeling such anguish tore through his own body. Elsie, for all her bravado and independence, needed support.

He led Agata towards the door. 'We're here for you,' he said, looking deep into Elsie's blue eyes. 'And when you need us, we'll be there.'

Elsie scoffed and turned her back on them all, and Mack lowered his head with sadness and walked out of the room.

When they were outside, he heard smashing from inside the apartment, drowned out only by Elsie's tortured screams.

'We can't leave her like that,' implored Agata, but Sid shook his head.

'Take it from me,' he said softly to Agata. 'She needs time. She needs to let everything out. She's hurting in ways we can't even imagine, and when she's ready, she'll let us know.'

'But what if she doesn't?' said Agata.

'Then we'll be here to tell her we're not going anywhere. Now, come on, let's get out of this cold and find somewhere to have a drink.'

***

They'd decided against a drink in the bistro. It was too close for comfort, well, Elsie's comfort, and they wanted to be able to speak freely and without fear that something they said might be overheard by somebody that Elsie knew. The last thing that she needed was for more people to know of her illness. They found a little café two streets away and ordered the strongest coffee on the menu, sitting in the far corner away from the door where blasts of freezing air swept in whenever someone came in or left.

Agata, like him and Sid, was relatively new in Elsie's life, and Mack realised that Elsie had probably only taken the leap in forming friendships purely because of what was happening to her. He was attracted to Agata the moment she'd walked into Elsie's apartment the previous evening; with her long blonde hair and alluring Polish accent, he had found himself thinking about her long after she and Elsie had left to go to the cocktail bar. Not that it mattered now.

'I don't think she should be on her own. She might hurt herself,' said Agata, but Sid shook his head at the suggestion.

'I don't think she will. It seems to me that she's a woman who has spent a lifetime keeping things to herself. She's gotten so used to being on her own that the fact that she's been forced into a position to talk about something so devastating is what's difficult for her to handle right now. She needs space and time alone because that's how she's used to handling things.'

Mack was surprised at how astute Sid was. 'How can you tell Elsie's like that?'

He shrugged. 'It's one of the few perks of being on the streets for so many years. You get used to sizing people up. You get used to spotting the signs when somebody's hiding something. It becomes more than instinct in the end; it becomes second nature.'

Mack raised his eyebrows, impressed. Sid was full of surprises.

'Where will you go now?' Agata asked them.

'Where we always go,' said Mack. 'Back to the car park. No. Don't be like that,' he said, seeing a look of terror wash over Agata's face. 'We're used to it. And to be fair, we never expected our stay at Elsie's to be longer than a few days. We knew we'd have to leave at some point. She was more than kind and generous towards us. I just wish that it hadn't ended like this.'

Agata reached over the table and took Mack's hand. 'I wish I could help. If it was my house, you could have come and stayed with me. But I live in my employer's home and look after their children.'

Mack squeezed her hand. 'Please. Don't worry. We'll be fine,' he replied.

It was kind of Agata to think of them, but the possibility of any stranger agreeing to let them stay in their house was non-existent. Elsie was the only exception to that rule.

Agata reached into her bag, pulled out a notepad, and scribbled down her mobile number. She tore off the paper and slid it over the table towards Mack.

'Here' she said. 'We keep in touch.'

Mack picked up the paper and gave a polite smile. 'Neither of us has a phone,' he said. His face flushed with embarrassment at how primitive he probably seemed to her.

Agata's hands flew to her mouth. 'Oh! I'm so sorry. I should have guessed,' she gushed. 'I didn't think.'

'Finding a charging point can be a little tricky where we stay,' joked Sid, trying to lighten the mood. 'You weren't to know.' He sat back in the chair and ran a hand through his short hair. 'But Agata's right. We should stay in touch. Any ideas?'

Agata's eyes drifted up to the ceiling. Suddenly, she clicked her fingers.

'The park! That's where I met her. She always go there. She say she meets her friend there,' she said.

'Yes! You're right,' said Mack. 'What was his name again?' He looked at Agata and Sid but was met with blank faces. 'Nevermind. That doesn't matter. But it's a good idea, Agata. We should go there. That way, Elsie will know that we're still thinking of her.'

Sid shook his head. 'No. If that's where Elsie goes to be with her friend, it's her safe space. We can't ruin that for her.'

Mack rubbed his hands over his face. 'Then what? What are we supposed to do?'

'We wait,' said Sid.

Chapter Twenty-Two

Agata

When Agata finally returned home after leaving Mack and Sid, she walked back into the house and was met with a scene of chaos. George was running around wearing a pirate hat and eye patch, brandishing a wooden sword, and chasing after Isabella and Penelope, who were screaming in fear as though their older brother was actually about to slice them in two. Little Arthur was naked save for his sagging nappy and crying heartily from the baby prison that was his playpen. Mrs King was laid out on the purple chaise lounge with a damp flannel resting over her forehead, and she was either too doped up on Diazepam to hear the racket that her children were making or was ignoring it altogether. Agata's head was thumping to its own beat. The effects of last night's alcohol, coupled with everything that had happened with Elsie, had taken its toll on her. She didn't need this right now. All that she wanted to do was go upstairs, take a long hot shower, crawl into bed, and try to sleep her headache away.

'Ta Ta,' cried Arthur, seeing Agata standing in the living room doorway. He reached up and opened and closed his pudgy hands, begging her in his baby way to pick him up.

Ta Ta was Arthur's way of saying Agata's name, and upon hearing it, Arabella flung off the flannel on her forehead and sat bolt upright.

'Oh, thank goodness you're back,' she said.

Agata took in her crumpled loungewear, her bloodshot eyes, and her bare face, which was devoid of any makeup. In short, she looked atrocious.

'Arthur has had me up all night with his whinging, and those three out there,' she flung her hand out in the direction of the high-pitched screams emanating from the kitchen, 'they've been climbing the walls all morning. Please. Can you do something?'

Every instinct in Agata's body wanted to tell Arabella to go fuck herself, but she knew that she would be spiting the children if she did, especially Arthur, who it seemed had been left to sit in his own filth for hours. No wonder the poor thing was traumatised.

'I sort them out for you, and then I go bed.' Agata said sternly.

She went over to the playpen and picked up Arthur. 'You see this,' she said, pointing to the bulging nappy. 'This is why he cry.'

She lay the child down on the rug and reached for his changing bag from the side of the playpen. His nappy was sodden with urine, and his little bottom was red and sore. She gently used a cool wipe over his skin, applied some cream to soothe the irritation, and secured a new nappy in place.

'There, there,' she said to Arthur, wiping away the tears from his cheeks. 'That's better. Now, would you like a treat? Shall we get banana?'

Arthur nodded and smiled, and Agata lifted him and carried him out of the living room and towards the kitchen, cutting Arabella a scathing look as she passed. Inside the kitchen, she found George standing precariously on one of the stools at the breakfast bar. He was holding his sword high in the air and bearing down on his two sisters, who were screaming and clinging to one another.

'What is this?' shouted Agata at the top of her voice.

The three children stopped immediately and looked at her as Arabella hovered in the doorway behind her like a nervous animal.

'George, you get down from there right now,' Agata instructed.

George gave a devious smile and held his sword higher in the air.

'You'll never take me alive,' he shouted back at her.

Agata shrugged. 'Okay. Fine. Maybe I call police and let them know that there is somebody in the house who is threatening little girls with sword. Maybe they send policemen with guns and burst into the house and shoot to save them.' George's eyes peeled back with horror. 'And maybe they accidentally shoot you with their gun. Pow Pow. And then I don't have to worry about looking after you any more.'

Agata had never spoken to any of the children like that before, especially in front of their parents, but she was past caring. She was sick of being disrespected or treated like a workhorse and tired of worrying about what people thought of her or whether or not she was going to keep her job. What did it matter? Like Elsie, Agata could wake up tomorrow with some incurable disease or be run over by a bus, and none of the King family would care. They'd find another Au Pair to replace her. They'd have her bedroom emptied before the ink had even dried on her death certificate, and the whole household would carry on as normal as though she'd never been there in the first place.

Under Agata's unflinching gaze, George slowly lowered his sword and jumped off the side.

'Mummy,' he whined to Arabella. 'Agata is making me feel sad.'

Arabella's eyes softened, but when she saw Agata's cold stare, she coughed and straightened her back.

'No. You've all been absolute terrors today. Unless you all behave, then Agata is well within her rights to do exactly what she says. In fact, I'll hand her the phone to call them.'

Isabella and Penelope exchanged worried glances, and Agata resisted the urge to smile at the naivety of them all. Sometimes, a white lie was a parent's best defence when it came to keeping children under control.

'Now. You tidy up all of the mess you have made, and if you have done good job then I make lunch. If not, you will wait until dinner.'

The children gasped and rushed from the room, their little feet pounding up the stairs. A series of loud thumps and doors being opened and closed drifted through the floorboards.

'You really are a marvel,' said Arabella, paying Agata the first compliment she'd ever received since she'd started working there. 'Now. I'll pop upstairs and try and get forty winks before Esra comes home.'

She went to walk out of the door, but Agata blocked her way.

'No. I don't think so,' said Agata, handing Arthur over to his mother. 'Today is my day off, not yours. I make the children their lunch, and then *I* go and lie down – not you.'

***

After her shower, Agata climbed into bed and waited for the sleep that she so desperately needed to come. The light from outside permeated through the pink curtains and cast a warm haze about the room, and even though the mayhem in the house she had walked into had ceased, her eyelids refused to close. All that she could think about was Elsie. She had no idea what it must be like to deal with that. If Agata was ever unlucky enough to find herself in such a position, she knew that she'd jump on the next plane out of the UK and rush back into the arms of her family.

But unlike Agata, Elsie had nobody. She'd never mentioned any family or boyfriends. The only person in her friend's life was the mysterious Jack, who, so far, Agata had never set eyes on. But they must be close for Elsie to trek all the way to the park to meet him. Did he know that she was dying? If he did, why didn't he make more of an effort to visit Elsie in her home? Mack and Sid told her that they'd never seen him, but she supposed that they hadn't been staying with Elsie for very long. It might be that Elsie had put him off from visiting while they were staying with her. After all, regardless of how nice both men appeared to be to Agata, they were still strangers and homeless to boot. Other people might not understand, and it stood to reason that a person might want to keep something like that to themselves.

Ingrid had told them everything from the first day she'd met Elsie to her ever-diminishing life expectancy. It was bleak to listen to. At best, Elsie had around seven months left. How does anybody cope knowing something like that? How did Elsie manage to find the strength to carry on each day? Agata doubted that she would have been able to. It was all very well for healthy people to say that a dying person should make the most of each day, but would they be as optimistic if it were happening to them? If it were Agata, she'd probably reach for the nearest bottle of pills. She'd much prefer to die on her own terms.

Elsie had come into her life in such an unexpected way and just when she needed somebody the most. She knew only too well the impact that loneliness could have on a person. It'd only been since meeting Elsie that Agata had reignited her old self back into action. She didn't feel the need to explain herself or people-please any more. She couldn't give a shit what the King family thought of her, and if they sacked her tomorrow, they'd probably be doing her a favour. Sometimes, for reasons unknown, a person can just become stuck to the point that they can't see any other possibility or options. Agata had certainly done that. She'd been so scared that her move to the UK would be a failure that she'd been prepared to accept anything that would stop that from happening.

Elsie may have pushed them all away, but Agata wasn't about to accept it. She wasn't going to let her do that. Ingrid was right; it would be the biggest mistake she would ever make, and although Elsie couldn't see it now, she would when her anger dissipated.

She, Mack and Sid had already arranged to keep in touch. She felt a fresh round of embarrassment course through her blood at handing over her mobile number to two men who couldn't even afford to feed themselves each day, let alone pay for a phone. They'd both been polite about it, of course, and made out that it was nothing, but Agata was annoyed at her stupidity. She'd been instantly attracted to Mack the second she'd met him. He had kind eyes and a softness beneath his weathered surface that she wanted to discover more about. She smiled at the thought of him, and Agata tutted at her selfishness. This wasn't about her. It wasn't about Mack and Sid. It was about Elsie.

Tomorrow, she intended to visit Ingrid at the residential home. Ingrid had taken a verbal battering from Elsie that morning, and whilst in some ways she understood why, it must have been difficult for her when all she was trying to do was help. Sid had advised her to avoid the park, but Agata felt it would be a mistake. She didn't want to upset Elsie or take that safe haven away from her. She would keep well away, but she needed to find out who this Jack character was and discover precisely what he knew. Was he as in the dark as they had been? Possibly. But if Jack didn't know, Agata had no qualms in telling him. Jack was the closest thing Elsie had to a best friend right now, and if she valued his friendship as much as Agata believed she did, then he was perfectly placed to try and make his friend see sense.

Chapter Twenty-Three

Jack

W ell, this was something that Jack hadn't been expecting. The first day that Elsie didn't show up, he'd put it down to her having a hangover. Elsie had told him the day before that she was going on a night out with Agata, and he just assumed that Elsie had drunk to excess as she so often did. When the following day arrived, and Elsie had failed again to meet him at the park, he was a little confused but not overly concerned. She was a grown woman, after all. But then it was the same the following day and the one after that, until slowly the days turned into weeks and the weeks into several weeks. In fact, it had been almost eight weeks. This wouldn't do. It wouldn't do at all!

Elsie was on the cusp of disappearing, and there was still so much left for her to do. In his head, he'd been confident that he'd finally reached her; that he'd finally got his message through to her, but now? Now, he didn't know what to think. Clearly, something had gone drastically wrong, and he wondered whether it was Elsie's relationships that were at the root cause of it all. Four new friendships were a lot for an emotionally closed person to handle, especially when each of those people had their own personal struggles to deal with. It might have just been too much for Elsie to process. He should have done something, said something, to put Elsie off. He'd misjudged her and her capabilities, which was frustrating. He'd never done that before.

He'd come to the park every day, knowing in his soul that Elsie wasn't going to turn up, but he went along anyway. He sat on the bench and waited, watching everyone go about their daily lives, coming and going, not even realising that he was there. He'd seen the Polish woman several times. At first, she'd come by herself, walking around the park and searching. On a few occasions, she had brought the Smythe-Owen lady with her, but regardless of how much they looked, they never found what they were looking for. It always amazed Jack at how most people could look for something but not see what was right under their noses.

What to do about Elsie though? She was wasting her time hiding away in that barren apartment of hers, and whilst he knew that she had a good reason to do so, why hadn't she come to see him? Why was it that she felt the need to push Jack away as well? If only there were a way that he could give her a little nudge to make her see sense. There had to be something he could do to make this better, well, maybe not better as such, but something that he could do that would guide Elsie back onto the path that she should be on.

A teenage girl walking a springer spaniel strolled down the path, her face focused on the phone in her hand. The dog stopped in front of Jack at the bench, sat down, and stared intently at him. The girl hadn't noticed that her dog had stopped walking and only found out when she was suddenly jerked backwards when the slack on the lead tightened.

'Come on, Muffin,' she said to the dog, gently tugging the lead.

The dog refused to budge and continued to stare at Jack as it happily wagged its tail.

'Muffin!' the girl said with impatience. This time she pulled more forcibly on the lead, dragging the dog as it still sat until it finally submitted to its owner, accepted defeat and walked away.

You see! Just like he said. People never saw what was right under their noses.

Chapter Twenty-Four

Elsie

Pretty much everything that could be sorted had been. All of her clutter had been thrown away or donated to charity, and she'd finally stipulated the terms of her will and signed away her generous estate to several local charities. She hadn't received any offers on her properties, but that was hardly surprising given the current housing market and the hike in interest rates. It made no difference to Elsie anyway. She had plenty of money in her bank account, earning interest, to see her through until the end.

Despite searching, she hadn't been able to find another home that came remotely close to what she'd seen at The Orchids, and although she didn't want to cut her nose to spite her own face, she just couldn't face seeing Ingrid again. She couldn't face seeing anyone again. She'd go back to being friendless Elsie. The woman who had nobody to think about other than herself, and even then that wouldn't be for long. She'd even decided against seeing Jack again despite him knowing everything. Elsie couldn't cope with people. She couldn't even bear going to the local shops. She'd withdrawn into her bubble of safety where she didn't have to listen to people's sympathetic monologues or watch them cry for her. Elsie intended to leave this world in the only way she knew – alone. So, no, the care home wasn't an option any longer, and instead, Elsie had found a company which provided in-house palliative care. It was all very detached and formal and just what she needed.

Even Julian had gone. He'd finally closed the bistro for good a few weeks previously, and the building stood obsolete, dark and empty inside, which was just how Elsie felt about herself. She was glad that she didn't have to see him anymore. At least he wouldn't be around to watch her get sicker and sicker.

'There we are,' he said, dropping the keys into Elsie's palm. 'It's been an absolute pleasure, but I won't pretend I'm not glad to say goodbye.'

'You've had a tough time,' said Elsie, pocketing the keys. 'But at least you've got the rest of your life to find something new to do.' She noted the slight edge of bitterness in her voice and cringed.

Richard draped a loving arm over his husband's shoulder, unphased by Elsie's tone. 'Exactly, and we intend to make the most of it. Don't we?' He planted a kiss on Julian's cheek.

'When do you set sail?' she asked, keen to end the conversation and return to the quiet lull of home.

'Friday,' replied Julian. 'And then it's six months of excitement.'

Richard pulled up the cruise itinerary on his phone and held it under Elsie's nose. Elsie had to admit, it looked amazing. France, Germany, Spain, Greece, and then over to the Caribbean islands before stopping at various other ports on their journey home. Why hadn't she ever done anything like that? She briefly closed her eyes and allowed herself to imagine sailing away from Southampton Port. She thought of the Captain's dinners, looking out over a calm sea and waking up to find herself transported to another country. There wasn't enough time left for her to consider a world cruise, but perhaps she could squeeze in a week-long mini-cruise somewhere. Somewhere hot and sunny, and where nobody knew her. But a pain suddenly ripped through her chest, and the sunshine that she envisaged warming her skin disappeared.

'Well. I guess this is goodbye then,' she said abruptly.

Julian and Richard were too excited and engrossed in their own world of adventure to notice her eagerness to leave, and even if they had said something, Elsie was past caring. All she could think about was going back inside and swallowing a load of painkillers. They pulled her forward, enveloping her in a three-way hug, and she winced as the pressure in her chest intensified beneath their arms.

'Fare thee well,' said Julian, releasing her. 'When I get back, we'll arrange to meet up, and I'll bore you to death with the endless photographs of everywhere we've visited.'

By the time you get back, you won't have to worry about boring me to death. The cancer would have taken care of that already, thought Elsie.

***

She had spent the last half an hour unboxing and setting up the new television in the living room. She'd bitten the bullet and ordered a new one after finding out just how difficult it was living without one now that she spent so much time at home on her own. There was only so much online surfing she could do to keep herself occupied, and even if she didn't watch much TV, at least it would provide a welcome noise in the background.

She picked up the remote control and followed the set-up instructions, and within a couple of minutes, BBC One filled the screen. She sat back, relieved. It was an old recording of *Homes Under the Hammer*, where people buy properties at auction and renovate them, with the production company returning sometime later to find out what they did with the property and how much its new value was. It wasn't the most thrilling programme in the world, but Elsie sighed as voices filled the living room and drowned out her thoughts.

Three hours later, Elsie was still channel hopping. There was a half-eaten ham sandwich next to her on the sofa, which she made only because she thought she ought to, but in reality, she had no appetite whatsoever. It had become a constant battle when it came to food, and her once healthy figure was becoming skinnier each day. Her clothes now hung from her frame, which only served to accentuate the fact that she was ill, and Elsie started to hate what looked back at her in the mirror. The sicker she looked, the sicker she felt; a deathly reminder that her body was being taken over and soon she'd have no control over it whatsoever.

She changed the channel yet again, and the screen filled with the familiar image of Canon Hill Park. It was the local news reporting on a 5k annual fun run that was taking place. The shot cut from the reporter and onto a steady stream of joggers, smiling for the camera as they made their way around the park. Elsie thought of Jack and wondered if he was sitting down and watching the events unfold. He probably was, knowing him. She thought back to the food festival last year. It was a beautifully warm June day, and the air around them was filled with the delicious smells that wafted from the stalls. Jack, as usual, had politely declined her offer to buy him any food, but Elsie made up for it, practically gorging herself with food samples from a number of different vendors. She smiled as she remembered walking home in the afternoon sun with a bloated stomach and a stain on her white t-shirt from a splodge of curry sauce that she'd accidentally tipped on herself.

Did Jack remember that day too? Would he be there today, hoping that Elsie would turn up? She felt a pull in her heart at how he must be feeling. Was she being fair to him? All Jack ever seemed to want to do was help Elsie. Okay, all Jack wanted to do was talk, but it was the same thing. His words were what pulled Elsie back from the brink of collapse the first time she was diagnosed. He'd soothed her pain, not in the physical sense, but mentally. Her meetings with him were what kept her going through the treatments that she had to endure. They were what pushed Elsie to keep going. But now, what was the point of seeing him? There was nothing to fight this time – she'd already lost. There weren't going to be any treatments for him to help her get through. There was no light at the end of the tunnel. No silver lining, not unless it was on the inside of her coffin. And what would Jack gain from her still seeing him? Nothing but hurt, and pain, and heartbreak. She wouldn't do that to him. He was too important to her.

She pushed Jack out of her mind and turned the television over again. This time, she found herself staring at an advert for MacMillan cancer support. What was this? A conspiracy? She switched the TV off altogether. That was enough of that for today. She went into the kitchen, opened the fridge, and tutted at the almost empty bottle of wine. Had she really drunk another bottle? Not a day seemed to go by without her buying one lately. In reality, she knew that she shouldn't be drinking at all. Not when her liver was already struggling to cope with the swarm of cancer cells, but what difference did it really make? All she was doing was hastening a foregone conclusion, and Elsie couldn't care less if she died with a swollen belly and amber skin; the end result was always going to be the same.

She pulled the stopper out of the top of the bottle and downed the remaining wine, not bothering to waste time finding a glass and dropped the bottle into the recycling bin. Reaching for her purse on the side, she headed out the door.

Hannigan's was a local newsagent which had been in existence in precisely the same side street spot for over one hundred years, or so the plaque screwed into the brickwork outside declared. However, Elsie doubted that it was the same Hannigan family running it. It sold everything a small corner shop needed to satisfy the community, mainly newspapers, cigarettes, milk, bread, chocolate and alcohol. Although its selection was small, it was always busy, and today was no exception. Elsie stood impatiently in the queue to pay with two bottles of Rosé wine tucked beneath her arm as the man at the front of the queue argued with the cashier.

'I gave you a twenty,' the man said to the woman behind a Perspex screen.

'Love. I can assure you it was just a tenner,' replied the woman.

'You can assure me? Why the hell would I take the word of somebody I don't know? No. I'm not going anywhere. You can call the police if you want, but I want my money,' he bellowed.

The woman rolled her eyes, causing Elsie to smile; customer service at its best.

'How about,' she said, 'I reconcile the till. If there's an extra ten pounds in there that shouldn't be, I'll happily hand it over.'

There was a round of disgruntled huffs and groans from the queue, and Elsie joined in. It would take ages to sort out. She sighed and looked up at the ceiling as she weighed up the pros and cons of leaving the shop without the wine. Her eyes settled on the black orb mounted right above the till.

'Wouldn't you be able to see on that?' said Elsie, pointing at the camera. 'It could save a lot of time.'

The cashier looked above her head and nodded. 'That's a good call. Thanks, love,' she said to Elsie, sticking up her thumb in gratitude, and she disappeared into a back room.

'Let's hope that she can see what note that guy handed over,' said a voice over Elsie's shoulder.

She turned and saw an attractive middle-aged man standing behind her.

'Fingers crossed,' she replied, smiling sweetly.

He's cute, she thought to herself. Would it be out of the question to do some serious flirting when she was trying to buy two bottles of wine? Or did it scream desperation? You never know, she might even get an unexpected fumble out of it. It'd be nice to have sex one last time before she was too ill to even think about it.

'I only came here to get Missy here some Smarties,' he continued.

Elsie looked down and saw a little girl wearing a thick woolly hat by his side, holding his hand. The girl proudly held up the Smarties to Elsie. Well, that answered her question. There'd be no illicit sex going on that night.

'Are they for you?' she said to the child, which was a stupid question because, of course they were for her.

The girl nodded and flashed a big smile.

'Daddy said that I could have a treat for being a good girl at the hospital today.'

Elsie looked up at the man.

'It was a pre-op check-up,' he told her.

The girl grabbed the pom pom on the top of the hat and whipped it off, revealing a hairless head save for a few wisps. Elsie's breath caught in her throat as she stared down at the child, who had to be no more than eight years old.

'Oh! I mean...Wow! What a total superstar you are,' Elsie managed to say.

The girl beamed and spun around in a circle, causing the tube of Smarties to fly out of her hand and spill all over the floor.

'Sorry, Daddy,' she said solemnly.

'Don't worry about it, Sweetheart. Why don't you go and get another one off the shelf.'

The girl's smile resurfaced, and she skipped off toward the chocolate aisle on the other side.

'I take it, it's...' began Elsie.

'Cancer? Yes,' he replied. 'But she's been completely amazing. Responding well to treatment, the doctors say.'

Elsie wanted to ask the man a ton of questions. She wanted to ask him where his daughter's cancer was in her body. She wanted to ask him what stage it was. How long had she been having treatment, and what treatment was she undergoing? How was he coping with his daughter's illness? How was his daughter coping? She had a thousand questions she wanted to bombard him with, but the one thing she wanted to know above all else was, would his daughter live? Had they caught the cancer in time? But the time it took for the girl to return with her new tube of sweets stopped her from asking a single thing.

'Hold on tightly to those ones, please,' he instructed her as she shook them like a maraca at him. 'There won't be any more if you drop them again.'

The girl protectively clutched them to her chest, and Elsie smiled. Don't cry, she told herself. For God's sake, don't cry in front of them.

'And normal service is resumed,' said the cashier, returning to the checkout with another person in tow. 'It was just a ten-pound note you gave me, and if you'd like to go with my manager to view the CCTV, you'll see that I'm not lying.'

There was a small chorus of quiet cheers among the customers waiting in line, and the man, with a face red with embarrassment or fury, Elsie couldn't quite tell, snatched up the change from the side and shook his head.

'Fuck it,' he spat, stomping out of the shop.

'Daddy,' the girl whispered. 'He said a bad word.'

'I know, Elsie. Some people are just never happy even when someone tries to help them.'

Chapter Twenty-Five

Elsie

E lsie must have been on autopilot all the way home. She remembered muttering a convoluted excuse to the man about forgetting to bring her wallet with her, and she recalled setting down the two bottles of wine and rushing out of the shop. The rest of the journey was a blur as her thoughts raged with shock, disbelief and injustice.

The chances of meeting another cancer sufferer were high in this day and age, and the cancer sufferer being a child was entirely possible, but that child having the same name as Elsie was just too much for her to comprehend.

It was as though she was being reminded that she wasn't the only person in the world to be in her position. No. Not reminded. It was as though she was being taunted. Taunted by the invisible man in the sky who decided who lived and who died in this world. It was as though he was saying to her, 'Oh.

Look here. Her name's Elsie, and she's sick too, but she doesn't appear to be feeling sorry for herself. Does she?'

Should she feel sorry for little Elsie for having such a severe illness and still smiling through it all? Or was she supposed to look on the bright side for having had the opportunity to have lived a longer life than the child? Elsie didn't know what she was supposed to think anymore, and little Elsie's father's parting shot about people never being happy even when people were helping them was like a final slap in the face. It was as though he'd stared into her soul, frowned on her behaviour and launched a weaponised attack on her with his words.

Should she feel ashamed for not being as carefree as the little girl? It was easier for kids not to be as phased by serious situations. They were children, for God's sake. The most they had to worry about was how many presents Santa would leave for them under the tree at Christmas. It was easier for them to process stuff when they didn't understand the seriousness. Look at what happened in the shop where a packet of Smarties brought a smile to the child's face. If only her happiness were as easy to buy.

It had happened almost two hours ago, and now Elsie cursed herself for not buying the wine. At least she could have drowned her thoughts rather than being forced to sit with them. She hadn't moved from her place on the floor, leaning up against the kitchen cupboards, where her legs had buckled the second she'd walked back inside. The evening sky had darkened, plunging the whole apartment into an eerie dusk, illuminated by the passing headlights of cars outside on the square.

Elsie imagined that she was dead. That this was what it would be like when she was gone. Her apartment, chilly and empty, and the people outside who carried on with their lives not knowing that Elsie ever existed.

Her funeral would be quick and undoubtedly quiet, seeing as she'd already arranged for the funeral directors to collect her body and arrange an immediate cremation the second that they were informed of her death. There would be no notice of her death posted in the local paper. No invitation to friends and family to attend the crematorium and celebrate her life. Elsie would be ashes before anybody realised, let alone intervene.

Was it the right thing to do? She was second-guessing herself now and all because she went out to buy wine. Was she doing her friends a kindness by pushing them away? Were they even friends anyway? She hardly knew them, for crying out loud. It wasn't as if they'd grown up together. But then she thought back to Agata's laughter and bizarre dancing when they'd gone out for cocktails, and Mack's kind eyes and the way he watched for her reaction whenever he'd cooked something new for her to try, and then there was Sid; The man who looked like he needed a good sheep dip when she'd first met him. Sid, with his wit and his barbed comments, and his endless need to bathe which had infuriated Elsie no end. And then there was Ingrid, whose compassion and concern for Elsie saw her break a cardinal and legal rule. Elsie remembered when Ingrid had held her in her arms when she had broken down the day she first went to check out the care home. She remembered the softness of Ingrid's green cardigan under her chin and the smell of Lavender on her skin. Ingrid didn't have to do that for her, and yet she had. That had to mean something? Finally, she thought of Jack. Her Jack. The first person in Elsie's life to never let her down. The man who had always been there, whatever the weather, waiting. Who had sat with her and listened to her pouring out her heart or made her laugh and whose words made Elsie make sense of her situation.

It was a hodgepodge of people who all had their own quirks and who, as a collective, shouldn't go together, but in some odd way, they slotted together perfectly. It was Elsie's own little gang, a clique that she had never had before. Maybe that was why she'd grown so attached to them so quickly. Perhaps somewhere inside, there was a young Elsie who had always craved friendship but had been too scared to allow the connections to form.

Elsie cried then. She cried for little Elsie, not just the child she'd met in the shop but the one inside her. She cried at the wasted years. At the friendships that she never allowed to happen. At the boyfriends she'd dumped. At the wedding dress she would never wear. At the children she'd never had. At the new friendships that she'd pushed away and how much more intense the pain of isolation was now that she had briefly tasted the joy that friends had given her. And then she howled as the realisation of just what she'd lost hit her.

***

October the first brought with it an unseasonably warm day. Not that it was unwelcome by Elsie, but she noted how much more pleasant it was to sit in the park not having to wrap up as though she was about to trek through the Antarctic.

After the agony of the evening before had subsided in the early hours of the morning, Elsie had lay on the kitchen floor deciding on what she should do to get things back to where they were. Until recently, she'd never apologised for anything in her life, and it was daunting for her. It wasn't so much about the saying sorry part; it was the abject terror of it not being accepted that made Elsie tremble inside. What if they all individually told her to fuck off? Okay, maybe she couldn't imagine Ingrid and Agata saying that to her, but she could think it of Sid, and Mack too, at a shove. Should she buy an apology present? Was there even such a thing as an apology present? Or would that be seen as trying to buy friendship?

She needed an expert opinion on the matter. Well, that was the excuse that she was going to use with Jack. Out of everybody, she knew that Jack would never judge her over what happened.

He wouldn't berate her for not meeting him in all these weeks. He'd just sit down next to her as if nothing had happened, and they'd pick up right where they'd left off.

She was early, almost a whole hour, so she wasn't surprised to find the bench empty. She swept away the leaves that had fallen from the branches above with her hand and sat down. It was quiet there that morning, and Elsie had only spotted a couple of dog walkers and one hardened jogger whom she'd seen there many times before. Being a Sunday, even the main road outside was quieter, and Elsie closed her eyes, tilted her head towards the sun and listened to the merry chirps of the birds in the trees.

When she opened her eyes again a few seconds later, she jumped at the sight of Jack staring down at her.

'Jesus!' she cried. 'Why don't your shoes make any noise when you walk? You're like a ninja.'

'And you're a sight for sore eyes,' he retorted with a smile, sitting beside her.

He went to say something, but Elsie grabbed him and hugged him tightly.

'I'm sorry,' she whispered in his ear. 'I'm sorry for everything. For the way I've treated you recently. For not being in touch. And for generally being a monumental bitch since you've met me.'

'I think the word monumental is a bit much,' joked Jack, and Elsie laughed, pushing him away.

The jogger ran past and gave a quick lift of his chin in Elsie's direction. She nodded, mildly annoyed that Jack had been excluded from the morning's greetings.

'So,' said Jack. 'What happened? I mean, I'm not saying I'm a psychic or anything, but I assume that something happened which made you want to stay away?' he asked her.

Elsie told him everything: Ingrid's arrival at the apartment and telling the others about her cancer. She told him about how vile she'd been to them and how she'd unceremoniously evicted Mack and Sid. She told him how cruel she'd been to Agata. She told him about hiding away in the apartment, venturing outside only to collect takeaways or bottles of alcohol. And then she told him all about the little girl and her father in the shop.

Jack's head gave an all-knowing nod. 'And how did that make you feel?'

'It made me feel, I don't know, conflicted,' she replied. 'I mean, I still feel bad about me, of course I do. But it made me realise that there are other people out there just like me. And that, in certain cases, it might be worse for them than it is for me. I felt bad for feeling sorry for myself, knowing that I was going to die at an age, which I consider young, and then I meet a little girl, little Elsie, and her life hasn't even started yet,' she sat back and sighed. 'I suppose what really got me was how her father made her smile. He made her feel like everything was okay and normal, taking away her fear. It made her feel that everything was going to get better. And it was like an epiphany hitting me square in the face. That was the power of having a positive relationship in your life. That was what friends did. They don't just comfort you, but they make you feel normal. They make you feel that everything will be okay, no matter what. And when I realised that, I finally got it. I finally understood what you meant about living. And it's taken for me to lose everyone to figure it all out.'

'You haven't lost everyone,' said Jack. 'You've still got me. For a brief second, I thought that *I'd* lost *you*. I even came up to the square and sat outside in the hope that I'd see you.'

'You did? I didn't realise that you knew where I lived,' she was touched by his thoughtfulness. 'But what about the others, Jack? I've definitely lost them.'

'If they're as good a people as you say they are, you haven't lost them. I guarantee it. '

Elsie felt an urge to cry, but thankfully, her tear ducts had run dry the night before, or at least that's how it felt.

'What do I do, Jack? Do I just turn up on their doorstep and say, "Hey. I'm sorry for treating you like a dickhead. Forgive me?"'

'It's a start,' agreed Jack. 'Although, I'd leave out the dickhead part.

He was trying to make her smile, and Elsie wanted to smile, she really did, but her mouth didn't want to adjust from the grim line that had been permanently set for almost two months.

Jack grabbed Elsie by the hands. 'Just go to them and say sorry,' he said to her. 'It's as simple as that.'

'Will you come with me?'

Jack shook his head. 'You need to do this part on your own, sweet girl. Trust me.'

She looked down at Jack's hands as they held onto hers. She trusted him completely.

'Okay. But one day, I'd like you to meet them.'

'And when that day comes. I'll be there,' replied Jack. 'Hey. What's the matter? Don't be sad. They'll be absolutely fine with you. It'll all work out. I promise.'

'It's not that,' replied Elsie. 'I never even asked the girl's dad if his daughter would be alright.'

He patted her on the hand. 'I told you. It'll work out. My promise extends to that Elsie as well.'

Chapter Twenty-Six

Ingrid

Ingrid knelt in the garden, scooping up fox poo from the grass into little bags. The gardener wasn't due for another week, and she couldn't just leave it. It sent out the wrong message to the friends and families of her residents and also to prospective new residents who came to view the home. It was the first thing people would see, and what did that say about the standard of care if they couldn't even be bothered to keep the gardens clean and mess-free? Ingrid loved all animals, and she thought that foxes were such beautiful creatures, especially urban foxes who had learned to adapt to sharing their once free and open landscape with humanity. However, the constant deposits left in her garden were frustrating. Even more so when she was the only person who cleaned it up. In fairness, she could hardly blame the staff for not volunteering for poop patrol, they were trained nurses and carers, after all, and she knew that the clearing of animal mess hadn't been part of their training.

A silhouette shadowed the lawn in front of her, and she looked up, squinting into the sunlight that bounced off her eyes.

'Hello, Ingrid,' she heard the voice say.

She recognised it immediately.

Ingrid threw the bag onto the grass, peeled off her gloves, and rushed forward to embrace Elsie. If she were being honest with herself, she truly didn't expect to see her again. Elsie was possibly the most fiercely complex person that she'd ever met, and she'd been afraid that Elsie wouldn't be able to see past her anger to come back, preferring to withdraw back into herself instead.

'I'm so sorry that I betrayed your trust,' said Ingrid with sincerity. 'I hope that you understand why I did it though.'

She felt Elsie's arms wrap around her back, and her body relaxed.

'I do,' replied Elsie. 'It just took me a while to see it.'

'Bloody hell,' she heard Amanda say. They turned to see her standing in the doorway with her hands on her hips. 'You'd do anything to get out of picking up that shit.'

***

Elsie had stayed for a couple of hours. She'd apologised profusely for what she'd said to Ingrid that day in her apartment despite Ingrid waving it away. Elsie had nothing to apologise for, in her opinion. Everything that had occurred resulted from Ingrid's behaviour, and the guilt had always weighed heavy in her heart. What if Elsie had never understood? That poor girl might have gone to her grave alone and all because Ingrid thought she knew what was best. But at least everything had righted itself now. Ingrid had every intention of making it up to Elsie. That girl would want for nothing when it came to her care from now on. Ingrid would be there every step of the way. She would cater to every wish and whim that Elsie desired. Elsie may not have experienced much love coming into this world, but by god, she would have it going back out again.

They'd sat in the staff room, away from the residents who were making use of the communal living room that day. Amanda, helpful as ever, had made them a pot of tea and had even laid out a small selection of finger sandwiches and mini cakes as though it was royalty who'd come to tea. Ingrid noted Elsie's half-eaten cheese and cucumber sandwich and the untouched minuscule cupcake on her plate but said nothing. It was never a good sign when a person's appetite deserted them. She eyed up Elsie's gaunt face, the thinness of her wrists and the yellow pallor of her skin.

'I know you said that day you'd keep my room available, but I just wanted to check...'

Ingrid smiled. 'It's very much still available, so don't worry yourself. Would you like to see it?'

'Yes. I would,' Elsie said eagerly, and Ingrid wasn't sure whether it was because there was a genuine want to see the room or because she didn't want attention drawn to the fact that she had hardly eaten a thing.

Ingrid led her up the staircase and into the bedroom. It was Ingrid's personal favourite of all the rooms. It was painted in neutral soft stone with large black and white photographs taken of the house in the late eighteen hundreds hanging on the wall. Despite the age of the house, Ingrid had opted not to furnish it as such and had added modern and robust white furniture, with a large double wardrobe, bedside cabinets and a wide chest of drawers. But it was the windows which really were the focal point of the room. Unlike the rest of the bedrooms, this room was so large that it had two long Georgian sash windows, allowing the natural light to flood inside, and the fact they overlooked the back garden provided a tantalising view.

Elsie went slowly around the room and ran her hand over the soft bedding and furniture. Ingrid watched her closely, trying to judge whether or not she liked it, but her unspoken question was answered when Elsie turned around and smiled softly.

'It's perfect,' she said to Ingrid.

'I thought that you'd like it,' she replied.

'I may start bringing some of my things over if that's okay. I'd rather do it now while I'm still able to.'

'Of course,' replied Ingrid. She was pleased that Elsie had started to accept her situation and was taking action rather than putting it off. At least she could familiarise herself with her new surroundings, making the transition of living there full-time easier to process. 'Have you spoken to any of the others?'

They hadn't spoken about Agata, Mack and Sid until that point, but over the past weeks, Ingrid had built a real connection with the three of them, even Sid, and they'd promised each other that they would contact one another if any of them heard from Elsie.

'Not yet. I'm on my way to do that now. Do you think they'll be as forgiving as you?'

Ingrid spotted the nervousness in Elsie's eyes, and she gave her a warm smile.

'Sweetheart. Don't you worry about them. You've managed to build up your very own network of stalkers. They can't wait to hear from you.'

Chapter Twenty-Seven

Agata

Agata was enjoying the peace of the afternoon. George, Isabella and Penelope were all at school, and as they had a swimming lesson straight after, they wouldn't be home until five that evening. Arthur, too, was enjoying the quiet and had fallen asleep for his afternoon nap watching *In the Night Garden*, clutching his Iggle Piggle teddy.

Arabella was out who-knows-where and with who-knows-who. Not that Agata cared. Mrs King could do whatever the hell she wanted so long as she stayed out of her way and didn't take advantage of her anymore. It was as though Agata had been transported into another house, in another time and with other people. The children, now that she was allowed to discipline them, had converted into better-behaved and more respectful little people. George still had moments though, like when he emptied a jar of frog spawn into Penelope's bath – while Penelope was still in it. Lord! The screaming that girl had done that day.

Arabella hadn't dared go against Agata since the day she'd caught her bringing in her secret beau for a bit of rough and tumble. It wasn't that Mrs King was being overly nice to Agata, that would have made her nauseous, but she'd stopped the outright nastiness. She'd also kept to their agreement and given Agata a huge but fair increase in her wages, much to her husband's confusion, but dear old Mr King had learned over the years never to argue with his wife.

The doorbell shrilled, and Agata flinched. She looked over at Arthur, who, apart from an initial twitch at the noise, remained asleep. A trail of dribble was trickling out of his mouth and straight onto Arabella's expensive silk cushions. Agata went to answer the front door before the person rang it again. It was probably another delivery for Arabella, who was constantly online clicking the 'buy it now' button on pretty much every website that she went on.

When she opened the door and saw Elsie standing there, a little squeak escaped from Agata's mouth.

'Hello, stranger,' said Elsie.

Agata found that she couldn't speak, and instead of replying with words, she replaced them with tears and promptly started to cry. Elsie rushed up the stone steps to the front door and took Agata in her arms.

'No. Please don't,' Elsie said, holding Agata tightly.

But Agata couldn't stop. For weeks, she and the others had been praying frantically for Elsie to turn up or at least call or text to let them know that she was okay, and just when they all thought that Elsie had disappeared from their lives forever, here she was standing on her doorstep.

'I thought that we would not see you again,' sobbed Agata. 'I thought you didn't want to know me anymore.'

'That's all on me, and I'm so sorry for what I said and did to you and the others,' said Elsie. 'Is there anywhere we can talk? Or would you get into trouble if I came into the house?'

Agata broke away from Elsie, grabbed her hand and pulled her inside.

***

After the initial shock of Elsie's appearance had worn off, Agata had finally managed to find the words that she'd rehearsed in her head over and over again.

'I was sorry to see you upset, but I'm not sorry that we care for you. And I'm not sorry that we have all conspired together to try and make you change your mind.'

Elsie laughed. 'Ingrid told me what you've all been up to. I'm touched, truly.'

'You've seen Ingrid?'

'Yes. But only just. I asked her not to tell you I was coming to see you.'

'And Mack and Sid?' asked Agata.

'They're next on my list. But I'm nervous about seeing them. After all, I kicked them back out onto the streets. It makes me look like a heartless bitch.'

'They don't think that. They'll be glad to see you, believe me,' said Agata. 'Especially Sid. He thinks the world of you.'

'Sid?' said Elsie with surprise. 'Sid thinks the world of me? Are you drunk?'

Agata laughed and shook her head. 'Honestly. You wouldn't believe the change in him. I think there is something about your illness. I think he has lived through it before, with somebody else. But he won't say who. I've asked him many times.'

The front door opened and closed, and Agata braced herself. Arabella didn't like strangers in her house, and it was an issue that Agata had never really had to contend with, seeing as she'd never had anyone in her life to invite around in the first place. There was the familiar clicking of heels against the tiles and then a pause as Arabella presumably stopped at the living room to see who was inside, before continuing straight into the kitchen.

'Oh,' she said, looking Elsie up and down when she saw her. 'And who is this?'

'This is Elsie. She's my friend,'

Elsie stood and went over to her. She held out her hand, 'Pleased to meet you,' she said.

Arabella looked down at Elsie's hand with disdain. 'I thought I was clear about not having guests,' she said, ignoring Elsie. 'I won't have just anyone around my children.'

Agata was on the cusp of reminding Arabella about the man in the hallway when Elsie suddenly spoke.

'But I'm not just anyone, Mrs King. I'm a senior investigator for the Employment Standard Commission, and I'm carrying out an investigation into the conditions of Agata's employment with you. So, as I heard with my own ears, you don't like Agata to have friends come to visit her. Is that correct? And I've also heard that until recently you were severely underpaying staff in your employ. Would you like to clarify that for me so I can put it all in my report?'

Arabella stood wide-eyed. 'Now. Wait a second. I didn't mean...you're twisting my words.'

'No. I don't think I am. I think that you're one of those disgusting human beings who believes that because a person is from abroad, you can take advantage of the situation and exploit them.'

Agata was impressed with how professional Elsie looked and sounded. Arabella looked as though she was about to faint, but then suddenly, her face flushed with rage.

'How dare you. You come into my house and make all of these wild accusations. I'll have your job for this. I've been bamboozled. Hoodwinked! You've tricked me into saying things that I didn't mean. I'd call that entrapment.'

Elsie gave a hearty and mildly overdramatic laugh. 'Oh no, Mrs King. I'd call that a lawsuit. I'll see you in court for breaking several Employment laws. Bye bye now.'

Elsie walked out of the kitchen, and Agata hurried behind her. On one hand, Agata was in complete awe of Elsie. That had been absolutely genius, but then reality hit her.

'I think now I am really in the shit. I think Mrs King will fire me,' she whispered to Elsie.

Elsie shrugged her shoulders. 'So what. Fuck it. You're better than this. Listen, Agata. You can stay here if you want, working for somebody who doesn't appreciate you and in a job that you don't even like. Eventually, it'll suck away your soul, and before you know it, all of those dreams and aspirations that you had when you first came to this country will be gone. You'll be at the end of your life and wondering where in the hell it all went wrong. Look at me, Agata. Look at what's happening to me. God forbid, but this could be you one day. It's time to start living – really living. Don't waste any more time.'

Agata's heart was beating wildly. This was it. This was her chance to leave. To start afresh. As Elsie said, it was time for her to start living.

'Wait here. I'll go and pack my things.'

Chapter
Twenty-Eight

Mack

Agata had texted him to say that they needed to meet. There had been no further explanation, even when Mack had sent her a response of just three question marks. The phone that Agata had bought for him had turned out to be a real lifeline. It was only a cheap model with a pay-as-you-go sim card, which Agata topped up every week, but it made such a difference to Mack's life. It meant he didn't have to worry about organising pre-arranged times and places. Contact with other people was just the click of a button away.

Mack hurried to the café around the corner from Elsie's apartment with Sid in tow. It had become a regular and favourite venue for them to meet. They'd even come to know the owner, Tony, who had always made them feel welcome despite Mack and Sid's appearance and had even told the men to stop by each day before closing for food that would have otherwise been thrown away.

'Stop walking so fast,' complained Sid. 'You don't know that anything is wrong.'

Mack's stomach had swirled with nerves the second the text had come through. They hadn't been due to meet until the following day, and they'd all promised to contact each other if they heard anything about Elsie, regardless of whether that news was good or bad.

'Then why didn't Agata say why she wanted to meet up? Why all the secrecy?'

Sid shrugged. 'Who knows! It's probably to do with the fact that she fancies the arse off you.'

Mack gave a quick scoff. 'Don't be ridiculous,' he replied but feeling secretly ecstatic at the mere suggestion of it. 'Now hurry up. Otherwise, I'll go ahead without you.'

'You never leave a man behind,' joked Sid. 'And besides, I know you. It's an empty threat so for the love of God, will you slow down a little bit.'

Sid was right; Mack wouldn't dream of leaving Sid behind, so he slowed his pace to a brisk walk. They were minutes away from the café now anyway, and he'd soon find out from Agata just what was going on.

As they turned onto the side street, Mack's eyes scanned to see if Agata was waiting outside for them. She wasn't, and he had no idea why he'd expected her to be. When it came to Agata, Mack seemed to have lost all rational thought. He'd felt it the first time he'd seen her: a pang of something in his heart that he hadn't felt for such a long time. In his dreams he imagined them living an idyllic life where he cooked her romantic dinners, renting beautiful cabins and cottages all around the UK for weekend breaks, and where he woke up to the beauty of her each morning. Even now, when Agata would hug Mack goodbye, he'd squeeze her just a fraction tighter than he ought and wondered what it would feel like to run his hands through her golden hair. But that's all Mack ever did: imagine, dream and wish. Agata was the first woman to make him feel this way for years; he'd never been this attracted to his ex. Maybe it was because Agata felt so unattainable to him that it intensified his connection to her? Who knew what it was. All Mack did know was that he'd rather harbour his feelings in total secrecy than run the risk of Agata laughing in his face and telling him that her feelings for him only went as far as friendship.

They pushed open the door to the café and stepped inside.

'Afternoon, gents,' said Tony with a broad smile. 'You're just in time. Barbara has plated you up two lovely plates of chicken curry with rice. Grab a seat, and I'll bring it over to you.'

Mack's eyes glanced across the tables, but Agata wasn't there. 'Not just yet, Tone. We're supposed to be meeting Agata here. Have you seen her?'

'Agata?' replied Tony. 'Nah, mate. She's not been in. Take a seat, and I'll bring you fellas some coffee over if you don't fancy the grub just yet.'

Mack would have preferred to sit in front of the window. At least that way, he could have seen Agata's approach and guess whether it was good or bad news from her expression. One of her purest qualities was her inability to hide her emotions. If she was happy, sad, angry or frustrated, then everybody knew it. Agata's poker face was non-existent, even though she claimed that she had never been like that prior to meeting Elsie. Elsie had managed to bring out the best in all of them, it seemed.

Globules of rain began to fall outside, dropping heavily onto the cars on the road. Passers-by hastily put up their umbrellas or the hoods on the coats, and those unlucky enough to have neither rushed along the pavement shielding their faces from the rain and sought shelter from the doorways of the buildings.

Tony brought over their drinks. 'Stinking day. How do you guys cope when it's like this?'

'You get used to being damp,' replied Sid. 'You wake up damp. You walk about damp. You got to sleep damp. In the end, you don't even notice it.'

Mack wondered if the repeated use of the word damp was entirely necessary but kept his counsel on the matter. He wasn't in the mood to make idle chatter with Tony, no matter how nice he was. All Mack cared about was finding out why Agata wanted to see them. Please, God, don't let it be bad news. He

229

knew that he should have been more forceful with Elsie. He should have pounded on her front door until she opened it, but as Sid reminded him, Mack would have probably just ended up getting arrested. All Elsie's neighbours would have seen was a homeless man hammering on the door in a rather upmarket area, and who could blame them for wanting to make sure that the person behind the door was safe?

There was a blast of cool air as the door opened, but Tony's hefty frame was blocking Mack's view.

'And when it's like this,' continued Sid, pointing to the rain splattering against the window. 'It's just a run-and-cover tactic. The nearest public toilet, or shop, although we usually get kicked out of them – some people are heartless fuckers.'

Elsie's head popped up from behind Tony's shoulder. 'I hope you're not talking about me.'

Chapter
Twenty-Nine

Elsie

'So, how's it going?' asked Jack.

'Truthfully? It's like an episode of *Friends*, only funnier,' said Elsie.

'I've never watched it, so I'll have to take your word for that,' replied Jack drily.

'You're such a dinosaur.'

It had been almost a month since Elsie had invited Agata, Mack and Sid to live with her. At first, it hadn't been an easy transition, going from being constantly alone to sharing her home with three very different people, especially when it came to the sleeping arrangements. Mack and Sid had resumed their joint occupation of the spare bedroom, leaving Agata with no choice but to share Elsie's bed. Well, that wasn't strictly true.

Agata had stated that she would sleep on the sofa, which Elsie said she wouldn't hear of. And then Mack and Sid had offered to give up their room to Agata and, instead, insisted that they sleep on the sofa, to which Elsie also refused. There had been a rather vocal disagreement between the four of them on the subject in which Elsie told them that if they didn't all shut up, she would sleep on the bloody sofa to make them all feel bad. Thankfully, that threat ended the debate, so Mack and Sid were in one bedroom and Elsie and Agata in the other.

Agata, thank god, was an easy bedmate. She slept on her back, arms flat by her side, and barely made a noise, but it was still an eerie sight for Elsie when she turned over in the middle of the night, still half asleep and saw Agata laid out in her Dracula-esq pose.

But apart from the sleeping arrangements and the mild annoyance at sharing the bathroom with so many people, the four of them had settled into an amicable and easy routine. Mack, for obvious reasons, had been designated the household chef. Sid, for less obvious reasons, had appointed himself as the cleaner, and Agata's new role was to do all of the shopping and washing.

Elsie, now with no role of her own, felt as if she'd been relegated and spent her time ensuring that the bills were paid and dealt with the paperwork side of the home. It was far from what she was used to, but her pain was almost daily now, and she practically rattled inside with the number of different painkillers that she was taking. It wasn't a surprise that it was happening; it was an inevitability, but the fact that it limited Elsie in what she could physically do was a difficult thing to accept, and letting go of her independence was an admission that the end was creeping ever nearer.

Elsie had bought a little Ford Focus for them all. She had always had zero interest in learning how to drive, but Mack, Sid, and Agata all had their licenses, so it seemed sensible to purchase a mode of transport to make everybody's life that little bit easier. They were all whizzing somewhere these days, and it helped Elsie no end to be dropped off at the park to meet Jack rather than making her ritual walk, and then there were the endless visits to the GP, or the hospital, or all of the day trips that they now filled their spare time.

'I'd hate to be the one to cover old ground, but how are things going with your living list?' continued Jack.

'Quite well, I'd say. I've made the lives of four people much easier than it was before. Agata is happier not working as an au pair, and Mack and Sid are like different people now they're off the streets,' beamed Elsie proudly.

Jack paused, and Elsie knew that something was coming. She braced herself.

'Is that enough?' he said. 'Is that really what you'd call a legacy?'

Yes, actually, Elsie would consider that a legacy. She pushed down her initial anger at the suggestion that what she'd done was somehow insufficient in Jack's eyes, reminding herself that, as always, he was only trying to make her see the bigger picture. Unfortunately, that picture was blurred and obscured by the smiles that she saw on her friend's faces every day. Surely, if they were happy, that had to count for something? Elsie had already made another appointment to see her solicitor about altering her will to leave part of her estate to each of them, Jack included.

'They won't have to worry about money for the rest of their lives, provided they're sensible and don't put it all on black at the casino. Honestly, Jack. I can't see what more you want me to do.'

'It's not about what I *want* you to do; it's about what you *can* do. You can do much more than leave the four of them money in their bank account, not that they wouldn't appreciate it, I'm sure. But take some time to figure out how to extend it. Make it bigger so that it grows outside the bounds of just being money. Start hearing instead of just listening. Start seeing instead of watching.'

Elsie nodded because it was just easier to agree with Jack than question him, but in truth, she had no idea what the hell he was on about. Elsie didn't walk around in a bubble. She saw and heard things all the time. She'd been paying attention to what Jack had said and look at what had happened as a result. She'd broken down barriers that she thought were unbreakable. She'd made strong connections and friendships with four strangers. And those strangers were on the cusp of inheriting a very sizable sum. And yet, Jack had made her feel as though it wasn't good enough.

'I should be going,' said Elsie, getting up from the bench. 'Sid will be waiting for me.'

Jack consulted his watch. 'It's too early yet. You've got another hour at least.'

'Not today. I have some other stuff to do, so I asked to be picked up a little earlier than usual.'

It was a lie, of course, and by the unconvinced look on Jack's face, she knew that Jack knew that too. Sid wouldn't be waiting for her in the car park, but she could text him as she walked, and it would only take him ten minutes or so to reach her.

'I think you're fibbing,' said Jack.

'And I think you're preaching, but hey ho,' she retorted.

She started to walk away, but Jack jumped up and blocked her path.

'Elsie. I'm sorry. Let's not do this again. You know I'm not being unkind. Just take some time and think about what I've said. You already know the answer to it all. You've already seen the answer. You just don't know that you know.'

Elsie had had enough of the riddles. Her back was aching, her head was thumping, and it felt as though her bones were crumbling inside her body. She wanted to pop a couple of painkillers and climb onto the sofa and watch some trashy TV before drifting off to sleep.

'Come with me,' she said to him. 'Come with me and meet them all. You promised ages ago that you would, but every time that I mention it, you say you can't.'

'Is that why you're asking me now? Because you know that I'll say no, and that'll give you a valid reason to be mad with me and go off in a huff.'

For fuck's sake. Was Elsie silently transmitting Morse code or something?

'So, will you?'

'Arrange to see them? Elsie, I've already told you that I will. But it has to be at the right time, and that's not now,' he replied.

She gave a heavy and dejected sigh.

'Fucking hell. Fine. Have it your way. But it's starting to wear thin, Jack. It's starting to look like you don't want to meet them. I've told them all about you, and they want to put a face to the name that I keep talking about. I've only ever said good things about you, but they're starting to find it weird that you're reluctant to come over. And they also find it weird that we have to meet here, even though it's fucking freezing most days now that it's winter.'

He gave a non-committal shrug. 'That's fine if they think that.'

'You're infuriating.' She turned and started to walk away, and took out her mobile to send a quick text to Sid, asking him to come and pick her up.

'Will I see you tomorrow?' Jack shouted after her.

'Yes!' Of course you bloody well will,' Elsie angrily shouted back, but she couldn't tell whether she was angry at Jack for being so annoying or herself for allowing him to be.

***

Elsie had done exactly what she said she was going to do and returned home, taken painkillers and fell restlessly in and out of sleep. When she finally woke, it was to the sweet cinnamon scent of the moussaka that was bubbling away in the oven. Her stomach grumbled, which pleased Elsie. At least this evening, she had an appetite, and she wouldn't be faced with the nagging of the others.

'Hello, sleepy head,' said Sid, who was laying the table ready for dinner. 'You woke up just in time.'

Elsie sat up and rubbed the sleep from her eyes. 'Was I asleep for very long?' she asked.

'Almost two hours,' said Mack from the kitchen. 'Which is good for you. You must have needed it.'

She must have done, she thought to herself. She was sleeping so much more lately. She'd never been one for taking daytime naps, preferring to use all of her available time on her business, and naively, Elsie had told herself that her cancer wasn't going disrupt her life in that way. She believed that she would be able to carry on as usual and that one day, she would just lie down, go to sleep, and never wake up again. How stupid it made her feel now that she knew differently.

Agata came out of the bedroom and into the living room with her wet hair wrapped in a towel. Elsie, now manoeuvring herself to the dining table, spotted the shy smiles exchanged between her and Mack, and she found herself smiling too. Their mutual attraction was obvious to everyone apart from Agata and Mack, it seemed, because, as far as Elsie knew, neither of them had taken it further. She wondered whether this was because they felt it might be insensitive to embark on a new relationship under her roof, given the circumstances. Perhaps they might have believed it inappropriate to be cuddling and canoodling on the sofa next to her and Sid? Or perhaps, and possibly more likely, they didn't realise their interest in one another was entirely reciprocal. Not that they were stupid people, far from it, but Elsie supposed that when it came to matters of the heart, it was always sensible to proceed with caution. There was no worse feeling in the world than being told by somebody you have feelings for that they didn't feel the same about you.

Mack advised that dinner was ready, and they all took their seats at the dining table as he brought over a large bamboo bowl of salad and, finally, the steaming dish of moussaka. He spooned a generous pile onto his, Agata's and Sid's plates and a smaller and more manageable portion onto Elsie's. Thank goodness he was getting control over his portion distortion where she was concerned. They tucked in, and a chorus of appreciative groans sounded around the table from everyone except Mack, who was too busy checking out how his hard work was being received.

'You really do enjoy it, don't you?' Elsie said to him.

'Enjoy what?' he replied.

'Cooking for people. I mean, you really love the whole process. The preparation, the cooking, and then seeing people's reactions. It must mean a lot to you.'

He nodded. 'It's the only thing that I've ever been good at. For me, food is more than slapping something in the oven and hoping for the best. It's an art form. Understanding where it comes from, how it's grown, or how meat is reared. It's about understanding what seasonings, spices, and herbs complement the dish. I'm at my happiest when I'm in a kitchen. Apart from,' he paused momentarily. 'Apart from when I messed up.'

Mack plunged a forkful of his dinner into his mouth.

'You should go back to restaurant work? You too good to be stuck inside normal kitchen,' Agata said to him.

It had been something that Elsie had frequently thought about. Mack himself had said many times about getting a job, citing that he couldn't live off Elsie's generosity forever, but the jobs he was looking at were in warehouses or operating industrial machinery. They were totally not a Mack job, and she'd never pushed the issue with him. Mack clearly thought that he wasn't ready mentally to go back to working in restaurants, and Elsie wondered whether it was fear, shame, guilt, or possibly all three that were stopping him from doing so.

'No. Not a restaurant,' he replied. 'I don't think that I could work for somebody else in an industry that I once had my own business in. It'd make me feel...I don't know...inadequate or something.'

'Inadequate?' said Sid. 'How could you possibly be inadequate when you make food that tastes like this.' He jabbed a moussaka-covered knife towards his plate.'

'But everyone would know that I couldn't make it on my own. I couldn't deal with that.'

'Then make it on your own,' Agata said sharply. 'Do it again. Things will be different this time. Elsie, do you agree?'

Elsie glanced at Mack. The muscle in his jaw tensed, and she knew that it was subject which he'd preferred to be dropped. She completely agreed with what Agata and Sid had said. Mack was wasting his time working in any other industry that didn't involve food, but she wasn't that blinkered to understand where his personal feelings of inadequacy stemmed from. The man had worked his arse off, set up his own business and watched as his world came plummeting down around him. Who wouldn't be fearful about being reminded of that? Owning and running a business was hard work, especially when you'd never run one before. It was all very well being good in one area, but as a business owner, in the early stages at least, your job description had to cover a broad spectrum of different job roles. But in the same breath, Elsie knew that often, failure made a person better. Failure highlighted weaknesses, and if you knew why a business failed, then you were halfway there in making the next venture successful. But still, she didn't want to push Mack.

'I think that your life would feel very unfulfilled if you settled for just any job. But you have to do what's right for you,' she said diplomatically.

Sid rolled his eyes at her comment, and Agata looked downright furious. Elsie was going to leave it there and change the subject, and then they could all carry on eating the beautiful dinner in relative peace. But there was something niggling inside her. Why shouldn't she say exactly what she thought? If she believed that Mack was making a mistake, then was she being a good friend by not telling him her opinions? Screw this, she thought to herself.

'Actually,' she blurted out. 'I think you'd spend the rest of your life regretting not being a chef. You'll be unhappy in any other job until the day you die, and I think Agata's right. You could do it again. You could open up a new restaurant and make it a success because you know exactly where you failed last time. Don't be the person who, at the end of their life, spends their last day listing all of the regrets of things they wished they'd done. Don't be like me.'

If Mack disagreed with anything Elsie had said, he didn't mention it. In fact, he said nothing in response. He solemnly looked down at his plate and continued to eat his dinner in silence. An awkwardness was hanging in the air, and Elsie cursed herself for creating it. Thankfully, it didn't last long.

'Great speech. It was a nice touch with the guilt-trip at the end,' said Sid, winking at her.

Chapter Thirty

Elsie

E lsie folded the last of her clothes and lowered them into the cardboard box on her bed, destined to be taken to her new room at the care home later that day. In total, she'd filled ten boxes with her possessions, which mainly consisted of accessories to decorate her room. For clothes, it seemed sensible to pack comfortable jogging bottoms, oversized t-shirts, loungewear and nightclothes, seeing as she was hardly likely to be venturing far from the home after she moved in. On the door of her wardrobe hung a dress bag, inside which contained a long, plain black dress with lace detail. It was for her funeral. In true Elsie fashion, she wanted to add a pop of colour to the predictable funereal couture, and she'd purchased a pair of shocking fuchsia Jimmy Choo stilettos for contrast. The front formed into a severe point, the type of shoe which Elsie had always veered away from, and she'd struggled to squeeze her wide feet into them when she tried them after they'd first arrived. Hopefully, the funeral directors could push her trotters inside when the time came.

Pain ripped through her chest, and she lowered herself onto the bed. The agony was a daily occurrence, and she looked over at the empty blister packs that littered her bedside cabinet. She'd taken a couple of pills only an hour or so ago, too soon to consider taking more, given the strength of them. When she got to the care home, she vowed to speak to Ingrid about some more suitable pain relief. Perhaps she could start having morphine instead?

There was a gentle knock at the bedroom door, and Elsie forced herself to sit up straight.

'Come in,' she said.

The door pushed open slightly, and Mack poked his head through the crack.

'I'm not disturbing you, am I?' he asked.

Elsie shook her head. 'Of course not,' she replied. 'I'm just sorting through the last of my things.'

Mack opened the door and walked inside, holding a cup of coffee. He placed it on the bedside cabinet, pushing the blister packs to one side.

'For you,' he said.

He sat on the bed next to Elsie and clasped his hands together, lowering them between his legs. 'I wanted to talk to you about what you said yesterday. About work and starting up again.'

Elsie adjusted her position. This was going to go one of two ways. Mack was either going to ask her for help setting up something new, or he was going to ask her politely, at least she hoped politely, to keep her nose out of his business.

'I didn't disagree with what you've said, but you have to understand it from my point of view. I lost so many things when my business failed. I didn't just lose a business. I lost my home, my girlfriend, my family. It felt as though everything had just been snatched away from me. But it was as though that wasn't enough of a punishment. I lost my pride, my dignity, my reason for waking up in the morning, and then after everything had gone, I lost my self-respect and my mind. Ultimately, I lost myself, and in the end, I didn't even care if I lost my life. It had no value for me at all. I can't describe how destructive it is to feel like that.'

Elsie rubbed his leg. 'It doesn't mean the same thing will happen if you try again.'

'But who's to say that it wouldn't? I worked so hard on myself. I got off the drugs, and I stayed clean, even though I was still living on the streets. Do you know how difficult it is for an addict when there's so much temptation around to stay on them? Drugs take away the pain you feel inside. It's no different to those,' he pointed at Elsie's packets of painkillers. 'They may be a different type of drug and for a different pain, but they're taken for the same reason.'

'So what's the answer then, Mack? If you don't do what you love, then you've still lost yourself. There's still a part of you that's missing.'

Mack's eyes narrowed as he digested what Elsie had said.

'I just think that you don't give yourself enough credit for what you *have* achieved,' continued Elsie, keen not to let it go when she seemed to be reaching him. 'And I don't think that you'll ever be able to see just what that is while you're still living in the shadow of what was and not what is or what could be. You're an inspiration in the way that, despite everything that you went through, you've still managed to turn your life around and come through to the other side. Not many people in your position can say that. I mean, how many people did you meet on the streets who, if you went to their patch right now, would still be there? Their circumstances are no different to yours. You chose to change your life, and you did it without any help whatsoever. You've got so much more to give. Don't let your story end when there's still a few more chapters to write.'

Mack gave a half-hearted smile. 'But what if it's a tough read? What if people don't want to read it, and it just ends up sitting on a dusty shelf, or worse, what if it's pulped?

Elsie tilted her head to the side. 'You only need one person to pick it. Wouldn't it be worth it then if that one person changed because of what you'd written?'

They were silent for a moment. Mack went to speak but was abruptly stopped when Sid appeared in the doorway with a plunger in his hand.

'I don't wish to alarm anyone, but we've got a bit of an incident in the bathroom. Give me five minutes,' he said to them before disappearing from the room.

Mack let out a soft chuckle and gently shook his head. 'I honestly don't know how he always manages to say the right thing to break the tension. Come on, you. Let's load the car up and get this stuff to Ingrid's.'

***

Even with Sid, Agata, and Mack in Elsie's bedroom at the care home, there was still plenty of room for them all. They all helped unpack her things and put them away under Elsie's strict instructions, and it had been quite a seamless process apart from when Sid, in his ever-annoying way, had inadvertently been given the box which contained Elsie's underwear.

'I'm not sure this is my colour,' he said, holding a black bra to his chest.

She marched over to him and whipped it from his hand. 'The colour's fine, but I dare say that you'll need a bigger cup size.'

'Touché,' said Sid, impressed. 'I think Ingrid mentioned something about a cream tea. I'll go down and see if it's ready.'

'That translates as Sid's had enough and wants to do something else,' said Mack and Sid stuck up his middle finger and walked out of the room.

'You don't have to move in here,' said Agata. 'You could stay at home. It's where you belong, and we could make sure we look after you properly.'

Oh no. We were going to have this conversation again, thought Elsie. She'd nipped it in the bud several times over the last few weeks, but she had to give it to Agata; she was persistent.

'Agata. I have no desire to die in my apartment. It's the last place on earth I would choose to end my days. That place, until recently at least, holds no special memories, and I don't want you all to be reminded of me every time you walk past my bedroom. For crying out loud, Agata, you can't watch *Eastenders* without getting upset sometimes. How do you think you'd be able to cope with a real-life death? You'd be living on your nerves.'

'And what if I promise not to cry?' Agata asked Elsie.

'What? Like now, you mean,' said Elsie, pointing to the tears on Agata's face. 'We both know that that'll be a promise that you won't be able to keep.'

'Elsie's right,' Mack chipped in. 'You're an emotional being, which isn't a bad thing. It's what makes you beautiful...person. A beautiful person, I mean.'

Mack's face reddened, and Elsie suppressed, rolling her eyes.

'See. Mack thinks you're beautiful,' she said to prolong his embarrassment, and Agata smiled. 'There. That's better. No more crying. At least, not for today. Come on, we'd better get downstairs before Sid snaffles all the scones.'

Downstairs, they found Sid sitting at the dining table in the communal room. The table had been laid like a Mad Hatter's tea party with sandwiches piled onto a floral-tiered cake stand. There was a ridiculously oversized Victoria sponge cake, a plate of fruit scones and two matching floral teapots, complete with tea cosies, all crammed onto the table.

Elsie sat next to Ingrid, who was chatting merrily away to Amanda, who, every so often, snuck one of the finger sandwiches off the plate and popped it into her mouth. Sid was listening intently to the conversation between the two women, and Elsie spotted the faint twitch of a smile form in the corners of his mouth, even though she was unsure why: They were only discussing the flurry of prospective buyers who had come to view the vacant property next door.

'I didn't like the look of that second couple,' whispered Amanda, not very successfully, as they could all still hear what she was saying. 'They looked a bit snooty if you ask me. And the ones this afternoon! Mark my words – they're all property developers. Before you can say 'sold subject to contract', they'll have ripped the heart out of the place and turned it all into separate flats.'

'You can't know that,' said Ingrid. 'How do you know they're not just looking for their forever home for their family?'

'The guy was wearing workmen's trousers. You know, the ones—heavy duty and with loads of pockets. And I saw him whip out a measuring tape as he walked through the front door. Who does that? Property developers, that's who.'

Ingrid shook her head. 'I'll believe it when I see it,' she said, reaching for one of the scones.

A buzzer sounded in the hallway, signalling that one of the residents in their bedroom needed assistance, and Amanda began to head out of the room.

'Don't say that I didn't warn you,' she said as she walked out. 'And I'll remind you daily that you refused to listen to me when I told you you should have bought it.'

'You're interested in buying the house?' asked Sid. He had sandwich crumbs sitting on his beard, and Ingrid reached over and gently brushed them away.

'It was a pipe dream, that's all. I would have been able to extend into next door and expand the home, and that way, we'd have been able to help more people.'

'So why don't you?' asked Agata. 'That would be a wonderful thing to do.'

'Alas, as knowledgeable as my gardener is, he hasn't yet been able to grow me a money tree successfully,' she replied. 'It'll have to keep, I'm afraid.'

They whiled away another hour, eating far too many cakes that were good for them and talking about almost everything apart from illness. It was one of Ingrid's few rules in the home. People didn't need to be reminded of it, she told them all sternly. Elsie would have to remind Agata to be a little bit more upbeat in future, or at least try and stop the crying. Sid tapped at his stomach with satisfaction and stood up.

'We're not leaving just yet, are we? Only I said that I would read to, whatshername in room four. She was wandering on the landing outside the room with a book in her hand. She told me she was waiting for her son to come and read to her but that he was running late or something. So I said that if he hadn't come by five, I'd do it instead.'

Ingrid let out a loud scoff of derision. 'He's not running late. He stopped visiting her weeks ago. He said it was too much for him to see his mother like she was. The poor woman doesn't even realise.' Her face softened as she looked up at Sid. 'Thank you for doing that, though. It's a kind thing to do.'

Sid gave the broadest smile that Elsie had ever seen. She could almost see his wisdom teeth poking out of his gums. In his eyes, Elsie recognised the same soppy expression that Mack had every time he saw Agata. This couldn't be happening. Not Sid and Ingrid! Her life had become an episode of *Take Me Out*!

'You'd better go and get reading then,' Elsie prompted him. 'We'll be leaving soon.'

Sid nodded and walked out of the room, glancing backwards at Ingrid, who was engrossed in conversation with Agata about the shortage of reliable accountants in the area.

Chapter Thirty-One

Elsie

M ack fancied Agata. Agata fancied Mack. Sid fancied Ingrid and Ingrid? Well, Elsie wasn't sure about the answer to that one yet. All in all, everybody, it seemed, fancied each other, apart from her. She fancied nobody, and nobody, to her knowledge, fancied her. There had been that driver who used to deliver to the bistro downstairs when it was open. Still, he was around twenty years older than her, had a receding hairline, by which she meant it had receded to the back of his neck, and one of his eyeballs refused to keep in sync with the other. She wasn't a fussy person when it came to attraction – actually, that's not true at all. She was an extremely fussy person, and her boyfriends had always been over six foot tall, with a thick head of hair that she could run her fingers through and whom she expected to have either large biceps or a six-pack, or, better still, both.

Elsie pined to know what it was like to feel true love for another person. All of those years that she wasted and all because she was too scared of the heartbreak that might have happened had this imaginary relationship failed. She was a fuck up. Or rather, she used to be a fuck up. The irony of realising this now that there was nothing she could do about it hadn't gone unnoticed and had played heavily in her thoughts in recent weeks. Where would she be now had she tried a little harder in some of her former relationships? Probably still single, thinking about it, she mused. Elsie had a knack for picking the wrong person.

Like the rather gorgeous Jamie, whom Elsie had met while standing in line at her bank when he'd accidentally bumped into her. He'd apologised a little too profusely, and Elsie had given a polite smile and turned back around. Seconds later, Jamie tapped her on her shoulder and made some inane comment about the weather. Again, Elsie smiled and gave an equally inane comment back, but it seemed that Jamie liked to talk, and before they knew it, they were chatting like old friends, which was briefly interrupted when it was Elsie's turn at the counter.

'Wait for me,' he pleaded, and Elsie, who never let anybody tell her what to do, found herself loitering by a large Areca palm for him to finish whatever he was doing when it was his turn at the cashier's desk.

Jamie, as he told her over a coffee in a café around the corner from the bank, worked for a London-based investment firm, holidayed six times a year in destinations all over the world, and owned a small portfolio of properties which he rented out. He was, in short, Elsie's type of person. It wasn't that he was rich that she'd found attractive, but she couldn't deny that it went a long way. In truth, she and Jamie shared so many of the same qualities; hardworking, successful, financially secure, that it would have been difficult for any woman not to be drawn to him.

Jamie took her to expensive restaurants and treated her to pricey gifts that glistened in the light—their first few weeks had been wonderfully idyllic ones filled with bouquets of roses delivered to her apartment every Friday afternoon, incessant texts and calls between them both, and rampant sex that left Elsie breathless, exhausted, and still wanting more.

As they approached their six-week 'anniversary', the first and only crack appeared after Jamie booked a five-star hotel to celebrate. He'd proudly pushed open the door, holding it open for Elsie to enter, where a bottle of champagne chilled in an ice bucket on the side next to two sparkling flutes. On the bed, he'd laid out red rose petals in the shape of a heart, and inside the heart, further petals spelt out their initials. Elsie's first thoughts of how incredibly tacky the whole thing looked were swept to the side when Jamie suddenly dropped to one knee and opened a small black box.

'I love you, Elsie Bellamy, and want to spend the rest of my life with you. Will you marry me?'

He lifted the engagement ring higher towards Elsie and looked hopefully up at her.

'Jamie. I don't know what to say,' she replied.

She didn't have a clue how to respond. Up until that point, their relationship had been fun but non-committal. Elsie had always been open about what she expected in a relationship, and an engagement ring was certainly not on her list of expectations. They hadn't even mentioned the 'L' word. This wasn't just unexpected: It was downright ridiculous.

'Jamie. No. Just no,' she said, deciding there was no nice way of saying it.

Jamie's face clouded with confusion. 'I'm sorry, what? 'Are you fucking kidding me?'

'Jamie. It's not that I'm not touched by the...gesture,' her eyes glanced at the tiny solitaire diamond. 'But I thought I made it clear about where I stood on the whole marriage thing.'

'You fucking ungrateful bitch,' Jamie spat back at her. 'Don't tell me that you didn't know this was going to happen. How could you humiliate me like this? You seemed happy enough letting me pay for the meals out, and the presents, and the flowers, but now, all of a sudden, you don't want commitment? What sort of person are you?'

Elsie knew precisely what sort of person she was: An honest one. And she also knew exactly what sort of person Jamie was. He was a narcissist. She'd had plenty of experience with them thanks to her mother, who she'd watched beg and plead with men, offering her forgiveness for something that she hadn't even done. Elsie should have spotted it sooner, in truth, but she had to hand it to Jamie, he'd done well to hide it from her. But in the end, their true colours always emerged, blazing like a beacon, and suddenly Elsie realised that Jamie hadn't doted on her – he'd love-bombed her. He hadn't showered her with gifts to express his feelings for her – he'd bought them to lure her into the mistaken belief that they had something special. But like all abusers, when their victim was suitably under their spell, the onslaught of gaslighting, guilt-tripping and abuse would start.

'Goodbye, Jamie,' said Elsie, and she turned and walked straight back out of the bedroom door.

She knew he wouldn't leave it there. Men like him couldn't allow a woman to win anything, and as she walked along the corridor towards the lift, she counted down.

'Three. Two. One.'

The bedroom door opened and a furious Jamie bounded towards her.

'Are you really going to do this? Are you just going to let things end this way?' he said, grabbing her wrist.

'Yes, I am. And for the record, Jamie. I didn't do this. *You* did this.'

Elsie yanked her wrist free from his grasp. Another bedroom door opened, and a tall man with the perfect set of abs stepped into the corridor with wet hair and just a hotel bath towel wrapped around his waist.

'Is everything alright here?' he asked, his eyes darting between Elsie and Jamie.

'We're good, thanks,' replied Elsie, unable to take her eyes off his body. 'This moron thought that it would be a great idea to propose even though we've only been dating for six weeks. This is his reaction because I said no.'

Jamie took a cautionary step backwards, just as Elsie had expected him to do. That was another thing with abusive men; they never got into a fight with somebody they knew they couldn't beat.

'Fuck this,' said Jamie, throwing the ring box on the floor. 'Keep it. You're not worth it.'

The man kept a steely eye on Jamie as he stomped off down the corridor, disappeared into a lift and from Elsie's life altogether from that point onwards. On the plus side, Elsie left the hotel with Mr Bath Towel's number, but knowing she'd been so easily duped bothered her. She even created a Facebook post about Jamie to warn other women and set it to public. It was shared by her friends, whose friends then shared it with their friends, and within a few days, Elsie had received half a dozen direct messages from other women who had also dated Jamie and had experienced the same thing. Sadly, a few of them had taken months to find the courage and inner strength to end the volatile relationship, but at least they'd got out, she supposed. Sometimes, not everyone was that lucky.

Consequently, Elsie had never allowed herself to get remotely close to other men. She used men as and when she needed them. If Elsie needed a date for an event, she'd find one, and if she were feeling particularly lonely or yearning for touch, she'd flirt with the first attractive man she could find and have sex with him. Did that make her a bad person? Not at all, she believed quite the opposite, seeing as everybody knew where they stood from the beginning, and the vast majority of the men she saw were more than happy with that arrangement.

No. It was too late now. Everybody else around her was enjoying the thrill of the chase and the unknown, and she was glad for them. People should be happy. They should have that special somebody to go home to and cuddle up in bed with on cold nights.

Elsie was becoming used to being faced with her inadequacies lately. She'd love to say that it was an enlightening experience, that somehow the epiphanies lightened the emotional loads that weighed her down, but most days, like today, it was a painful reminder of all of her failures.

She bustled herself, trying to shake away the negativity that encased her.

'No. I won't have this anymore,' she said quietly to herself.

Elsie realised that it was her past that kept dragging her back. Her memories were like stubborn relatives, refusing to let go of her and refusing to be let go of at the same time. Memories of being hurt, used and abused kept her caged, preventing her from flying away, and all Elsie wanted more than anything was to be free. She wanted to know what it would be like to live, albeit briefly, without the sombre reminders that shackled her to a half-lived life. She wouldn't be that woman anymore. She wouldn't be another victim born out of other people's failures.

Elsie went to her bag and pulled out a notebook. It was filled with her handwritten lists of things she needed to do, things she had to buy, appointments she needed to make, doodles and general scribbles. She flicked it open to the next available blank page and, with her pen, scrawled '*The Living List of Elsie Bellamy*' across the top and started to write.

Chapter Thirty-Two

Mack

M ack punched the end call button on his phone and tossed it across the bed. Yet another failed job application. He wouldn't have minded so much, but the jobs that he was applying for were menial ones: warehouse pickers, machine operatives and the like. They were jobs that he'd deliberately chosen because they required little-to-none experience, and with a high-staff turnaround, they were always readily available. They were the less desirable jobs, reserved for those who needed work and money quickly, and it was because of those reasons that he mistakenly believed he'd be snapped up for them.

Unfortunately for him, his CV betrayed him each and every time, exposing one tiny detail that, as it turned out, was quite important to these prospective employers: The gaping hole in his employment history was quite the red flag, it seemed, and in every interview, he'd been questioned about why he hadn't worked for almost six years.

It was at this point that Mack could have taken the deceitful approach. He could have lied and told them he was ill or that somebody close to him was ill. He could have even told them that he was working in Europe. Anything but the truth, but that therein lay the problem. After everything that he had been through, after all of the lies, and stealing, and hurt he had caused other people, Mack had always promised himself after he got clean, he would never tell another lie again. Well, not a big lie anyway. Little ones, like the ones he told the others about not being attracted to Agata, didn't count.

Mack understood the destructiveness of lies better than most people. For years, he had lied and stolen from people that mattered to him the most, and he'd lost them as a result. Secrets always had a knack of coming back to bite you on the arse when you least expected them to. He'd be damned if he ever put himself in that position again.

Elsie had told him that it was admirable of him to stick to his own unwritten rule. Agata had said that it showed that he had principles that he should be proud of. Ingrid had said that she'd give a job in a heartbeat if she'd been told that by a prospective employee. Sid had told him that he was being a dickhead and said that principles never put money in your wallet. Mack hated it when Sid was right, even though he should be used to it by now. Sid was never wrong. Well, rarely wrong.

The simple fact was that Mack was growing tired of surviving off another person's generosity. He'd been living that way for such a long time now, and even though Elsie had never directly or discreetly asked Mack to start funding himself, he couldn't help but feel that all of these months of being supported by Elsie was enough. His pride took a battering every time he had to ask her for a few pounds to buy anything from a new toothbrush to ingredients for that night's dinner. It was embarrassing, and as Elsie so morbidly reminded them all the time lately, she wouldn't be around forever. At some point, she'd be gone, and then he'd find himself being sucked back down to the depths of lack and want, and who knew where that would lead. It was also his pride that stopped him from claiming the welfare benefits that he would undisputedly be entitled to. He'd grown up in a working household where both of his parents had instilled into Mack and his brother that benefits were reserved only for those who *couldn't* work and that unless their legs had fallen off, his parents expected them to do just that. Mack may not be in contact with them, but what if he bumped into them one day? He could just imagine the look of disappointment spread across their faces when they discovered their son had gone from the dizzying heights of business owner to dole dosser.

Sid, as usual, had taken a completely different approach to claiming welfare benefits and had clicked the submit button on his online application form without hesitation.

'I served my country for years. I've earned that,' he'd told Mack. 'Every tour that I did, every bullet that whistled past my ear, and for every mate that I've lost, that's my eligibility. Besides, I'm a pensioner. I don't have to find a job, but I do need to survive when you lot have all got your shit together and buggered off.'

At least Mack wasn't on his own on the job front. Agata was having problems too, but she'd been trying to get a job for years now, which didn't exactly fill Mack with much hope.

Ah. The beautiful Agata. It didn't take much for his mind to wander where she was concerned. She filled his waking thoughts and danced around in his dreams at night, which was awkward on so many levels when you shared your bed with a grumpy pensioner.

Each day, Mack told himself that that was the day he'd tell Agata exactly how he felt. He'd tell her how she was the most beautiful creature ever to grace the earth's green grass. He'd whisper in her ear how her hair wafted a fruity scent every time she walked past him. How her smile made his stomach somersault. How her accent made him want to take her to bed every time she uttered a word. But by the time the sun broke through the curtains in the morning, Mack had already lost his bottle. He imagined her laughing uncontrollably at his confession. The 'thanks but no thanks' conversation, or worse still, the 'it's not you, it's me' cliché.

Apart from the job situation, Mack was in a good place, possibly the best that he'd ever been in, and there was no way that he would risk ruining it.

He tapped the steering wheel with impatience and glanced at the clock. It was almost half past one. Elsie was usually done by now. Actually, that wasn't totally true. Sometimes, she overran her visits at the park, but intrigue and general nosiness were starting to get the better of him.

This Jack character that Elsie thought so highly of was, in his opinion, taking the royal piss out of her. Who else would insist that a dying woman visited him in the middle of a public park in the winter?

They'd all brought it up several times now with her, but Elsie was always quick to shut the subject down. It was as if she was under a spell where Jack was concerned, but Mack, Ingrid, Agata and Sid all agreed that something wasn't quite right with the man.

'Maybe he's a murderer? And Elsie is going to be his next victim,' Ingrid said during one of their secret 'anti-Jack' conversations.

Sid scoffed and then attempted to hide it behind a forced cough.

'I doubt that a murderer would wait over three years before killing their target,' he said to Ingrid. 'They tend not to have that kind of restraint, and I also think that killing somebody who is terminally ill wouldn't give them quite the same thrill.'

'I think he's a secret relative,' said Mack. 'Elsie didn't know who her father was, and her mother died when she was young. Maybe it's a long-lost grandfather or something?

It was both plausible and possible, he believed, until he saw the unconvinced look on Agata's face and he felt a flush of embarrassment.

'Then why doesn't he tell her that?' said Sid. 'No. I think he's a pervert. He gets off on talking to young women in the park. He probably bench hops and spends the whole day there.'

Agata let out a loud huff. 'I don't think this man exists.'

This time, Sid didn't attempt to stifle his laughter and began chortling. Agata, not impressed with his response, stuck up her middle finger.

'What is he then? A ghost?' replied Sid.

'No. Not a ghost,' she said. She flicked her hair behind her shoulder, sending a fresh, fruity wave into Mack's nostrils. 'I think she imagines him. I think she believes she sees him, but he's not really there. I think that perhaps the cancer, it is here...' she tapped the side of her head with her finger.

Mack, Sid and Agata all looked at Ingrid. 'I don't know why you'd think I'd know anything about that,' she said, holding her hands up in defence. 'And even if I did, you know that I wouldn't be able to talk about it with you. Look at the mess I made the last time.'

'We're not asking you to discuss Elsie personally,' said Mack. 'But you have experience with this illness. Would cancer on the brain make her see things that aren't really there?'

Ingrid let out a long sigh. 'Yes. It can make a person misremember things. It can make them see things and hear things that haven't happened. So it's a possibility.'

They'd spent a further half an hour discussing the pros and cons of allowing Elsie to keep her imaginary friend but ultimately agreed that if Jack brought Elsie comfort, they should leave her alone to get on with it. They didn't want to upset her unnecessarily. So what if she looked crazy sitting on a bench in the park talking to herself?

But that day, Mack couldn't shake the need to find out for certain. He got out of the car and headed into the park, pulling his coat up as the wind slapped against his face. Surely, even if Jack wasn't real, there was a way of getting through to Elsie that she and her 'friend' should perhaps meet up in a Starbucks on days like these.

As he rounded the corner, he saw Elsie walking towards him. Fuck. Had her eyes not locked with his, then Mack would have spun around and hurried back to the car, but it was too late for that now. He smiled and gave an exaggerated nod, but all that was returned was a terse stare. Elsie had given them all a stern warning to leave her alone for these few hours after she'd caught Agata lurking not too successfully behind a large Rhododendron shrub a few weeks previously.

'I wasn't checking up on you,' Mack defensively said as he neared. 'You were taking a little longer than expected, so I thought I'd check that you were okay. Hey! Don't look at me like that,' he added, spotting a subtle rise of Elsie's eyebrow. 'You'd be thanking me if it turned out you slipped and hurt yourself.'

Elsie checked her phone. 'I'm a whole five minutes over. I'd hardly say that constitutes a welfare check.'

'Seriously? Elsie, you can't be angry with me for wanting to check that you're safe. It may have escaped your notice, but it's freezing cold, this place is practically deserted, and you're not a well woman.'

'Fine. I'll let you off this time,' she replied. 'But you needn't worry, you know. Jack always makes sure that I'm with somebody before he leaves.'

'That's good of him,' said Mack flatly. He took a quick glance over his shoulder and was met with an empty footpath right up to the bench and beyond. 'But do you think you could have a word with him and see if he can agree to meet up somewhere that doesn't require you to wear a ski suit? It's getting too cold for you to keep doing this. We're heading into November now.'

'Fine,' said Elsie, exasperated. 'I'll see what he says, but I wouldn't hold your breath. We like it here. It's not just him. And I'm really starting to see things so clearly now.' Her tone lightened, and Mack saw an excitement dancing behind her eyes. 'Everything is going in the right direction, and I don't want to mess it up.'

'Mess what up?'

But Elsie used her finger to pull an imaginary zip across her lips. 'Never you mind. It's a work in progress, and there's still so much to do.'

And that's just what I'm worried about, thought Mack.

Chapter Thirty-Three

Ingrid

S id entered the kitchen carrying a tray piled high with dirty plates, cups and cutlery. He placed it on the kitchen work surface and slid the tray over to Ingrid, who was busy loading the dishwasher.

'That's the last of it,' he told her. 'Apart from number three. He hadn't finished, but I said I'd grab it off him when I take his beer up in half an hour.'

'Beer? Who said he could have a beer? He's not supposed to be drinking.' admonished Ingrid.

'Says who?' retorted Sid.

'His bloody doctor, that's who.' Honestly, this man infuriated her at times.

'Exactly. A doctor! What about what *he* wants? The man has, according to what you've told me, one week left? Maybe two? And he's asked for a beer. Him. The patient has asked for it. He's not asking for much. He just wants one final treat before you know...he's gone. Who are we to deny him that?' said Sid.

'We're his caregivers,' said Ingrid, resisting the urge to head-butt him. She'd never head-butted anybody in her life but she imagined it to feel quite satisfying. 'Correction. I'm his caregiver. Not you. You're a visitor. I'll get into trouble if something goes wrong.'

'And if it goes wrong, you can blame it on me. You can say that it was the *visitor* who plied him with booze when your back was turned. Don't worry about it. It's only the one. It's not like I'm taking him for a night out on the town,' he said sarcastically.

'It wouldn't surprise me in the slightest if you did. That sounds like something you'd do.'

'I absolutely would, but I think the drip might cause a few problems.' He gave a coy smile, and Ingrid scowled, even though secretly she wanted to smile with him.

That was the problem with Sid. He had the most annoying habit of frustrating the life out of you, only to whip it away and replace it with a joke seconds later. Ingrid had increasingly found herself going from frown to smile within microseconds. It probably looked like she was having a stroke when she was around him for too long.

Sid had been a frequent visitor to The Orchids for weeks now. She'd been touched by the offer, and an extra pair of hands was always welcome, especially when they were free. Sid busied himself with general handyman work in the morning, and in the afternoon, he visited the residents. He'd spend a good hour with each, reading, talking, or even simply watching the television with them. And after dinner had been served and cleared away, Sid would say his goodbyes and catch the bus back to Elsie's.

He'd never asked for anything in return, apart from a spot of lunch, that is, and Ingrid couldn't help but feel moved by him. Sid's manner with the residents was no different to how he was with his friends. He joked, he swore, and no doubt he probably pissed some of them off from time to time, but oftentimes Ingrid had walked past a bedroom and heard the cackle of laughter from inside. Sid just had this knack for making people feel comfortable. In some ways, she was a little bit jealous of the fact that he didn't have to conform to rules, regulations, or professionalism. Sid was just Sid, regardless of who was sitting in front of him.

Mrs Foster had a particular fondness for him and had now started to apply shocking shades of makeup. Bright pink lipstick extended beyond her thin lips, which, when coupled with the heavy coral rouge on her cheeks, gave her a clown-like appearance, but Sid, ever the gentleman, had never referred to it apart from the once when Mrs Forster stepped out into the corridor from her bedroom, all made up, and giving Ingrid and

Amanda the shock of their lives. Sid's eyes had widened with surprise, but he expertly suppressed them again and held out his arm for the old lady to hold.

'Wow,' he had said. 'Look at you! You look just like a film star.'

Mrs Foster had blushed and batted the comment away with her free hand. 'What? I always make an effort no matter how I'm feeling.'

Sid had led her back into her bedroom, and Amanda and Ingrid followed them inside. She watched as he ushered Mrs Foster to her armchair and eased her down gently as though she was made of brittle glass. She had to hand it to him. He certainly had a way with people.

Everybody just seemed that little bit happier with him around. Not because The Orchids was ever an unhappy place, but Sid managed to bring a bit of spark back to residents. Sid wasn't a worker. He wasn't paid to visit them, and that, it appeared, made the world of difference. Even Ingrid had found herself warming to him, much to her surprise, and she'd found herself watching the clock each day to see how long it would be before he walked through the door. She'd even started to gaze out of the window when the number fifty-three bus pulled up at the stop across the road. Good grief. She was starting to behave like a teenager! And although it bothered her that she was starting to look at Sid through different eyes, she couldn't deny that she was enjoying the dizzying feeling attraction brought.

'Well, if Mr Sanderson drops down dead from an alcohol-related complication, I'll hold you entirely responsible,' Ingrid said, just a little too forcefully.

'If Mr Sanderson drops down dead from an alcohol-related complication, I expect he'd come back in ghost form and shake me by the hand. Sometimes, some people want to carry on as normal. They don't want to sit in bed all day or be stuck in front of a television waiting for death to pounce on them. They want to be with friends, having a drink or a smoke, talking about the old days. It takes them away from what's really happening to them, and if I can make somebody feel like that, no matter how brief, then what's wrong with that?'

What *was* wrong with that? Ingrid pondered momentarily as Sid stared intently back at her, waiting for her response. She didn't have one. There was no way that she could argue with that, so Ingrid did the only thing that she could think of: roll her eyes, huff loudly, and flounce from the room. She was sure that she could feel Sid smiling behind her back.

She went into the front room and began plumping up the sofa cushions even though they didn't need it. Sid followed her, picked up one of the magazines from the coffee table, and dropped heavily onto the sofa opposite. She huffed again. He was only sitting down, but Sid was trying to provoke a reaction from her. Well, he wasn't going to get one this time, she thought to herself, and Ingrid made a mental note to refrain from any further huffing and puffing in order to prove herself right.

'Will you look at that? That went quickly,' said Sid. She turned to him and saw that he was now by the window and looking outside. She followed his gaze to where a man was erecting a sold sign in the garden next door, and her heart sank. That was that dream dashed. The images she'd conjured of knocking through walls, extending the peace garden, and expanding her little empire evaporated from her mind.

'I'm sorry. I know how much you wanted it,' came Sid's soft voice behind her.

'Thank you. But it was never going to be mine. Not really. It was just a dream. Silly of me to think that it might actually happen.'

'There's nothing silly about dreaming. It's what drives us forward,' he replied.

She felt a burning tinge behind her eyes, and she fought to push her sadness to one side. What a fool to behave like this, and in front of Sid of all people. She knew he wouldn't mock her – quite the reverse, but she hated feeling weak in front of anybody, let alone him. There was no way that she was ever going to be able to afford something like that, so why on earth did it hurt her so much knowing that within a few months, it was going to be somebody else's dream? She just prayed that it wasn't the property developers who'd bought it. What if they converted it into flats? It would be a tragedy for that to happen to such a beautiful building, making that pill all the more difficult to swallow.

'Fancy a cuppa?' Sid asked, and she nodded.

'Yes. That would be lovely.'

'I'll make it extra sweet for you, although I think you're perfectly sweet enough,' he said before scurrying from the room.

Ingrid's eyes sprang open, and she felt a flutter of excitement spread inside her. Maybe Sid had said it to be nice? Maybe not. But he had said it at just the right time, and Ingrid found herself crying. She angrily wiped the tears away with the back of her hand, worried that he might walk and see her.

'You silly old woman,' she whispered to herself. 'One nice word to you, and look what happens.'

She took one final gaze at the sold sign and went to join Sid in the kitchen.

Chapter Thirty-Four

Agata

It wasn't like Agata to snoop, but she couldn't help herself. Each day that passed, Elsie's illness was becoming more and more apparent. The new clothes, which were a size smaller than last month, were now hanging off her, and her bones were starting to poke through the material. Her skin was almost the colour of a sunflower, as were her eyes, and Elsie's beautiful vivid blue irises now seemed dull and listless next to the whites, or yellows to be precise. Elsie barely ate, and when she did, it was no more than a few mouthfuls before she declared that she was too full to continue. Up until recently, Elsie had disguised her pain well, but now the doctor's appointments were becoming more frequent, and the painkillers stronger, and which never lasted her as long as they should. Agata had seen how Elsie screwed up her face in agony when she pushed herself up from the sofa, or the bed, or the dining chairs, and she'd noted how much slower her steps had become. It took her an age to walk the shortest of distances, and Agata wondered whether or not she should broach the subject of getting a wheelchair for her.

And yet, despite all of the pain and the suffering, Elsie somehow seemed totally at peace with everything. She never complained, well, at least, she hadn't said anything to them, and she still insisted, much to all of their annoyance and frustration, that she saw Jack almost every day. Elsie even planned her doctor's appointments around her visits with him.

Agata had tried, and failed, on several occasions, to put Elsie off the visits or at least move them to somewhere more suitable, but Elsie, as defiant as ever, refused point blank even to consider it.

'It's mine and Jack's special place. I don't want to stop going there,' she told Agata after yet another 'discussion'. 'If there is such a thing as heaven, I hope it looks just like the park, and then I'll spend eternity in a place that means so much to me.'

Elsie had said it with such passion that Agata found herself too scared to ask her to consider the possibility that Jack was nothing more than a figment of her imagination: that he was a visual representation of the father figure that had been absent from her life. It was her brain's way of making sense of her situation; a subconscious reaction to help her accept her fate. Agata was sure of it. The others were a little less receptive to the suggestion.

The difference between Agata and the others, though, was that Agata had witnessed it all for herself. She'd seen Elsie several times in that bloody park before summoning the courage to talk to her. Each time, Agata had only ever seen Elsie either walking into the park, walking out of the park, or sitting on the bench. Each time she'd been alone, and when Agata queried this with Elsie, she'd told her that she must have just missed Jack. She supposed that could be true; she was minding the children then, and god knows how much of her attention they'd demanded. But if she was wrong, why hadn't they met Jack yet? He'd never even been to the apartment to visit Elsie. Something just wasn't right.

Mack had taken Elsie out to yet another doctor's appointment, and with Sid over at Ingrid's, she decided that it was the perfect time to have a look through Elsie's things to see if there was anything, anything at all, which might help her discover the truth. Mack and Elsie would probably only be half an hour or so before they returned, so Agata set to work. She started a cursory search in the living room, but with so little of Elsie's possessions left, she doubted that she'd find anything. She pulled open the drawers on the sideboard and glanced inside, but they were relatively empty. For good measure, she went to the bookcase and systematically removed each book and flicked through the pages, just in case Elsie had stashed something inside one of them. Agata had once seen a television detective solve the murder of a family of four by finding one lowly Post-It note stuck between the pages of an A-Z; Agata had found nothing other than a sweet wrapper, which she assumed Elsie had used as a makeshift bookmark.

She didn't bother to check the kitchen drawers and cupboard; she'd seen inside them often enough, and if Elsie was hiding anything, it was highly unlikely that she would leave it next to the cups and plates. She headed straight for the bedroom. It was more lived-in than the rest of the apartment, but the majority of the things in there were Agata's. She had been a little hesitant when Elsie had first suggested Agata take more of the wardrobe space and the empty drawers, but as Elsie had pointed out, there were so few of her things remaining that it seemed silly for Agata to live out of suitcases. Even so, Elsie still used a couple of the drawers, and there was also her bedside cabinet, which, every time Elsie pulled them open, seemed fit to burst.

She went to the chest of drawers first and riffled through quickly, but inside there were only clothes. So she went over to the bedside cabinet and pulled open the bottom drawer, removing it completely, and placed it on the bed next to her. She made a mental note of everything's position. The art of mooching was to ensure nobody knew that you had mooched. Inside, there was a mix of old makeup, instruction manuals and costume jewellery, and just a quick glance confirmed there was nothing of importance inside. She placed everything back into the drawer and slid it into its place in the cabinet. Drawer number two looked a little more promising. It was filled with paperwork; she grabbed them and sifted through the pile. There were solicitor's letters that dated back years concerning the purchase of the apartment, as well as the one above and the now defunct bistro. There were several months' worth of bank statements, and Agata flicked past them without looking at the balances; There were limits to her prying. At the back of the pile was a blank hard-backed envelope. She delved her hand inside, and her fingertips brushed against paper. Using her thumb and forefinger, Agata plucked it out and discovered it was an article snipped out of a newspaper. The paper was yellowing, and she unfolded it gently. It was a report, no more than a couple of paragraphs long, concerning the death of one Caroline Bellamy.

Woman's Body Undiscovered for Three Weeks

The body of Caroline Bellamy, 39, lay undiscovered in her council flat for as much as three weeks, according to the findings of the coroner's inquest. Bellamy, a known drug addict, was believed to have died in early November. Neighbours stated that Bellamy rarely left her property, and her absence, therefore, went unnoticed. Concerns were raised by social workers who were visiting another property at the address and noticed a suspicious smell originating from Ms Bellamy's residence.

Police forced entry and discovered her body lying on the sofa. One officer on the scene gave evidence describing the flat as 'in a delipidated and disgusting condition.' A post-mortem confirmed that Ms Bellamy had died from a heroin overdose. Ms Bellamy had one child, a daughter, who was taken into care the year prior to her death. The coroner recorded a verdict of death by misadventure.

Agata had never been so astounded that the life, and more importantly, the death, of a person could be reduced to a few sentences. There were no kind comments from concerned neighbours. In fact, there was no concern at all if they hadn't even bothered to question the pungent smell coming from the flat. Poor Elsie. Agata could only imagine the horror of her childhood. No. She couldn't imagine it at all. She couldn't imagine what it must have been like to have had a mother who was addicted to heroin, who lived in squalor, and who, as a result, was whipped away from the only thing she had ever known and forced to live with strangers. No wonder Elsie hadn't wanted to talk about her family.

Agata also noted that there was no mention of a father. No kind words from neighbours. Or Caroline's family. Nobody, it seemed, had cared enough for Caroline Bellamy to at least pretend that her loss would be missed. Caroline had been easily forgettable and just another casualty of a broken society.

She carefully refolded the newspaper clipping and returned it back into the depths of the envelope, placing it, along with the other letters, back into the drawer.

Agata opened the last drawer and was both excited and surprised to find a notebook placed on top, crushing down the other contents. She took out the drawer and drew a deep breath.

This was akin to reading somebody's diary – a total no-no by anyone's standards. But seeing as Agata had already searched through all of Elsie's things, it hardly seemed to matter now.

She turned the pages, and her initial excitement downgraded into disappointment. It was a doodle book—a book of nothing: A book where you jotted down all sorts of silly things. Page after page, there were lists about one thing or another, dotted with crude drawings of stars, flowers, or swirly lines. Agata could imagine Elsie absent-mindedly drawing them while on the phone. She picked up her pace and, within seconds, reached the last page. It was blank. She huffed loudly and threw herself back on the bed. What a waste of time.

She sat up again on the bed, mindful of the time. Mack and Elsie would probably be back soon. She was about to close the notebook and return it inside the drawer when something caught her eye. She tilted her head and ran her fingertips across the page, feeling the soft ripples of indentation beneath them. Turning on Elsie's bedside lamp, she held the paper up to the light and saw neat lines of writing. It was out of sorts with the scrawls on the previous page, where Elsie had written down a reference number for who-knows-what, a telephone number for who-knew-where and a sketch of a massive cock and balls.

Agata tore out the page, making sure that the little remnants of paper caught within the spiral bounding were also removed. There was a slam of the front door on the street and the soft thuds of footsteps coming up the stairs to the apartment's main door, and Agata pushed the notebook inside the drawer and closed it. As the key turned in the lock, she folded the paper and thrust it inside her jean pocket, straightened the duvet to remove the tell-tale crumples of her having sat there, and headed back out of the bedroom.

Chapter Thirty-Five

Jack

'So? What do you think?' asked Elsie.

Jack nodded his head. He was impressed. Seriously impressed.

'I think you've done a grand job,' he replied, and Elsie beamed back at him. 'And how far have you got with sorting this out?'

She leaned over him and jabbed at several sections. 'Done. In progress. Done. Done. In progress. And those two there – they're good to go.'

Jack wanted to hug her, but he was scared that, at this point, it was likely to cause her physical pain. Elsie had put a brave face on everything, as she always had done. Pain was just like every other emotion that she'd managed to suppress or hide over the years, but she wasn't able to conceal everything. Jack had spotted her slower movements and her hesitancy when she sat down.

Thank goodness she had finally picked up on all of the little hints he'd given her over the past months. At one point, he felt sure she would miss them altogether and what a catastrophe that would have been. He would have found himself in serious trouble for that, and in all of his years of doing this, not once had Jack ever failed.

Time was no longer on Elsie's side. The option of her having months to live had been stripped to just weeks, and Jack prayed that all of the paperwork could be sorted in time. If Elsie died without finalising it all officially, then everybody would suffer.

'The only thing that needs to change is that one,' he said, pointing to the paper. 'You need to rethink that.'

Elsie's smile faded, replaced with the crumpled brows of a petulant teenager. 'Absolutely not. That needs to stay. Non-negotiable.'

'Everything is negotiable. It just all depends on the price to exchange,' said Jack.

Elsie leaned back against the bench, took a packet of Polos out of her pocket and popped one into her mouth.

'Not for me, thanks,' said Jack when she offered the packet to him. 'So? Are you going to take that one out?'

'I'm thinking,' she said as she sucked away on the mint.

They remained silent as Elsie mulled over his proposal. It was a pointless exercise because Jack knew exactly what she would say. He'd prepared for it a long time ago.

'Okay. I'll drop that one if...' she left a dramatic pause, 'you agree to spend Christmas day at mine with the others. And you can't say yes now and then back out on the day. Otherwise, I'll just re-write this and add it back in again.' She wiggled the paper in the air, and it fluttered against the breeze.

'Deal. I'll be there on Christmas day.' He offered out his hand to a surprised Elsie and she shook it slowly.

'That'll be a deal then. It's official. We've shook hands, so you're not allowed to change your mind.'

'I won't change my mind,' Jack told her.

'You promise?'

'I thought the whole hand-shaking thing would answer that one.'

'Promise me, Jack,' insisted Elsie.

He turned to her and looked her in the eyes. 'Elsie. I promise you, with my hand on my heart,' he said, placing a hand on his chest, 'that I will be there on Christmas day.'

Jack would have said anything to her to get her to make the changes on that list in her hand. He was an expert at convincing people to do what he wanted without them realising it. It was the benefit of being an old man. Nobody ever saw it coming because they couldn't believe that a pensioner could mislead them so easily. There was an illusion of safety with age, and Jack had capitalised on it whenever he deemed it necessary.

Elsie's eyes filled with excitement, and she did a series of happy claps in her gloved hands. 'I can't wait to tell the others. They won't believe it.'

'The proof of the pudding is in the eating, as they say,' he replied because he couldn't think of anything else to say without it being an outright lie.

Chapter Thirty-Six

Mack

S id had taken Elsie to meet Jack, leaving Mack alone in the apartment with Agata. She'd been acting odd ever since he and Elsie had returned from the doctor's surgery that morning. If Mack hadn't been as experienced as he was with drugs and their effects, he would have sworn that Agata was totally wired. But her pupils were normal, and she wasn't sweating or suffering any breathlessness or palpitations, but there was definitely something putting her on edge.

He went to the fridge. It was a far cry from the fridge he had first opened when it had been nothing more than a giant wine chiller. Now it was filled to the brim with vegetables, salads and fresh meat, and Mack loved the sight that greeted him when the door opened, and he was met with bursts of colour from peppers, carrots, broccoli and red onions.

He took out a shin of beef he'd picked up from the butchers the previous afternoon. Today, he was going to slow-cook it in one big pot filled with vegetables and lashings of red wine gravy. Mack loved one-pot cooking. It reminded him of when he was younger, watching his mother haphazardly chop vegetables and meat and throwing them into a large Pyrex dish. She'd cook it on low for hours on end while she went about her business cleaning the house. Even now, after all of these years, if he inhaled deeply enough, he could smell his mother's cooking all around him in the air. It was the smell of childhood. The smell of when things had been simpler. It was the smell of home.

Mack began by peeling the carrots. His hands moved quickly and subconsciously, and he glanced up and saw Agata sitting at the dining table, staring vacantly out of the window as she bit her nails. She looked so beautiful today in her fluffy black polo-neck jumper and leggings. On her feet, she wore a pair of slippers with sheep's heads at the front. It was one of those many silly things that Agata did that made Mack want her all the more.

'What's up with you?' he asked.

Agata stopped biting her nails but continued to stare out of the window. Still, she remained silent, and Mack set down the peeler and the carrot.

'Agata?'

'I don't want you to be angry with me,' she replied.

'Angry? I could never be angry at you,' he replied. 'Tell me what's wrong.'

Agata reached into her pocket, pulled out a piece of folded paper, and held it out to Mack. Still, she didn't move or look at him, so he walked over and plucked the paper from her fingers. His stomach clenched. What was on it that worried her so much? He unfolded it and his face clouded with confusion.

'It's blank, Agata. Why would I be angry at that?' He said as he turned it back and forth.

She jumped up from the chair and snatched it away from him. 'It's not blank. Look – feel.' She grabbed his hand, and Mack's heart quickened. Her skin felt so soft as she rubbed his fingers over the surface.

'You feel that?' she said.

'Feel what? Agata, you're confusing me. Can you just tell me what this is all about?'

She took a deep breath. 'I found it in Elsie's notebook.'

'Elsie doesn't have a notebook,' he replied.

'She does. It's in her bedside cabinet.'

His face darkened. 'You went through Elsie's things? Agata, what the fuck? Why?'

She threw her hands up in the air dramatically. 'Because something is wrong. I don't know what, but I feel it here,' she said, patting her chest. 'Something with this Jack person. I think he's lying to Elsie. I think he's a bad man, and I don't want to sit here and let him hurt my friend. That's not what friends do. So

I go through her things to see if I can find something that tells me I'm right, and then I find this.'

Agata flapped the paper in the air, 'You found a piece of blank paper, Agata. What does this prove?'

She went to the window and pressed it against the glass. 'There,' she said, 'You see writing? Elsie must have written in notebook and it pressed through to the next page.'

Mack joined her at the window and squinted his eyes. 'You can barely make anything out. I don't see what all this fuss is...' his voice trailed off as the invisible words appeared before his eyes. He could see Elsie's full name on the top of the page. Numbering down the side, and there on the first line, he could see Jack's name. The following few words were illegible apart from *'the sum of five hundred thousand'*.

Mack took the paper and tore it in two.

'Mack. Please don't,' gasped Agata, as she tried to grab it back from him, but he pulled his hand away.

'Agata. This is Elsie's private business.' He was furious. Elsie had shown them all nothing but indiscriminate kindness. She'd trusted them. She opened up her home, her life, to them when most people would have just turned their backs. How could Agata betray her like this? 'You had no right going through her things.'

'It's her will. You see it. She leave her money to this man, and I think that was always his plan all this time. I think that is why he doesn't meet us. That is why he says he doesn't have a phone.

Or why he has never told Elsie where he lives. This is why they meet in park. And why he is so careful not to be seen.'

Mack rolled his eyes at her. 'The other day you were trying to convince everyone that Jack was a figment of Elsie's imagination, and now he's this criminal mastermind trying to syphon her money from her. Make up your fucking mind, Agata. You're starting to sound crazy.'

His words came out harsher than he intended, and Agata visibly winced. Mack wished he could snatch them back, but the damage was already done. Her eyes turned cold, but behind her glare, he could see a teary film forming.

'Keep it,' she said, gesturing to the paper. 'You think I am stupid for thinking these things. You think I have no business looking through Elsie's papers, and maybe you are right. Maybe it is not my place, and maybe this would make Elsie angry. But I rather her be angry at me for being good friend, than disappointed that I didn't even care.'

'Agata, I didn't mean...,' he started to say, but it was too late. Agata was already walking out of the room. He heard the slam of her bedroom door, and his heart sank.

He shouldn't have spoken to her like that, but he did stand by his opinion. Agata shouldn't be going through Elsie's things regardless of the good intentions behind it. It was Elsie's decision what she did with her money. Having both had money and lost it all, Mack no longer desired vast wealth. He wanted to be able to put a roof over his head and live a little, but the

293

grand things, the dreams of big houses, flashy cars and expensive watches that weighed more than he did, no longer excited him. All Mack wanted was to wake up in the arms of the woman whose opinion of him he'd just managed to destroy in the space of seconds.

If he were any kind of man, he'd stride right down the corridor, open the door with one strong kick, and pull a shocked Agata into his arms. He'd move her golden hair away from her face and gently wipe away the tears that he'd made her cry, and then he would slowly bring his head closer to hers and kiss her tenderly, pulling away only to tell her that he was sorry.

But Mack wasn't that kind of man. He was a coward. He wasn't this imagined superhero character who kicked down doors and whisked women up in his arms. He was the man who was about to let the woman he loved cry alone in her bedroom because he'd spoken to her like shit. He was *that* kind of man. He was a total prick.

Mack angrily tore up the paper into tiny pieces and watched the remnants flutter into the bin from his hand. Whatever Elsie had written on that there, it wasn't likely to be a bloody will. She had a solicitor for things like that; Mack had driven her there often enough. He'd sat there and waited patiently in the swanky reception area, looking at gaudy pieces of 'art' on the wall while getting eyeballed by the receptionist whose makeup was as orange as, well, an orange, as he waited for Elsie to sign whatever it was she needed to sign that day. Elsie wasn't about to start writing wills on scraps of paper when she was paying a solicitor £200 per hour to handle her affairs. Maybe he could have explained it that way to Agata rather than flying off the handle. It was all too late now. Everything was crumbling away from him. This new little life was falling apart; Elsie would be gone, Agata now hated him, and Sid was at Ingrid's more than he was here. Mack knew that given half the chance, Sid would move into The Orchids without a backward glance, and where would that leave him then? Alone, that's where.

He went back to the vegetables on the side and continued peeling them, but before he'd even chopped the first carrot and added it to the pot, he knew that it was going to taste terrible. Even after slow cooking for hours and all the juices mixing and bubbling away, he knew that when he forked the first mouthful onto his tongue, it would taste bitter and soiled. It didn't matter what the others said about it, Mack would know. That was the thing about food; it needed love and care for it to work, and today, at that moment, Mack felt neither.

Maybe he would speak to Sid about it later. He'd leave out the bit about whisking Agata off her feet; he didn't need to know all the details. Maybe Sid would offer to speak to Agata on his behalf? Or would that seem too teenager-like?

He roughly cut up the beef shin and covered the pieces in flour. He flash-fried the chunks, waiting for them to turn golden brown; the butter sizzled loudly in the pan, and it wasn't until Mack heard the front door close that he realised that he hadn't heard Agata come back into the living room and slip past him until it was too late.

He should have hurried after her and shouted that he was sorry. He should have dashed barefoot down the staircase, looked her in those beautiful eyes and begged for her forgiveness. But he didn't. Mack stood firmly at the cooker, flipping pieces of beef in a pan, thinking about all of the things he should have done but that he didn't have the balls to do in reality.

Chapter Thirty-Seven

Elsie

The beginning of December swept in along with the coldest temperatures on record and three feet of snow, which blanketed the city like a duvet, and for the first time that Elsie could recall, she was excited about celebrating Christmas.

In the Christmastime of old, Elsie had rarely bothered to get up and had spent most of the day laying on the sofa watching the festive favourites that were always guaranteed to be televised. She'd watched *Oliver* more times than she cared to remember, and who could forget the classic *The Snowman*, which seemed so outdated compared to today's animated films and cartoons. For dinner, she would eat whatever she could find in the freezer, but more often than not, it was simply a couple of slices of cheese on toast, and if she was feeling particularly naughty, she sometimes heated a small tin of baked beans and threw them on top. In the evening, Elsie would go to any party she was invited to, but those were few and far between as people tended to celebrate the holiday with their families and not work associates. All in all, it was a tedious and tiresome affair, and Elsie would count down for the season to be over, the shops to fully reopen and for normal service to be restored.

This year, however, was going to be the Christmas she'd never known. It was going to be that one that made up for all the missed moments as a child where excitement fluttered inside at what presents waited for her under the tree, the copious amounts of chocolate that seemed perfectly acceptable to eat, and the silly family games played in the evening after all of the Christmas specials had been aired and watched on television. Although she realised she would never be able to relive those moments, Elsie could create her own version of Christmas happiness with Agata, Mack and Sid. She hadn't asked Ingrid to join them. Ingrid's business didn't clock off for the holidays, and she didn't feel the need to put her friend in the difficult position of saying no.

Elsie had ordered an artificial tree, baubles, and trimmings, and the moment they arrived, she set to work and decorated the whole apartment, hanging lines of foil trimmings from the ceiling and setting the LED tree lights to the flashiest setting she could find. When she had finished hanging the last bauble, Elsie sighed, placed her hands on hips and surveyed her work. It looked as though there'd been an explosion in a tinsel factory somewhere close by. It was tacky beyond belief, but it was how Elsie wanted it. As much as she didn't want it to be, this was likely to be her last Christmas, and she intended to throw everything at it to make it the most memorable for everyone. She'd successfully set her plans in motion, and she was within weeks of everything coming together, but she needed to tread carefully with some parts of her scheming. Otherwise, she might find herself eating turkey alone this Christmas.

She sat down with a glass of water – wine was strictly off the menu for her now, and waited for everyone to return home. Mack had gone to pick up Sid from The Orchids, and Agata was out on yet another job interview. Poor Agata, Elsie thought to herself. She was an intelligent woman, clearly qualified for her job. Yet, interview after interview, she returned home with sour dejection: 'She wasn't what they were looking for right now,' or Agata had 'been pipped to the post by somebody with slightly more experience' or 'thanks, we'll be in touch,' were all common responses she received when Agata asked for feedback at the end of an interview. Elsie couldn't help but feel that unconscious bias played a part in the lack of success for her. All she needed was one break. One chance to prove that she was indeed the woman for the job.

Sid, bolstered by his unspoken love for Ingrid, even though it was completely obvious to the rest of them, spent much of his spare time online shopping in the apartment, spending his well-earned pension money on new clothes. And his love of bathing was more acute than ever, though thankfully, Elsie had managed to convince him to swap to showers instead so at least she could stop imagining the never-ending spinning of her water meter. But as a consequence, she had walked into the bathroom and caught a glimpse of his bare arse practically pressed against the glass of the shower screen more times than was healthy. Thank goodness for small mercies, she reminded herself; it could have been frontal nudity that she'd been subjected to.

There was tension between Agata and Mack, though, which baffled her. She hadn't been present for any argument between them so presumably, this was something that had occurred when she hadn't been around. Their feelings for each other were as transparent as Sid's were for Ingrid, and the way that they continued to cast furtive glances at each other gave Elsie a smidgeon of hope that all was not lost. Yet still, it appeared that whatever was going on between them was something they wanted to keep to themselves. Normally, Elsie despised secrets, but considering she had so many of them dancing around in her head, she felt it was a little unfair of her to pass judgment. Hopefully, whatever it was would right itself and soon! There were only a few weeks until Christmas, and if her little gang weren't getting along, it would scupper everything.

Mack and Sid were the first to return. Their heated debate on the merits of air-frying food halted immediately the second their eyes settled on the Christmas decorations.

'Ta da,' exclaimed Elsie excitedly.

Sid stepped deeper into the apartment and turned slowly, taking in every chintzy, glittering decoration.

'This is what I imagine it would look like if Santa Claus vomited,' he said flatly.

Elsie threw a cushion at him, and it bounced off his head. 'I should have known you wouldn't like it.'

Sid flashed a smile. 'No. It looks...nice...in an odd sort of way.'

'And what do you think?' she asked Mack.

'It looks alright, I suppose,' he said, giving a quick shrug of his shoulders.

'Gosh. I'm surrounded by heathens,' replied Elsie. 'I hope you're more excited when I give you your presents.'

'Elsie,' said Sid. 'We've talked about this. Being here and spending Christmas with somebody other than grumpy bollocks,' he thumbed towards Mack, 'is more than enough.'

She smiled at him, keeping the fact that she knew Sid had bought her a gold necklace from Argos quietly to herself; he'd left the page open on her laptop. She'd gone one further than him in the gift stakes, but hers wasn't the type that would fit underneath a tree, neatly wrapped and secured with a bow. Elsie prayed that she hadn't overstepped the mark with this one.

'Fine. No presents,' she lied.

The door swung open and in walked Agata, and immediately Elsie could tell that she didn't harbour good news but her face did brighten when she saw the decorations.

'I love it. Elsie. It looks beautiful,' she said, gazing in awe at the Christmas tree.

'How'd it go? Elsie asked her, although she already knew what was coming.

'Not good. They said I interview well, but they worry I might not be so up to date with all the new rules even though I tell them that I check legislation all the time. They say no, anyway. Fuck them. It look like a shithole.'

Mack stepped toward Agata and brushed her arm with his hand, and Elsie spotted her tense under his touch.

'I'm sorry to hear that. You'll find something soon.'

'Thank you. You say nice things...sometimes,' she replied, and Mack immediately looked at his feet and stepped back again.

Jeez-Louise. These guys needed to sort themselves out, thought Elsie.

***

Dinner, which consisted of roast lamb, cabbage, sprouts and roast potatoes, was, as always, utterly delicious. Elsie had managed to eat a slither of lamb, half a potato and two sprouts, and even that was a struggle. She knew that her hourglass was on its last few grains and had already spoken to Ingrid about moving into The Orchids on boxing day. She just prayed that she could last until then.

Agata helped Sid clear away the plates and clean the kitchen. It was the rule of the apartment that as Mack cooked, he was excused from cleaning duties. It was a rule that was universally accepted by them all, mainly because Mack cleaned as he went along, so it wasn't the most taxing of chores to undertake. Elsie was excused for obvious reasons, and so she and Mack took a moment to relax on the sofa together, him with a glass of beer and Elsie with water.

'Elsie. I've been thinking about what you said about work.' Mack shifted his position on the sofa to face her. 'I'm thinking about working with homeless shelters or charities. Whoever will have me, really. Having been through it, I'm in the perfect position to help other people. I mean, who better to know the struggles that homeless people face than somebody who's lived through it.'

The conversation that had flowed freely between Agata and Sid reduced to nothing, and Elsie knew they were listening.

'I know the places where they sleep at night. I know the daytime hangouts. I know what they need. I know what they're looking for. From food for themselves, food for their animals, where they can get a shower, or wash their clothes. I think I could do a good job. I could really make a difference.'

Who was Elsie to argue with that? Deep down she knew that Mack would always long for the heat of the kitchen cookers and a shouting match with the maître d. But how could she tell somebody that doing something so wonderfully selfless was wrong for them? She couldn't.

'I think that's a wonderful idea,' she told him and Mack's face lit up. 'You're right. You'd make a huge difference.'

'Damn right, mate. I'm so proud of you. I'll help in any way I can just don't ask me to walk the streets at night. My bones aren't quite what they used to be,' said Sid.

'I think that it is a really amazing thing to do,' Agata chipped in. 'I think people would be glad for you helping them.'

'Thank you,' replied Mack, holding her gaze. Agata's eyes dropped back down to the tea towel in her hand.

Honestly, those two needed their heads smacking together. Elsie vowed to have a quiet word with Agata that night when they were alone in the bedroom. With any luck, she might be able to sort out what was wrong. Otherwise, that would be another one she'd have to cross off her list. It had been bad enough crossing out the one that Jack had suggested, but, she reasoned, at least he was coming over for Christmas dinner. Then all of this gossiping about Jack can finally be put to bed. Elsie was going to tell them all about it that evening, but Mack's news had put her off. She didn't want to look like she was stealing his thunder, so tomorrow would have to do instead.

Chapter Thirty-Eight

Ingrid

Ingrid watched Sid work away in the garden from the safety and warmth of her bedroom. She'd been standing at the window for around ten minutes, unable to move from her spot. She was pretty sure it didn't constitute as spying, merely checking up on an employee's work, but then she remembered that Sid didn't actually work for her. He was a volunteer—a good Samaritan—one of those generous and selfless souls who helped other people in need.

Sid was sweeping up the golden leaves that had blown in from next door's scruffy garden. Hopefully, the new owners would have it landscaped, maybe even hire a gardener, and in the future, she wouldn't have the persistent battle that plagued her beautiful space whenever the wind blew.

He knelt next to the small pile of leaves and debris that he'd studiously collected and began to deposit them into a garden bag, which was being viciously whipped around by the breeze. She smiled as the bag was snatched from his hand by a sudden gust and catapulted to the other side, stopped only by the hedges that lined the edges of her garden. Sid's annoyance was clear even from her position in the upstairs window, and Ingrid watched him mouth 'fucking hell' as he rose to his feet and went to retrieve the unruly bag. By the time he'd returned, the pile that he had so carefully compiled had fluttered away like disobedient children refusing to come inside when playtime was over, and he threw his head back towards the sky muttering something that Ingrid couldn't make out. She chuckled to herself.

She hadn't realised how little she had laughed, properly laughed, since her husband had passed away. When Phillip had died, she'd channelled her grief into a self-made mission of helping the dying pass with love, dignity, and, above all, expert care. As crusades went, it was a worthy one, but it also meant that Ingrid faced dying and death every single day. She lived on a treadmill of perpetual grief; it turned like a never-ending cycle of sadness as her residents came only to leave in a private ambulance destined for the undertaker.

It wasn't that Ingrid viewed her residents as numbers rather than people, far from it. She provided all the necessary facilities and support that they needed, but Sid gave them something that Ingrid didn't have enough time to give herself. Normality. He'd been right when he'd said that all that they wanted was to have a friend to talk to. A friend who listened, who played board games or helped with oversized jigsaw puzzles. It eased their loneliness and made them feel less of a burden.

It wasn't for the want of trying on Ingrid's part. She loved nothing more than to sit with her residents, but the logistics of running The Orchids often made it impossible to find the time to do those things. Her days were filled with organising doctor's appointments or arranging transport to the hospital, speaking to food suppliers and waste companies, paying bills, balancing the books, talking to families, and a whole host of other daily tasks that needed to be done just to make sure that everything was running smoothly.

Sid was the type of person that every care home needed. He was the jester. No. That sounded unkind. Sid was nobody's fool; he was so much more than that. He was the glue that seeped around the inner workings and the turning cogs and secured them all together. He did the essential jobs that were so often lost amongst the general administration.

She turned her wedding ring around her finger, watching Sid as he once more swept up the leaves that littered the footpaths. Breakfast would soon be over, and he'd be back inside making his own morning rounds after the nurse had finished administering that morning's medication.

She went to her dressing table to check her appearance, tidying her hair and ensuring her clothes looked okay.

'What the hell are you doing, you silly cow,' she admonished herself, moving towards the door. But suddenly, she stopped, returned to her dressing table, and sprayed liberal amounts of *Jimmy Choo*, Flash – a present from Amanda the previous Christmas.

'It's a beautiful scent,' she'd told Ingrid as she watched her spray some onto her wrist. 'All the men will be chasing you if you wear this.'

Well. Let's just test that little theory out and see if it's true, shall we?

***

Sid came into the staff room not long after Ingrid. He rubbed his hands together and let out a shudder.

'Bloody freezing out there today,' he said. 'I've bagged up all of the leaves. Well, most of them. The buggers kept blowing away. It's a losing battle, I tell you.'

'Thank you. You didn't have to. I'm sure Dave could have seen to that when he comes in next week. Tea?' she said, holding up the kettle.

'Yes, please,' said Sid. 'It's no skin off my nose – the leaves, I mean. I know how much you hate your garden looking untidy.'

Ingrid filled the kettle with water, trying to recall the time when they'd spoken about the garden. She frowned as her brain found nothing.

'Did I say that to you?' she asked him.

'No. Not in words. I saw you doing it yourself the other week. I thought I'd save you the hassle and just get the job done instead. You've got far more important things to be getting on with, I'm sure.'

Ingrid's stomach flipped at the thought of Sid secretly watching her, but she kept her composure and took the now-filled kettle back to its base and flicked it on.

'That was kind of you. Thank you,' she said, praying that her neck hadn't gone that hideous patchy red that it so often did when she was nervous.

Amanda bustled into the staff room with a clinical waste bag in one hand and a laundry bag in the other.

'Morning, both,' she said as she dashed past them into the utility room. 'Mrs Foster has had a bit of an accident,' she shouted back to them from inside the room. 'Alice and I have cleaned it all up, but honestly, I'd burn the bedding. It's past saving.'

Sid wrinkled up his nose. 'I'll go and see her after I've finished with Adrian,' he said to Amanda as she rejoined them. 'Can you make sure you crack a window and light a candle or something for me, though? I'm not good with smells.'

'You get used to it in the end,' said Amanda. 'Anyway, have no fear. Alice is spraying a liberal amount of air freshener as we speak. Oh,' she said, pausing to look at Ingrid. 'What's wrong with your neck?'

Ingrid's hand darted to her neck. Thanks for pointing that out, Amanda, Ingrid silently seethed, knowing full well that it would probably get worse now that she'd highlighted it.

'I think I've reacted to that perfume you bought me. You remember?' she said, thinking quickly. 'It started to come up after I put it on this morning.'

'Really? That hasn't happened before. Not that I've noticed, anyway. I recognise the scent, so I know when you're wearing it, but I thought it was just for special occasions? That's what you told me anyway. You only put it on for something important.'

Piss off, Amanda!

As amazing as that woman was, she wished she could just sack on her the bloody spot but reasoned that she didn't have the energy or money for a lawsuit, so instead, Ingrid smiled sweetly and turned as the kettle gave a satisfying and much-welcomed click.

'I've no idea why it's reacted today,' replied Ingrid, as she poured the boiling water onto the teabags in the cups.

'Don't you?' Amanda said cryptically, and Ingrid closed her eyes tightly. 'Oh well. I better get back up there,' said Amanda, 'Sid, Adrian has got a 1000-piece cat puzzle out for you to do today. So brace yourself.'

'I hate cats,' said Sid. 'They shit in everyone's garden.'

'Same,' agreed Amanda. 'But have fun anyway.' And she left the room, leaving Sid and Ingrid alone once again.

Ingrid squeezed the teabag against the side of the cup and dropped it into the waste bin, added milk to the cups and stirred them liberally. The silence only served to emphasise the tension, and she frantically thought of something to say to break it, but her brain came back with a useful nothing.

She turned to Sid and handed him his tea, and as he took it from her, his fingertip brushed hers. Again, her stomach fluttered, and Ingrid knew without hesitation that her neck was probably now a horrifying shade of red.

'Any joy with Elsie and trying to get her to move in before Christmas?' asked Sid. 'I'm seriously worried that she won't...' his voice trailed off.

Ingrid knew how that sentence ended. Sid was worried that Elsie wouldn't make it to Christmas. It was a thought that she'd had herself many times. She was no fortune teller, but she was experienced in estimating a person's life expectancy. Specific indications made it an easy thing to guess, and judging by the muscle wastage, her skeletal frame and her jaundiced skin, Ingrid gauged that Elsie had possibly two weeks, three at best, before passing. It was a morbid skill that Ingrid had formed over the years, a blessing and a curse all at the same time, but this was the first time she'd wished she'd never developed it.

'I've asked her repeatedly, but she refuses to listen. You know what she's like. She's a stubborn soul,' she replied.

'You could try again,' suggested Sid.

'I could. But it'd be pointless. Agreeing to move in for Elsie would be like her accepting that her death is imminent, and as true as that might be, it'd be hard for anybody to accept. Elsie has told me, time and time again, that she doesn't intend to die before Christmas, and as crazy as it sounds, I think she'll probably do it. Sometimes, the human mind is more powerful than people realise. I don't think it'll be by much, though. But I won't force her to change her mind.'

Sid looked thoughtful as he blew the steam away from the top of the mug.

'Okay. I'll trust your judgment,' he told her. 'Right. I better see what this puzzle is like. God give me strength.' He walked past Ingrid but paused at the door. 'You know, that perfume does smell beautiful,' he said, not turning to look at her. 'Even if it does bring you out in hives.'

Chapter Thirty-Nine

Elsie

I t was an audacious plan. Crazy. Mental. And it led totally into the unknown. Elsie would be lying if she said that she wasn't nervous about it all. There had been many sleepless nights when she'd lay awake staring at the ceiling as she listened to Agata's gentle snores and wondered if she was doing the right thing.

Elsie had managed to cross the first hurdle in total secret. Phone calls were difficult to keep private when she shared a home with three other people, but thankfully, there had been times when she was left completely alone in the apartment, albeit only briefly. Texting had been much easier to conceal, but it had still been tricky. Elsie had to speak to a total of four people in order to make this happen. Four separate lots of phone numbers. Four separate series of chat messages.

Agata was out for the day, and Mack was on 'Elsie' duty, which basically meant that he was babysitting her. It was a term that she'd eventually come to accept after her pleas to use another term went ignored. Sid was also knocking around the apartment thanks to Ingrid, who'd agreed to tell a little white lie to him about there being a stomach bug doing the rounds at The Orchids, and he'd reluctantly stayed at home that day.

'What's this all about?' Ingrid had asked her when Elsie first broached the subject with her.

'Never you mind,' she replied. 'But it's not a bad thing. Well, at least I hope it's not a bad thing. I'm sure you'll find out all about it, but I'll need you to keep it to yourself for now. No dobbing me in. I'm counting on you.'

'Whatever you want. As long as you promise to tell me all about it,' said Ingrid before she hung up the phone.

The stage was set and ready to go. Now, all she needed was the cast, and her apprehension began to set in. Elsie took a glance at her phone. It was nearing 1 p.m. Finally, it gave a satisfying buzz, and she checked the message.

Here.

Her fingers quickly typed out a reply.

All of you?

All of us. Came the response.

She heaved herself off the sofa, and Sid glanced at her over the top of his book. *A Tale of Two Cities*, no less. He was wearing

Agata's sheep's head slippers, which would constitute a hanging offence if Agata ever found out.

'I'm just going to check and see if the post has come,' she told him, pre-empting his question.

Mack was in his bedroom, so at least she didn't have to worry about him. She went out of the front door, partially closing it behind her, and crouched down and retrieved a set of keys she'd hidden earlier that morning behind the pot plant containing an artificial Bird of Paradise.

She went down the stairs and, as quietly as she could, opened the front door that led out onto the street and went outside.

**

'I need to go down to the bistro and get a meter reading for the gas and electricity company,' she told Mack and Sid half an hour later.

'Right now?' asked Sid.

'I'll go and do that for you,' offered Mack, but Elsie shook her head.

'I want to go and check on the place anyway.'

Sid looked at her perplexed. 'Why?'

'Why not? It'll probably be the last chance I get.'

'It'll probably be the last chance I get,' along with, *'What if I die tomorrow?'* and not forgetting *'I won't leave this world*

315

regretting that I didn't do it,' were all well-used sentences that Elsie threw out every so often when she needed to get away with something. Distasteful? Absolutely. Wrong? Well, that depended on who was judging. But sometimes, it was a necessary tactic that needed to be utilised every so often to loosen the 'Elsie Duty' Gestapo.

The other day, Sid had offered to put her socks on her feet for her because she'd grunted in pain when she'd bent over to do it herself, and Mack, she noticed, had now started to cool down her cups of tea with extra milk because he was worried that she might tip it over herself.

All kind and highly considerate things to do, and had Elsie been infirm or completely incapacitated or even semi-incapacitated, she would have welcomed their little interventions. But as it stood, she wasn't out of action just yet, simply slower, and she'd be damned if she was going to let any of her friends put socks on her bloody feet.

'Why don't you both come with me if you're so concerned?' she suggested.

There, the bait had been dropped. All she needed now was to hook two fish.

Sid wiggled Agata's slippers. 'We both know she'll kill me for wearing these. So long as I stay inside, then I'm safe, but woe betide me if I step outside. She'll know in a heartbeat, and then we're all screwed because if I go down, then I'm taking you all down with me.'

'I'll go with you,' offered Mack and Elsie forced a smile.

One fish hooked. Not a bad start, but she needed both of them. She wracked her brain.

'No problem,' she replied as calmly as possible, and she headed out with Mack.

On the stairs, Elsie deliberately took the stairs slowly. More slower than usual, and Mack glanced back at her with concern.

'Are you alright?' he asked as he reached up and grabbed her arm to steady her.

'Yes. Yes. I'm fine. It's just...ow!' she said dramatically. 'Everything is a little bit achy today.'

'Maybe we should go back?' said Mack.

But Elsie refused, vehemently shaking her head. 'No. I can't. I need to do this today. What if I die tomorrow?'

There. She'd said it—two terminally ill guilt-tripping statements in one day! She'd be tumbling straight down to hell at this rate.

'Sid!' Mack shouted up the stairs as Elsie feigned greater pain as she took another step down. 'Come and give us a hand.'

Sid materialised by her side in seconds. He hooked his arm under Elsie's, and for extra emphasis, she allowed her weight to bear down on his arm.

'Will someone tell me why we're going down instead of straight back upstairs?' asked Sid.

'I won't leave this world regretting that I didn't do it,' replied Elsie.

There. A hat trick! She'd better pack her bikini because it'd be hot where she was going.

The three of them hobbled down the stairs, out the front door and onto the street. Elsie kept up the pretence as they slowly walked the few steps to the bistro door, and then she stopped, stood up straight and turned to face them both.

'Just remember this. Whatever I've done, I did it because you're my friends, and I love you,' she told them.

'Shit. She's not going to ask us to bump her off is she?' said Sid.

Chapter Forty

Mack

Whatever Mack was expecting to be waiting for them beyond the bistro doors, it wasn't this. He and Sid stepped inside, leaving Elsie, who'd seemed to have made a remarkable recovery, to beat a hasty retreat back into the apartment.

The lights were already on, and from the blast of warmth that greeted them, the heating had been turned on too. The majority of the tables and chairs had been removed by Julian and Richard when they'd closed the business, but a few that formed part of the fixtures and fittings when Julian had taken on the tenancy remained.

Two tables had been placed in the centre of the almost empty space. Sat at one was a man that Mack didn't recognise. The man gave a teary smile, and Mack instinctively smiled back. It took milliseconds for him to realise that the man wasn't smiling at him at all, and he turned to the sound of Sid's gasp beside him.

'Chris?' Sid cried as tears spilled from his eyes. 'Chris?'

The man pushed back his chair and stood. 'Hello, Dad,' he said.

The two men rushed towards each other and embraced; their arms wrapped around each other's backs, clutching and grabbing and patting as though the years of silence that had passed between them had never happened.

A lump of fear rose in Mack's throat. So far, he hadn't looked at the occupants of the other table. He didn't need to. Elsie's subterfuge was apparent. If she'd arranged for Sid's son to meet his father, then it was obvious who the three people were sitting at the other table. Mack was frozen with fear; too scared to move, too scared to turn, too scared to look.

The lights were dazzling in his eyes, and he blinked them away, releasing his own torrent of tears.

'Son?' he heard his mother's soft voice say.

A firm hand landed on his shoulder and squeezed.

'Mackenzie. Look at us,' said his dad. 'We're here and we're not going anywhere.'

Mack was a kid again, standing in front of his parents, upset at being caught doing something he shouldn't have; Like when he snuck a whole packet of biscuits up to his room or when he took that ten-pound note out of his mum's purse so that he could buy the new Right Said Fred single and a McDonald's happy meal. The disappointment in their eyes as they stared down at him after he'd been caught out had etched itself into Mack's brain for the rest of his life. He couldn't face seeing it again.

'Fucking hell, Bro. Open your eyes,' his brother Marcus said.

Marcus! His little shadow. His partner in crime. There may have been two years separating them in age, but visually, when they were younger at least, there had only been half a foot and a beauty spot on Marcus's cheek between them. Marcus was more than just a brother. He had been Mack's best friend. They'd done everything together as brothers often did. The illicit, stolen biscuits had been shared, and the happy meal had been bought solely for Marcus to enjoy.

Mack opened his eyes. There were no frowns of disappointment. There was no anger or fury. Just a palpable relief, where sadness mingled with overwhelming happiness. It was just a jumble of emotions swirling in one big family pot.

He smiled through his tears at them all. He felt a trickle from his nose running down onto his lip, and his mother, as she'd so often done when he was a child, plucked out a tissue stuffed up the sleeve of her cardigan and wiped it away.

'Oh, my boy. Thank God you're alright,' she sobbed and then threw herself against his chest. His dad leaned over her and hugged him, and his brother joined the embrace from the side. A 'Stewart sandwich', as his dad used to call it when Mack and Marcus had been kids. His mum had called it a 'home hug'.

'You'll always know that you're home when you have one,' she'd said when Mack was around thirteen years old.

Mack, full of hormones and mild rebellion, had no idea what she was talking about. He was far too cool for home hugs now that he had grown an extra foot and his face had filled with spots. He had his reputation to think about, and just what would his friends say? He'd have the piss ripped out of him for eternity if they ever found out. So the hugs that Mack had adored when he was younger had been shrugged away until, eventually, his mum got the picture and stopped giving them altogether.

But now, in her arms, feeling the rise and fall of her chest against his, the smell of her Charlie Red perfume drifting up his nose, the cigarette smoke ingrained in his father's coat, his brother's muscular back under his arm, he realised his mother had been right all along. Mack *was* home.

***

'We had to move in the end. The house was too big for us with you two boys leaving home. But we downsized to a two-bedroom, just in case you ever came home,' said his mother, reaching out and holding Mack's hand across the table.

So far, his parents had apologised around ten times for moving. They hadn't moved to get away from him, they assured

Mack, even though he repeatedly assured them back that he already knew they wouldn't do that. They'd only moved to a house around the corner, two streets away, they continued to tell him, just in case he went back to his childhood home.

His dad had done the thing that he'd always threatened to do – retire, and now spent his spare time watching true crime documentary's, endlessly decorating whatever room his wife told him to, and babysitting Marcus's son when he and his wife were at work.

It had been a shock to learn that in his absence, Marcus had met and married Leona, who was a lovely woman, according to his mum. They had one toddler, Riley, and another baby on the way, which also, according to his mum who relied heavily on old wives' tales, was a girl because Leona was carrying all around the sides. Mack hadn't realised how much he'd missed his mum's pearls of wisdom and general scatter-brained behaviour.

'Will you come home?' his mum asked, looking at him hopefully.

But Mack shook his head. 'I'm good where I am Mum. And even if I wasn't I wouldn't leave Elsie. Not now,' he replied.

'That poor woman,' his mum replied.

'She seems like a such a nice girl. It's awful how bad things happen to good people,' added his dad.

'She told us everything you know?' said Marcus. 'She found us; hired a private detective no less. He knocked on the door one

Saturday afternoon. Dad was in the middle of cooking on the barbeque, weren't you Dad?'

Mack's father nodded. 'It was going bloody terribly. I couldn't get the coals to stay alight. The sausages were all pink in the middle.' He said, shaking his head with shame.

'Private detectives don't look the way you expect them to,' added his mum. 'They don't wear long coats or wide-brimmed hats. It was such a surprise.'

Marcus rolled his eyes, and Mack chuckled.

'Anyway. As I was saying,' continued Marcus. 'Elsie told us everything that you'd told her. About you getting clean, leaving rehab.' He paused. 'Why you felt you couldn't come home. And we just want you to know we understand. We understand why you stayed away.'

'Although, I still think you should have come home,' said his mum.

'Yes. You certainly would have been useful to have around, if only to make sure that the barbeques ran smoothly,' joked his dad. 'There would have been no pink sausages on your watch.'

'There wouldn't have been sausages on my watch, period!' replied Mack. 'Gourmet burgers served with balsamic onions, American cheese, and on a brioche bun.'

'Brioche!' said his mum, wrinkling up her nose. 'I can't stand them. It's like eating a burger on a slice of cake.'

'It's nice to hear that you still love cooking,' said his dad. 'Elsie told us that you've decided not to go back to it, though. It surprised us to hear that. Didn't it, Margaret?'

Mack's mum nodded her head. 'A waste of talent if you ask me.'

'I don't want to push you either, Mack,' added Marcus. 'But I have to agree with them. I couldn't imagine you doing anything else. It's all you've ever dreamed about.'

Mack looked down at his hands. Up until that day he'd been so sure about his decision never to work in a kitchen again. It may have been where his heart lay, but his head had drifted to pastures new; across to greener fields where the past lay far behind him, totally out of reach. But sat there now, with his family just an arm's length away, with the bistro's stainless steel kitchen glinting at him through the pass behind the bar, Mack felt that familiar pull inside. He was the sizzle of a pan away from reaching for his chefs' whites and striding behind the oven. Yet, he had been so fixated on working with the homeless that he would have felt like a traitor to betray that promise.

'Never say never,' he told them all in a bid to placate them. 'Who knows what the future holds for us? Elsie's a good example of that.'

They'd spent all afternoon together until the dull day dimmed into darkness, and the street lamps turned on and cast an orange glow all over St Paul's Square and beyond. In the end, they'd pushed their tables together and formed one big group with Sid and his son Chris.

Mack had introduced Sid to his family and started to tell them how they'd met, only to be halted by his mum, who told them that Elsie had already explained everything to them. How thorough Elsie had been, mused Mack.

Sid's ex-wife, Patricia, had passed away from a heart attack some six years previously, leaving Chris, as he'd told them, parentless. Sid looked into his lap when his son had said this, but Chris draped an arm over his father's shoulder.

'I never held it against him,' he explained. 'I joined the army back in 2016, following in the old man's footsteps, as it were, so I know just what it's like. When I'm out on leave, it feels as if I've stepped out onto an alien planet. They make you so used to routine and structure and orders that when they're gone, even temporarily, it's as though you lose all sense of your identity. I completely understand why Dad would have found it difficult. Nobody prepares you for that.'

Chris himself was engaged to be married to a woman called Tania, and she was three months pregnant with their first child. Sid had jokingly asked if that was why Chris was marrying her, but Chris had laughed and dismissed the comment away with a wave of his hand.

'We got together just after you left. High school sweethearts and all that. I just thought it was about time, plus it was her birthday, and I'd forgotten all about it, so it was all a little bit spur of the moment. But don't tell Tania that.'

It was nearing 9 p.m., and Mack was exhausted. They'd drank two bottles of warm white wine that they'd managed to find tucked away in the back of one of the kitchen cupboards, and several glasses of tepid tap water, but Mack's stomach was starting to grumble. All he wanted to do was eat toast, drink a warm cup of tea and fall into bed. All of the emotion of the day had drained him, and no doubt by the force of his mother's yawn, she was equally exhausted.

'Perhaps, we should call it a night?' he suggested to them.

His mum, visibly relieved, immediately began to pull on her coat.

'Yes. I think that's a good idea. Muffin has been on her own all afternoon, and I'm pretty sure that your dad forgot to leave the kitchen light on so she's going to be in the dark. And she's got to have her dinner too. Of course, it'll be too late now for your dad to take her out for a walk so the back garden will have to suffice tonight.'

'Muffin?' said Mack.

'Muffin McStuffin,' said his mum. 'A Cockerpoo. Mad as a box of frogs that one, but she keeps your dad healthy and moving now that he's retired.'

'That bloody dog,' his dad muttered under his breath.

Mack had missed the banter between his parents. He stood and hugged them both, swapped mobile numbers with each other and said their goodbyes. He followed them out onto the street and hugged his brother once more.

'I'm glad you're back,' Marcus whispered into his ear. 'I've told Riley all about you. I kept showing him your picture so that he'd recognise you when he saw you in person. He licked the photo and then babbled some nonsense at it, so I think it's worked.'

Mack laughed.

'Just look at this, Graeme!' he heard his mum shout at his dad. She strode over to the car and pulled off a parking fine stuck to the windscreen. 'I thought that you said you'd bought a parking ticket?'

'I did. It's there in the window,' he shouted back, pointing to the little printed sticker stuck on the window of the driver's door.

'Then what's this all about?' she asked, waving the parking fine at him.

'It's probably due to the fact that we've been here eight bloody hours, Margaret, when we only paid for two.'

His dad pressed a button on his key, and the doors clunked unlocked. They both got into the car, still arguing over the fine as they did so.

'That'll be about seventy pounds, Graeme. You do realise that we'll have to cancel that day trip to Weston now to pay...'

The car doors slammed closed and silence was once again resumed on the square.

'It's good to see that not everything has changed since I last saw you all,' said Mack.

'Yep,' replied Marcus. 'You missed it?'

'More than you could ever realise,' said Mack.

Chapter Forty-One

Agata

Agata had been livid when she first got home that afternoon and discovered Elsie alone in the apartment. But before Agata had time to react, Elsie explained where Mack and Sid were and what she'd done. Her anger immediately evaporated, and instead, nervous anticipation swirled inside her.

They'd waited hours and hours, wondering how it was going, theorising what was being said and whether or not there had been any heated debates. Then both men had come home, all smiles and thanks to Elsie for, as Sid put it, being an interfering cow, and Elsie had retorted by saying she'd been called worse and by better. They'd hugged Elsie, and as they did, Agata's eyes drifted down to Sid's feet and saw that he was wearing her sheep's head slippers. That fucking man! She knew that somebody had been wearing them when she'd once slid her feet inside and they were still warm. Initially, she'd thought it had been Elsie, so she'd kept it to herself. She could hardly complain about that now, could she? But discovering that it had been Sid's old-man feet soiling the fluffy lining was too much. And the worst part was that she couldn't even complain or make a fuss. Mack and Sid had just been reunited with their families after years apart. How would Agata look if she were to cause a stink over a pair of slippers? It'll keep, she said to herself, dropping the subject. For now!

She went over to Sid first and hugged him and congratulated him, making no reference to 'slipper-gate' even though she could tell by Sid's eyes that he'd just realised that he was still wearing them in front of her. Then she went over to Mack and held him tightly. His body felt good pressed against hers. It had been the first time that there'd been any proper contact between them since they'd fallen out, and it felt nice to have the excuse to be close to him again. They held their embrace a second or two longer than necessary, and Agata only broke away when she opened her eyes and saw Elsie staring back at them with a smug smile plastered over her face.

Agata had made them all cheese on toast and teas and coffees, and they'd sat in the living room as they told Elsie and Agata about what had transpired. Mack's face was more animated than Agata had ever seen before, and right then and there, she realised just how much in love she was with him. She could sit and watch him and listen to him talk until the end of time.

Seeing his family again had unlocked a side of Mack that she'd never seen before. His whole energy had been lifted. His movements seemed more fluid; his body now at ease with itself as the part of him that had been missing had been returned, slotting back into its original place in his heart. Agata just hoped that there'd be enough room in there for her as well.

Mack and Sid showed them pictures that Mack had taken with his phone. His parents seemed, for want of a better word, normal. Then again, how else were they supposed to look? Marcus, Mack's brother, looked scarily like Mack, only with less worry lines and a silly little freckle on his cheek, which looked like an ink splodge and which Agata would have had removed with a laser years ago had it been on her face.

As they continued to talk, her imagination wandered into a world where Mack was introducing her as his girlfriend. They'd be seated around a table as Mack cooked a grand meal while Agata busied herself with keeping their wine glasses topped up. Riley, Mack's newly discovered nephew, would sit on her lap, and he'd nestle into Agata's chest, and everybody would coo at what a natural mother she looked like. And Agata would give Mack a knowing look, aware of the secret they shared of what was growing in her stomach.

'Agata?' Are you okay? You're off in your own little dream world there,' said Mack.

Agata's imaginings disappeared, jolting her back to the present. 'Yes. Sorry. You were saying?'

'This little man here,' Mack said, holding the phone up to her face, 'is Riley. Isn't he cute?'

Agata looked at the screen. Riley was standing next to Mack's dad, who was crouched by a flower bed in the garden. He was presenting Riley with a freshly plucked daffodil, and Riley's face was filled with delight at the gift. His pudgy hand was reaching out to grab it as Mack's dad smiled lovingly back at his grandson.

Agata imagined a similar scene where it was her and Mack's child playing in the garden with Mack's parents, but before her mind drifted away again, Mack pulled back the phone, breaking her fantasy.

'When will you see them next?' she asked.

'Soon,' replied Sid. 'Chris hasn't stopped texting since he left.' His phone pinged again, and Sid smiled proudly as another message came through. 'See,' he said as if they needed to see the evidence.

'Can I just say something?' said Elsie. She shifted forward on the sofa. 'I understand that this is a monumental thing, and I couldn't be happier for you. You both know that, right? But they're your family, so I completely understand if you want to spend Christmas with them. It's honestly not a problem if you want that to happen. I don't want you to feel guilty about anything. Me, Agata and Jack will be fine on our own.'

Me, Agata and Jack will *not* be fine on our own, Agata silently fumed. The thought had never even crossed her mind. These past few months, all she'd ever dreamed about was spending Christmas with Mack. Well, not just Mack, the others too, but mainly Mack, if she were being honest. She'd conjured up her own series of events where she'd wake Christmas morning, and they'd all be giddy with excitement as a heavy sheet of snow fell outside. She'd set the tree lights to warm white to cast a nice calming glow and turn on the radio and listen to Christmas songs all morning as she stood next to Mack in the kitchen, helping him prepare the vegetables for their Christmas dinner. They'd drink Buck's Fizz all morning until they were mildly drunk, and then Agata would 'accidentally' stumble, and Mack would reach out to steady her. They'd be in each other's arms as they looked up at the mistletoe hanging from the ceiling above their heads, and Mack's head would lower to hers, and he'd lean in, and then...

'Agata? We'll be alright on our own. Won't we?' repeated Elsie.

'Yes. Yes. Of course. Fine on our own,' she replied, forcing a smile on her face.

She held her breath.

'We spoke about this just before we came back up,' said Mack. 'And of course, our families have asked us to spend Christmas day with them.'

Agata felt her heart sink to the soles of her feet. She felt sick.

'But,' he continued.

She held her breath again. There was a 'but'.

'We said that we wanted to spend Christmas with you guys so we told them that there was no way that we could contemplate not being with you both that day.'

Agata's heart now leapt straight back up and thumped wildly.

'But...'

For fuck's sake.

'What Mack is trying to say,' interrupted Sid. 'Is that we want to spend it with everyone. So, we were wondering if it would be okay with you if we spent it together? All of us. Together. Families and friends. Obviously, it'd be a little tight with everyone being in here,' he gestured towards the six-seater dining table, 'so we thought it might be better if we had it downstairs in the bistro?'

'Yes!' Agata blurted out and then realised it sounded far more enthusiastic, or desperate, depending on how you looked at it, than she intended.

'Elsie? What do you think? It's your call. I know how important this Christmas was to you, and we won't be offended if that's not what you want,' said Mack.

Elsie's face broke into a big smile. 'Not what I want? That would be amazing. Of course! I'd love that. One big happy family on Christmas day.'

'From my experience, Christmas is never one big happy family day,' said Sid. 'There's always an argument somewhere along the line. Me and Patricia once had a blazing row over what time we should put the turkey in the oven. It was a right shit show that year, let me tell you,' said Sid.

'I like the thought of arguing over the turkey, or who pulls crackers with who, and sore losers at afternoon charades. It's everything I've never had,' said Elsie. 'Bring it on.'

Mack clapped his hands together and then immediately started to type out a message on his phone.

'Be prepared to be that sore loser. I'm an expert at charades,' said Sid.

Agata laughed, not knowing what on earth charades was, but made a mental note to Google it at the first opportunity she got.

Chapter Forty-Two

Ingrid

Ingrid added the little bow to the final present, sat back, and sighed. Some people might have said that she was super-organised for her to have finished all of her Christmas shopping with two weeks to spare. Amanda had told her that she was usually up all night on Christmas Eve frantically wrapping all her presents while half drunk on sherry. But for Ingrid, this was actually late.

Normally, she'd wait for the last bang of Bonfire Night fireworks to finish and then immediately get to work on her Christmas list. Within the space of a week, every present had been bought, wrapped and set aside ready for when December came around. She hated rushing, but this year, Ingrid's mind had been everywhere other than where it should have been.

She glanced at the pile in front of her. There were presents for her residents, mainly night clothes, books and magazines. There were courteous boxes of chocolates wrapped for the postman, delivery men and her gardener, a token gesture to say thank you for servicing The Orchids. There was a small pile of presents for her staff which didn't look like much but had actually cost the best part of £300: designer perfumes again. Let it not be said that she wasn't a creature of habit. Then there were the presents she'd bought for Elsie and Agata (perfume again) and Mack (aftershave). And finally, there were Sid's gifts.

His pile was more substantial than the others, and by that, Ingrid meant that he had five gifts to everyone else's measly one. There was a bottle of aftershave (standard), a Lynx deodorant set (Christmas law), a pair of sheep's head slippers (Agata had ranted to her on the phone that he'd been wearing hers), a copy of Shakespeare's, *Romeo and Juliet* (subtle hint), and cat and kitten jigsaw puzzle for a bit of fun.

Okay, so it hadn't cost her a lot of money, and people might question why she'd bought him so many presents, but at least she could say that it was because Sid had done so much work around the home without being paid for it. It was just her way of saying thank you to him. Or at least that's what she kept telling herself.

Ingrid wondered whether he'd think to buy her anything. But then again, this was Sid we were talking about. Not that he wasn't thoughtful in some ways, but try as she might, she just couldn't see him standing in shop windows mulling over what made a decent present. He was more of a 'pick up the first thing you see' kind of guy. Ingrid would probably end up with a festive tea cosey, or a new iron or something like that – that's if he even bothered to buy her anything in the first place.

To be fair, she reasoned, Sid would probably be spending his pension money on presents for his son and his almost daughter-in-law. His pregnant almost daughter-in-law! How amazing that must have been for him. Ingrid wondered how they must feel, knowing that by the following summer, his title would transform to Grandad. There'd be a little baby, full of gurgles and giggles, growing up and not knowing anything of the past. It was like a clean slate for Sid, and it was his opportunity to prove to his son, and himself, that he wasn't just an ex-serviceman or an ex-homeless man. He would simply be Grandad.

Ingrid wasn't being selfish but she prayed that it wouldn't take him away from The Orchids and, ultimately, her. Okay. She was being selfish: A disgustingly selfish, self-centred cow.

She heaved herself up from the floor and shook away the pins and needles that stabbed at her legs after being knelt for too long and placed all of the presents into a large carrier bag, hauling it over to the side of her wardrobe.

She headed downstairs and strolled past Elsie's room, or what would be Elsie's room, the second that Christmas was over. Sid had told her that morning that he'd watched her stumble into a wall, clutching her chest, as she walked to her bedroom the evening before. The crease between his brows silently told

Ingrid just how concerned he was for her, and she made a mental note to herself to once again speak to Elsie and see if she could speed things up and get her to move in a little earlier than she'd planned. The turn of events with the introduction of both Mack and Sid's families, especially with them joining them all for Christmas dinner, had seen Elsie take on more tasks than was healthy for her.

'All done?' asked Amanda as she came out of one of the bedrooms.

'Done,' she replied. 'But there's probably someone that I've forgotten to buy for. There always is.'

'As long as it's not me,' she replied gaily, trotting off to the ground floor with Ingrid following closely behind her.

She found Sid in the dining room, staring at his phone and smiling.

'Another message from Chris?' she asked him even though she already knew the answer.

'He wants to know if I'd like to go over this weekend to meet Tania,' he beamed, and Ingrid felt her own heart warm.

'I'm pleased for you, you know. To get a second chance like that must be such an amazing feeling,' she told him.

'Thank you. I'm pleased too,' Sid paused and averted his gaze from hers. 'Listen. I've been thinking...well, if you're not busy, which I know you are. I was wondering if you'd like to...you know...come with me. To meet Chris and Tania with me. Just for moral support, obviously.'

Would Ingrid like to go with him? She'd bloody love to go with him!

'Oh, Sid,' she replied. 'I don't know. What would Chris say? Would it bother him that you've brought a...' she paused, carefully deciding which word to use, 'friend with you.'

Yes. Friend. That was entirely the right word.

'I'd already told him about you,' he replied.

He's spoken to his son about me!

'He told me that I'm more than welcome to bring you along, seeing as you're my...friend.'

'Then I'd love to join you. Thank you for asking me,' she replied.

'Great,' said Sid.

They stood and stared at each other; an awkward silence loomed between them.

'I'd better get on then,' he said, finally breaking it. 'Adrian's wardrobe door is dropping down on one side, so I said I'd look at it for him.'

Sid grabbed a screwdriver from the side and gently threw it in the air like a cheerleader's baton. It slipped through his fingers and clattered to the floor. He reached down, picked it up and left the room without saying another word.

Ingrid stood smiling as she looked out of the window. All of the little solar lights that lined the garden were starting to flicker into action as dusk drew in, and she stared, mesmerised as they lit one by one, as if on cue.

'Wow. Off to meet the in-laws, are we?' said Amanda from behind her.

Ingrid jumped. 'For fu...will you stop doing that! she fumed.

'I'm just saying. That's not what friends do. Nobody takes their...*friends*,' she made inverted commas with her fingers, 'to meet their son and his wife. It all sounds a little formal to me.'

'Don't be ridiculous. I'm going there to support Sid. Nothing more. Now get on and do some work before I seriously consider wrapping up a P45 for your Christmas present.'

'It'd make a refreshing change from the perfume. Love you,' said Amanda blowing a kiss at Ingrid as she sauntered from the room.

Chapter Forty-Three

Elsie

Elsie made two big ticks on her list with a gold gel pen that she had bought especially for the occasion. She'd always been a big fan of writing lists: lists for shopping, lists for work, lists that numbered the lists in order of importance, and not forgetting her bucket list. But this list, Elsie Bellamy's Living List, was the list of all lists! She got a different sense of satisfaction with ticking off her completed tasks, hence the requirement for a special list-ticking pen.

If she was being entirely truthful, she'd been terrified that day when she had covertly arranged for Mack's family and Sid's son to meet them in the bistro. It could have all gone so terribly wrong and potentially left Elsie with two friends down and one spare bedroom up.

Her trepidation was high during that first half-hour, and she spent the time sitting on the sofa biting her nails and waiting for either Mack or Sid or worse, both of them, to kick in the front door and confront her with a wrathful vengeance.

After an hour, Elsie had stopped biting her nails but kept her eyes fixed on the door, and her ears pricked, listening out for the sound of heavy footsteps thumping their way up the stairs.

Two hours later, and following the return of Agata, both women had sat exchanging what-if scenarios. What if Sid's son rejected him? What if Mack couldn't face seeing his family and turned and ran off somewhere? What if he went off to score drugs? What if Sid got into a fistfight over it all? What if the families had only agreed to come so they could say a proper goodbye and get closure for themselves?

Eight hours and several sweet cups of tea later, Elsie and Agata sat binge-watching episodes of *Married At First Sight*, convinced that given how much time had elapsed, it could only mean that everything was okay.

So, two gorgeous golden ticks down with another two that could technically be ticked were left 'tickless' as Elsie's unspoken rule was that the task had to be completed in full before she would even consider taking the lid off her special pen, but still, they were tantalising close.

Was it enough though? She looked down at the scrap of paper in her hand. Jack had been right. She needed to think big, but even if she did come up with other things to add, did she have enough time left to make sure they happened?

This piece of paper was what kept her going; Elsie was sure of it. It was like a magical talisman, giving her the strength to carry on, easing her pain. Elsie wasn't stupid. She knew that it didn't have mystical powers, but while there were still things left to complete and while her mind was occupied, Elsie wasn't thinking about the cancer. She wasn't thinking about feeling ill, *being* ill, or dying. She wasn't thinking about what she couldn't do or what she'd never get to do. All that filled Elsie's mind was what else she *could* do. It was from a place that served other people rather than herself, and it was this which spurred her on.

She refolded the paper taken out of her pocket so many times that the creases were precariously close to tearing. Perhaps she should tape it to hold it together? She carefully tucked it back into her jeans pocket, the only safe place in the apartment, seeing as she was certain that somebody had been looking through her things. It had probably been Agata. She was perfectly placed, seeing as she shared a room with Elsie, and try as she might, she just couldn't envision Mack or Sid coming into her room and rummaging through her personal effects, or what was left of them.

Mack came into the apartment, holding a bulging bag of groceries in each hand. He whistled as he entered, and he closed the front door with his foot and placed the two shopping bags on the work surface.

'Good morning,' he said cheerily to Elsie.

'Hey,' she replied.

Mack had transformed, metamorphosised into a more beautiful and pure version of his former self, like a squidgy caterpillar into a butterfly.

'What do you have there?' she asked him.

'Lots and lots of food that you're probably not going to eat much of but that I'm going to put in front of you anyway,' he said to her, smiling. 'I thought a nice homemade stew for dinner this evening. It's the perfect meal when the weather is this cold.'

'Good call,' she replied. Elsie preferred it when Mack cooked stews and soups. Liquid-based food were much easier for her to manage. There was a lot to be said for chew-free dinners.

Mack stopped unpacking the bags and joined Elsie in the living room. 'I need to talk to you about Christmas,' he told her. 'While there's nobody else around. I need you to be on board with this before I speak to the others.'

Elsie hoped that he wasn't going to say that he wouldn't be joining them for Christmas dinner after all. Agata's heart might not take it; she'd seen the look in her eyes the other week when Mack was about to potentially spend Christmas elsewhere.

'I think since reconnecting with my family, I'm seeing things in a new perspective,' he continued. 'They've been talking to me, well, my mum has been berating me actually, about me choosing not to work in restaurants, and my dad has been saying the same thing but mainly because Mum would go mad if he went against her.'

Elsie smiled. Yes. The Margaret and Graeme marriage dynamic was one of the most heart-warming yet hilarious things she'd ever seen. She loved it when they came over, which they did – frequently. Not that it mattered to Elsie. She loved them visiting.

'And I suppose I've been listening to what everybody has said about it all. You, Sid and Agata, included. And I think you're right. But I also feel that I was right about what I said about working to help homeless people. And I just don't want to give up on that.'

'So what were you thinking?' asked Elsie.

She was delighted that Mack was reconsidering returning to work as a chef. No, she wasn't delighted. She was fucking ecstatic.

Mack gave a nervous laugh. 'I don't know how you'd feel about this because I know how excited you are about having a proper family Christmas, and I don't know how the others are going to receive this, but if it's a no from you, then I won't even broach it with them.'

'For fuck's sake, Mack. Spit it out,' pleaded Elsie.

He took a deep breath. 'I was thinking that instead of a traditional Christmas dinner with family, why don't we put on a Christmas dinner for the city's homeless? You've no idea how tough it was for me and Sid on that day. The roads would be deserted, and it was eerie being smack bang in the middle of a major city and hardly seeing any cars drive by. And with the shops all closed, it was a silent reminder of how life carried on without you. How just because you didn't have a roof over your head, you were somehow unworthy of celebrating. It was like we didn't matter. Me and Sid used to buy food in advance so that we'd have something to eat on Christmas day. We'd try and make it as Christmassy as possible. Know what I mean? A turkey and stuffing sandwich or something like that. Stupid really. Don't get me wrong, there are charities; church groups and whatnot that would put on a soup kitchen or do the rounds with hot food, but it's not the same. You know what I'm trying to say?'

Elsie nodded. She couldn't possibly imagine what it must have been like. She, like the majority of the population, never gave a thought to the people who didn't have homes or families. People were selfishly too busy on Christmas to think about anybody else. How blinkered had Elsie been all of these years? These were real people with real lives, histories, and problems. These were people who lived in the harshest of conditions and adapted to survive. They were strong and resilient. If only she'd taken time to stop and talk to some more of them on the streets over the years rather than stroll past without giving them a second glance. How many Mack and Sid's could have potentially been in her life right now if she had?

'I think it's an amazing idea,' she told Mack. 'I couldn't think of anything more perfect. If that's what you want to do, Mack, then you have my full support, and I know the others will think the same. We can all chip in and serve the food and drinks...'

'No. Not you,' interrupted Mack. 'Sorry, Elsie, but you won't be lifting a finger that day. You can help organise it, of course. You're good at stuff like that. And on the day, you can mingle if you're up to it, but all of the manual stuff, you'll have to leave to the rest of us.'

She held up her hands, admitting defeat. 'Fine,' she said, realising that it would be pointless to argue. 'I'll organise and mingle – it's right up my street.'

'I'll tell Agata and Sid this evening, but I better call Mum and Dad and see what they make of it all.'

'Do you think they'll be upset?' asked Elsie. 'They might have been looking forward to one big family meal.'

Mack looked at her and smiled softly. 'But I suppose, in a way, they're my family too.'

'Yes,' replied Elsie quietly. 'I suppose they are.'

Chapter Forty-Four

Mack

Mack had been nervous about telling everybody about the drastic alteration to their planned Christmas, but most of his anxiety lay with his parent's reaction. After all, this was to be their first family Christmas in years. It was supposed to be a scene of bliss, like a picture postcard, where, for once, all of them were getting along, laughing, drinking, eating and playing games; a far cry from the days of Christmas past when Mack was either as high as a kite or sneaking out of the back door to score off his local dealer who, it seemed, was still very much open for business that day.

When Mack had texted his brother, his response was a thumbs-up emoji with the words, *'I'd look like a right dick if I said no to that. Count me in.'* But Marcus followed up with a second text, advising him that it would probably be best if Mack spoke to their parents in person about it.

Mack wasn't sure whether Marcus was suggesting that because the personal touch was just the better approach when it came to their Mum and Dad or whether it was because they were both god awful when it came to mobile phones. Mack's mum had recently accidentally pocket-dialled him, and he'd listened to the briefest of conversations between her and her friend, Betty, about the perils of vaginal dryness; Mack was still recovering from the trauma.

He'd gone to visit them in their new house, a house he didn't recognise from the outside but which felt like stepping back in time when he walked inside. Pictures were hung on the walls in exactly the same rooms and in exactly the same place as in their old house. The curtains were the same, and they'd even kept the same green velvet sofa, which his mother insisted on having professionally cleaned once a year even though the arms were now almost threadbare. The carefully placed doilies draped over them were fooling no one.

"But I've already bought the turkey,' his mum had said after Mack sat them down and explained what he wanted to do.

'You can cook it the next day,' suggested Mack. 'Have boxing day turkey sandwiches or the turkey curry that you always used to do.'

His dad rolled his eyes at his wife. 'I thought you'd love not cooking on Christmas day? You always moan that it's left to you. Think of it as having a day off.'

Mack coughed. 'I wouldn't say it was a day off exactly. I'm going to need everybody's help with this.'

'Doing what?' asked his dad.

'Plating up food, serving, making sure everyone has a drink, clearing dirty plates away,' replied Mack.

'You want *me* to be a waiter?' replied his dad, his eyes wide with surprise. 'But it's Christmas.'

Suddenly, the thought of her husband doing more than sitting on his arse and watching re-runs of Christmas specials seemed to placate Margaret, and she sat up straight in the chair, leaned over and tapped Mack's knee.

'I think that it's a wonderful idea, Mackenzie. Of course, we'll be there to help out. You can count on us. Can't he, Graeme?'

She shot him an icy glare, and Graeme gave a solemn nod. 'Yes, son.'

'You'll all get to eat too. After we've fed everyone, we can sit down together and have our dinner then.'

Graeme grunted in response. 'Aye. Whatever you think's best.'

'Now,' said Margaret, focusing back on Mack. 'I've only got a box of eight crackers. But I can pop out and get some more?' she offered, but Mack shook his head.

'No need, Mum. We'll sort all that out.'

'Are you sure? They're the good ones,' she added. 'They've got silver egg cups and bookmarks in them.'

'Honestly. It's fine,' he assured her. 'Keep them for another year.'

She leaned back in the armchair and fiddled with the doily. 'I might open the top and take them out instead. You can never have too many bookmarks,' she said, looking thoughtful.

***

Sid and Agata had taken the news surprisingly well when he'd spoken to them. Sid's face beamed with pride, and he hugged Mack, holding him tightly to his chest and gave him manly pats on his back.

'I couldn't think of anything more perfect,' he whispered in his ear.

Sid was his comrade, and having lived on the streets longer than Mack, he knew only too well just how bleak Christmas day could be when you were holed up in the corner of a car park or a shop doorway. Although still cantankerous and a generally arsey fucker when he wanted to be, Sid had mellowed over these past few months. Not only because of Ingrid. His love for her was a by-product of being given the chance to blossom into a better version of himself. He'd missed out on so many opportunities over the years to be a man of value after leaving the army. To be a man who could express love and be loved in return, and now that he'd been given the chance,

Sid had grabbed it with both hands and not only embraced it but submersed himself within it. Sid had walked into Elsie's apartment that first evening as a shadow; a silhouette, black inside, with a hard, impenetrable border. Meeting Elsie had allowed him to erase those lines and colour himself to be whatever shade and brightness he wanted. It was amazing to witness the effect that one person could have on another person's life. They still spoke about their former lives when they were alone at night in the confines of their bedroom. Reminiscing about the people they used to be, the people they became on the streets, and the men they had become now.

'If a man who needs help is given that help and then chooses not to pay it forward to other people in need, then he's no man at all,' Sid had told him one night when they were both feeling particularly sentimental.

The words had imprinted themselves into Mack's psyche like a tattoo.

Agata had taken the news in an altogether non-philosophical manner.

'If that is what you want. Then I am happy also,' she'd simply told him.

She reached out and hugged him, but it was brief and tinged with hesitation. Mack didn't think that she'd totally forgiven him for the way that he'd spoken to her, but it was a start. She'd started to smile at him again when he walked into a room and had also resurrected saying good morning, so at least they were heading in the right direction. But Mack realised he needed to pull something major out of the bag to get it back to the way it was before. A declaration of love, perhaps? Of course not. Mack wasn't an idiot. Agata didn't look at him in that way, and he wasn't going to humiliate himself by putting his heart on the line only to be told that she saw him as a friend or, worse, a brother. There'd be no coming back from that. At least if Mack kept it all to himself, he could love Agata from afar, which was a damn sight better than just being afar, which is what would happen if he ever told Agata how he truly felt about her.

'I can cook with you,' she offered. 'I am a good cook.'

Was she? Mack didn't know. He'd never given anybody the chance to cook dinner in the apartment. Did that make him look conceited? Selfish? Maybe tomorrow, he should let Agata take charge. Is that what she was secretly asking? Fucking hell, Mack. Get a grip and stop overthinking everything!

'I'd like to see you in the kitchen for once,' said Mack, and then realising that it probably sounded a little passive-aggressive, he added. 'I'd love someone to cook for me for a change.'

Nope, that still sounded like he was having a dig.

Agata's mouth twitched at the corners, and he wasn't sure whether it was a twitch of amusement or utter contempt. It was just...twitchy. Giving nothing away. Best just to walk away now, Mack, he told himself, and he brandished a wide smile at Agata, which no doubt made him look a little demented, and without saying another word he turned and went into the kitchen.

He heard the click of Agata's shoes going into the corridor and down towards her bedroom.

'Are you on drugs again?' asked Sid. 'You sounded like a right twat just then.'

Mack tutted. 'Don't Sid. Just don't.'

Chapter Forty-Five

Agata

Mack hated her. That was much obvious. Well, maybe hate was a little too strong a word, but he definitely thought that Agata was an idiot.

Just then, in the kitchen, he'd insinuated that Agata was lying when she said that she was a good cook, and just when she thought it couldn't get any worse, he'd made out that she never did anything to help in the kitchen. Was Mack saying that Agata was lazy?

She thought back to all the times that he'd cooked them dinner. Agata thought he liked doing all the chefy stuff? That was the impression that he'd always given them. Mack did all the cooking, and she and Sid would do the cleaning afterwards. That was what they'd always done. But now it materialises that Mack wasn't happy at all about it. Should she have intervened?

Or at least offered her help? Why didn't Mack say anything about it if it bothered him so much?

'Fucking men,' she muttered under her breath as she kicked off her shoes.

She needed to lie down for a moment. Her feet throbbed after all that walking today, and wearing those shoes hadn't helped. They were bright red, three-inch heels that formed into a severely pointed triangular tip at the front. Technically, it had been Elsie's fault she was wearing them, as it had been she who'd told Agata that wearing statement shoes meant that you were always remembered in job interviews: 'Who was that amazingly clever woman who outshone everybody else today? You know, the one who wore those beautiful red shoes.' 'Oh, her! That was Agata Rutkowski.' 'That's the one. Phone her up and offer her the job immediately. She's just what we're looking for.'

Yeah. They'd remember her alright, especially when they thought back to her nearly breaking her ankle when one of her heels got stuck in a carpet grip. Agata had careered straight into a woman returning to her desk with a steaming cup of coffee she'd just made for herself.

No more squeezing her pudgy feet into tiny little shoes from now on, no matter how gorgeous they were. She'd wear trainers the next time. Agata doubted it would make a difference either way. She was never going to be offered a job by anybody the way things were looking for her.

She sighed and rubbed her feet against each other, hoping that it would somehow ease the toes out of the triangle shape that they'd moulded themselves into.

She was due to pick Elsie up from the park in an hour. Actually, it'd been Sid's turn to pick her up, but Agata had offered to do it for him because she knew that he wanted to go shopping for a new shirt. Not so lazy now, Mack, thank you very much!

God. He could be such a dickhead to her at times. Why did she even entertain liking him, seeing as he thought so little of her? Thinking about it, it was like being in an abusive relationship, where one person always goes back for more...minus the relationship part, of course.

It was becoming clear to her that there was nothing between her and Mack. He couldn't stand Agata, and at that precise moment, she couldn't stand him either. If Mackenzie Stewart walked naked into her room right now and begged for Agata's body, she wouldn't give him, or his penis, a second glance. Well, maybe she'd take a peek at his penis. What woman wouldn't?

'I'd like to see you in the kitchen for once,' she said, mimicking his voice.

That was it! Agata was seriously pissed off now. She jumped up and slid her aching feet into a pair of trainers. She'd meet Elsie earlier than planned; she wouldn't text her to let her know. Agata would just turn up and see if she could catch sight of Jack. Yes, he may have told Elsie that he would join them all for

Christmas, but Agata still had her suspicions and was doubtful that Jack would make an appearance.

If just one of them could see what he looked like, then at least, if he was planning to swindle Elsie out of a tonne of money, it would go a long way to providing the police with a description of what he looked like.

Afterwards, she could drive to the supermarket and get some ingredients for dinner. She'd show Mack precisely what she was capable of. Maybe she'd cook them kotlet schabowy? That had always been her favourite Polish dish to cook. With any luck, Mack – the super-duper superior chef, hadn't heard of it.

***

This is ridiculous. Agata thought to herself. Actually, it wasn't ridiculous. It was an utter disgrace.

Agata was wrapped up in a heavy woollen coat, a jumper, vest, jeans, thick socks, a long scarf wrapped around her neck four times, gloves and a hat, and still she was bitterly cold.

What sort of person insisted that somebody like Elsie, who was ill, meet them in these types of conditions?

Agata parked the car and hurried into the park with her hands plunged deep inside her coat pockets and her face half-hidden in her scarf. There were, unsurprisingly, few people there today, which would make it even more difficult for her to go unnoticed.

As she walked, she diverted from the path onto the grass and proceeded towards where she knew Elsie and Jack sat. Hopefully, they wouldn't see her approaching if she kept close to the trees.

A woman walking a beagle gave Agata a suspicious look, and Agata tutted at her in response. The beagle stuck its head in the air and started to howl, and Agata cringed.

'Can you control your dog, please,' she told the woman.

'He only howls like that when he senses danger,' the woman responded in a flat, unamused tone.

'I'm just walking. How is that a danger to anybody?'

'That all depends on where you're walking to and what you intend to do when you get there,' replied the woman.

'I'm walking to where my business is and where yours isn't,' replied Agata. 'Now, kindly go about your day, and I'll go about mine.'

The woman looked Agata up and down and sniffed through her bulbous nose, red from the cold, and stomped off in the opposite direction.

Agata crouched down, although she wasn't sure why. If Elsie did turn around, then there was no bush or tree for her to hide behind, so she may as well have just remained upright, but for some reason, for the purpose of snooping at least, it felt right to be slightly hunched when spying on somebody.

She continued to head towards the infamous bench, expertly avoiding as many twigs as she could. The bench came into view, but from Agata's angle, she could only make out Elsie. She continued taking tentative steps forward, closer and closer, until the whole bench became visible.

Agata's eyes opened with surprise. She stopped walking and stood up straight.

A hand landed heavily on her shoulder, and Agata jumped.

'Excuse me, Miss. This lady has some concerns about your behaviour,' came a man's deep voice behind her.

Agata turned and saw a man in a fluorescent yellow jacket, flanked by the red-nosed dog owner, with her annoying beagle by her side. She folded her arms across her chest and gave a smug smile to Agata, who, in response, stuck her middle finger up to the woman.

'You are a busybody,' whispered Agata to the woman, and then turning to the man, she said. 'I'm here on a special mission. That lady over there is my friend. I am simply checking that she is okay.'

'Sounds like she's some type of pervert if you ask me,' the woman told the man. 'I told you something wasn't right about her.'

'Hey! I'm not a pervert,' said Agata in horror. 'Why don't you, and that silly nose of yours, fuck off and mind your own business.'

'Listen to that aggression. She's trouble. You'd better watch out for that one,' the woman said, almost goading the man.

'You better come with me, Miss,' said the man, gently pulling on Agata's arm. 'We don't want to have to call the police now, do we?'

'Will you be quiet, or my friend will hear,' she pleaded quietly.

'Your friend indeed! I bet she doesn't even know you're here,' the woman continued.

'Oh, will you just...fuck off!' Agata shouted, shrugging the man's hand away from her arm.

The dog started to howl.

Agata wanted to kick it but decided against it. She was probably going to be arrested for something, although she had no idea what for. Making a public nuisance seemed to fit the bill, but she didn't want to add animal cruelty to the charge sheet.

She looked back at the bench and was greeted by Elsie's thunderous face.

'Fuck,' Agata said quietly. 'Look what you've gone and done now.'

Chapter Forty-Six

Ingrid

Sid had picked Ingrid up at precisely 6 p.m. on the dot. Actually, to be factually correct, he'd come to the front door at precisely 6 p.m. on the dot but had, in fact, arrived fifteen minutes earlier but had remained seated in the car until their pre-arranged time had come around.

Ingrid had been nervously peeking through the front window for a while, waiting for Sid to arrive so she knew how long he'd been out there. His delay, albeit because he was keeping to his impeccable timekeeping, had only served to heighten her nerves, and those last few minutes ticked perilously slowly along.

Finally, with a minute to go, Ingrid heard the slam of a car door, and she held her breath until the shrill of the bell rang out in the hallway. Even so, Ingrid took the time to make Sid wait a second or two longer. She checked her reflection in the mirror, straightened her hair with her fingers even though there was absolutely nothing wrong with it, and repositioned her necklace in the centre of her chest. Well, it wouldn't do to look too eager now, would it?

When Ingrid finally opened the front door, she found Sid standing in front of her with a bunch of flowers in his hand. He said nothing as he thrust them forward, practically throwing them at her; he seriously needed to work on his dating skills.

'Thank you,' she said, touched that Sid had even bothered to think of such a thing.

She looked him up and down and took in his shiny brogues, denim jeans, and, if Ingrid wasn't mistaken, a new checked shirt that still had creases embedded from where it had been folded in its packaging.

'You look very smart,' she told him.

'Thanks,' he replied.

She waited for him to return the compliment. He didn't.

'I'd better go and put these in some water, and then we can get going,' she said.

Ingrid turned and walked towards the staff room, and she heard Sid follow her inside and close the door. She waited for him to say something – anything, but Sid remained uncharacteristically silent. She prayed that it wasn't going to be like this all night.

She took out a vase from the cupboard, filled it with cold water, and removed the flowers from their packaging: purple freesias and crisp white roses. They were beautiful. She ruffled them into place in the vase and then placed it on the table.

'There,' she said, smiling. 'They're gorgeous. I'll take them up to my room when I get home.'

She glanced back at Sid and found him staring back at her. Ingrid's smile faded.

'Are you alright?' she asked him.

Sid strode over to her and pulled Ingrid's body to his. Oh, my lord! This was it. This was really happening. His head tilted towards hers, and he planted his soft lips on hers. His kiss was warm and gentle and everything that Ingrid had dreamed it would be. She kissed him back and shivered as his hands lowered down her back.

'Sorry to disturb you,' she heard Amanda say.

They jumped away from each other. Amanda was standing in the doorway with a sheepish look and holding a yellow bag of clinical waste.

'Mrs Foster had another accident,' continued Amanda.

Sid and Ingrid's moment was over.

***

The evening at Chris and Tania's house had been more than Ingrid could have ever wished for.

Chris had cooked that night as Tania, as Chris had informed them, couldn't boil an egg. However, later that evening, Tania leaned over to Ingrid and whispered that she'd actually attended catering college after leaving high school and was quite a good cook.

'Start as you mean to go on,' she'd told Ingrid with a cheeky wink.

Chris had cooked a beef Wellington with mushroom stuffing, dauphinoise potatoes, and spinach for the main, entirely from scratch as it transpired, and which had taken him the best part of the day to do. For pudding, they'd had apple crumble with custard – Aunt Bessie's, because Chris said that after the Wellington, he couldn't be bothered to cook anything else.

They chatted about what they did: Chris worked in IT but didn't go into further details, and Tania was a self-employed lash artist, although Ingrid wondered whether 'artist' was an appropriate use of the word when it came to gluing fake eyelashes onto a person's lash line. Still, she was a nice girl, and she also let Ingrid rub her pregnant stomach, even though being at such an early stage, no bump was yet visible.

They asked about Ingrid's business and how The Orchids came to be in existence, and Ingrid explained everything about Phillips's illness and the difficulty in finding a facility that could provide the level of care that he needed outside of a hospital environment.

'Very admirable,' said Chris. 'That must be an amazing thing to do for other people, but tough too, I expect, watching people pass away. How did you find the strength to do that after losing your husband? Mum and Dad could barely function after Katie passed away.'

'I'm sorry, who?' said Ingrid.

Chris's eyes darted over to Sid and then back to Ingrid. 'Sorry. I thought Dad would have told you.'

Ingrid looked at Sid. He was looking down at his empty plate.

'It's not that I didn't want to tell you, and I would have eventually. It's just a difficult thing to talk about, not the type of thing that tends to crop in conversations easily. You know what I mean?'

'Yes, of course,' agreed Ingrid.

'Katie was my daughter. She was nine years old when she died,' said Sid.

Ingrid gasped, and her hand flew to her mouth. 'Oh Sid. I'm so sorry.'

'It was leukaemia. I was in the army then, away on duty. It all happened so quickly. I remember going back to the barracks after my leave had ended, and I waved Chris and Katie off. I remember her crying, holding onto me tightly, and begging me to stay. Well, kids do that, don't they? They don't want their parents to go anywhere away from them. And I told her not to be silly and that I'd be back soon, and I left. I left my little girl sobbing in the road as I got into a car and drove away, just like that. And then, one day, I phoned home, and Patricia told me that Katie had started to get all these bruises over her body. We both thought that she was being bullied at school; you would think that wouldn't you? You wouldn't think it'd be anything else. And then, Katie was tired all of the time. And so Patricia took her to the doctors, who took her blood and ran all kinds of tests. And then the results came back and she had to go for more tests at the hospital. And it came back that she...'

Sid's voice broke, and Ingrid wrapped her arms around him. 'You don't have to talk about it, Sid. Not if you don't want to.'

'Thank you,' he mumbled as he gently squeezed her arm. 'It's not that I don't want to. But there never seemed to be the right time. And tonight –' he coughed and wiped away a tear from his cheek. 'Tonight is about being together again. It's about happiness and new life,' he gestured towards Tania's stomach. 'So, no sadness tonight, eh?'

Ingrid nodded and held back her own tears. 'Not tonight,' she repeated.

***

Sid pulled up outside The Orchids and switched off the engine.

'Thank you for a lovely evening,' said Ingrid.

'Thank you for coming,' he replied. 'I hope that it wasn't too...overwhelming.'

'Not at all,' she replied. 'Chris seems lovely – very welcoming. And Tania, well, what a funny one she is; smart, kind and generous. Chris is a lucky man.'

'Yeah, but – a lash artist? What's that all about?' joked Sid. 'It's not like you'd see her work hanging in the V & A or anything. Wrong word, artist.'

Ingrid chuckled. 'I thought the same.'

They were silent for a moment. Ingrid reached down for her handbag from the footwell and began to rummage inside for her house keys. She suddenly stopped and turned to Sid.

'You could have told me. About Katie,' she told him.

Sid sighed. 'I know. I know that I could have spoken to you, but some things are just too difficult to talk about. Some things I can't go back to. All I see when I think of my beautiful girl is the last time that I saw her, crying, running after the car as I drove away from her. The guilt inside is like a punch to the guts when I think about her. I left her. I wasn't there for her when she was sick. Not until the end, anyway. The army gave me compassionate leave. I walked into the hospital and saw a little girl that I didn't recognise lying in that bed. It wasn't my daughter. It wasn't Katie. It couldn't have been. She was so thin and pale, and all of her hair,' he touched his head, his eyes staring out in a trance. 'It was all gone.'

'Is that why you left?' asked Ingrid.

'You have no idea what it was like,' said Sid. 'A few weeks after the funeral, and I'm back with the army. Back at the barracks, making out that everything was okay. Training. Shooting. Sleeping. Yes, Sir. No, Sir. More training. I was functioning on autopilot. Doing what I was told so I didn't have to think for myself. And then I left, eventually, many years later. And I went home to a house that didn't feel like mine. To a son, I didn't recognise. And to a wife who despised me. She blamed me for what happened to Katie. She didn't have to. I blamed me too.'

'You're being unfair on yourself. There's nothing you could have done,' said Ingrid.

'I could have been there. I could have supported Patricia. I could have helped look after Katie. I should have been there reading bedtime stories every night to Katie, not hiding behind a uniform as though that had a greater importance, a greater meaning, than my own child. No. Patricia was right to feel the way that she did.'

'And then all of this with Elsie. It must be a painful reminder for you?' she said.

Sid gave a slow nod, still avoiding her gaze. 'Painful, yes. But strangely, it's my chance to put things right. To do for Elsie what I didn't do for Katie. It's a chance to prove to myself that I'm not a selfish bastard who was too scared to face how it might affect him. Too scared to know how it might feel to watch somebody you care about, somebody you love, slip away from this world.'

Suddenly, Sid made complete sense. The rude, brusque man. The man who had always managed to come across as uncaring or thoughtless when he spoke, and yet he came around to

The Orchids every day and sat with residents and talked, and laughed, and played silly games with them. He sacrificed his time and donated it to them, all in the name of redemption.

'I think you're done proving yourself,' she told him. 'You don't have to do it anymore.'

He turned to her now. 'No. I'll never be done. Not while there's a single breath left in my body.'

Ingrid took his hand. She should have told him that he was wrong and that Katie wouldn't have wanted him to blame himself for an illness nobody could have stopped. She should have told him he'd long since stepped out from behind the shadow of the man he once was. But she didn't. She knew that Sid wouldn't have believed her even if she had. This was something that he had to do. He had to be this man. He'd been given a second chance at not just life but living. His life had a purpose, and Ingrid would be damned if she was going to try and persuade him otherwise.

She squeezed his hand. 'Don't go home tonight,' she told him instead.

Chapter Forty-Seven

Elsie

It was Christmas Eve, and the run-up to the big day had been a hectic one. Elsie's list-creating capabilities had once more been called into action, and it had felt good to be busy making calls and speaking to suppliers and catering companies. She was useful once again and not the decrepit burden that she had become, and who recently had to rely on support to walk up and down the stairs or Agata's help to get undressed and into bed.

Granted, all she was doing was making phone calls, so it wasn't the most energetic of tasks, but it gave Elsie a sense of satisfaction being more than just the woman who lived in her pyjamas every day.

For her part, she'd ordered the food, organised the loan of tableware, cutlery and glasses, hired a small kitchen team to work under Mack, and bulk-bought socks, gloves, scarfs, hats, and other essential items to make small parcels for each guest to take away at the end of the evening.

Agata had been responsible for designing and organising the leaflets which housed the details of their Christmas dinner event: A pretty little notice with a Christmas tree and snow for decoration, both of which she'd illegally downloaded to use, but hey, it was Christmas! So, it was completely acceptable, in Elsie's opinion.

Mack and Sid had done the rounds, visiting old haunts, handing out the leaflets to the city's street sleepers and liaising with charity organisations, soup kitchens and church groups so that they could also pass on the message.

They'd become a band of Christmas warriors, determined to bring happiness, if only for one day.

Elsie had also arranged for a team of waiters and waitresses to work alongside Mack's parents, his brother Marcus, and Sid's son Chris. Marcus's wife, Leona, and Chris's girlfriend, Tania, were both exempt from duty owing to the growing babies in their bellies. As was Elsie, for obvious reasons, and Jack, for less obvious reasons other than it being at the insistence of Mack, Sid, and Agata, who Elsie secretly believed doubted that Jack would show. Ye of little faith, Elsie thought to herself. She'd pressed Jack several times on the matter, and each time, he'd promised faithfully that he'd be there Christmas day, come rain or shine, and the conviction in his eyes had convinced her that he was telling the truth.

That just left Agata, who, at her insistence, was to be in the kitchen helping Mack as his unofficial sous chef, but to be fair to her, she had cooked a rather marvellous Polish dish the other week.

Elsie had only just forgiven Agata for her spying on her and Jack in the park. Thank god for that howling dog. Otherwise, Elsie wouldn't have known she'd been lurking. She'd been so engrossed in her conversation with Jack that she hadn't noticed her there.

It was a little embarrassing for Elsie, trying to convince the park worker that Agata wasn't a sexual deviant, just a nosey cow who couldn't mind her own business. But at least Agata had finally seen Jack, and she could tell the others that he was indeed a living, breathing person, and her brain hadn't turned to slush just yet.

Ingrid, and rightly so, would be spending Christmas with her residents, and so they'd all arranged to go to The Orchids on Boxing Day instead. Elsie had asked Jack to join them, as a matter of courtesy, really. She hadn't expected him to agree, but Jack had beamed back and said that he'd be there too. All that Christmas spirit had finally gotten through to him!

Elsie glanced at the clock. It was just coming up to 8 p.m., and Agata, Mack and Sid, who were down at the bistro setting up the tables, would soon be back. She heaved herself out of the chair and shuffled over to the kitchen, gripping every available surface to steady herself.

The pain was constant now. Her bones ached as if they were set to splinter at any second. She'd developed a bark-like cough, and every time she inhaled, there was a bubbly sound inside her lungs. Her head throbbed most of the day, and no amount of painkillers seemed to ease her agony.

Elsie turned on the tap and filled a glass with water. She reached for her pills and popped four of the painkillers out onto the side; it was more than she should have taken, but she knew that two wouldn't touch the sides anymore. In many respects, she was looking forward to moving into Ingrid's just for the stronger stuff. Bring on the morphine, Elsie joked to herself, even though she knew that it was the beginning of the end the second that it was administered.

She dropped the now-empty pill packet into the bin and shuffled back to the sofa. Water sploshed out the side of the glass, spilling on the floor, and she wiped it away with the sole of her slipper. Lowering herself back down, more water spilt over the top of the glass and onto her lap. Christ. She couldn't even carry a glass of water without making a mess.

The front door opened, and her three roommates walked back inside.

'Done and done,' declared Mack, running a hand through his hair. He looked exhausted. But in a good way, Elsie decided.

'Have you been okay on your own?' asked Agata, and Elsie nodded back at her.

'As you can see, I'm still in one piece,' she replied.

Sid's eyes drifted down to the wet patch in her lap. 'Had a little accident, have we?' he joked, and Elsie narrowed her eyes at him and stuck out her tongue.

'It's water,' she said, holding up the glass. 'I'm not quite that bad just yet.'

'Right. It's Christmas Eve, so I'm excused from cooking duties tonight,' declared Mack.

'I didn't agree to that,' said Sid.

'Shut up. It's an unwritten rule at Christmas,' retorted Mack. He delved into one of the kitchen drawers and pulled out a takeaway menu. 'Who fancies a Chinese takeaway tonight?'

They all murmured their agreement, but Elsie couldn't stomach the thought of eating anything. Maybe she'd get away with some egg-fried rice and a sweet-and-sour chicken ball?

Mack phoned through the order and then joined Elsie on the sofa.

'Are you sure you're going to be alright with tomorrow?' he asked her. 'It's going to be a long day, and you're looking a little peaky.'

Peaky? She looked like death warmed up. Elsie didn't need a mirror to know that.

'I'll be fine. I'll be sitting down for most of it, so don't worry about me. Just do what you have to do. Besides, it'll be fun seeing how it all pans out, and,' she added, 'I'll have Jack to keep me company.'

Elsie saw the exchange of unconvinced glances but chose to ignore them.

'It'll be a Christmas to remember. That's for certain,' said Sid.

And Elsie nodded. It would indeed, and that was all that mattered.

***

Agata had woken everybody up on Christmas morning with all the excitement of a Labrador puppy. Elsie had smiled through her pain, not wanting to ruin the moment for her, but the second Agata had left the room and bounded into Sid and Mack's bedroom, she reached for her pills.

Half an hour later, they were all gathered in the living room, exchanging presents. Of all the moments of the day that Elsie had been looking forward to, it had been this.

The central heating was on full blast, and the Christmas lights blinked away merrily as they sat there, coffees and teas in hand, as they took turns to delve under the tree and hand out the presents they'd bought for each other.

Sid received a pair of new brown trousers, a white shirt with light blue stripes and a pair of Christmas socks from Mack. A hot air balloon experience day for two from Agata (although none of them really knew why, as Sid had never expressed an interest in floating hundreds of feet in the air in a little basket) and a Kindle reader from Elsie.

Mack had three Jamie Oliver cookbooks from Sid, a voucher for dinner for two at Gordon Ramsey's, The Savoy Grill in London from Agata (Elsie didn't need a degree to figure out that Agata was hoping Mack would choose her as his plus one), and a set of professional kitchen knives from Elsie.

Agata had opened a bright pink pair of flamingo slippers with matching flamingo pyjamas from Sid, a silver heart pendant from Mack, which, judging from Agata's flushed and somewhat gushy reaction, had been more than she'd been expecting from him, and a laptop from Elsie.

Then, it was Elsie's turn. She looked down at the small pile of neatly wrapped presents in her lap. This was her first proper Christmas. Her first Christmas when she'd felt truly loved and the presents that had been bought for her had come from a place of genuine tenderness rather than duty. It was the first Christmas that excited her when she saw a Christmas advert or heard the Christmas songs playing on the radio stations. It was the first time she'd enjoyed saying Merry Christmas to strangers on the street and listening to the carollers as they sang harmonised Christmas songs in the square. It was a Christmas of firsts for Elsie, and it was the realisation that it would also be her last that stung the most.

She slowly unwrapped the first gift, savouring the moment. It was from Mack—a Polaroid camera with two packets of film.

'To capture all of your memories from today,' he'd told Elsie as she stared at the box.

From Agata, Elsie received a charm bracelet. On it dangled three charms: A Christmas tree, a heart and a little house. Their meanings didn't need explaining to Elsie, and she took it out of the box and attached it around her thin wrist.

Sid's present was a copy of Charles Dickens's *A Christmas Carol*. She'd read it once, back in high school and hadn't paid much attention at the time, but now. Now, it felt as though Dickens had written it personally for her.

'Not saying you were a Scrooge or anything, but, you know...' said Sid in true Sid fashion.

They were gifts from their hearts, and they seeped straight into Elsie's.

If only things weren't like this, she thought to herself.

If only things could be different.

Chapter Forty-Eight

Elsie

The bistro was heaving. Busier than it had ever been before. Elsie could well imagine Julian's shocked face at the sight of every table and chair being occupied by the type of people who, when it had been his business, he'd never let past the threshold. She might take a picture on her phone and send it over to him just to piss him off.

So far, they'd served over seventy homeless people in two separate sittings. An orderly queue had formed outside the front door as men and women patiently waited their turn. There was even a local news crew outside interviewing people, and a burst of impromptu carol singing pierced the cold Christmas afternoon, although Elsie assumed it was just for the benefit of the onlooking cameras.

She'd been placed on a table in the corner with Leona and Tania, close to the toilets, making it easier for them to navigate their way should the need arise. An empty chair sat opposite Elsie, taunting her. So far, Jack had failed to make an appearance. Nobody had made reference to it, but she'd spotted Agata, Sid, and Mack periodically peer over to check if he'd turned up throughout the day.

Her pain was now at intense levels. Elsie had munched her way through all of the painkillers that she'd brought with her, and with everybody so busy, she didn't feel she could ask any of them to go back up to the apartment for her. She rubbed at her swollen stomach, a sign of her failing liver, if the yellow skin wasn't obvious enough. She'd had it drained just the other week and was surprised when it swelled again just a few days later.

Leona made a joke, something about Marcus, although Elsie wasn't listening. Tania broke into a fit of giggles, and Elsie, feeling that she ought to, joined in. Pain ripped through her body as though she was being torn in two. She gasped, but it was lost amongst the other women's laughter and the loud conversations around them. She took slow, shallow breaths and waited for it to subside.

Where are you, Jack? She thought silently to herself. He knew how important today was for her. Surely, he wouldn't let her down? He wouldn't leave her looking foolish. Not today.

Elsie had run out of excuses to make for him. He wasn't ill or lying dead wherever it was he called home. He wasn't stuck in traffic or had lost his way. Jack was either going to come, or he wasn't, and if that chair at the table remained empty for the rest of the day, then as far as Elsie was concerned, she was done with the man. There'd be no second chances. No forgiveness.

She thought back to all the times she endured sitting in the park. All the times she'd battled the grim weather, sitting there on the bench as the unforgiving rain pelted down on them. Not once had he ever come to her. It was as though she was there for his convenience, not hers.

He'd promised her that he'd be there today—a promise which she'd believed, which she still believed. Jack had to come today. He just had to.

Waiters and waitresses bustled around the tables, clearing away the empty plates, resetting the tables, and refilling empty glasses with water.

Mack's Dad, Graeme, sweating under his ill-thought-out reindeer hat, ushered another four people to a recently vacant table next to Elsie's. A group of four men sat down, took off their coats, and draped them over the backs of their chairs. A letter fell out of one of the men's pockets, and Elsie instinctively bent down to retrieve it for him. Immediately, she regretted it as the pressure in her chest tightened. She winced, stopping halfway down.

The man, seeing her discomfort, eased her back up into an upright position.

'I can get that. Don't you worry yourself,' he told her, kneeling to pick it up and placing it on Elsie's table. 'Are you alright?'

Elsie could have lied. Perhaps she should have? After all, it was Christmas.

'I've been better,' she told him.

Not a lie. But not the harsh truth. The perfect answer.

'I can see that,' he replied.

He looked Elsie up and down and stared. His eyes were a dazzling blue. The type of blue you would see on a bright, crisp morning in springtime. He held her gaze. It was as though he was staring into her soul, and the world around Elsie seemed to slow. The man pulled out Jack's chair and sat down.

'Gabe,' he said, offering his hand out to her.

Elsie took his hand and felt a flash of warmth run through her fingertips.

'Elsie,' she replied.

'Ah, the famous Elsie! I hear that you're the one who's responsible for all of this,' said Gabe, gesturing around the packed restaurant.

'Not me. You have that man to thank in there for this,' she pointed over to the kitchen where Mack was angrily shouting at somebody about overcooked sprouts. 'It was all his idea.'

'Maybe it was his idea, but you made it happen. A man with an idea is only as good as his execution,' said Gabe.

'So I'm an executioner?' joked Elsie.

'Yes. But not in a chop-your-head-off kind of way. So, it's all good.' said Gabe. 'You must be feeling very proud of yourself to have achieved all of this?'

'I'm feeling very proud of my friends. *They* did all this. The only thing that I'm feeling is tired,' she said.

'Because you're ill?' said Gabe.

'Because I'm ill.'

'Can I ask what's wrong with you?'

'No. It's Christmas. Not the right time for sad news,' she told him.

'So sad news means bad news, I take it?'

'What do you think? I weigh about seven stone, and I have the skin colour of the inside of a mango. It doesn't take Columbo to work out that it's bad news.'

'At least it hasn't affected your humour. I'll say that for you,' said Gabe, flashing a smile.

She smiled back at him. 'My humour is the only part of me that still works.'

'I'd say that mouth of yours is still doing a pretty good job,' retorted Gabe.

'Shouldn't you be eating Christmas dinner with your friends?' she asked.

'They won't miss me. And besides, aren't we friends? You invited me here. I've got the leaflet to prove it.'

'But that seat's taken,' said Elsie.

'Then I can move when they get here.'

'Are you always so pushy?'

'Are you always so rude to people on Christmas day? I'm homeless. You're supposed to be nice to me.'

Elsie saw Margaret hurrying to the table. 'I just thought I'd check that everything's alright over here while I get a chance. It's chaos here. Chaos. Graeme is on the verge of fainting, but he won't take off that ridiculous hat. There's a sprout catastrophe in the kitchen, but I suppose Christmas without sprouts would be a catastrophe, wouldn't it? And Marcus accidentally jabbed his finger with a knife and is bleeding all over the carrots. They've all had to be chucked in the bin, of course. Such a waste.'

'You're doing a wonderful job, Margaret,' said Elsie. 'Don't panic. Everything is going wonderfully. Everybody seems to love the Christmas crackers you bought.'

Margaret glanced around the restaurant and smiled at the discarded silver trinkets adorning the tables. 'Mack told me not to, but I couldn't help myself. They're the premium crackers, you know. Not the cheap ones that only have the paper hats and a sticker inside.'

'You can never have too many bookmarks,' Elsie told her, remembering what Mack had told her his mother had said when he'd relayed the story to her.

'My thoughts exactly! Must dash. People to seat, and tables to clear,' said Margaret and she dashed away to the doorway where a very flustered Graeme was dabbing his head with a handkerchief.

'She seems nice,' said Gabe.

'She is. I wish I'd had a mother like her.'

'As opposed to?'

'A mother who was most definitely *not* like her,' Elsie said sardonically.

'No two people are the same,' said Gabe.

'Thank fuck for that. I wouldn't wish for two of my mother in this world.'

'Why's that?'

'None of your business. And no. I don't have to be nice to you just because you're homeless before you say it.'

'I get it. She was a terrible mother. But have you ever thought that she never had the chance to change? Have you always been the person you are now? Or did something happen that gave you an opportunity to change? Perhaps she was presented with an opportunity and didn't see the value of it until it was too late? So many potential reasons why she was the way that she was. And so many potential outcomes that could have been, but that wasn't,' said Gabe.

'Why are we talking about this?' asked Elsie.

'Because you brought up your mother.'

'No. I referenced her. It's not quite the same thing.'

'Isn't it? I always find that mentioning a person means that they're still in our mind in some way. Some things we struggle to find peace with – struggle to let them go.'

'And how can someone let someone go when it's a struggle?' asked Elsie.

'You have to change the scenario. Look at it with a different ending. If your mother had been different, then it stands to reason that your life would have been different as well. If your upbringing had been different, you wouldn't have made the decisions that you did, and you wouldn't have become the person that you became. And all of those little inconsequential decisions would have veered you off onto a whole different path, and who knows whether that would have been a good path or a bad path? Nobody can answer that. But what I *can* tell you is that had you had a different mother, you would have been a different person, and none of this would have happened. None of us would have been sitting here. You wouldn't have met the friends that you met. You wouldn't have been presented with an idea to help people on Christmas day. They wouldn't have this special memory imprinted in their minds. None of it would have happened but for the fact that your mother was an awful woman who never had the chance to be a better version of herself.'

Elsie tilted her head and stared into Gabe's eyes. 'You remind me of my friend, Jack. He says things like that.'

'Is he the friend who should be sitting here,' he replied, pointing down at his chair.

Elsie nodded. 'He hasn't turned up. He promised he'd be here, and as usual, he's let me down.'

'He promised to come here?'

'Yes. Well, sort of. He promised he'd see me on Christmas day,' Elsie corrected herself.

'Then, as far as I can tell, he hasn't broken his promise. There's still plenty of time.'

'Unfortunately, time is something that I don't have a lot of.'

'Elsie. You strike me as someone who has always lived on her own terms. You won't go anywhere until you're ready. And you've already decided when that'll be. And you wouldn't have chosen Jack as a friend if you thought he was the type to let you down. He'll keep his promise. You've plenty of time.' said Gabe. He rose from the chair. 'Talking of time, I've taken up enough of yours.'

'It's not been the most Christmassy of conversations,' she told him.

'True. But it's been an honest one – a gift from me to you,' replied Gabe.

'A box of chocolates would have been a better one.'

Gabe turned out his pockets. 'Empty. Unfortunately. But you can keep that instead,' he told her, pointing down to the envelope still on the table. 'Another gift from me to you.'

Elsie looked down at the tatty and discoloured paper. 'Wow! You're spoiling me,' she said, smiling.

'I try my best.' said Gabe as he rejoined the others at his table, leaving Elsie staring at the back of his head.

She slid the envelope nearer to her and picked it up. Leona and Tania were now discussing the benefits of water births over natural ones, and she felt hopelessly excluded. Elsie slid her finger underneath the flap and slid it along, plucking out a single sheet of paper inside.

Two neat lines of the most beautiful writing Elsie had ever seen adorned the page.

'We all die. The goal isn't to live forever. The goal is to create something that will.' – *Chuck Palahniuk*

Instinctively, she turned and reached out to tap Gabe on the shoulder, but when she looked up, he'd gone. Her head scanned the restaurant. She couldn't see him.

'Excuse me,' she said, leaning forward to the other men sitting at the table. 'Where's your friend gone?'

A man with deep wrinkles etched into his skin crumpled his brow, emphasising them even more. 'What friend?'

'The one who I was just talking to. He was sitting here,' she pointed to the empty chair.

The man burst out laughing, causing the others to join him. 'Sounds like you've had more booze than me,' he replied. 'Nobody has sat there. It's just us three.'

Elsie stared back at him. 'But he was sitting there. I've been talking to him for the last five minutes.'

The man gave a throaty laugh. 'Maybe it was the ghost of Christmas present?'

He turned and continued to talk to his friends, and Elsie leaned back in her chair as her brain tried to make sense of everything. She looked around the room again. The men could be playing her up, she thought to herself. Gabe might have just popped into the toilet. He might have seen somebody he knew outside in the queue. There were hundreds of possibilities.

Margaret was standing at a table a few feet away, scolding one of the waiters for sneaking off for a cigarette.

'Margaret,' Elsie called out and waved her hand to get the woman's attention.

The waiter, relieved at the interruption, hurried away before Margaret could stop him.

'You just can't get the staff these days,' she said to Elsie. 'Mackenzie said you're paying triple time for all the staff too! It's a bloody liberty. He's been out the back four times, that one. He thinks I haven't noticed.'

'Margaret. Did you see where that man went,' asked Elsie, ignoring her concerns.

'What man?'

'The one I was just talking to. He was sat here when you just came over to check on us,' said Elsie.

Margaret shrugged her shoulders and gave a blank look at Leona and Tania. 'I didn't see anyone. Did you two?'

Leona and Tania shook their heads.

'There's been nobody here but us three, Elsie' said Leona.

'But he was sitting right there,' insisted Elsie, jabbing at the empty seat with her forefinger.

Tania placed a sympathetic hand on Elsie's arm. 'Honestly, Elsie. Nobody has sat there. Not a man. Not a woman. Nobody,' she said softly.

Elsie's head began to spin. This wasn't right. He'd been there. She'd seen him! Spoken to him. He'd given her the envelope with the quote inside, with beautiful handwriting that drifted over the paper like a wave on the ocean.

Elsie looked down at her hands to where she'd clutched the envelope only seconds before and found that they were completely empty.

Chapter Forty-Nine

Mack

Whatever Mack's concerns had been about working back in the kitchen, they'd dissolved into the air around him the second that he'd put on his chef's whites and unfurled the set of knives that Elsie had bought him for Christmas.

The small team that she'd hired from the agency for the day weren't as experienced as the cooks he'd worked with before, but seeing as this was a Christmas dinner and not a dainty minuscule plate of micro herbs and scallops, he figured that they were more than capable to cook roast potatoes, chop vegetables and carve slithers of turkey onto a plate.

Agata had been a godsend. Standing by his side, she'd quickly picked up the pressures of working in a professional kitchen and had mutely taken his orders, plated up, and when the need had arisen, assertively instructed the other kitchen staff on their orders.

Plate after plate had gone out quickly, and Mack felt his confidence surge every time he shouted 'service' at the pass.

His brother, Marcus, was less skilful even though his duties only extended to peeling and cutting potatoes and carrots. So far, he'd cut two of his fingers, dropped a freshly peeled bowl of carrots all over the floor and slipped on a wet patch by the sink, landing heavily on his side.

'Working in a kitchen is more dangerous than going to war,' Marcus declared.

'I'll bet you a tenner it isn't,' Sid had said drily, himself busy washing a huge bowl of sprouts.

Agata chuckled, and Mack turned to look at her discreetly. He'd been doing it all day – not very successfully either, as Agata had caught him on several occasions. She'd flashed a shy smile back at him and continued working as the heart pendant he'd bought her dangled delicately around her neck. Mack was glad that their little spat appeared to be over.

His parents were doing a fantastic job in front of house. Well, strictly speaking, his mum was doing a fantastic job while his dad was busy doing what his wife told him to. As soon as one table left, his mum had waiting staff stood by, ready to strip it down, clean, and set it up ready for the next sitting, while his dad ushered in the next group of people who'd been waiting patiently in the queue outside and were no doubt hungry for their lunch.

Mack assessed the diminished line of people outside the window. They probably had another eight, maybe ten tables left to feed. How many people would that mean they'd served that day? It had to have been at least a hundred and fifty, he guessed.

His pride swelled. This would be a day he would never forget. If he never stepped inside a kitchen again, he would always have this memory: the most rewarding thing Mack had ever done. He didn't want it to end.

He'd been keeping a watchful eye on Elsie as well. Initially, things appeared to be going well. When they'd first arrived, Elsie had stood and greeted the first group of guests, but Mack spotted the unsteadiness in her legs and how she'd held onto a chair for support. And through her smiles, he could see the pain she was trying to hide. In the end, she hobbled slowly over to the table, where she was later joined by Leona and Tania and where she remained for the rest of the day.

He'd caught Elsie a few times taking painkillers when she thought that nobody was watching, and it worried him. Elsie had been taking them like a child would sweets, and he was surprised that she was still functioning.

Almost two hours later, Graeme had bid farewell to the last remaining table of the day. He locked the doors behind them as they left, leaned his back against them and let out a heavy sigh.

'And that's a wrap, folks,' he declared, and a small round of cheers went up amongst them all.

'Let's not get carried away,' Mack said firmly. 'You've all been wonderful, and I'm sure you're all eager to get home. So let's clean down as quickly as we can.'

Motivated by the ending that was now within their reach, the staff busied themselves with cleaning. Mack began clearing down his section at the pass and looked up to see his mother approaching.

'Thanks, Mum. You've been an absolute star. You really have,' he told her.

But Margaret brushed the comment away.

'She's not well, Mackenzie. She really isn't,' she told him. 'She's been seeing ghosts, talking about a conversation with a man. But there was nobody there with her. I promise you there wasn't, and that's not just me being a little silly and not seeing things, which your father tells everybody that I sometimes do. Leona and Tania said the same. They didn't see anything either.'

Mack looked over at Elsie. Her arms were wrapped around her chest, and she rocked back and forth on the chair as her face twisted in pain.

'Mum. I think she needs an ambulance.'

A wave of panic washed over Margaret. 'I'll get my phone. It's my handbag,' and she dashed across the room, through a door and out of sight.

Sid and Agata were chatting as they wiped down the stainless steel workstations. Mack went over to them.

'I think this is it,' he whispered under his breath and motioned his head towards Elsie.

Agata dropped the cloth she was holding and rushed into the restaurant, and Mack and Sid followed. She knelt in front of Elsie and took her hands in her own.

'Hey, you,' said Elsie weakly.

'Hey,' she replied.

'I think it's time we got you out of here,' Agata told her, but Elsie shook her head.

'No. We haven't had our dinner yet. I won't ruin it.'

'Don't be silly,' said Mack. 'You haven't ruined anything. We've all had an amazing day.'

Sid leaned forward, his head inches away from Elsie's ear. 'Elsie, sweetheart. It's time to go.'

She looked up at him and smiled softly.

'I know it is,' she said. 'I know.'

Chapter Fifty

Elsie

E lsie remembered the ambulance arriving. She could see a sea of concerned faces bearing down on her, telling her everything would be okay. She remembered the paramedic hovering above her, looking through various compartments above her head, and shouting medical jargon through to the driver. She recalled the brightness of the hospital lights flashing by as she was wheeled along the corridor. The beeps of machines. The hushed tones of doctors who spoke amongst each other at the foot of her hospital bed.

Elsie drifted in and out of consciousness. One second, there seemed to be a hive of people, and in the blink of an eye, she was alone again. At least the pain had gone, and she turned her head and saw the tube of a drip snaking down towards her hand.

She was so tired, as though all the energy had been stripped from her body. Elsie could barely move. She closed her eyes, finding comfort in the machines as they bleeped rhythmically, guiding her into sleep.

She blinked again.

Sid, Agata, and Mack were all at her side. Agata's warm hand on hers.

'What man?' she heard Agata ask Mack.

Mack shrugged his shoulders. 'She didn't say who.'

'Do you think it was this Jack fellow?' said Sid.

But Mack shook his head. 'Elsie told Mum that it was one of the homeless guys.'

It was one of the homeless guys. I saw him. He gave me a letter, she thought to herself.

'She's seeing more and more things,' said Agata. 'I should have done something when I saw her that day in the park. I should have insisted that she see a doctor then.'

Mack folded his arms over his chest. 'What day in the park? What happened?'

Agata was rubbing her thumb across the top of Elsie's hand. It felt so soothing.

'When I went to pick her up. I left early to get her to see if I see this man Jack.'

Sid tutted. 'She asked us not to do that,' he whispered.

'I know. But I had to know. Elsie caught me. She was so angry,' said Agata.

'What did you see?' asked Mack.

'I saw,' started Agata and then she paused, and Elsie strained her ears. 'I saw Elsie sitting on bench. She was alone.'

Mack moved closer to Agata and lowered his voice. 'So, she hasn't been meeting anyone? She made it all up?'

'Worse than that,' said Agata with a slow shake of her head. 'She was talking as if there was somebody there. I watched her. She was laughing and leaning as if somebody sitting next to her. But there was nobody. Just an empty space on the bench.'

Elsie wanted to scream. He *was* there! Jack had always been there. He'd been sitting and waiting for her to arrive when she'd walked into the park that morning. She hadn't imagined it. This wasn't her brain deceiving her; she knew the difference between reality and fiction. Jack was as real as she was.

'You should have told us earlier,' said Mack.

'What difference would it have made?' said Sid. 'None. 'It would have only distressed everyone, especially Elsie. The doctors would have done a brain scan and seen that the cancer had spread, and it would have made absolutely no difference. This day was always going to come, and even if Elsie did look like a lunatic talking to thin air in the middle of the park, at least she thought it was real. At least she was happy in that reality.'

'But...' started Mack, but Sid held up his hand to stop him.

'But nothing. Elsie was happy, and that's all that mattered.'

Elsie's breath caught in her throat. Her heart hammered against her chest. She thought back to all of the times she'd sat there. She thought of all the people who'd walked past:

dog walkers, families, people enjoying the festivals and fayres organised at the park. They must have seen Jack!

Agata was wrong. She must have been distracted by the dog woman and the park warden, who'd threatened to call the police on her. Elsie remembered only seconds before that first bark echoed from behind her, she was discussing her latest addition to her list. She could see Jack's face as clearly as if he were sitting next to her right now. His face had broken into a dazzling smile, the creases in the corners of his eyes. He'd been there. Sitting next to Elsie.

But as she remembered, she struggled to find a single instance of when anybody had interacted with Jack. Her memories presented images of curious looks, of the parents who steered their children further away from the bench, the dogs that had sat down in front of Jack and stared at him, the dogs that hadn't even paid him any attention at all, the jogger who had almost careered into Jack even though he was looking straight in Jack's direction.

'So,' continued Sid. 'Regardless of what happens next, none of us tell her the truth. We make her as comfortable as possible. We even lie if we have to, tell her that Jack has been to visit. Whatever it takes. This is for Elsie.'

She heard Agata and Mack mutter 'For Elsie' in unison.

Elsie felt a numbness travelling around her body as a fresh wave of exhaustion seized hold of her. She tried to fight it away in her mind. *No. Not yet. I don't understand what's going on,* she pleaded. But the invisible demon was too strong, and before she knew it, she drifted away again.

***

She opened her eyes again. Her friends had gone. It was dark outside, and the lights in the hospital ward had been lowered. The bustle of movement in the corridor had diminished into silence.

'They've gone home,' she heard Jack say. 'They tried to put up a fight, but the doctor insisted. He threatened to call security if they didn't leave.'

Elsie turned her head. Jack was sitting in the armchair next to the bed.

'You're not real,' she said to him. 'Go away.'

'Says who?'

'My friends. Agata spied on us in the park, and she said that I was on that bench alone. You're all in my mind,' said Elsie.

'Just because they can't see me doesn't mean I'm not real.'

She tried to smile but failed. 'I think you'll find that's exactly what it means.'

'If a single person witnesses an avalanche, but nobody else is around to see it, does that mean it never happened?' he asked her.

'But there were people to see it – in the park, I mean. There were other people around. Nobody else saw you.'

'Okay. That's a bad choice of analogy on my part,' he replied.

'You could have showed up today. That would have proven to everybody. But you didn't. You broke your promise.'

Jack consulted his watch. 'It's quarter to midnight. It's still technically Christmas Day. I kept my promise.'

Elsie shook her head. 'Hardly worth it.'

'And anyway, I did come,' continued Jack. 'I came in and sat down at your table. We talked about your mother. Remember?'

Elsie's eyes widened. 'Gabe? But...'

He leaned towards and took her hand. 'But why didn't I come as me? Because the first thing you would have done is stand up and proudly introduce me to everybody, and all they would have seen was you gesturing into a space. You would have been carted off to the nearest psychiatric clinic.'

'I don't understand what's happening.' Elsie felt as though she was going insane. It must be the morphine, she thought to herself.

Jack gave a soft laugh. 'It's not the drugs. Sometimes, people aren't meant to see what others see. This was for your eyes only. This was for you to experience.'

'Are you God?' she asked him.

'No, Elsie. I'm not God.' He laughed again.

'Are you Death?'

'Nope. That's somebody else. A nice girl, so I'm told. What?' said Jack, catching the surprise on Elsie's face. 'And I thought you were a feminist? Not all the big jobs go to men, you know.'

'So, you're not God, and you're not Death. Are you an angel then?'

He tilted his head and considered the question. 'No. Not an angel. But I do come here to help people.'

'Have you met God?'

'No.'

'Why not?'

'It's a big place up there. There are protocols and rules to follow just as there are here. Have you met the King? No. Of course not.'

'But he is real, though? God, not the King. I know that the King is real. We all watched him give his Christmas speech on television.' she said.

'God is as real as you and me. Or maybe, more accurately, a combination of both. He's all around us and nowhere at all at the same time. He intertwines with our lives. He watches. He guides. He lives within all of us.'

'Humph,' grunted Elsie, displeased with the response. 'A simple yes or no would have sufficed. Why bother with me? I'm nothing special.'

'And you thinking that way is exactly the reason why I came,' replied Jack. 'You're not the same person that I met, Elsie.'

'I'm exactly the same person. Still little old Elsie Bellamy dying with cancer.'

'That's who you were, who you still are, but you're not the same person,' insisted Jack. 'Do you realise how many lives you've transformed? How many lives you'll continue to transform?'

'But I won't be around to see it.'

'In the same way that I'm not around to see you. And yet, here I am.'

Elsie squeezed Jack's hand. 'I don't want to die here, Jack. I don't want to die tonight.'

He brought her hand to his lips and kissed it. 'Then don't, my beautiful girl. I told you earlier you've already decided when you want to go. Just hold onto that.'

'I'm scared to close my eyes,' she told him.

'Don't be. I'll be by your side the whole time.'

Elsie's eyes fluttered closed. Whatever people did and didn't see, whatever they thought of her, whether Jack was real or not, Elsie trusted him.

'Stay with me, Jack,' she whispered.

'Always,' he replied.

Chapter Fifty-One

Ingrid

Elsie had lasted longer than the doctors had predicted. Initially, they'd informed Mack, Sid and Agata that Elsie wouldn't be expected to live through the night. Two days later, Elsie's heart kept giving reassuring bleeps through the monitor, and the doctors looked on with surprise as they checked the charts and readouts.

Reluctantly, and after much persuasion from the four of them, the doctors agreed that Elsie could be transferred to The Orchids.

'She didn't want to die in a hospital,' Ingrid had told them. 'It was her only wish.'

'Elsie wouldn't make the short journey,' 'It would be safer for her to stay in the hospital,' and 'it wasn't in her best interests' were all counter-arguments to their requests, which eventually fell on deaf ears, and conceding defeat, they'd reluctantly agreed to discharge Elsie from the hospital and into the care of Ingrid and her staff.

The ambulance ride was a slow one, and almost an hour after they'd first left the hospital grounds, they finally pulled up outside The Orchids.

Sid, Agata, Mack, and Amanda were all waiting outside the front door when they pulled up and, in muted voices, watched as Elsie was taken out of the back of the ambulance and brought inside. They hovered nervously behind, neither helping nor assisting for fear of getting in the way. All apart from Amanda, who had gone ahead of the medics and into the bedroom to prepare to transfer Elsie onto the bed.

Elsie hadn't woken, but with her being pumped full of morphine, they hadn't expected her to. Ingrid had brought extra chairs into the room for them all to sit down around the bed, and for the rest of that day and the next, the four of them had taken it in turns to sleep, as one stayed awake, keeping a watchful eye over their friend, promising to wake the others if there was any change.

Elsie was the second admission that week, along with a rather regal-sounding Edward Mayhew-Blake, who'd been admitted the previous day, and with all of the extra workload and the fact that Ingrid was currently unavailable for the duration of Elsie's stay, she'd employed an extra care worker and a nurse to help cover the workload.

Edward, like Elsie, was suffering from terminal cancer, and also like Elsie, despite his rather old-fashioned sounding name, had only turned thirty that year. He was a handful, that man, Ingrid thought, smiling to herself. On the day that he'd arrived, he'd knocked on the other resident's doors and introduced himself, which was all rather pleasant and orderly, but by the end of the day, he'd taken a thrilled Mrs Foster for a ride on his electric scooter and had gotten stinking drunk with Adrian in his bedroom on a bottle of Remi Martin that his younger brother had snuck in for him.

Let him be like that, she thought to herself. Let him have fun and whizz an old lady around the house in his wheelchair, and have a drink with other residents and laugh, and be silly and free. Although, she'd prefer it if they didn't end up vomiting in the pot plants next time. Within weeks, that young man would be in the same position as her dear Elsie, neither in this world nor out of it. He'd be stuck in limbo as his friends and loved ones stood by the side of his bed and whispered their goodbyes into his ear.

Towards the end of the second day, Amanda tapped on the door and entered.

'I'm off now,' she told Ingrid. 'I'm sorry that I can't stop longer and be with you all.'

Agata grabbed her hand and squeezed it. 'You've been on shift for almost eighteen hours. We're all grateful to you,' she told her and Sid and Mack nodded in agreement.

'Go home and get some rest, love,' Sid told her. 'Elsie wouldn't want you to exhaust yourself.'

She went over to the bed, leaned down, and gave her a gentle kiss on the forehead. Ingrid fought to hold her tears back. Clearly, Amanda didn't expect Elsie to last the night.

She left the room, and Ingrid followed her downstairs. 'How long do you think?' she asked, but Amanda slowly raised her shoulders.

'I'm not sure. You never can tell.' She hugged Ingrid tightly. 'You know where I am if you need me,' she told her.

Ingrid gave her a soft smile. 'Of course,' she replied, even though she had no intention of calling Amanda if Elsie passed away during the night as Amanda was expecting. That woman had been her rock throughout all of this, but she needed to go home and spend time with her own family.

She walked into the kitchen to make them all hot drinks and sandwiches, which would undoubtedly go uneaten. A few minutes later, she felt Sid's arms wrap around her waist. He nestled his face into her neck, and she leaned into him. They'd kept their relationship secret from everyone; it didn't feel appropriate somehow.

'How are you doing, my love?' he asked her.

'Struggling,' admitted Ingrid.

'You're allowed to let go. You're allowed to be sad. Try not to be so stoic in front of people. Mack and Agata are hardly likely to say anything.'

'The tears can come after Elsie's gone. Not before. They can hear everything. I'm certain of it. And I won't give that girl a reason to hold on any longer. She has to feel peace inside to pass. I won't ruin that moment for her,' she told him.

Sid squeezed her tighter. 'Then I'll wait for that time. I'll open my arms, and you can rush straight into them when you're ready.'

'Has anyone told you, you're a soppy sod, Sid *Mason?*'

'No. They know they'd get a smack in the mouth if they did,' he replied. 'Come on. Let me give you a hand with this lot.'

They'd drank the drinks and had a nibble of a few sandwiches when the door knocked, and in walked the new nurse that Ingrid had employed.

'I'm not disturbing you am I?' she said, poking her head through the crack in the door.

Ingrid rose from her chair. 'Not at all. Come in. I want to introduce you to everyone. This is Agata,' she said, pointing at Agata. 'Sid,' he waved back. 'And Mack. And this,' she said, walking over to the bed, 'this is Elsie. Everyone, this is Marion.'

Marion went over to the bed and stroked Elsie's arm.

'Elsie Bellamy. Yes. I remember now.'

'You know Elsie?' asked Agata with surprise. 'How?'

'I see a lot of people coming and going in the hospital. But this girl right here, she's always stuck in my mind. I was there in the room when the doctor first told Elsie that the cancer had returned...when he said that there was nothing else that could be done,' explained Marion. 'And I just remember feeling so incredibly sad for her, not because of the diagnosis. Well, not just that. But I remember the impression she gave that nobody was there for her. That she had no support, it's plagued my thoughts for so many months.'

'She didn't have anybody. Not then. But now...' said Mack.

'You found her,' finished Marion.

But Sid shook his head. 'No. She found us. She saved us, all of us.'

Marion nodded, looked down at Elsie, and smiled. 'Then she's lucky. She found the right people.'

Chapter Fifty-Two

Jack

It was a little after 1 a.m. when Jack stepped forward to Elsie's bedside. Mack, Agata and Sid were all fast asleep in armchairs dotted around the bedroom, and Ingrid had just left the room to go to the toilet.

They were a dedicated bunch; he'd say that about them. Elsie was a lucky woman. The nurse, Marion, had been right about that. It hadn't taken much organising to arrange that she applied for a job at The Orchids; one failed MOT and a hefty bill from the garage had seen to that. Although, sometimes, he did feel bad about doing that to people, but needs must.

Elsie had said that she'd wanted Marion with her when she passed. Granted, she'd said it to herself in her head when she was first coming to terms with everything, and Jack was wrong for eavesdropping, but again, needs must.

He hadn't accounted for the strength of Ingrid's bladder, though. That woman was like a camel, and as he waited for the copious amount of teas she'd drunk to take their effect, Jack had waited in the corner of the room among the shadows cast onto the walls from the soft glow of the bedside lights.

Jack had been assigned Elsie the second that the cancer was first diagnosed. Although assigned was probably not the right word. You sort of just found yourself somewhere: no discreet conversation, no instructions, just wham, and you're there. Almost four years of playing the long game with one of the most stubborn people he'd ever met.

He never thought he'd get to this point if he were being honest. Elsie had been one of his trickiest customers. Stubborn was actually an understatement, but then he supposed that was the thing with childhood trauma; It embedded behaviours for protection, regardless of how destructive they were in the long run.

What a long way Elsie had come. He looked around her friends as they slept in blissful, oblivious peace. They'd been the perfect friends for Elsie. All feisty and independent in their own way – just like she was.

Jack had chosen them all. Agata's loneliness. Mack's fear of failure. And Sid's hidden guilt – and also his humour. He'd made Jack smile so many times over these past months, and it wouldn't do for it to be all doom and gloom. They all needed that comedic touch somewhere along the line.

If Jack had chosen correctly, and not one to blow his own trumpet, which he indeed had, then Elsie's bond to them had been strengthened because she could relate to all three.

All that it needed was the one person who would bring them all together and bind them like glue. Cue Ingrid: Kind, caring, compassionate. She was the mother hen who fussed over them all and wanted nothing in return. Jack liked her. He'd sent a few people her way before.

He had to admit, though, he hadn't expected all of these love matches. Ingrid and Sid? Who'd have thought it? But then, fate and love matches weren't his department.

He had less than two minutes before Ingrid returned. Elsie desired to pass without them knowing. She hadn't wanted them crying over her bed, sobbing as her chest rose and fell for the last time. She wanted that moment for herself. Jack couldn't remember now if she'd thought that or had told him directly. It didn't matter either way. It was Elsie's wish.

He felt it then: An icy stillness in the air, the kind you feel when walking on a frosty winter's morning. Jack never saw them, not in person, but he knew that they were there waiting for Jack to give the signal that they could go ahead.

It was a beautiful thing to watch. It didn't happen every time. Sometimes, they showed up, and other times, they didn't. It was as simple as that. But when Jack felt them materialise beside him, he always felt privileged.

When he'd asked people before what they thought Death looked like, they'd described the stereotypical caricature depicted in works of art: An image which had been drummed into them at some point as they'd sat on hard-backed wooden pews in a chilly British church. And who was to say that Death wasn't like that? Jack had never seen them. Perhaps, once, one person did, and the myth was born. But then again, that image had been around for centuries when fashion had been somewhat different. Death may have caught up with the times and had a makeover or two as the centuries ticked by. He could well imagine the latest incarnate donning a pair of jeans, a hoody, and a pair of Doctor Martins.

One minute left before Ingrid returned. He had to act now; otherwise, he'd run out of time, and Elsie's final wish wouldn't be honoured.

He stepped forward and leaned over the bed.

'Time to let go now, Elsie,' he whispered. He kissed her on the forehead and then, with the gentlest of touches, placed another on her cheek. A light began to glow inside her chest, and Jack stepped back.

The coldness by his side moved past him, and Jack gave an involuntarily shiver. The coldness transformed into a fluid-like state, like a magnificent fountain on the verge of freezing.

'Beautiful,' Jack gasped as he watched on.

The figure's hand hovered above the light in Elsie's chest, guiding it higher, up through her throat. Elsie's mouth opened slightly, allowing the light to waver close to her lips. The figure swiped its hand, absorbing Elsie's soul into its own and with another whoosh of bitter air, the figure had gone.

And so had Elsie Bellamy.

Chapter Fifty-Three

The Living List of Elsie Bellamy

Dear Agata, Mack, Sid and Ingrid,

If you're reading this, or to be factually correct, if this is being read to you, then I am where I was destined to go, wherever that may be. In truth, I hope it's like you see in the movies, and I'm up there, wearing a toga, sitting on fluffy clouds with the sound of harps all around me. I'd be pretty disappointed with anything less.

In any case, I am going to be sad to not be with you anymore, but I count my blessings that I had you at all. Jack encouraged me to see the positives in everything, and I assure you that was a bitter pill to swallow at times, but in the end, I understood. And yes, I said Jack. That international man of mystery that you were all so intrigued by. Whether you believe Jack is real, whether you believe him to be a con man or a figment of my own cancer-riddled imagination, Jack's influence on me is what led me to all of you. So, he can't be that bad, can he?

Hopefully, by this point, I've made it past Christmas day, and you would have met him. He'd promised to be by my side that day, and I have no reason to doubt that. He also promised he'd be around to read this letter to you, so you'll have had two opportunities to scrutinise him.

Talking to Jack made me realise the limited life that I'd been living. I was existing in an autonomous world, wandering around aimlessly and blaming other people for the void that I'd created in my own heart. Jack helped me heal that wound, and I won't lie; it wasn't easy. At times, I hated him and everybody around me, and I've no doubt that during those times, the people I hated, hated me right back. But eventually, I could see the beauty and the possibilities and everything that was wedged in between.

I'd been given a second chance at living, regardless of how short a time I'd been granted. Those months I had with you all were the equivalent of a lifetime of happy memories that had escaped me before.

Jack taught me that to really live, you had to think beyond the boundaries of existence and my own mortality. The only way to live was through other people, creating a generational change with the decisions that I make today. My legacy means that I could never truly die.

So, my darling group of misfits, here is my living list, and here's to eternal life.

- *To Sid, Agata, and Mack, I transfer ownership of my apartments. The short time that we shared there has imprinted on the bricks and floorboards, and I could never imagine another person, other than you, living there. I shall remember with fondness all of the special times we shared there, especially the sight of Sid's bare arse greeting me in the morning because he failed to lock the bathroom door as he so often did.*

- *Sid and Mack. By now, you would have been reunited with your families, and hopefully, provided everything goes to plan, I would have had the pleasure of seeing your reactions and watching your relationships blossom. If, for some horrific reason, it all went terribly wrong, then you can live safe in the knowledge that I would have taken that shame to my grave, and I will be eternally reprimanding myself for being the interring busy-body that I once was.*

- *Sid. The man who says he wants so little from life other than love and access to his State Retirement Pension. It appears that I'm surplus to requirements, seeing as you've done a pretty fine job of sorting both of those* out for yourself. And I'm completely going to blow your cover because I know that you're not just talking of the rekindled love for your family but also love for Ingrid. It's been both beautiful and exciting watching your relationship grow from friendship into something more meaningful. All I can say to both of you is good luck and bon voyage! I've booked you both a three-month world cruise, which I wish I'd done for myself. So go and explore for me! And know that wherever you are in the world, I will always be right behind you...apart from in your bedroom. Even spooks have limits.

- To my darling Agata. You're the bravest person I know. From leaving your country to come here and start a new life to enduring raising Arabella King's womb goblins, you never lost sight of your goal. You're resilient and strong, and all you need is that one chance to show everybody just how wonderful you are. I have therefore made provision to fund your own accounting agency. The funds are ready and waiting in the capable hands of my solicitor. Go forth and conquer my love, and where possible, make sure that people pay their fair share of corporation tax.

- Ingrid. I have so many reasons to thank you, even though I was possibly one of the worst residents you've ever had. I *never did as I was told and frequently went against your advice, but I did pay my bill. (Don't think I didn't notice that you hadn't cashed my cheque. My solicitor should have deposited the money directly into your account today, so nice try!). You have such a special gift, and that's why I imagine your rooms are always filled. Sid told me of your dreams with The Orchids and your disappointment when the next-door property sold. I'm sorry that you felt that way, especially as I'm the one who caused that feeling because it was me who bought the property. Surprise! I, of course, transfer ownership over to you, and as with Agata, there is a separate account to fund the required renovation work.*

- *Mack. By now, the Christmas day dinner would have been an utter success, and you would have realised that I was 100% right about you not being able to work anywhere else outside of a kitchen. Now, I don't want to sound like a know-it-all, but hey, if the cap fits! I transfer ownership of the bistro into your capable hands. What you choose to do with it is entirely up to you, but I have a feeling deep down that whatever course of action you take, it will be the right one.*

And that's it!

If you're wondering why I never left anything to Jack, it's because he refused to entertain the suggestion for reasons known only to himself. But I'm sure you'll be able to ask him all about it when he's finished reading this to you.

All that sneaking around was a tad exhausting, so I'll bid you a final farewell: my friends, my family, my heart.

Your ever loving

Elsie

P.S. Mack and Agata. For the love of God, will you tell each other how you feel about one another? It's getting silly now.

Chapter Fifty-Four

One Year Later

T hey all raised their glasses and chinked them together in the centre of the table.

'Congratulations to you both,' declared Sid. He sipped at the wine and wrinkled his nose. 'Bloody horrible stuff champagne. I don't know how anybody drinks it.'

Ingrid rolled her eyes at him. 'You heathen,' and then turning to Agata, she added, 'Let me see it again.'

Agata held out her left hand, and Ingrid admired the solitaire diamond that glistened under the restaurant lights. 'It's beautiful. I couldn't be happier for you both.'

Mack smiled and reached across to his new fiancée and gently stroked her shoulder with his fingertips. 'Your turn next,' he said to Sid and winked.

Sid pulled a face and sipped again from his glass, pulling the same look of disdain he had the first time.

'I've only just gotten him used to using a laundry basket,' joked Ingrid. 'Let's not push him. He's a work in progress.'

They'd all gone to The Spice is Right, their local Indian restaurant. Mack would have preferred something a little more upmarket to celebrate his and Agata's engagement, but they all took turns to choose the destination, and today had been Sid's choice. Still, the food was tasty, and he knew that Agata loved going there, so he let it slide.

What a difference one year could make, he thought to himself. In the grand scheme of things, twelve months wasn't a long time and yet the changes to their lives had been astronomical, thanks in no small part, to Elsie.

When the solicitor had first knocked on the apartment door on that cold January morning, just a week after Elsie's passing, they hadn't known what to expect. Elsie had always been generous when she'd been alive, and in truth, none of them had expected it to extend beyond her death.

The solicitor, Jacob, had sat them down and read out a beautiful letter that Elsie had written, and as the rain battered down on the windows, he revealed the true extent of Elsie's kindness.

Agata had burst into tears, and Mack prayed that it wasn't because Elsie's statement in her postscript was wrong. In any event, he grabbed her and held her tightly to him, kissing her tenderly on the top of her head.

Sid, not generally known for public displays of affection, excused himself and went to the bathroom, but Mack heard him repeatedly blowing his nose, and when he came back out to join them in the living room, his nose was bright red and his eyes watery.

'She shouldn't have done that,' Agata said to Jacob. 'Now it looks like we were only here for her money.'

Jacob shook his head as he refolded the paper and slid it back inside its envelope. 'Elsie was a clever and astute woman, and I think she chose the right people,' he told them.

'The right people for what?' asked Sid.

'To create her legacy. It all starts with you,' he gave them a serious nod. 'However you proceed from this point is entirely up to you, but if I may give one piece of advice, create something that extends into the lives of others; facilitate the change in their lives just as Elsie has done with you.'

'I think we could all do with a drink.' said Ingrid. 'We're all in shock. It's a lot to process.'

But Jacob waved his hand in refusal. 'Not for me, thank you, Ingrid. I only popped in to introduce myself and pass on Elsie's wishes. She was quite excited about it all. No need,' he added as they all rose from their seats. 'I can see myself out. But please make sure you make an appointment with the office soon to start finalising the arrangements.'

Jacob left, leaving the four of them standing in the middle of Elsie's apartment, correction, their apartment, bewildered.

'What do we do now?' asked Agata.

'Exactly what the man told us to,' said Sid. 'We start creating a legacy.'

It was strange that nobody had heard of Jacob when they visited the solicitors the following week. Maybe they'd misheard his name? Who knew? But the mystery was soon forgotten, lost amongst the months of organisation and planning that followed. Every spare second was filled with meeting contractors, liaising with project managers, dashing from one supplier to the next—meetings upon meetings—instruction after instruction. But as everything fell into place, with every last stroke of a paintbrush and every finishing touch added, they'd done it. They just hoped that everything they had done would make Elsie proud, just as she had asked in her letter.

The Orchids had indeed extended into the neighbouring property and now boasted a further ten bedrooms, seven extra staff and gardens which wouldn't have looked out of place at Kew. There had been a big feature in the newspaper and on the local news station, which outlined the pioneering Ingrid Smythe-Owen's vision. Agata and Mack had watched the televised interview as they snuggled together on the sofa, laughing only at Sid's awkwardness as he stood mutely by Ingrid's side as she confidently spoke about the expert care that residents could expect to receive from her and her staff.

'And what about you, Mr Mason? What do you make of it all?' the reporter asked him. She held the microphone next to

Sid's chin, and his eyes darted between the microphone, Ingrid and then back to the reporter.

'I'm just the handyman,' he'd managed to stammer.

Mack prayed that someone somewhere turned that clip into a viral meme.

Agata's business was flourishing. She'd started in much the same way as Elsie, operating as a one-man band from the comfort of the dining room table in the apartment as she took over the accounts for The Orchids for Ingrid. Within weeks of her official launch, she secured two major contracts with local firms. The following month, she took on her first employee, Stacey, a ditzy twenty-one-year-old but whose administration skills were second to none.

In a bid to follow Elsie's wishes, Agata began to approach local charities and offered to take over their accounts for free. Stacey quickly saw the opportunity to capitalise on this and plastered the offer all over the business's Facebook page, even paying for an ad which covered the whole of the West Midlands. Soon, the kind-hearted accountant and her free accounting services for charities was all over social media, and as interest in the business soared, the paying contracts poured in, all keen to work with such a philanthropic company. Stacey now found herself managing a small team of administration assistants, and Agata hired an additional four accountants to cope with the increased workload.

Mack had indeed reopened the bistro, but the thought of working with the homeless was something that he couldn't shake. He had reopened the bistro, aptly naming it, The Streets. It was made up of a small team of experienced kitchen staff, but peppered amongst them was a selection of homeless men and women.

Mack went out onto the streets and worked with homeless charities, offering training and accommodation to any of the homeless who were keen to work their way off the streets. They would train and work under Mack and his team and live in the apartment above theirs. They could only train six people at a time, and he had to liaise with all manner of counsellors to make sure that people didn't struggle with the adjustments. The Streets received critical acclaim, not only for the standard of the food but also for the fact that Mack was single-handedly providing homeless people with a skill which could change the course of their lives. With that under their belt, earning a wage and a home to live in, it made it easier for them to transition to finding their own employment elsewhere when they were ready. And as one person left, the space was filled with the next. It was a never-ending carousel, but Mack was glad that the ride would never stop.

Elsie Bellamy, the rude woman who had thrown coins at him, even though she'd said she hadn't, had hurtled into all of their lives like a hurricane. She'd swept them up off their feet, spun them around and placed them back down into a different world that they may not have recognised but they most certainly appreciated.

Everybody was happier having met her. However, the fact that Elsie wasn't around to share their happiness with them was bittersweet.

Mack raised his glass again at the table, bidding everyone to do the same.

'Don't make me drink any more of this crap,' said Sid, but Ingrid quickly shushed him.

'I'd just like to make a toast,' said Mack. 'To absent friends,' he continued. 'Or more precisely, to Elsie. Our kooky, maddening friend. I hope that you're looking down...'

'Or up,' interrupted Sid.

Mack shook his head with dismay. 'Ignore him, Elsie. You know what a pain he can be. I hope that you're looking down and are pleased with everything that we've done. I hope that we've made you proud.'

They all clinked their glasses together again.

'To Elsie,' they said.

They continued to chatter and laugh as the waiters placed their main courses in front of them. Ingrid and Agata were discussing possible wedding venues. Sid was asking Mack for his opinions on buying an electric armchair now that his hip was causing him so much pain.

None of them noticed the flicker in the lights above their heads.

Chapter Fifty-Five

Elsie

Elsie sat on the bench, waiting. The cruel winter weather had finally retreated, making way for the first glimpses of Springtime warmth. She heard familiar footsteps walking towards her, and she turned her head and squinted her eyes against the low-morning sun.

'Hello stranger,' said Jack, sitting down next to her.

'Hello you,' she replied. 'I have to be honest. I'm a little surprised to be back here.'

'You're back here because you wanted to be. That's how it works,' he told her.

'It it? I'm still getting used to it all.' She leaned back on the bench and kicked her legs in front of her. 'Is this how you see everything?' she asked him.

She turned her head slowly, taking in the vibrant bright lights that surrounded the trees, the sparkles that danced in the grass, and the mixture of colours that surrounded every person as they walked mindlessly by, not noticing that they were even there.

'The colours all mean something,' said Jack. 'Blues, greens, reds, indigos, they all represent a particular emotion or feeling. Even the shape of the aura has meaning. People are walking rainbows. It's quite beautiful.'

A Labrador surrounded by orange came bounding towards them, dragging his small-framed owner along with him. He stopped running abruptly as the owner pulled on the lead, dragging him to a halt.

'Fucking hell, Pepper. You nearly broke my neck then,' the owner shouted.

But Pepper wasn't listening. He sat down and stared at Elsie and Jack, and Jack nudged Elsie with his elbow.

'I love it when this happens,' he said to Elsie, smiling.

'Pepper?' continued the owner. He knelt beside Pepper and followed the dog's gaze. 'What you looking at, boy? What can you see?' Pepper barked, causing his owner to jump and stumble over. 'Stupid dog,' he said, brushing away the dirt on his legs. 'Come on.'

After much tugging on the lead, Pepper finally submitted and reluctantly went back onto the grass with his owner.

'Have you been back to see them?' Jack asked her.

Elsie nodded and smiled softly. 'Many times.'

'I popped to see them the once. Read out your living list to them. It's funny how they didn't make the connection, but then, they didn't know that Jack was my nickname. How do you think they're doing?'

'Better than I could have imagined,' she admitted.

'Understatement,' said Jack sardonically.

He was right. It was an understatement. In every aspect, Sid, Mack, Agata, and Ingrid had created something so pure that it affected the lives of everyone they met: Agata offering free accounting for charities might not have sounded like a lot, but those charities now had extra money to help people. Ingrid, with the additional rooms at The Orchids, could now help countless more families. And Mack's restaurant had been genius. How many people had he helped off the street already? How many people between them had their lives affected by the kindness of those four magical people? How many people were yet to be helped?

'Thousands upon thousands,' said Jack, answering the unspoken question she'd been pondering.

'How do you do that?' she asked him. She'd been trying to figure out all the nifty tricks since passing, but it was as if she were a baby learning to walk and talk again.

Jack shrugged his shoulders. 'I don't know exactly. It sort of just happens. You'll figure it out as you go along.' He stood up.

'Where are you going now?' she asked him.

'You know what it's like. People to meet. People to see. I thought I'd pop in and see how little Elsie was doing.'

Little Elsie! The girl from the shop who'd dropped her Smarties all over the floor.

'You see her? How is she?' asked Elsie eagerly.

Jack gave her a wide smile. 'She's doing wonderfully well. The doctors are expecting her to make a full recovery. I promised you she'd be okay. And you know me, I never break a promise.'

Elsie's heart warmed. 'Good. I'm glad.'

'Anyway, I'd better get out of your way. Here comes your first customer,' said Jack, pointing to a man walking towards them in the distance.

Elsie looked to where Jack was pointing and saw a man ambling towards them. He was too far away to guess his age, but from the loose-fitting jeans, zip-up hoody and trainers, she'd put him in his early twenties. His hands were pushed deep inside his pockets, his head lowered to his feet, and he walked with the same solemn stride as a funeral director leading the cortege. All around him, his aura was devoid of any dazzling bright colours that Elsie had seen around other people, and instead, the man's field was bulging with dirty, muddy colours. Elsie felt sad just looking at him.

'What am I supposed to do?' she asked.

'You do exactly what I did with you?' he told her. 'Listen. Then listen again. And finally, listen some more. You'll be surprised just how much that helps. And when you think he's ready for more, that's when it's your turn to talk.'

She shuffled uncomfortably in her seat. 'Jack. I don't think I can do this.'

'Elsie, my sweet girl. This is what you were made for.'

He turned and walked down the path, past the dog walker and the spritely Pepper, past a woman pushing a little girl in a pram and straight past the man with a soul full of sorrow, unnoticed by them all. With each step that Jack took, he became lighter and lighter until, eventually, he vanished into mist and whooshed up into the sky above, carried by the gentle breeze.

The man was coming closer to Elsie now. Head down and about to walk straight past Elsie.

'Please stop,' Elsie whispered to herself.

Surprisingly, he did just that, and she straightened herself on the bench. You did pick these things up, after all!

The man turned and sat beside her, leaned forward, and let out a heavy sigh.

What now? She thought to herself. *Say something!*

Her thoughts seemingly transferred straight onto the man, as after a second, he turned to Elsie.

'Don't suppose you've got a light, have you?' he asked.

Closer up, he was younger than Elsie had initially thought, probably no more than eighteen. Dark circles framed each eye, and his mouth was set in a sorrowful downward position.

'Sorry,' she replied. 'I don't smoke. Not good for your health.'

The man shrugged. 'You only live once.'

Elsie smiled back at him. 'Do you?' she said cryptically, reminiscent of some of her conversations with Jack. 'That all depends on who you ask.'

Afterword

If you've made it this far, then you've presumably read the book for which I thank you wholeheartedly. I hope that you enjoyed the story. If you did, it would be fantastic if you could leave an honest review on Amazon to let other readers know exactly what you thought. Leaving a review can take as little as five minutes but can have a huge impact on an author's visibility.

If you'd like to find out more about upcoming releases, then feel free to follow me on Facebook at: https://www.facebook.com/tamiablaineauthor

or Instagram at: https://www.instagram.com/tamiablaine/

It'd be great to connect and engage with my readers, so please click those like buttons, and I'll try my best to keep you entertained.

Alternatively, you can email me at tamiablaine@gmail.com if you have any queries or questions.

Lastly, I'd like to thank you again for purchasing this book. Here's to the next one...and the next one...and the next.

All my love

Tamia